THE MORNING AFTER

Abby rolled onto her side to study the man who slept at her side. No, not man, she fiercely reminded herself. Vampire. Studying the wickedly perfect features in the dim light, it seemed impossible that she hadn't guessed the truth before. He was every woman's fantasy.

Barely aware of what she was doing, Abby silently lifted the duvet to reveal the lean, muscular form. Although the jeans rather disappointingly remained, he had removed his silk shirt to reveal a chest that was just as lethally beautiful as she had imagined in her heated dreams.

"Good morning, lover," a husky voice abruptly intruded into the silence.

Jerking her head up, Abby took in the slit of silver glittering beneath the heavy black lashes. She abruptly dropped the duvet as if it might scorch her fingers.

"I . . . didn't realize that you were awake."

"I may be dead, but not even I can sleep while a beautiful woman ogles me. Tell me, sweet, what were you searching for? A horn and tail?"

"I suppose I was curious. You seem so . . . normal."

"You mean human?"

"Yes."

Without warning, she discovered herself rolled onto her back with Dante looming above her, his hands planted on either side of her head.

"Perhaps I don't possess three eyes or have acid dripping from my fangs," he said, his beautiful features unexpectedly somber, "but you should never make the mistake of pretending that I'm human. I am a vampire, Abby, not a man . . ."

Books by Alexandra Ivy

WHEN DARKNESS COMES

EMBRACE THE DARKNESS

DARKNESS EVERLASTING

DARKNESS REVEALED

DARKNESS UNLEASHED

BEYOND THE DARKNESS

DEVOURED BY DARKNESS

BOUND BY DARKNESS

And don't miss these Guardians of Eternity novellas

TAKEN BY DARKNESS in YOURS FOR ETERNITY

DARKNESS ETERNAL in SUPERNATURAL

WHERE DARKNESS LIVES in
THE REAL WEREWIVES OF VAMPIRE COUNTY

Published by Kensington Publishing Corporation

When Darkness Comes

Alexandra Ivy

ZEBRA BOOKS
Kensington Publishing Corp.
www.kensingtonbooks.com

ZEBRA BOOKS are published by

Kensington Publishing Corp.
119 West 40th Street
New York, NY 10018

All Kensington titles, imprints, and distributed lines are available at special quantity discounts for bulk purchases for sales promotion, premiums, fund-raising, educational, or institutional use.

Special book excerpts or customized printings can also be created to fit specific needs. For details, write or phone the office of the Kensington Special Sales Manager: Attn.: Special Sales Department. Kensington Publishing Corp., 119 West 40th Street, New York, NY 10018. Phone: 1-800-221-2647.

Zebra and the Z logo Reg. U.S. Pat. & TM Off.

ISBN-13: 978-1-4201-2529-0
ISBN-10: 1-4201-2529-X

First Printing: January 2007
20 19 18 17 16 15 14 13

Printed in the United States of America

Prologue

England, 1665

The scream ripped through the night air. Pulsing with a savage agony, it filled the vast chamber and tumbled down the vaulted corridors. Servants cowering in the lower halls of the castle clamped hands over their ears in an effort to block out the piercing shrieks. Even hardened soldiers in the barracks made the sign of the moon, the protector of the night.

In the southern turret, the Duke of Granville paced across his private library, his shadowed features lined with distaste. Unlike his servants, he did not cross his forehead in an effort to ward off the evil eye. And why should he?

Evil had already struck. It had invaded his home and dared to taint him with its filth.

The only thing left was to purge the infestation with a ruthless strike.

Tugging at the hood to his robe to ensure his marred countenance was fully hidden, he grimly squared his shoulders. Patience, he told himself over and over. Soon enough the moon would move into the proper equinox. And then the ritual would at last be at an end. The child he had sacrificed to the witches would become their precious Chalice, and his suffering would be at an end.

Turning abruptly on his heel, he marched back toward the slotted window that offered a fine view of the rich countryside. In the distance he could witness the faint glow of fires. He shuddered. London. Filthy, peasant-infected London that was being punished for its foul sins.

A punishment that had spewed out of the ramshackle whorehouses and swept its way to his sanctuary.

His hands clenched at his sides. It was untenable. He was a just man. A godly man who had always been richly rewarded for his purity. To have that . . . vile disease enter his body was a perversion of all that was due to him.

That, of course, was the only reason he had allowed the heathens to enter his estate. And to bring with them that creature of evil that was currently shackled in his dungeon.

They promised him a cure.

An end to the plague that was consuming his life.

And all it would cost him was a daughter.

Chapter 1

Chicago, 2006

"Oh God, Abby. Don't panic. Just . . . don't . . . panic."

Sucking in a deep breath, Abby Barlow pressed her hands to her heaving stomach and studied the shards of pottery that lay splintered across the floor.

Okay, so she broke a vase. Well, perhaps more than broke it. It was more like she shattered, decimated, and annihilated the vase, she grudgingly conceded. Big deal. It was not the end of the world.

A vase was a vase. Wasn't it?

She abruptly grimaced. No, a vase was not just a vase. Not when it was a very rare vase. A priceless vase. One that should no doubt have been in a museum. One that was the dream of any collector and . . .

Freaking hell.

Panic once again reared its ugly head.

She had destroyed a priceless Ming vase.

What if she lost her job? Granted, it wasn't much of a job. Hell, she felt as if she were stepping into the Twilight Zone each time she entered the elegant mansion on the outskirts of Chicago. But her position as companion to Selena LaSalle was hardly demanding. And the pay was considerably better than slinging hash in some sleazy dive.

The last thing she needed was to be back in the long lines at the unemployment office.

Or worse . . . dear God, what if she was expected to pay for the blasted vase?

Even if there was such a thing as a half-price sale at the local Ming outlet shop, she would have to work ten lifetimes to make such a sum. Always supposing that it was not one of a kind.

Panic was no longer merely rearing. It was thundering through her at full throttle.

There was only one thing to be done, she realized. The mature, responsible, adult thing to do.

Hide the evidence.

Covertly glancing about the vast foyer, Abby ensured that she was alone before lowering herself to her knees and gathering the numerous shards that littered the smooth marble.

It was not as if anyone would notice the vase was missing, she tried to reassure herself. Selena had always been a recluse, but in the past two weeks, she had all but disappeared. If it wasn't for her occasional cameo appearances to demand that Abby prepare that disgusting herb concoction she guzzled with seeming pleasure, Abby might have thought that the woman had done a flit.

Certainly Selena didn't roam the house taking inventory of her various knickknacks.

All Abby needed to do was ensure that she didn't leave any trace of her crime and surely all would be well.

No one would ever know.

No one.

"My, my, I never thought to see you on your hands and knees, lover. A most intriguing position that leads to all sorts of delicious possibilities," a mocking voice drawled from the entrance to the drawing room.

Abby closed her eyes and heaved in a deep breath. She was cursed. That had to be it. What else could possibly explain her unending run of bad luck?

For a moment she kept her back turned, futilely hoping Selena's houseguest, the utterly annoying Dante, would disappear. It could happen. There was always spontaneous combustion, or black holes, or earthquakes.

Unfortunately, the ground didn't open up to swallow him, nor did the smoke detectors set off a warning. Even worse, she could actually feel his dark, amused gaze leisurely meandering over her stiff form.

Gathering her battered pride, Abby forced herself to slowly turn, and keeping the broken vase hidden behind her as she regarded the current bane of her existence.

He didn't look like a bane. God's truth, he looked like a delicious, dangerously wicked pirate.

Still kneeling upon the floor, Abby allowed her gaze to travel over the black biker boots and long, powerful legs encased in faded denims. Ever higher she skimmed over the black silk shirt that hung loosely upon his torso. Loose, but not loose enough, she acknowledged with a renegade shiver. Much to her embarrassment, she had caught herself sneaking peeks at the play of rippling muscles beneath those silky shirts during the past three months.

All right, maybe she had indulged in more than

mere peeks. Maybe she had been staring. Gawking. Ogling. Occasionally drooling.

What woman wouldn't?

Gritting her teeth, she forced her gaze up to the alabaster face with its perfectly chiseled features. A wide brow, a narrow aristocratic nose, sharply defined cheekbones and lushly carved lips. They all came together with a fierce elegance.

It was the face of a noble warrior. A chieftain.

Until one noticed those pale, silver eyes.

There was nothing noble in those disturbing eyes. They were piercing, wicked, and shimmering with a mocking amusement toward the world. They were eyes that branded him a "badass" as easily as the long raven hair that carelessly tumbled well past his shoulders and the golden hoops he wore in his ears.

He was sex on legs. A predator. The sort that chewed up and spat out women like her with pathetic ease.

That was, when they bothered to notice women like her in the first place. Which was not very damn often.

"Dante. Do you have to skulk about like that?" she demanded, desperately aware of the priceless clutter just behind her.

He made a show of considering her question before offering a faint shrug.

"No, I don't suppose I *have* to skulk about," he murmured in his husky midnight voice. "I simply enjoy doing so."

"Well, it's a very vulgar habit."

His lips twitched with amusement as he prowled ever closer. "Oh, I possess far more vulgar habits, sweet Abby. Several that I don't doubt you would enjoy fully if only you would allow me to demonstrate."

God, she just bet he did. Those slender, devilish hands would no doubt make a woman scream in pleasure. And those lips . . .

Abruptly she was squashing the renegade fantasy and stirring up the annoyance she most certainly should be feeling.

"Ack. You're revolting."

"Vulgar and revolting?" His smile widened to reveal startling white teeth. "My sweet, you are in a very precarious position to be tossing about such insults."

Precarious? She battled the urge to glance down and discover if any shards of her crime were visible.

"I don't know what you mean."

With a flowing elegance, Dante was on his knees before her, those disturbing fingers lifting to lightly stroke her cheek. His touch was cool, almost cold, but it sent a startling flare of heat searing through her.

"Oh, I think you do. I seem to recall a rather precious Ming vase that used to sit upon that table. Tell me, lover, did you hock it or break it?"

Damn. He knew. She desperately attempted to think of some feasible lie to explain the missing vase. Or for that matter, any lie, feasible or not. Unfortunately, she had never been particularly skilled at prevarication.

And it didn't much help that his lingering touch was turning her brain to mush.

"Don't call me that," she at last lamely muttered.

"What?" His brows lifted.

"Lover."

"Why?"

"For the obvious fact that I'm not your lover."

"Not yet."

"Not ever."

"Tsk, tsk." Dante clicked his tongue as his fingers moved to boldly outline her lips. "Has no one ever warned you that it is dangerous to dare fate? It has a tendency to come back and bite you." His gaze drifted over her pale countenance and the soft curve of her neck. "Sometimes quite literally."

"Not in a million years."

"I can wait," he husked.

She gritted her teeth as those skillful fingers traveled down the arch of her throat and along the neckline of her plain cotton shirt. He was merely toying with her. Hell, the man would flirt with any woman who possessed a pulse. And maybe a few who didn't.

"That finger moves any lower and your stay in the world is going to be considerably shorter."

He gave a soft chuckle as he reluctantly allowed his hand to drop. "Do you know, Abby, someday you're going to forget to say no. And on that day, I intend to make you scream with pleasure."

"My God, how do you possibly carry that ego around?"

His smile was purely wicked. "Do you think I don't notice? All those covert glances when you think I'm not looking? The way you shiver when I brush past you? The dreams that haunt your nights?"

Conceited, puffed-up toad.

She should laugh. Or pooh-pooh. Or even slap his arrogant face. Instead she stiffened as if he had hit a nerve that she didn't even know she possessed.

"Don't you have somewhere you need to be?" she gritted. "The kitchen? The sewers? The fires of hell?"

Surprisingly the pirate features hardened as his lips twisted into a sardonic smile.

"Nice try, my sweet, but I don't need you to

condemn me to the fires of hell. That was accomplished a long time ago. Why else would I be here?"

Abby gave a lift of her brows, intrigued in spite of herself by his hint of bitterness. For God's sake, what more could he want? He possessed the sort of cushy life that most oversexed playboys could only dream of. A glamorous home. Expensive clothes. A silver Porsche. And a sugar mommy who was not only young, but beautiful enough to make any male hot and bothered. His life was hardly in the gutter.

Unlike her own.

"Oh yes, you must really suffer," she retorted, her gaze flicking over the silk shirt that cost more than her entire wardrobe. "My heart simply breaks for you."

The silver eyes flashed with a startling heat as the fierce power that always smoldered about him prickled through the air.

"Do not presume to speak of things you know nothing about, lover," he warned.

Just let it be, Abby, she sternly warned herself. Whatever his easy charm, the man was dangerous. A genuine bad boy. Only fools deliberately toyed with fire.

Of course, when it came to men, she might as well have the word *idiot* tattooed on her forehead.

"If you dislike being here, then why don't you leave?"

He regarded her in unnerving silence before his eyes slowly narrowed. "Why don't you?"

"What?"

"I'm not the only one suffering here, am I? Every day you seem to fade a bit more. As if your frustration and sadness has taken another piece of your soul."

Abby nearly tumbled backward at his sharp perception. She had never dreamed that anyone could possibly have noted her desperation at her tedious existence, nor the budding fear that she would soon be too old and tired to care that she was going nowhere.

Certainly not this man.

"You don't know anything."

"I know a prison when I see one," he murmured. "Why do you remain behind the bars when you could so easily slip away?"

She gave a short, humorless laugh. Easily? Obviously he was not nearly so perceptive as she had given him credit for.

"Because I need this job. Unlike you, I don't have a generous lover to pay my bills and keep me in style. Some of us have to earn our pay with actual work."

If she thought to insult him, she was far off the mark. In fact, her sharp words merely returned that mocking humor she found so damn annoying.

"You believe me to be Selena's whore?"

"Aren't you?"

He lifted a broad shoulder. "Our . . . relationship is a bit more complex than that."

"Oh yes, no doubt being a boy toy to a rich, glamorous woman is astonishingly complex."

"Is that why you try to keep me at a distance? Because you believe I share Selena's bed?"

"I keep you at a distance because I don't like you."

He leaned forward, until his lips were nearly touching her own. "You may not like me, sweetness, but that doesn't keep you from wanting me."

Her heart forgot to beat as she struggled not to close that shallow distance and put herself out of her misery. A kiss. Just one kiss. The tingling need was nearly unbearable.

No, no, no. Did she really want to be a poor joke

to relieve his boredom? Hadn't she played that humiliating game before?

"Do you know, Dante, I've met my share of jack-asses in my time, but you—"

The rather tidy insult was brought to a stunning halt. In the air there was a sudden, crackling heat. As electrifying as a strike of lightning.

Unnerved by the prickling sensation, she turned her head toward the stairs just as a thundering concussion ripped through the house. Caught off guard, she tumbled backward, her breath knocked from her body.

Just for a moment she lay perfectly still. She half-expected the ceiling to come crumbling down upon her. Or the ground to open up and swallow her.

What the blazes had happened? An earthquake? A gas explosion?

The end of the world?

Whatever it was, it had been enough to tumble the pictures from the walls and knock over tables. Suddenly the Ming vase she had broken matched every other priceless object.

Giving a shake of her head to clear the ringing in her ears, Abby sucked in a deep breath. Well, at least she seemed to be alive, she told herself. And while she was certain to be sporting a few bruises, she didn't think anything vital was actually missing or punctured.

Lying flat on her back, she barely heard the low feral growl, but it still managed to make the hair upon her nape stand upright. Dear Lord, now what?

Struggling to push herself upright, she glanced about the littered foyer. Astonishingly it was empty. No wild animal. No approaching madman.

And no Dante.

With a frown, Abby ignored her wobbly knees and forced herself toward the nearby stairs. Where had Dante gone? Had he been hit by the explosion? Or thrown from the foyer?

Had he simply disappeared in a puff of smoke?

No, no, of course not. She pressed a hand to her aching head. She was thinking crazy. She must have been knocked unconscious for a moment. That would explain it. No doubt he had gone to check on the damage. Or to call for assistance.

Her job was surely to ensure that Selena was not injured.

Concentrating upon placing one foot in front of the other, a startlingly difficult task, she managed to climb the sweeping marble stairs and awkwardly make her way down the hallway. At the end of the long east wing, the door to Selena's chambers was already open and Abby stepped over the threshold.

She got no farther.

A gasp was wrenched from her throat as her wide gaze swept over the demolished room. Like downstairs, the pictures and various objects had been tumbled to the ground, most of them smashed beyond recognition. But here the general mayhem had left the walls blackened and in places crumbled to dust. Even the windows had been blasted from their frames.

Her gaze flew to the large bed that was tumbled onto its side and at last to the center of the room where Dante was kneeling beside a limp, battered form.

"Oh my God." Holding her hands to her mouth, Abby stumbled forward, her heart firmly lodged in her throat. "Selena."

Noticing her presence for the first time, Dante

jerked his head up to regard her with a frown. Almost absently, Abby noted the even sharper pallor of his skin and the oddly hectic glitter in his silver eyes.

Obviously he was as shaken as she was.

"Get out of here," he growled.

She ignored his warning as she fell to her knees beside the burned body. Whatever her secret dislike for the beautiful, coldhearted woman, it was forgotten as tears streamed down her cheeks.

"Is she . . . dead?" she croaked.

"Abby, I said to leave. Now. Get out of this room. Out of this house . . ."

The dark, furious words continued, but Abby was no longer listening. Instead she watched in fascinated horror as one of the charred hands twitched upon the carpet. Holy freaking hell. Could the poor woman still be alive? Or was it some horrible trick of her imagination?

Frozen in shock, Abby stared at the fingers that continued to jerk and spasm ever closer. It was like something out of a nightmare. A sensation that only deepened when the hand snapped upward and grasped her wrist in a painful grasp.

Opening her mouth to scream, Abby discovered her breath wrenched from her body. A coldness was spreading from the fingers that dug into her flesh. A coldness that crawled through her blood with a searing, ruthless agony. With a groan, she desperately attempted to tug herself free of the brutal grip.

She was going to die, she realized in stunned disbelief. The pain was clawing at her heart, slowing its beat until it was doomed to halt. She was going to die, and she hadn't even bothered to start living yet.

What an idiot she was.

Raising her head, she met Dante's shimmering metallic gaze. His beautiful, wicked features appeared grim in the dim light. Grim and edged with something that might have been fury, or regret, or . . . desperation.

She tried to speak, but a bright flare of light burst through her mind, and with a strangled scream she plunged headfirst into the welcoming darkness.

Chapter 2

Surrounded by a silver fog of pain, Abby floated in a world that was not quite real.

Was she dead?

Surely not. She would be at peace, wouldn't she? Not feeling as if her bones were being slowly crushed and her head about to explode.

If she were dead, then this whole afterlife thing was a big, fat rip-off.

No. She had to be dreaming, she at last reassured herself. That would certainly explain why the silver fog was beginning to part.

Curious despite the vague taste of fear in the air, she peered through the shimmering light. Moments later she could see a dark, stone chamber that was only dimly lit by a flickering torch. In the center of the stone floor lay a young woman in white robes. Abby frowned. The woman's pale face was remarkably familiar, although it was difficult to determine the exact features as the woman twisted and screamed in obvious agony.

About her prostrate form sat a circle of women in gray cloaks, holding hands and chanting in low voices. Abby could not make out the words, but it appeared as if they *were performing some sort of ritual. Perhaps an exorcism. Or an enchantment.*

Slowly a gray-haired woman stood and held her hands toward the shadowed ceiling.

"Arise Phoenix and bring forth your power," she called in booming tones. "The sacrifice is offered, the covenant sealed. Bless our noble Chalice. Bless her with your glory. Offer to her the might of your sword to fight the evil that threatens. We call. Come forth."

Crimson flames swept through the chamber as the women continued to chant, hovering in the thick air before surrounding the screaming woman upon the floor. Then, just as abruptly as they had appeared, the flames melted into the woman's flesh.

Abruptly the gray-haired woman turned her head toward a darkened corner.

"The prophecy is fulfilled. Bring forth the beast."

Expecting some horrid, five-headed monster that would fit right into the bizarre nightmare, Abby caught her breath as a man attired in a ruffled white shirt and satin knee breeches was brought forward, a heavy metal collar and chain hung about his neck. His head was bowed, allowing his long raven hair to cover his face, but that didn't halt a shiver of premonition from inching down Abby's spine.

"Creature of evil, you have been chosen above all others," the woman intoned. "Wicked is your heart and yet blessed are you. We pledge you to the Chalice. In fire and blood we bind you. In the shadow of death we bind you. Through eternity and beyond we bind you."

The torch suddenly flared, and with a terrifying growl, the man lifted his head.

No. It was not possible. Not even in the strange and ridiculous world of dreams. Especially not ones that felt so horrifyingly real.

Still, there was no mistaking his terrifying beauty. Or the smoldering silver eyes.

Dante.

She shuddered in horror. This was madness. Why would these women have him chained? Why would they call him a monster? A creature of evil?

Madness, indeed. A dream. Nothing more, she attempted to convince herself.

Then without warning, the unease tracing her spine turned to consuming terror. In pure fury, Dante tilted back his head, the perfect alabaster features bathed in flickering light. The same flickering light that revealed his long, deadly fangs.

When Abby at last woke again, the silver fog, and the sharpest edges of her pain, had disappeared.

Still, with uncommon caution, she forced herself to remain perfectly motionless. After the day she had already endured, now didn't seem to be the best time to be charging and blundering about in her usual style. Instead she attempted to take stock of her surroundings.

She was lying upon a bed, she at last decided. Not her own bed, however. This one was hard and lumpy and possessed a funky scent she didn't even want to consider. In the distance, she could hear the sounds of passing traffic and, closer, the muffled sound of voices or perhaps a television.

Well, she wasn't in Selena's charred house. She was no longer in a damp dungeon with screaming women and demons. And she wasn't dead.

That was surely progress?

Screwing up her courage, Abby slowly lifted her head from the pillow and glanced about the shadowed room. There wasn't much to see. The bed she was lying upon consumed most of the cramped space. About her were bare walls and the ugliest flowered curtains ever created. At the end of the bed was a broken dresser that held an ancient television, and in the corner was a shabby chair.

A chair that was currently occupied by a large, raven-haired man.

Or was he a man?

Her heart squeezed with a building dread as her gaze swept over the slumbering Dante. God. She would have to be demented to think what she was thinking.

Vampires? Living and breathing . . . or whatever it was that vampires did . . . in Chicago? Nuts. Full-out, engines-roaring madness.

But the dream. It had been so vivid. So real. Even now she could smell the foul, damp air and the acrid burning of the torch. She could hear the screams and chanting. She could hear the rattling of heavy chains. She could see Dante being pulled forward and the fangs that marked him as a beast.

Real or not, it had unnerved her enough to desire a bit of space between her and Dante. And perhaps several crosses, a few wooden stakes, and a bottle of holy water.

Barely daring to breathe, Abby sat upright and swung her legs over the edge of the mattress. Her head threatened to revolt, but she gritted her teeth and pushed herself upward. She wanted out of here.

She wanted to be in her familiar home, surrounded by her familiar things.

She wanted out of this nightmare.

Taking one unsteady step followed by another and another, Abby moved across the room. She was just upon the point of reaching for the doorknob when there was the faintest whisper of sound behind her. The hair on the nape of her neck tingled before a pair of steely arms wrapped about her.

"Not so fast, lover," a dark voice murmured directly in her ear.

For a moment her mind went blank, and she was paralyzed with fear. Then sheer panic took control.

Arching her back, she frantically attempted to kick at his legs. "Let me go. Let go."

"Go?" His arms merely tightened at her struggles. "Tell me, sweet, where do you plan to go?"

"That's none of your business."

Surprisingly he gave a short, humorless laugh. "My God, you don't know how I wish that were true. We were both released, do you realize that? We were free. The chains were broken."

Abby stilled at his rough, accusing words. "What do you mean?"

He brushed his face over the top of her head in an oddly intimate manner before he was firmly turning her to meet his shimmering gaze.

"I mean that if you had kept that beautiful nose out of matters that are none of your business, we both could have gone upon our merry way. Now, because of your Florence Nightingale act, where you go, what you do, what you bloody well think is now very much my business."

What the hell was he talking about? Unconsciously her wide gaze skimmed over the perfect alabaster features. The last thing she needed was more trouble.

"You're insane. Let me go or—"

"Or what?" he demanded in silky tones.

Good question. A pity she didn't have a brilliant answer.

"I . . . I'll scream."

The dark brows lifted in sardonic amusement. "And do you truly want to discover just what sort of hero is going to rush to your rescue in this place? Who do you think it will be? The local crackheads? The whores working the lobby? You know, I'd place my money on the drunk next door. There was a definite hint of rape in the air when I carried you past him in the hall."

Suddenly Abby understood the cramped room, the vile smells, and the echoes of despair. Dante had taken her to one of the endless seedy hotels that catered to the poor and desperate.

She might have shivered in disgust if it hadn't been the least of her worries.

"They couldn't be any worse than you."

He stiffened at her accusation, his expression guarded. "Rather harsh words for the man who might very well have saved your life."

"Man? Is that what you are?"

"What did you say?"

His fingers dug into her shoulders, and belatedly Abby realized that confronting Dante directly might not have been the wisest decision.

Still, she had to know. Ignorance might be bliss, but it was also freaking dangerous.

"You . . . I saw you. In the dream." She shivered as the memories burned through her mind. "You were chained, and they were chanting and your . . . your fangs—"

"Abby." He gazed deep into her eyes. "Sit down and I'll explain."

"No." She gave a frantic shake of her head. "What are you going to do to me?"

His lips twisted at her shrill tone. "Although

several enticing ideas have passed through my mind upon various occasions, for the moment I plan nothing more than talking with you. Will you calm down long enough to listen?"

The very fact that he hadn't laughed and told her that she had lost her mind only deepened Abby's terror. He knew of the dream. He recognized it.

Allowing instinct to take over, Abby forced herself to pretend a resignation she far from felt.

"Do I have a choice?"

He shrugged. "Not really."

"Very well."

Weakly following his lead toward the bed, Abby waited until Dante was convinced of his victory before reaching out to push him sharply away. Caught off guard, he stumbled, and in the blink of an eye, she was bolting toward the door.

She was fast. Growing up with five older brothers ensured she was well practiced in running from a potential massacre. But shockingly she had taken only a few steps when Dante's arms were wrapping about her and lifting her off her feet.

With a muffled scream, she reached her arms over her head and grasped two handfuls of his silky hair. He gave a low grunt as she gave a violent tug. Still keeping grasp of his hair with one hand, she shifted the other to dig her nails into the side of his face.

"Dammit, Abby," he muttered, his grip loosening as he sought to ward off her attack.

Not pausing for a moment, Abby wriggled free and, turning, she aimed a kick that over the years had proven to bring even the largest of men to a screeching halt. Dante gasped as he doubled over in pain. Not pausing to admire her handiwork, Abby lunged for the door.

On this occasion, she managed to actually touch the knob before she was roughly hauled up and over a broad shoulder and carried back to the bed. She screamed again as Dante easily tossed her onto the foul mattress, and then followed her downward to cover her struggling form with one much larger, and much harder.

More frightened than she had ever been in her life, Abby gazed into the pale face with its unearthly beauty. She was sharply, disturbingly aware of his lean muscles pressing against her. And the knowledge that he held her completely at his mercy.

Uncertain what was about to happen, she was startled when a slow smile curved his lips.

"You possess powerful weapons for such a tiny thing, lover," he murmured. "Have you practiced those rather nasty tricks often?"

Somehow his teasing managed to ease a portion of her rabid terror. Surely if he were going to suck her dry, he wouldn't be indulging in conversation?

Unless of course vampires preferred a bit of pre-dinner chat?

"I have five older brothers," she gritted.

"Ah, that would explain it. Survival of the fittest, or in this case, survival of the one with the dirtiest arsenal."

"Get off me.'"

He gave a lift of his brows. "And risk becoming a eunuch? No, thanks. We'll finish our discussion without anymore scratching, hair pulling, or low blows."

She glared into his mocking expression. "We have nothing to discuss."

"Oh no," he drawled, "nothing beyond the fact your employer was just barbequed to a crisp, the fact that I'm a vampire, and the fact that thanks to your stupidity, you now have every demon in the vicinity after your head. Nothing at all to discuss."

Barbequed employers, vampires, and now demons? It was too much. Way, way too much.

Abby closed her eyes as her heart squeezed with horror.

"This is a nightmare. Dear God, please let Freddy Krueger walk through the door."

"This is no nightmare, Abby."

"It's not possible." She reluctantly lifted her lids to meet the glittering silver gaze. "You're a vampire?"

He grimaced. "My heritage is the least of your concerns at the moment."

Heritage? She swallowed a hysterical urge to laugh.

"Did Selena know?"

"That I was a vampire? Oh yes, she knew." His tone was dry. "In fact, you could say that it was a prerequisite to my employment."

Abby frowned. "Then she was a vampire too?"

"No." Dante paused as if carefully considering his words. Ridiculous since he could have informed her that Selena was Beelzebub and she couldn't have twitched a muscle as long as he held her in his relentless grip. "She was . . . a Chalice."

"Chalice?" Her blood ran cold. The woman screaming in agony. The crimson flames. "The Phoenix," she breathed.

His brows drew together in shock. "How did you know that?"

"The dream. I was in a dungeon, and there was a woman lying on the floor. I think the other women were performing some ritual upon her."

"Selena," he muttered. "She must have passed

a portion of her memories onto you. That's the only explanation."

"Passed on memories? But that's . . ." Her words trailed away as a mocking smile curved his lips.

"Impossible? Don't you think we're beyond that by now?"

They were, of course. She had tumbled into some bizarro world where anything was possible. Like Alice in the Looking Glass.

Only instead of disappearing cats and white rabbits, there were vampires and mysterious Chalices and who knew what else.

"What did they do to her?"

"They made her a Chalice. A human vessel for a powerful entity."

"So those women were witches?"

"For lack of a better term."

Great. Just great. "And they put a spell upon Selena?"

The silver eyes shimmered in the shadowed light. "It was rather more than a spell. They called forth the spirit of the Phoenix to live within her body."

Abby could almost feel the crimson flames that had seared into the woman's flesh. She shivered in horror. "No wonder she was screaming. What does this Phoenix do?"

"It is a . . . barrier."

She eyed him warily. "A barrier against what?"

"Against the darkness."

Well, that made everything as clear as mud. Impatiently Abby wriggled beneath the man pinning her to the bed.

A bad, very bad move.

As if a lightning bolt had suddenly struck her, she was vibrantly aware of his hard body branding her own. A body that had haunted her dreams more than a few nights.

Dante's jaw tightened at her unwittingly provocative movements, his hips instinctively shifting in response.

"Do you think you could possibly be a little more vague?" she managed to choke out.

"What would you have me say?" he demanded in rasping tones.

She struggled to keep her thoughts focused. Good God. Now was no time to be thinking of . . . of . . . that.

"Something a bit more clarifying than *the darkness*."

There was a moment of silence, as if he were waging his own battle. Then at last he met her gaze squarely.

"Very well. The demon world refers to the darkness as the Prince, but in truth it isn't a real being. It is more a . . . spirit, just as the Phoenix is a spirit. An essence of power that demons call upon to enhance their dark skills."

"And the Phoenix does something to this Prince?"

"Her presence among mortals has banished the Prince from this world. They are two opposites. Neither can be in the same plane at the same moment. Not without both being destroyed."

Well, that seemed like a good thing. The first ray of hope in a very bleak day.

"So, no more demons?"

He gave a lift of his shoulder. "They remain, but without the tangible presence of the Prince, they are weakened and chaotic. No longer do they band together to attack in strength, and rarely do they hunt humans. They have been forced into the shadows."

"That's good, I suppose," she said slowly. "And Selena was this barrier?"

"Yes."

"Why?"

He blinked at the abrupt question. "Why?"

"Why was she chosen?" Abby clarified, not quite certain why she even cared. She only knew that at the moment it seemed important. "Was she a witch?"

Oddly Dante paused, almost as if he were considering not answering her question. Ridiculous after all he had already revealed. What could be worse than the fact that she was being held captive by a vampire? Or that the one person who kept away all the scary, bad things in the night was now dead?

"She was not so much chosen as offered as a sacrifice by her father," he at last grudgingly confessed.

"She was sacrificed by her father?" Abby gave a startled blink. Hell, she had always thought her father was a shoo-in for scumbag of the year. He had been a brutal jerk whose only redeeming act had been tossing aside his family for a bottle of whiskey. Still, he hadn't offered her up as fodder to a band of crazed witches. "How could he do such a thing?"

The elegant features hardened with ancient anger. "Quite easily. He was powerful, rich, and accustomed to having his way in all things. Or he was until he was struck down with the plague. In exchange for a cure, he gave the witches his only daughter."

"Holy crap. That's horrible."

"I suppose he thought it a fair trade-off. He was cured and his daughter made immortal."

"Immortal?" Abby caught in breath with sudden hope. "Then Selena is still alive?"

The beautiful features sharpened even further. "No, she is very much dead."

"But . . . how?"

"I don't know." His tone was rough with coiled emotions. "At least not yet."

Abby bit her bottom lip, attempting to wrap her aching brain around the consequences of such a death.

"Then the Phoenix is gone?"

"No, it is not gone. It is—" Without warning, Dante flowed to his feet, his head turning toward the closed door. A tense silence filled the room before he at last returned his gaze to her startled face. "Abby, we must go. Now."

Chapter 3

Dante fiercely cursed his stupidity.

For 341 years he had stood as guardian to the Phoenix. Not willingly, and not without a simmering fury at his fate, but with absolute dedication. It was not as if he had a choice. Those witches had seen to that.

But now, when the danger was at its greatest, he discovered himself barely capable of concentrating upon the threat very much at hand.

He impatiently shoved back his tangled hair. Bloody hell, there was little wonder he was distracted. In the past few hours, he had endured more shocks than he had in centuries. The death of the immortal Selena. The fierce, intoxicating joy as he felt the chains begin to loosen. And the horror of watching the Phoenix being branded into Abby.

Abby.

Double bloody hell. He glared down at her slender form. The woman had been a plague and pestilence since she arrived at Selena's estate. With her skin as soft as satin. Her honey curls that haloed her gamine face. Her vulnerable eyes. And the hot passions that smoldered just beneath her screw-the-world attitude. It called to him like the song of a Siren. A tasty morsel that he had had every intention of consuming at his leisure.

But now everything had changed. Now she was no longer a lovely diversion. No longer a bit of sport. She was his to protect. And he would do so until his very death.

"Come," he commanded in soft tones, summoning his ancient instincts. "Something approaches."

Struggling to her feet, she eyed him warily. "What?"

He grasped her arm in a firm grip. "Demons." He reached out with his senses, touching the approaching darkness. "And more than one."

Her face paled, but with that inner strength he had always admired, she didn't faint or scream or do all those annoying things that mortals were so prone to do when faced with the mystic.

"But they surely won't trouble us. We don't have anything they could want."

His lips twisted. "You're wrong, lover. We possess a treasure beyond all dreams."

"What—"

"I'm afraid the twenty questions will have to wait until later, Abby."

Pulling her close to his side, he silently crossed toward the nearly hidden door next to the bed. Reaching out, he turned the knob and thrust it open. Wood splintered as the dead bolt was ripped from the frame. Still holding Abby close, he tugged her through the shadows of the adjoining room, barely giving a glance toward the drunk who snored in vodka oblivion upon his bed.

Dante moved directly to the narrow window. Forcing it open, he turned to lean close to Abby's ear. "Stay close to me and don't make a sound," he whispered. "If we are attacked, I want you to stay behind me and don't run. They will be attempting to frighten you into a trap."

"But I want to know why—"

"Not now, Abby," he growled impatiently. "If we're going to get out of here alive, I need you to trust me. Can you do that?"

There was a moment of silence. In the gloom, Dante could sense the fragility of her control. She was near shattering, and he could only hope that her impending collapse could be held off long enough to get to safety.

At last she swallowed heavily and gave a grudging nod of her head. "Yes."

He gazed deep into her eyes, startled by the stir of something that might have been warmth.

"Then let's go."

Taking her hand, he helped her climb through the narrow window, waiting until she was standing upon the metal fire escape before following her into the darkness. He paused just a moment, peering down at the littered alley below. His instincts warned that demons lurked nearby. Unfortunately, to remain would mean being trapped and surrounded. They had no choice but to go forward.

Or in this case, down.

Grimly Dante gave a tilt of his head toward the nearby ladder. With reluctant steps, Abby moved across the platform and forced herself to climb down the rungs. He waited until she had reached the bottom before stepping off the edge and landing next to her shivering form.

As she opened her lips to speak, he reached out to press a finger to her mouth, giving a sharp shake of his head. Danger prickled over his skin. Something was near. Very near. Turning toward a large Dumpster, he took a slow step forward.

"Show yourself," he commanded.

There was a rustle in the shadows followed by a sharp scrape of claws upon the pavement before a large, hulking form slowly appeared. At first glance, it would be simple to dismiss the intruder as an awkward, brainless beast. With thick, leathery skin, seeping boils, and a misshapen head that sported three eyes, he was the poster child for the monster beneath the bed. But Dante was all too familiar with this particular demon and knew that beneath all the ugly was a cunning intelligence that was more deadly than any muscle.

"Halford." Dante offered a mocking bow.

"Ah, Dante." The deep, rumbling voice possessed a polished, elegant accent that would have been right at home in a posh boarding school. A ludicrous contrast to his brutish appearance. "I just knew you would be dropping in once you caught whiff of those hellhounds. I've tried for centuries to train them with a bit of discretion, but they must always rush in when stealth would serve best."

Ensuring that he stood squarely between Abby and the demon, Dante offered a faint shrug.

"Hellhounds have never been renowned for their intelligence."

"No. A pity, really. Still, they do have their uses. Such as flushing out prey so that I needn't muck about in such filth." Halford cast a disdainful glance toward the dilapidated hotel. "I must say, Dante, I had always believed you to possess better taste."

"What better place to hide from the scum than beneath their very noses?"

Halford loosed a rumbling laugh that echoed eerily down the alley. "A clever ploy except for the fact that every brother in the city can smell your beauty from a mile away. I fear there's no hiding."

Dante silently cursed. Although Abby carried the Phoenix, she had not yet fully acquired its powers or any knowledge of how to control those powers. Until she did, she would be a beacon to every demon in the area.

"You underestimate my skill," he drawled in silky tones.

"Oh no, I would never be so stupid as to underestimate you, Dante." The demon stepped forward, his claws grinding the pavement to dust. "Unlike many in the brotherhood, I can easily sense the power that you have been forced to keep leashed all these tedious years. Which is why I'm quite prepared to allow you to walk away. I have no wish to kill you."

Dante gave a lift of his brow. "You will allow me to walk away?"

"Of course. I have never taken pleasure in killing my fellow demons." Halford gave what vaguely passed as a smile, considering his triple rows of teeth. "Leave the girl and I can promise that you'll never be troubled again."

Ah. Dante abruptly grasped the truth. Halford was alone. And not at all certain he could best a vampire. At least not before the other gathering demons could arrive and complicate matters.

"A rather generous offer," Dante murmured.

"I think so."

"Still, I think that handing over such a priceless treasure should be worth something more tangible. After all, if you are forced to battle me for the wench, you might discover yourself having to share the glory with any number of demons rushing in this direction."

A sudden blow to the center of his back assured Dante that Abby had heard his taunting words. And naturally had jumped to the predictable conclusion. He was an evil vampire, after all.

Reaching back, he grasped one slender wrist in a tight grip. He could not risk having her bolt.

Halford narrowed his eyes. All three of them. "What could be more tangible than your life?"

Dante shrugged. "There's little point in living an eternity if I must be reduced to wallowing among the wretched. As you said, I'm accustomed to a rather more luxurious lifestyle that is about to come to an end without Selena."

"Why you . . ." With a low growl, Abby frantically struggled against his grasp, kicking him with a savagery that would have sent a mortal to his knees.

"Hush, lover," he commanded without ever turning his head. "Halford and I are about to start negotiations."

"Pig. Monster. Beast."

Dante ignored the kicks that punctuated each word as he met Halford's amused gaze.

"A spirited thing," the demon rasped.

"A character flaw that could be easily corrected."

Halford flexed his bulging muscles. "Quite easily. Now let us be done with this. What is your price?"

Dante made a show of considering. "A ready supply of blood, of course. In this day and age, it really is far too dangerous to be out hunting among the riffraff."

"Simple enough."

"And perhaps a few Shantong to keep my lair warm

at night," he murmured, deliberately choosing demons notorious for their insatiable sexual appetite.

"Ah, a vampire with exquisite taste. Is that all?"

Noting the triumph glittering in Halford's eyes, Dante at last judged the moment ripe. The demon was consumed with thoughts of the glory as he offered the Phoenix to his dark Prince.

"Actually, no. I shall also need this." Loosening his hold upon Abby, he bent downward and with one smooth movement grasped the daggers hidden in his boots. In the same motion, he was rolling forward, the daggers already leaving his hands as he came back up to his feet.

For a moment Halford merely stood silent in the darkness. It was almost as if he hadn't yet noticed the dagger deeply planted in his middle eye or the other that stuck in his lower stomach. But whether he was in shock or indifferent to the danger, the deadly missiles had done their duty; with a rasping moan, he collapsed onto the vile rubbish that littered the alley.

Dante never hesitated as he flowed forward. With efficiency, he sliced open Halford's throat and then cut out his heart. He was never stupid enough to presume a demon was dead until he held its heart in his hand. At last satisfied, he reached to retrieve his daggers and traced his way back to Abby. She hastily backed away from his approach, her eyes wide with distress.

"Abby."

"No." She held out her hands. "Stay away from me."

Harshly smothering his flare of impatience, Dante forced himself to return the bloody daggers to his boots and to smooth back his tangled hair before taking another step closer. She was a breath away from bolting. One misstep and he would find himself having to chase her through the maze of alleys.

A wickedly delicious thought under normal circumstances, he ruefully conceded. Tonight, however, was anything but normal.

"Abby, the demon is dead," he soothed. "He will not harm you."

"And what of you?" she demanded in uneven tones. "You were going to sell me to that . . . thing. For blood."

"Don't be a fool. Of course I wasn't going to sell you." He reached out to grasp her chin, forcing her to meet his steady gaze. "I merely wanted to distract Halford long enough to strike. In case you didn't notice, he was somewhat larger than me. It seemed best to avoid an ugly brawl."

Her tongue peeked out to touch her lips. It was a tiny, unwitting gesture, and yet it made Dante's fingers tighten upon her delicate skin. No matter what the danger about them, having her so close stirred a fierce, aching hunger. One that he feared wouldn't be appeased any time soon.

"Why should I trust you?" she rasped.

His lips twisted as he lowered his hand and held it out. "Because for the moment, lover, you have no choice."

There was a long moment when she battled her inner demons before at last accepting that the demons currently hunting them were far more dangerous than him.

Still, it was with obvious reluctance that she at last laid her hand in his.

Not giving her time for second thoughts, Dante grasped her fingers and, with a tug, they were slipping through the darkness. He was startled by the flare of disappointment that touched him at her lingering fear of him. What else did he expect from a mortal?

Unfortunately, the knowledge that she considered him only a step above the evil creatures chasing them, and maybe not even a whole step, more like a baby half step, left a hollow sensation within him.

Turning down a side alley, Dante continued to brood upon the woman struggling to keep pace with his long strides. Brooding and tingling with awareness of her warm flesh touching his own. That no doubt explained why he was taken off guard when the hellhound abruptly sprang from the building overhead and knocked him to the ground.

In a heartbeat, the deadly hound had him pinned to the ground, the acid from his teeth dripping onto Dante's flesh with searing pain.

"Bloody hell," he muttered. "You smelly, slimy piece of crap."

Reaching up, Dante was preparing to grasp the demon's throat and rip it out when there was a sudden whoosh of air, followed by the sickening crush of bone. He blinked as the hellhound tumbled to the side, obviously dead.

"Are you hurt?"

Like a vision from a dream, Abby was leaning over him, her face smeared with muck and her hair hanging in limp tangles, but her expression was one of gentle concern. Dante took a moment to savor the enchanting view before reluctantly pushing himself up to his elbows. Turning his head, he regarded the twitching demon before returning his attention to Abby.

"Nice swing, love," he murmured, taking in the

rusty pipe she clutched in her hand. "Demon killer extraordinaire, in fact. Almost as good as—"

"Say the name Buffy and I'll stake you," she warned, raising the pipe in a threatening motion.

He gave a low chuckle. "Very frightening, sweet, but if you truly want to get the job done, it has to be wood."

"That could be arranged."

"No doubt." Dante rolled to his feet, brushing off the clinging filth. "Unfortunately, it will have to wait until later. For now we must be on our way."

Taking her arm, Dante was once again moving down the alley, on this occasion keeping his senses alert. Sharply, excruciatingly alert.

Devil spit. He had been knocked down by a hellhound. In front of a beautiful woman. He wasn't about to be humiliated again.

Killed, maybe. Staked, slaughtered, or beheaded, maybe. But not humiliated. A far preferable alternative for a proud vampire.

For near half an hour they traveled in silence, moving ever deeper into the slums. There were no more surprise attacks, but Dante could still sense demons in the distance.

Damn, he needed to determine if they were still following them or if he and Abby had managed to cover their trail.

Slowing his pace, he searched the shadows until he discovered a narrow door cut into the back of a brick building. He glanced about to ensure they were alone before lifting his leg and kicking the heavy steel off its hinges. There was a dull crash followed by a choking cloud of dust, but he never paused. Pulling Abby within the abandoned garage, he leaned against the twisted frame to keep watch for any unpleasant nasties that might be lurking in the dark.

Tense moments passed before Abby at last came to the end of her strained patience.

"What are we doing here?" she demanded.

"Waiting."

"Do you even know where we're going?"

"Away from here."

Her teeth snapped together. "Stunningly ambiguous as always. I suppose you think it makes you all dark and mysterious?"

"Oh, but I am dark and mysterious." He risked a glance over his shoulder to encounter her smoldering glare. "Isn't that how you like your men?"

"I like them with a heartbeat and a taste for quiche, not blood," she readily shot back.

Dante chuckled as he returned his gaze to the alley. "How can you be so certain, lover? You have yet to try a vampire. I can promise you it will be an experience you will never forget."

"God, you must be mental. Or the most arrogant—"

Dante abruptly held his hand up in warning. "Sssh."

Instantly on alert, she peered into the darkness. "Is something coming?"

"Yes. Stay behind me."

They waited in tense silence until at last the muffled sound of approaching footsteps could be heard. Sniffing the foul air, Dante swiftly assured himself that the intruders were human rather than demon before relaxing his tense muscles. They couldn't pose a true danger to him.

Then, the silence was broken by the static buzz of a voice floating through a walkie-talkie, and he heard Abby give a small gasp.

"Dante, it's the police. They can help us," she hissed before abruptly charging from behind him toward the door.

With pure instinct, Dante reached out to wrap her slight form in his arms. Smoothly he hauled her back into the building and pressed her against the wall. Her hands reached up to angrily beat at his chest, but already anticipating the scream that was about to expose their presence, Dante lowered his head and covered her mouth with his own.

His intent was honorable. The kiss was merely a means to prevent disaster. But the moment he touched the satin enticement of her lips, all honor was forgotten.

A combustible heat flared between them as he tightened his grip, and he devoured her with a hunger that he couldn't disguise. Bloody hell, he wanted her. He wanted to taste, to seduce, to consume her until his dark need was sated.

Restlessly his hands trailed up her back, brushing the tantalizing skin of her nape before plunging into the honey curls. He held her head steady as he continued to plunder her mouth, all thoughts of danger forgotten in a haze of searing pleasure.

Pressed against him, Abby momentarily stiffened in shock at the sudden embrace, but with gratifying speed, she offered a low moan and wrapped her arms about his neck as she opened her lips to his. Almost as if she had been waiting for this moment with the same fierce intensity as he had.

At the unmistakable capitulation, Dante instinctively softened his lips, his kisses deepening with persuasive intent. She stirred restlessly against his hardening thighs as his lips moved to trail over her smooth cheeks and down the arch of her neck. He was drowning in the passionate fire she had released within him.

"Abby . . . my sweet Abby . . . I want to feel you beneath me," he rasped in raw tones.

He felt her shudder with longing beneath his touch before she was abruptly pulling away to gaze at him with wide, dilated eyes.

"Are you insane?" she rasped, pressing her fingers to her swollen lips.

Caught off guard by her sharp retreat, Dante gritted his teeth and shoved his hands roughly into the pockets of his jeans. It was a grim battle to master the desire still pulsing through his taut body.

A swift yank, a few heated kisses, and he would have her on the dusty floor and himself sheathed deep in her body.

Thankfully sanity slowly forced its way through his hazed mind; taking a careful step back, he regarded her with a measure of calm.

"I was attempting to keep you from getting us both killed. I couldn't allow you to call out to those cops," he explained in smooth tones.

Her brows furrowed together. "You think that demons have infested the Chicago police force?"

"No, I think the second you attempt to explain to those nice, unimaginative cops that we're being pursued by vicious demons and hellhounds, we'll find ourselves locked in a lovely padded room. If we aren't first tossed into jail for the murder of Selena. I don't know about you, but I'd rather not be strapped in a straitjacket or offered a cell with a spectacular view of the morning sunrise."

Her expression hardened, as if she longed to argue with his logic. Then wrapping her arms about her waist, she heaved an annoyed sigh.

"Fine. And what is your brilliant solution? To crawl through these disgusting alleys for eternity?"

He gave a shrug, moving back to the open doorway. "Not quite that long, I hope. I do know a place, but I must be certain that we've shaken our bloodthirsty friends."

"God, what a mess," she muttered.

Dante forced his fangs to shorten as the lingering shudders of desire tortured his body.

"For once, lover, we are in full agreement."

Chapter 4

Two hours later, Abby was spent.

She had endured a house exploding, the violent death of her employer, being chased by demons (one of which she had killed with her own hands), hours of walking through vile-smelling alleys, and a kiss by a vampire. And to be honest, she wasn't sure which unnerved her the most.

Now, however, a wrenching weariness invaded her entire being.

Her feet hurt, she smelled like an overripe landfill, and a numbing fog was clouding her mind. Hell, at the moment she would have paid a lurking demon to leap out and swallow her whole.

Unfortunately, the ghastly creatures who had seemed so determined to destroy them a mere three hours ago had seemingly disappeared the moment they might have come in handy, and she was left to trudge upon trembling legs behind a silent vampire.

Perhaps this was hell, she theorized. Perhaps she had indeed died in the mysterious blast and was now doomed to roam through darkened, demon-invested alleys for all eternity.

No, not hell, a treacherous voice whispered. Not if she were to be offered an eternity of kisses from a gorgeous vampire that had made her melt into a puddle of aching need.

Her heart skipped a renegade beat before she was giving a sharp shake of her head.

Obviously she was becoming delirious. Vampire kisses. God. No doubt the toxic stench had driven her over the edge. Enough was enough.

"Dante." Coming to a halt, she folded her arms over her chest. "I can't go any farther."

With clear reluctance, Dante stopped at the corner of the alley and turned to meet her stubborn gaze. As weary as she was, her breath caught in her throat.

Bathed in the dull golden light of the streetlamp, Dante was strikingly beautiful. His flowing raven hair. His fiercely elegant features. His silver eyes that shimmered with a lethal danger. It all combined to create a vision that was bound to weaken the knees of any woman.

Thankfully unaware of her treacherous thoughts, Dante reached out to grasp her hand.

"It is just a bit farther, I promise," he urged softly.

Her expression only hardened at his words. "You've said that for the past half hour."

His lips twitched with wicked amusement. "Yes, but on this occasion, I'm not lying."

"Ugh." She leaned against the brick building, too tired to care that she was only adding to the layer of grime that covered her. What were a few more nasty germs? "I should have staked you when I had the chance."

A raven brow arched at her petulant tone. "Do you know, Abby, you really are an ungrateful brat."

"No, I'm tired, I'm hungry, and all I want is to go home."

The chiseled features softened as he reached out and pulled her close to the hardness of his body. Tenderly he ran a hand over her tangled curls.

"I know, lover. I know."

Vampire or not, Abby discovered his touch oddly comforting. And deliciously wonderful. Without conscious thought, she leaned her head against his wide chest.

"Dante, will this horrible night ever end?"

"That much I can promise you," he assured her, giving a small tug until they were out of the alley and standing upon a narrow street. "You see the building on the corner? That's our destination. Can you make it?"

She regarded the plain building, at last concluding that it must have been a hotel in years past. A hotel that was now dank, moldy, and no doubt filled with entire communities of hungry rats. She heaved a sigh even as she gave Dante a reluctant nod of her head.

She was too weary to quibble. If a few rats and a rotting chair were the price of resting her aching feet, then so be it.

"Let's go," she muttered.

Readily accepting Dante's assistance, Abby limped across the street and around the building to the back. He ignored the narrow door that hung limply off its hinges and instead reached out his hand to touch one of the loosened bricks near the window. Astonishingly (well, perhaps not so astonishing on this particular evening), a silver shimmer filled the air, and before Abby could even question what had occurred, Dante had pulled her through the mystical veil into a vast crimson and gold lobby.

Stumbling to a halt, Abby glanced about her with wide eyes. It was impossible. There was nothing rat-infested about this place. Not with its black marble columns and crimson velvet walls and domed roof painted with beautiful naked women.

It was lush and exotic and, well, more than a little decadent.

"What is this place?" she breathed in wonder.

Dante smiled wryly as he took her arm and steered her toward a nearly hidden alcove at the back of the room.

"Better not to ask."

"Why?"

Ignoring her question, he brushed aside the gauzy curtain spangled with golden stars and pulled her down a darkened hall until they reached the last door. Tugging it open, he waited for her to enter before firmly closing the door behind them and turning on the lights.

Much to her relief, Abby discovered the large room considerably more comfortable than the lavish lobby they had left behind. There was a solid warmth to the satinwood paneling and leather furnishings that were scattered over an ivory carpet. More like an English country estate than a lavish bordello, she decided.

Absently wandering to study the leather-bound books that filled the shelves upon one wall, she drew in a deep breath before turning to meet Dante's guarded gaze.

"Will we be safe here?"

"Yes, the building is owned by an acquaintance of

mine. It possesses an enchantment upon it that will prevent anyone from sensing your presence here. Human or demon."

Enchantment? Well, that sounded . . . less strange than anything else that had occurred this bizarre evening. Still, Abby sensed there was a great deal he wasn't telling her. Always a bad sign.

"And your friend?" she demanded.

"What?"

"Is he human or demon?"

He gave a lift of his shoulder. "He is a vampire."

Abby rolled her eyes toward the open beamed ceiling. "Great."

With a silent grace, Dante was suddenly standing before her, his expression relentless in the muted light.

"I would suggest that you attempt to disguise that rather nasty prejudice of yours, lover," he warned in silky tones. "We shall need Viper's assistance if we are to survive the next few days."

Suddenly realizing that she had indeed been more than a bit rude to the man who had saved her life more than once in the past few hours, Abby caught her lower lip between her teeth.

"I'm sorry."

The silver eyes darkened as he tenderly ran the back of his fingers over her heated cheeks.

"There are some things I must do. I want you to remain here." The fingers slid beneath her chin as he gazed deep into her eyes. "And whatever happens, do not open this door until I return. Do you understand?"

A shiver inched down her spine. He was leaving her? Alone?

Good Lord, what if he didn't return? What if some demon attacked while he was gone? What if . . .

Grasping her shattered courage, Abby gave a lift of her chin. *Stop being such a spineless wimp,* she chided herself. Dammit. She had been taking care of herself since she was fourteen years old. Not only herself, but her mother as well, since the older woman discovered life easier to bear at the bottom of a whiskey bottle.

And all without the assistance of a sinfully beautiful vampire.

"I understand."

As if sensing the effort it cost her to appear brave, his fingers tightened upon her chin. Gazes locked, he slowly lowered his head.

"Abby," he whispered.

Softly he brushed his lips over her own. And over and over. His touch was featherlight, but it was enough to make her entire body tingle with pleasure. Tingle and shiver and lots of other exhilarating things.

At last he lifted his head and stepped back. Still reeling with the aftershocks, she watched in silence as he turned to leave the room. It was only when the door snapped firmly shut behind him that she recalled the need to breathe.

Well . . .

It seemed that her feet weren't nearly as tired as she had thought since her toes were firmly curled in pleasure.

A hysterical urge to laugh bubbled in her throat as she moved to flop herself upon a leather sofa. Vampire kisses, indeed. She was mad. That was the only explanation. She was stark, raving mad.

And thankfully too exhausted to even care at the moment.

Allowing her head to topple back onto the leather cushions, Abby breathed in deeply and closed her eyes. For the first time in hours, she wasn't searching over her shoulder for marauding demons or squashing through rotting trash. There was not even a vampire in sight.

For the moment she could simply relax.

Relax? Yeah, right, a tiny voice mocked in the back of her mind.

She sucked in a deep breath. No. She could do this. All it took was a bit of concentration.

Relax, relax, relax, she silently chanted. She snuggled deeper into the cushions. She slowed her breathing. She tried to imagine a beautiful waterfall, a peaceful meadow, the sound of whales (whatever the hell they sounded like).

All worthless efforts that were eventually disturbed when a cold rash raced over her skin.

A sudden certainty that she was no longer alone had her eyes fluttering open and her head lifting. Her heart halted as she realized her instincts had not been wrong.

There was a man standing in the center of the room.

No, not a man, she swiftly corrected. Now that she knew the truth of Dante, she could detect what those too-perfect features and fiercely elegant form meant.

Not that this vampire was the spitting image of Dante, she readily concluded. He was taller and leaner, with a ripple of hard muscles beneath the crimson velvet coat that flowed nearly to his knees and black satin slacks. His hair was worn long, but it was like the pale silver of moonlight and his eyes the startling darkness of midnight. And while his features were hauntingly beautiful, there was a starkness to his countenance that sent a chill down her spine.

This was not the charmingly wicked bad boy.

This was an exquisite fallen angel who held himself aloof from the world about him.

Slowly rising to her feet, she discovered herself nervously licking her lips as he strolled nonchalantly forward. His midnight gaze swept over her with unnerving intensity. It was not until he was a mere step from her that he came to a halt.

"Ah, Abby is it not?"

The dark voice flowed like warm honey over her. A voice as lethally fascinating as the rest of him. Yikes. He fell under the category of dangerous with a capital *D*.

Still, Dante wouldn't have left her here if he didn't believe she was in safe hands. She might not know much about her savior vampire, but she did know he wouldn't deliberately hand her over as dinner to one of his pals.

Would he?

"Yes, and you, I presume, are Viper?" she forced herself to murmur in polite tones.

"Very astute." The dark eyes swept over her slender features and tumble of honey curls. "And lovely."

Lovely? A faint frown touched her brow. Was he blind? Or was he indeed up to something nefarious? She had never been more than passably average. And that was when she wasn't covered in muck and reeking of back alleys.

"Thank you . . . I think."

His lips curled into a smooth smile. "You needn't

regard me with such distrust. I never feed upon my guests. It is rather bad for business."

Well, that was a relief. She cleared her dry throat. "And what is your business?"

"I am a procurer of pleasure," he said simply.

She choked, her eyes widening at the unexpected words. "You're a pimp?"

His soft laugh reminded her forcibly of Dante as he tilted his head to one side. "Nothing so mundane," he purred in low tones. "I offer . . . ah no, Dante would not thank me for exposing you to such sordid tales. He is astonishingly protective of you." Without warning, he reached up to lightly brush her cheek. "And it is little wonder."

She stiffened in unease. "What?"

"Such purity." His gaze drifted over her tense form before returning to linger upon her pale features. "A golden beacon to the dark."

First lovely and now pure? The poor, incredibly beautiful vampire really must be off his rocker.

Not a very comforting thought.

"I'm afraid you must have me confused with someone else," she said in slow, easy-to-follow tones.

His lips twitched as if realizing that she feared him mental. "I do not speak of chastity." He gave an elegant wave of his hand. "Such a tedious mortal obsession. Or even of the spirit that you now carry within you. I speak of your soul, Abby. You have known tragedy and even despair, but you remain untainted."

She took a careful step back, desperately wishing that Dante would return. There was something very unnerving about this Viper.

"I don't know what you're talking about."

"Evil, lust, greed—the darker passions that so easily tempt mortals."

"Well, I suppose everyone is tempted."

"Yes, and so few resist." He closed the small distance between them, his fingers once again tracing the line of her cheek. "Such innocence is bound to be an irresistible attraction for those who walk in the night. Wickedness always seeks redemption, even as the shadows seek the light."

Abby's brain was beginning to ache in an attempt to follow the obscure revelations. Holy crap, she thought Dante spoke in riddles.

"Ah . . . right," she muttered, taking yet another step back in their peculiar dance. "Where is Dante?"

Viper offered a shrug. "He did not give me his full itinerary, but I do know he has gone in search of breakfast."

Her stomach gave a sudden growl of relief. She couldn't even remember her last meal. Which meant it was far too long ago.

"Thank God, I'm starving. I hope he brings . . ." The delicious images of pancakes and eggs and bacon were suddenly tarnished by the thought of what Dante would be having for his predawn meal. "Ew."

Viper lifted a golden brow at her unmistakable shudder.

"Do not worry, lovely Abby. He is not on the hunt." Moving with mesmerizing grace, Viper flicked open a hidden panel in the wall to reveal a small refrigerator filled with dark bottles. "This is the home of a vampire. I always possess an ample supply of synthetic blood. The breakfast is for you."

Ridiculously relieved to know that Dante wasn't

out sucking the life from hapless pedestrians, she heaved a deep sigh.

"Oh, that's good."

Closing the panel, the vampire smiled in a mysterious manner as he once again returned to stand before her.

"You do not know, do you?"

Her brows snapped together. "Know what?"

"Since Dante was captured by the witches, he has been incapable of taking blood from a human. It is an element of the spell that binds him to the Phoenix."

"Oh, I . . . see."

"No, I don't believe you see at all," he murmured softly. "The suffering that Dante has endured for the past three hundred years has been immeasurable. He has been leashed and imprisoned by those who have no compassion, no ability to see him as anything more than a monster."

Abby stilled. Dear heavens. She had been so consumed with her own fears that she had never taken even a moment to consider what Dante must have endured all those endless years. He had been a prisoner, chained for eternity to Selena. God, it was a wonder he hadn't dumped her whining butt in the nearest gutter and left her as demon food.

"He's not a monster," she retorted in sharp tones.

"You have no need to convince me, my dear." He peered deep into her eyes. "I can only hope that you will understand his suffering and do what is possible to ease his burdens."

"Me?"

"You now possess the power."

She blinked, giving a faint shake of her head. "And I thought Dante was cryptic. No offense, but vampires are strange creatures. Not as strange as that Halford or hellhounds, but definitely strange."

He gave a soft chuckle as he reached out to touch her curls. "We are ancient beings. We have seen the birth and fall of nations. Witnessed endless wars, famines, and natural disasters. Surely we are allowed a few eccentricities?"

And what did she say to that?

"Or at least a Purple Heart."

The midnight eyes momentarily filled with something that might have been amusement. "There are also visions of joy, pleasure, and unexpected beauty. Beauty such as yours."

"Exquisite taste as always, Viper," a velvet voice drawled from the doorway.

Startled by the interruption, Abby turned her head to regard Dante slowly strolling toward them. With a casual motion, he tossed the suitcase he held in his hand onto the sofa, never pausing in his approach.

More relieved than she cared to admit at his return, Abby drank in the pale, wicked countenance. As ridiculous as it might be to accept, it was almost as if a part of herself had been missing during his absence. A part that now felt fulfilled.

She was barely aware that Viper had moved to stand behind her, his hands resting lightly upon her shoulders.

"So you return at last, Dante," Viper murmured. "We were worried."

The silver gaze narrowed as Dante pointedly glanced toward the hands intimately grasping Abby's shoulders.

"Your concern is quite touching, Viper." He slowly arched a brow. "And speaking of touching . . ."

There was no mistaking the menacing edge in the satin voice, but Viper merely laughed.

"You cannot blame a vampire for admiring such purity. It is quite . . . intoxicating."

"Then perhaps you should get a breath of fresh air to clear your mind," Dante warned.

"Always the warrior." Viper reached to pull Abby's fingers to his lips. "If you decide you prefer a poet, be sure to call for me."

"Viper," Dante growled.

With that mysterious smile, Viper offered his fellow vampire a faint bow before moving toward the door.

"I shall leave the two of you to rest. Don't worry that you'll be bothered. I promise to keep the wolves, or in this case the demons, at bay."

Left on their own, Dante paused a moment before he moved to take the hand that Viper had so recently caressed.

"You must forgive my friend," he said with a wry smile. "He believes himself to be irresistible to women."

Smothering the urge to reach up and touch the sculpted face, she offered a distracted shrug. "He is rather fascinating," she felt bound to admit. Surely not even a babbling idiot would believe she was utterly indifferent to the beautiful fallen angel?

"You find him attractive?"

"In an undead sort of way."

His expression hardened. "I see."

Abby shivered. "He also terrifies me. I think he would destroy anything or anyone in his path if it suited his purpose."

A smile touched his lips. "He will not harm you. Not as long as I am near."

"Where have you been?"

He gave her fingers a slight squeeze before moving back to the suitcase he had left on the sofa and sweeping it open.

"To Selena's to retrieve a few belongings I thought we might need." He pulled out several pairs of jeans and casual cotton shirts that had once belonged to her employer. "They might not be a perfect fit, but they should do."

She heaved a sigh of sheer relief at the thought of clean clothes. A small slice of paradise.

"Thank you."

He reached back into the suitcase to pull out a small plastic container. "I also brought you this."

"What is it?"

"Something I believe you shall soon have need of."

Hoping against hope that it was a hot fudge sundae, she took the container and slowly pulled off the lid. Her nose wrinkled at the foul smell that wafted from the green goo that most certainly was not a hot fudge sundae.

"Ugh. This is that vile stuff Selena used to drink."

"It will give you nourishment."

She hastily put the container onto a nearby table. "So will a cheeseburger and fries, and without any icky green aftertaste."

"Abby." Oddly Dante turned to pace across the large room, his fingers running a restless path through his long raven hair. "There is something you need to know."

Her blood froze at his raw tone. She might not know jack about vampires, but she did know that tone. It meant trouble. It always meant trouble.

"What?"

Slowly he turned to study her with a somber expression. "When Selena was dying, she touched you."

Abby reluctantly recalled those horrible moments in Selena's charred bedroom. It was something she had tried to put from her mind.

She gave a nod of her head. "Yes, I remember. Her fingers were moving, and then she grabbed my arm. It hurt."

"That was because she transferred her powers to you."

"Her . . . powers?"

"The spirit of the Phoenix," he said. "It now resides within you."

She stumbled backward as she waited for the punch line to the sick joke. There had to be a punch line, didn't there? Otherwise Dante would be serious. And that would mean she had some horrid creature setting up camp inside her.

Abby clutched her throat with trembling hands. She couldn't breathe. Couldn't think.

"No," she at last managed to gasp. "You're lying."

Easily detecting her distress, Dante moved forward, his hands held out. "Abby, I know this is difficult."

Abby loosed a hysterical laugh even as she bumped painfully into the paneled wall.

She had thought there was nothing left to shock her. How could it? Nothing could be worse than demons and vampires.

Or so she had thought.

Now she gave a violent shake of her head. "What could you know? You're not even human."

Chapter 5

Dante suppressed the urge to growl in frustration.

During his hurried excursion to Selena's, he had prepared himself for this confrontation. He hadn't pretended that Abby would do backflips of joy at being the Chalice for the Phoenix. Or thank him for offering the truth.

He knew she would be upset, even hysterical.

But that sudden fear in her eyes as she backed from him was enough to stir his most primal feelings.

Bloody hell, why did he care if she had returned to thinking him a monster? He had endured over three hundred years chained to the Phoenix without giving a damn about Selena as a person. Unless one counted the delicious dreams of draining her dry.

She had been no more than his captor. The tangible source of his smoldering fury.

But Abby . . .

It did matter, he grimly accepted. It mattered too damn much.

Reluctantly he studied the fragile, too-pale

features, knowing he would do whatever necessary to ease her distress.

"Please listen to me, Abby," he murmured.

She gave another shake of her head. "No, just stay away from me."

Stay away? The irony brought a wry smile to his lips.

"I'm afraid I can't do that. We are now bound together. Neither of us can leave the other. It's part of the spell."

Her eyes widened in horror before they abruptly narrowed. "Now I know that you're lying. You did leave me."

"I did not go far, and it was with the knowledge that I would soon return to your side," he said softly, subtly moving forward. "Had I deliberately intended to flee, the pain would have been unbearable. Trust me, I tried enough times over the centuries to be certain."

She licked her dry lips. "No."

"Abby, can you tell me honestly that you did not feel my absence? Deep within you?"

The truth was etched upon her pale features even as she shook her head in denial. "This . . . can't be. I would know if some creature was living inside me."

"Do you want proof?"

She pressed even tighter to the paneling. "What do you mean?"

Dante slowly held out his hand. "Come."

Abby paused, staring at his hand for long moments before at last placing her fingers on his own. Dante felt a rush of warmth at her unspoken display of trust. And another rush of warmth at the sensation of her soft skin brushing his own.

Heady stuff for a vampire who had been cold for an eternity.

With a gentle tug, he led her across the room to the large mirror hanging above the marble fireplace. Then, stepping behind her, he placed his hands upon her shoulders.

"Tell me what you see," he commanded in low tones.

She gave an impatient sound. "I see . . . oh." She leaned forward to peer into the mirror. "God, you have no reflection."

Dante rolled his eyes heavenward. "Of course not, I'm a vampire."

"It's just so weird."

"Abby, look at yourself," he rasped.

"What?" Her brows drew together. "You want me to see I'm a wreck? News flash, I already knew that."

"Look at your eyes."

"My eyes? I—" Her words abruptly broke off as she reached with shaking fingers to touch her reflection. And no wonder. The soft brown eyes that had always fascinated him were now a brilliant, sapphire blue. The same blue that had marked Selena. A visible sign of the Phoenix that she could no longer deny. "No. No, no, no."

She stumbled backward, straight into his arms. Gently Dante turned her about and pressed her head to his chest as he brushed his hand over her curls.

"Easy, love," he murmured. "It's going to be okay."

A violent shiver raced through her body before she pulled back her head to stab him with a tearful glare.

"How? How is it going to be okay? I have some . . .

creature inside me." She gave a sudden gasp. "Oh God, that's why the demons were trying to kill me, isn't it?"

His arms tightened about her. He could lie, of course. And for a few minutes she might actually be comforted. But in the end, he knew that she would have to know the truth.

"Yes. They sensed the spirit within you as well as the fact you are vulnerable. They will halt at nothing to regain their Prince."

A stark terror darkened the brilliance of her newly blue eyes. "I'm going to die."

"No," he swore in vicious denial. "I will not allow that to happen."

"And how long do you suppose we can fight off every demon on earth? Unless you intend for us to hide here for the next fifty billion years?"

Shifting, he placed his fingers beneath her chin and forced her to meet his stern gaze.

"It will not be necessary. With every passing hour, the Phoenix gathers its strength."

"The Phoenix is gathering strength?" She gave a short, humorless laugh. "Inside me? Is that supposed to be reassuring?"

A hint of tenderness eased his stark expression. "I only mean that it soon will be capable of masking itself so that the demons cannot sense its presence."

Far from comforted, Abby regarded him warily. "And what else will this thing be doing inside me?"

"I can't say for certain," he reluctantly admitted. "Selena did not consider me her confidant. I was merely her chained beast."

Her head dropped back onto his chest. "My God, what am I going to do?"

He laid his cheek upon the top of her head, readily surrounding himself in her sweet warmth. "I do have a suggestion."

"What?"

"We must seek out the witches."

He felt her suck in a shocked gasp. "The witches? You mean the women who put this Phoenix into Selena?"

His features hardened. Even after three centuries, he vividly recalled every moment he endured at the hands of the coven. The black dungeon. The chains that had burned his very flesh. The magic that had leashed him like a neutered dog.

His searing hatred had not eased, but his concern for Abby was even greater. There was no one else who could help her.

"Yes."

"But"—she pulled back to regard him with a frown—"surely they are dead by now?"

"Their powers are linked to the Phoenix. As long as it lives, so do they."

"And you think they could help me?"

"Perhaps," he offered cautiously.

"Then let's go to them." She reached up to clutch the lapels of his silk shirt. "Where are they?"

"Actually, I'm not entirely certain."

"What do you mean?"

"As I said, Selena kept most of her secrets to herself, but I do know that she met the witches on occasion. They must have a coven close by."

"In Chicago?"

He gave a faint shake of his head, having already considered the possible locations. "Not in the city. They will need a place that is well secluded."

"Why?"

Dante hesitated. Although he had determined

not to hide the truth from Abby, he conceded that there was no need for graphic details. Not when they were only bound to upset her further.

"They perform . . . certain rites that they would not want others to witness."

Thankfully she was too distracted to consider the nature of the rites. Instead she chewed her bottom lip until Dante shivered with the need to soothe it with a soft kiss.

"Then how can we possibly find them?"

Now it was Dante who was distracted. The scent of her satin skin, the feel of her soft curves, the delicious heat that stirred his passions.

"Leave that to me," he muttered, his hands slipping down the curve of her spine to rest upon the swell of her hips. "Now, what would you say to a hot bath?"

"A bath?" The frantic urgency faded as a dreamy longing settled upon her face. "I would say that it sounds like heaven."

Dante silently groaned at the thought of seeing that dreamy expression for an entirely different reason than hot water and soapy bubbles. Reasons such as his hands skimming over that silken skin and tumbling those honey curls while his lips blazed paths that had never been blazed before.

Abruptly he stepped away, not at all accustomed to restraining his passions. The witches might have stolen his lust for hunting humans, but every other lust remained in exquisite working order.

"Come along, lover. You shall have your bath."

Turning on his heel, Dante moved to a door neatly hidden by the paneling. A press on the hidden lever and the door swung open to reveal a narrow hall. With a glance over his shoulder to ensure that Abby was following, he led her past the various bedrooms to the master bathroom.

With a flick of the switch, muted light filled the room. From behind him he heard a faint gasp, and then Abby was stepping into the center of the room with a dazed expression.

For a moment Dante regarded her in puzzlement, but as she reached out to run a hand over the marble tub that was the size of a small swimming pool, a smile touched his lips. Of course. For one un-accustomed to Viper's extravagant taste, the perfect replication of a Grecian bath would be somewhat surprising. And perhaps just a tad overwhelming.

"Viper is never subtle," he murmured, sweeping past her to turn on the faucets that were shaped as goddesses.

"It's beautiful."

"Yes."

Pausing to pour a measure of scented bubble bath into the cascading water, Dante turned back toward Abby and then firmly reached out to begin unbuttoning her grimy shirt.

Her eyes widened as he nimbly dealt with the fastenings and stripped the offending garment from her slender form. Without hesitation, he performed a similar duty to her khaki pants and slid them down the length of her legs.

"Dante," she at last managed to croak, "what are you doing?"

Flowing to his knees, he removed her shoes and pulled away the slacks to toss them into a pile in the corner.

"Preparing you for your bath, my lady," he murmured, rising to tackle the lacy bra.

Instinctively her hands rose in protest. "You can't . . ."

His gaze collided with her own as he swept aside her hands and undid the clasp to her bra with one motion.

"Trust me, my love."

She swallowed heavily, but clearly too weary, or perhaps as caught in the spell-tingling moment as he was, she didn't protest. Still holding her gaze, he caught her silk panties in his fingers and slowly slid them down before at last lifting her in his arms and carrying her to the waiting bath.

With a careful tenderness, he lowered her into the water and reached for a washcloth that was folded in a pretty seashell.

He was forced to kneel upon the marble floor as he began the slow task of scrubbing her skin clean. Not that he noticed the hardness beneath his knees or the warm steam that was making his silk shirt cling to his body. His every thought was consumed with the sensual delight of touching this woman.

"So soft," he husked, rubbing the cloth down the length of her arm. "Like warm ivory."

Leaning back her head, Abby allowed her eyes to drift closed. "That feels wonderful."

Wonderful. Yes. And wicked. And sinfully tempting.

A slow, simmering hunger woke within Dante as he continued his self-imposed torment. Lying in the tub built for the worship of goddesses, she might have floated down from Mt. Olympus itself with her long, slender limbs and honey curls floating about her fragile face.

Careful to do nothing that might startle her out of her oblivion, he washed her creamy skin and then the honey curls. The warmth of her filled his cold body. Filled him and made his blood run hot as he rinsed the last of the shampoo from her hair.

Barely aware of what he did, Dante softly cradled her face and traced her cheeks with his thumbs. Such delicate beauty, he admired in silent satisfaction. Not the absurd physical beauty that humans held in such high regard and could change at the drop of a hat. Hell, anyone could buy that sort of beauty from a plastic surgeon. But Abby possessed a spiritual beauty that called to him with irresistible force.

Slowly, ever so slowly, he lowered his head and stroked his lips over her mouth. For a moment she seemed to stiffen, but even as he prepared to pull back, her lips astonishingly parted in silent invitation.

The capitulation was as soft as a whisper, and yet Dante felt a bolt of pleasure shimmer through his body.

Bloody hell. He had dreamed and ached for this woman for weeks. Months. Now he trembled with the sheer force of keeping himself from devouring her.

His fingers tightened upon her face. He could taste soap upon her lips and smell the heat of her blood. Sweet, forbidden magic raced through him as his kisses deepened with demand.

Beneath him Abby offered a sigh of appreciation as she lifted her damp arms to wrap them about his neck. Dante moaned his approval. He savored the fierce sensations clenching his body. His passions had always run high. He had enjoyed countless women over the centuries. But never had he been stirred with such a relentless force.

It was as if she had awakened a slumbering

hunger that would not be satisfied with anything less than absolute possession.

Parting her lips with his tongue, he explored the moist cavern of her mouth. He needed more. Her body pressed beneath him. Her legs wrapped about his waist. Her hips lifting to sheath him deep into her body.

Her fingers clenched in his hair even as his mouth shifted, tracing a path of searing fire over her cheek and down the curve of her neck.

He felt as if he were drowning as he nuzzled the frantic pulse at the base of her throat and moved his hands down to brush over her slender curves. Abby shuddered in response before her fingers were suddenly cupping his face and her body arching upward.

"Dante?" she demanded in soft confusion.

Lost in his heated passions, Dante wanted to ignore her whisper. It would be so easy. Beneath his hands he could feel her shiver with a longing that matched his own. Why shouldn't he provide the sweet release that lurked so tantalizingly close?

It was the unwanted memory of his own words that made his head slowly lift.

Trust me, he had commanded as he had prepared her for her bath.

Damn. He had urged her to put aside her natural caution and place herself in his hands. Perhaps the most difficult thing for a woman such as Abby to do. Whatever his desire for her, he could not risk any belated sense of betrayal. Both their lives depended upon her faith in him.

Grimly lifting himself upright, Dante gathered Abby carefully in his arms and wrapped her in a warm towel. "Come, it's time you were safely tucked into bed."

For a moment she stiffened, as if embarrassed by her blatant reaction to his touch. Then with a rueful sigh she allowed her head to drop onto his shoulder.

"I'm so tired," she muttered.

"I know, my sweet. We will rest here today."

He dropped an absent kiss on the top of her head as he moved through the door that connected directly with the master bedroom. Despite the fact that morning had long ago arrived, not even a stray hint of light marred the perfect darkness. Still he had no difficulty in finding his way across the lush carpeting to the bed. Sweeping aside the blankets, he laid Abby onto the satin sheets and pulled the duvet over her.

About to pull away, he was caught off guard when she abruptly reached out to grasp his hand.

"Dante?"

"Yes?"

"We will be safe here?"

"Nothing will harm you here."

"And"—there was a pause as if she battled something within herself—"you will be near?"

A small smile touched his lips. He knew this woman would rather have a root canal, a bad perm, and cellulite rather than confess her vulnerability.

"I'll be right at your side, lover," he promised as he gracefully moved to lie on the bed and take her into his arms. Covering them both with the duvet, he allowed her warmth to cloak about him. "For all eternity."

* * *

The once-proud Victorian church with its stained-glass windows and walnut pews had long since fallen into ruin. With the closing of the paper mill, the small town that had been called to worship had abandoned hope and faith and at last migrated to richer pastures. Even the attached graveyard was now only a shell of tumbled crypts and tenacious weeds.

Beneath the remains of stone and forgotten corpses, however, the vast catacombs were kept with meticulous care.

Not a rat would dare enter the maze of tunnels or stone chambers that had been polished as smooth as marble over the ages. No spiderweb would disturb the stark simplicity.

Hardly what one might expect from a demon's dark temple. But then Rafael, the master of the cult, was not a usual demon.

In truth, he wasn't a demon at all.

A tall sparse man with gaunt features, he had once been as drearily mortal as any other. But he had given his humanity and soul to the Dark Prince centuries before.

In reward for his cold cruelty, and perchance for evil, he had quickly risen through the ranks into a position of power. A power that had become all but impotent since the arrival of the witches and their damnable Phoenix.

Pacing through his shadowed chamber, Rafael absently stroked his thin fingers over the heavy silver pendant that hung about his neck.

So much depended upon him.

Upon his actions tonight.

He could not fail.

Hearing the sound of the approaching footsteps

that he had been awaiting, Rafael smoothed his features to a cold mask of invincibility. Now, more than ever, he needed to use the lethal reputation he had earned over the long years.

There was a tentative knock. Calling the visitor to enter, Rafael carefully surveyed the young apprentice.

He was standing as still and forbidding as granite as he watched the apprentice close the door and move toward the center of the room. The younger man did not yet have the shaved head of a convert. Such an honor would not be allowed unless he survived the trials. Many came to worship the Prince, but few survived.

His shrewd gaze easily pierced the modest demeanor of the younger man, discerning the sharpness to the countenance and the cunning in the pale eyes.

Oh yes, he would do quite well, he decided with an inward smile.

Clearly unnerved by the relentless gaze, the apprentice nervously shifted. "You summoned me, Master Rafael?"

"Yes, Apprentice Amil. Please, have a seat." Rafael waited until the student had moved to perch upon the uncomfortable wooden chair, then he slowly moved to stand before his guest. "You are comfortable?"

Amil shifted with a faint frown. "Yes, thank you."

"Be at ease, my son," Rafael drawled, folding his hands within the arms of his robe. "Despite persistent rumors among the brothers, I do not usually eat acolytes for dinner. Not even those who have dared to practice the dark arts forbidden even to us."

There was a moment of shock before the young man was abruptly sliding out of the chair and landing upon his knees.

"Master, forgive me," he begged in unsteady tones. "It was mere curiosity. I did not intend harm."

Rafael grimaced as the fool threatened to wrinkle the hem of his robes. It had been more fortune than skill that had led him to discover the overly ambitious apprentice slipping from the tower to recite the black spells. His first instinct had been to rip out his throat. Not only would it have been a fitting punishment, but it would have provided him a great deal of pleasure.

But in the end he had hesitated. A man in his powerful position was always in need of faithful servants. And no servant was more faithful than one who knew he was a breath away from death.

"Oh, do get up, worm."

Shakily the man forced himself to regain his seat, warily regarding Rafael.

"Am I to be killed?"

"That is the penalty."

"Of course, master," the man obediently agreed, although his sincerity was open to question.

"Dark magics are not a toy. They are dangerous to you and to those about you. You endangered us all with your stupidity and risked exposing our temple."

"Yes, master."

Rafael's thin lips hardened. "But you are ambitious, eh, Amil? You desire to wield the power that beckons just out of reach?"

The pale gaze covertly flicked toward Rafael's potent medallion, before recalling he was on the knife's edge of becoming dinner. Or worse.

"Only if the Prince wills it so."

"I sense your talent. It runs deep within you. A

pity it shall be wasted before it can ever bloom to its full potential."

"Please, master. I have learned my lesson. I shall not stray again."

Rafael slowly lifted his brows. "And you believe I should trust your empty promise? You who have already displayed an inbred treachery?"

Perhaps sensing a glimmer of hope, Amil leaned forward, his thin features flushed. "All I ask is a second opportunity. I'll do whatever you ask of me."

"Whatever? A rather rash promise."

"I don't care. Just tell me what I must do."

Rafael pretended to consider the plea. He had, of course, known that the pathetic apprentice would sell his soul. He had depended upon it. In some ways the youth reminded him of himself with his burning thirst for knowledge. But unlike this fool, he had possessed the wits to keep his secret studies well hidden. And the wisdom never to place himself in the power of another.

"Perhaps I could consider being lenient upon this one occasion," he slowly drawled. "With one condition."

"Bless you, master," Amil breathed. "Bless you."

"I do not believe you will be so grateful when you discover my condition."

"What do you desire of me?"

With measured steps, Rafael moved to take his seat behind the massive desk. He templed his fingers beneath his chin and regarded his guest with a piercing gaze. The next few moments would decide his fate.

If he was to be acclaimed as the savior of the Prince of Demons or as an arrogant failure. He could not afford a mistake.

"First I desire that you tell me what you know of the Phoenix."

Caught off guard, Amil blinked in surprise. "I . . . what all creatures of the dark know, I suppose. Nearly three hundred years ago, powerful witches gathered together to call for the spirit of the Phoenix and placed it within a human body. The presence of the vile beast has kept the Prince banished from this world and made his minions impotent."

"I am not impotent," Rafael snapped in annoyance.

"I do not understand." Amil regarded the older wizard with a wary frown. "Why do we speak of the Phoenix?"

"Because it keeps us from our true master."

The younger man shrugged. "He has been lost to us. What can we do?"

Rafael barely restrained his flare of fury.

Fools. The lot of them. While he had toiled and sacrificed to return his dark lord, the others had allowed despair to overwhelm them. No longer were they proud beasts who inspired fear and loathing among mortals. Instead they scuttled in the shadows like rabid animals.

They disgusted him.

"No, my son. The Prince has not entirely been lost to the world."

"What are you saying?"

"The vessel has been destroyed. The witches no longer have control of the Phoenix."

The pale eyes widened in shock. "It's a miracle."

"Indeed."

The apprentice gripped the arms of his chair. "The Prince will soon be freed."

"No." Rafael's voice was harsh. "The vessel placed

the spirit in the body of another mortal. The Phoenix yet lives, but it is weakened and vulnerable."

"It must be destroyed. And swiftly."

Rafael's expression hardened to grim lines, his thin fingers moving to stroke the heavy pendant about his neck.

"Certainly it must be destroyed."

"And what do you want of me?"

"I want you to bring the vessel to me. Alive."

The apprentice narrowed his gaze in a calculating manner. "Forgive me, master, but wouldn't it be best to call out the minions to crush the Phoenix before it can regain its strength?"

Rafael twisted his lips wryly. Like most who craved power, Amil was far too ready to resort to violence when cunning was needed.

"Certainly a simpler, if more bloodthirsty, solution," he agreed. "But consider, my son. It will be a great honor for the one who offers up the Phoenix to the master. And I intend for that glory to be mine."

Amil considered for a moment before giving a nod of his head. "Of course. A clever scheme. But, why me? Why do you not do this grave task yourself?"

"Because someone must ensure that the witches do not interfere. I am the only one with the power to challenge them." He shrugged. "And, of course, you have tampered with forces that will assist you in discovering where the woman is hiding."

There was a long pause before Amil folded his hands over his chest, a faint smile upon his lips.

"This is a dangerous thing you ask of me, master. The vampire is certain to be protecting the vessel. I risk more than just my life."

Rafael struggled to hide his disdain for the man

who would barter for power rather than earn it. Unfortunately, he possessed no other servants willing to call upon powers forbidden by even the Prince.

Sacrifices must be made, he reluctantly acknowledged.

Even if it meant being in league with such a pathetic fool.

"So you wish to know your reward?" he demanded in cold tones.

"I am a practical man."

Sacrifices.

Rafael grimly maintained his composure. "I shall personally take charge of your training. You wish to earn your medallion before all others? I can give you that."

The smile widened. "And a share of the Prince's gratitude?"

Rafael briefly glanced down at his hands, imagining them around the greedy Amil's neck. Then he gave a small shake of his head.

The future was poised upon the night ahead. He had to do whatever was necessary to ensure the return of his master.

"So be it."

The younger man rose to his feet, satisfaction engraved upon the narrow features.

"Then we have a bargain."

Rafael also rose, his own countenance as hard and dark as the stone walls.

"Amil, do not fail me. You have already faced death. If I discover you were unable to complete this task I set for you, then death will be the least of your worries. Do you understand?"

The apprentice possessed the sense to pale at the threat. "Yes."

Rafael waved an impatient hand. "Then go. You have much to do before the sun sets and the vampire is at his full strength."

Amil slipped from the room, and Rafael turned to pace toward the fire that burned in the center of the floor.

The Dark Prince would soon be returned to his place of glory.

And he would be leading the way.

"Soon, my lord," he whispered.

Chapter 6

It was some hours later when Abby stirred from her deep, thankfully dreamless sleep. Lifting her heavy lids, she was at first befuddled by the feel of satin sheets brushing her skin and the shadows that filled the vast room.

She was not the sort of girl who woke up in strange rooms. Certainly not those with satin sheets and an echo that could rival St. Paul's Cathedral.

Still, it was better than the lumpy mattress and foul stench that had greeted her last time she awoke, she wryly told herself. And with the added benefit of a pair of delicious male arms wrapped about her.

Not a bad way to awaken.

At least it wouldn't be if those rotten memories of demons, witches, and being invaded by a powerful spirit didn't come crashing back.

Grimacing, Abby rolled onto her side to study the man who slept next to her.

No, not man, she fiercely reminded herself. Vampire.

Studying the wickedly perfect features in the dim

light, it seemed impossible that she hadn't guessed the truth before. He was every woman's fantasy. Life had taught her that there had to be a catch somewhere.

Her lips twitched. All women knew that the sort of men who could steal a woman's heart with a glance had to be either gay, psychotic, or married. Now she supposed she would have to add vampire to the list.

Barely aware of what she did, Abby silently lifted the duvet to reveal the lean, muscular form. Although the jeans rather disappointingly remained, he had removed his silk shirt to reveal a chest that was just as lethally beautiful as she had imagined in her heated dreams. It was broad and smooth with enough chiseled muscles to satisfy the most demanding woman. Lordy, it virtually begged to be stroked.

And thankfully there were no odd bumps or scales that plagued other demons. Not even a tattoo marred the alabaster skin.

"Good morning, lover," a husky voice abruptly intruded into the silence.

Jerking her head up, Abby took in the slit of silver glittering beneath the heavy black lashes.

Well, this was embarrassing.

It was one thing to walk about with toilet paper stuck to her shoe. Or have lipstick on her teeth. Or even to destroy a priceless Ming vase.

But to be caught openly leering at a half-naked man while he slept . . .

It was downright lewd.

She abruptly dropped the duvet as if it might scorch her fingers.

"I . . . didn't realize that you were awake," she managed to croak.

"I may be dead, but not even I can sleep while a beautiful woman ogles me." His lips curved in a sardonic smile. "Tell me, sweet, what were you searching for? A horn and tail?"

The very fact that she had possessed a furtive need to assure herself he didn't have any peculiar oddities made her instantly defensive.

"No, of course not."

"Ah, then you were planning to take advantage of me while I slept, eh? Twisted, but I like it."

"No . . . I . . ." She wrinkled her nose, accepting that she had been well and truly caught. What was left but to admit the truth? "I suppose I was curious. You seem so . . . normal."

He stiffened at her reluctant confession. "You mean human?"

"Yes."

"Are you disappointed or relieved?"

She gave a faint shrug. "After Halford and the hellhounds, I'll have to admit to some relief."

Without warning, she discovered herself rolled onto her back with Dante looming above her, his hands planted on either side of her head.

"Perhaps I don't possess three eyes or have acid dripping from my fangs," he said, his beautiful features unexpectedly somber, "but you should never make the mistake of pretending that I'm human. I am a vampire, Abby, not a man."

Her heart stuttered as she stared at the dangerous warrior poised above her. Suddenly he did appear far from human. He was coiled, elegant death that held her life in his hands.

"What are you saying?" she whispered. "That I can't trust you?"

The raven brows snapped together. "Of course you can trust me. I will die before I ever allow anything to harm you."

"Then what?"

"I just don't want you to try and pretend that I'm something that I'm not." His metallic gaze pierced deep into her eyes. "It will only prove painful to both of us."

Pretend that he was not a vampire? Holy hell, what was he babbling about? She might pretend that eating a hot fudge sundae was a balanced meal as long as it had peanuts and whipped cream on top. Or that Johnny Depp was her true soul mate if only he would take the time to get to know her.

But the fact that this man was not a vampire?

Ha.

Oddly, however, as she opened her mouth to inform him that he was off his rocker, she abruptly hesitated.

Rats. Could she honestly say that she hadn't at times during the past few hours attempted to forget the truth of Dante? Times such as during his tender seduction in the bathtub? And when she had clung to him in the dark as if he were her guardian angel?

It was certainly her stock and trade to ignore what she didn't want to see.

Lowering her lashes, she battled a ridiculous urge to blush. "We should be getting up."

"Abby, please don't shut me out," he said, his voice softening to a dark, pleasant rasp that feathered down her spine. "I didn't mean to frighten you. It's just . . ."

Against her will, her eyes lifted to clash with his silver gaze. "Just what?"

"I want you to know me for who and what I am, not as some sugar-and-spice image of what you wish I could be."

"I saw you fight that demon, Dante. I know what you are."

Surprisingly he grimaced in the dusky shadows. "No, you don't, but you will before all this is said and done. And that's what I fear."

Suddenly Abby understood. This was about more than just her uncertain opinion of vampires. It was about faith. Trust. In him.

"We both know I would already be dead if you were a human. I'd be a hypocrite to wish you to be anything but what you are," she admitted, a reluctant smile touching her lips. "Besides, my record with men of the human species doesn't precisely make me anxious to be saddled with one for an eternity."

His features thankfully softened at her rueful confession. "No knights in shining armor?"

"Knights? More like mooks."

"Mooks?"

"Well, my last boyfriend dumped me for our mailman, and I do mean mail*man*, and the one before him stuck around just long enough to steal my ATM code so he could clear out my savings account."

"Worthless vermin." He narrowed his gaze.

"Unbelievably they were an improvement to my first boyfriend, who thought the best way to end an argument was with his fists."

There was a stark silence as he studied her face. "He hit you?"

"Only once. I at least learn from my stupidity."

"Do you want me to kill him?"

Abby blinked, not at all certain he was teasing. "Ah . . . well . . . a tempting offer, of course, but I suppose I should pass."

He shrugged. "It's an open-ended offer if you change your mind."

"Actually, I prefer to simply forget they ever existed," she assured him.

"A solution of sorts." His gaze swept down to the fullness of her lips before lifting. "But do you think it wise?"

Abby frowned. Surely to God she was not about to receive dating advice from a half-naked vampire who just happened to be perched on top of her?

A deliciously sexy half-naked vampire.

"I would say it's at least wiser than having them eaten," she forced herself to mutter.

"I only wonder if you truly have learned from your mistakes," he said.

"I've learned that I have rotten judgment when it comes to men."

"Or you seek out those who are destined to disappoint you so that you needn't worry about an emotional attachment."

"Oh God, please don't turn Dr. Phil on me," she grumped, not at all in the mood to consider he might be right. "The last thing I need is to be psychoanalyzed by a vampire."

He arched a raven brow. "It is the fact that I am a vampire that gives me some insight. You don't live among humans for four centuries without learning something of their peculiar habits."

"Well, you don't know anything about me."

"No?" His lips curled in a faint smile. "I know that you hate onions and tuna fish, that you consume your weight in chocolate every day without ever gaining a pound, and that you need a recipe to boil water. I know that you pretend to enjoy classical music but change the radio station to punk rock when you think no one is around. I also know that you hide yourself from the world and that you're lonely. You have always been lonely."

Abby dutifully tried to breathe. Unfortunately her lungs refused to cooperate.

Damn him. It was one thing for her to have spent the past three months watching him with covert fascination. After all, she had discovered nothing more intimate than the fact that he was shamefully gorgeous and possessed a haunting skill upon the piano. To think that he had seen so easily through her carefully erected barriers was more than a little unnerving.

"Fine," she muttered. "I have intimacy issues. Yadda, yadda. Now, can we get up?"

His smile only widened. "There is no hurry. The sun is just now setting."

"Well, you could use a bit of sun," she informed him dryly. "You are very pale."

"You would see me a pile of ashes, eh?" The silver eyes smoldered with a sudden fire. "And how would I protect you if—"

Mesmerized by his dark honey voice and the promise that softened his features, Abby very nearly missed the shadow that slowly rose up behind the raven head. But when it shifted and neared, her eyes widened and a scream ripped from her throat.

"No!"

Distracted by the sharp lust that so readily consumed him when this woman was near, Dante was unprepared when Abby's scream ripped through the air and she shoved herself upright.

Tossed onto his back, it took a moment to struggle with the blankets wrapped about him. A moment too long as Abby surged from the mattress and attacked the looming form.

"Abby, no," he commanded, flowing upright in a belated attempt to halt her impetuous assault.

He caught no more than a glimpse of a human male before she was shoving the intruder away from the bed and they both tumbled onto the floor. In a heartbeat, or what would be a heartbeat if he were anything but a vampire, Dante was lifting Abby away and crouching beside the unmoving body.

"Hold, lover, he is dead," he murmured, his gaze swiftly taking in the rotting black suit and gaunt hand that still clutched a wooden stake. A vampire assassin. "For the second time, if I don't miss my guess."

Holding on to her towel with the grip of death, Abby regarded the still form with revulsion. Not much of a surprise. Being attacked by a decomposing corpse tended to be a once-in-a-lifetime event.

"My God, what is it?"

"An abomination."

"What?"

"A zombie." His voice was edged with disgust. Even among the demon world, the use of such magics was condemned. To disturb the realm of the underworld was sacrilege. "A dead shell animated by powerful magic. More magic than most demons possess. It isn't alive or dead, which explains why I didn't sense it and how it managed to slip through Viper's spell of protection."

"Zombies." Abby gave a short, near-hysterical laugh. "Great. Just great. Now all we need are a few mummies and a werewolf to complete our official Hoyle deck of monsters."

Dante reached out to touch the cold body that had spilled face-first on the carpet. "Abby, I need you to tell me what happened."

"What do you mean?"

"After you saw the zombie, what did you do?"

He sensed her shift uneasily at his probing. "You were here. You know what happened."

Dante lifted his head to meet her bewildered frown. She was still in shock from the unexpected violence, but at the moment he couldn't comfort her as he desired. It was imperative that he discover all he could of this latest threat.

"Please, Abby, tell me exactly what you did."

"What does it matter?" She gave a shiver. "It's dead, isn't it?"

"As dead as Elvis on this occasion. The question is why he is dead."

"Well, it might have something to do with that gaping hole in his head."

"No, that killed him the first time. When he entered the room, he was animated by magic, not a heartbeat. Nothing could have killed him but fire, preferably of the mystic variety."

"Fire?" She gave a shake of her head. "All I did was push him."

Rolling over the body, Dante jerked open the formal white shirt the poor soul had been buried in. In the shadowed light, the decay of the chest was hardly visible, but there was no mistaking the deep burns that were in the perfect shape of two hands.

Abby's hands.

"That was quite a push, lover," he murmured.

She made a sound deep in her throat as she hastily backed away in horror. "Are you saying that I did that?"

The tight distress in her voice had Dante uncoiling to move directly before her, conveniently blocking out the nasty sight of the corpse.

"I'm saying that you saved me," he informed her sternly. "If you hadn't stopped Undead Walking there, I would be showered over you in a very unflattering shade of ash."

"But how?" she whispered. "How could I do something like that?"

His hands moved to her shoulders to stroke them in a soothing motion. "I did tell you that the Phoenix would find ways to protect itself. There's nothing to be frightened of, Abby."

The brilliant blue eyes flashed with a barely suppressed emotion. "I just burned huge holes in that . . . thing without even knowing what I was doing."

"You were protecting yourself. And thankfully me in the bargain."

She lifted her hands to stare at them as if they were foreign objects. "But I don't even know how I did it."

"Does it matter?"

"Of course it matters," she retorted in sharp tones. "I've seen *Firestarter*. Do you think I want to be some freaking human torch?"

Dante was swift to smother his flare of humor at her fears. For all her courage, Abby was hanging by a thin thread.

"Lover, calm down. You aren't a human torch." Gently he reached for one of her hands and placed it to the center of his chest. Sharp, smoldering heat flared through him at her touch, but it had nothing to do with the power of the Phoenix. "See?"

"But . . ."

"Abby." He rested his forehead upon her own, squeezing her fingers in silent comfort. "It's no different than your ability to stop a man with a well-aimed kick or using those nails as lethal weapons. It's just another tool. One that might very well keep you alive."

She remained stiff in his arms for a long moment, and then at last she gave a tearful chuckle. "Is there anything that ever bothers you?"

Pulling back, Dante traced the lone tear that ran down her cheek. "This bothers me. It makes me ache deep inside."

"Dante."

The vulnerability that softened her features was Dante's undoing. Before he could resist, his head was lowering to capture her lips in a soft kiss that shimmered through his very bones.

Slowly he tightened his arms about her shaking body, needing to comfort her in the only means possible. Bloody hell, he wanted to sweep her away from this devil-infested mess. An impossible desire, of course. Until they found the witches, all he could do was try to protect her and hope that she could endure the terrors yet to come.

Stroking his lips over her cheeks and down the length of her jaw, he patiently whispered words of encouragement until he sensed her trembling lessen.

"Abby, my love," he at last murmured, pulling back to meet her shadowed gaze. "We can no longer remain here. I think we should gather our things and prepare to leave. We don't know how many other zombies might be lurking about."

Although pale, Abby had once again regained her staunch courage. Wrapping her arms about her waist, she gave a determined lift of her chin.

"Where will we go?"

"To find the coven," he retorted without hesitation. "Which means I shall first have to speak with Viper."

Her brows rose in surprise. "He knows where the coven is?"

His lips twitched. "No. But he does possess what we need to find them."

"And what's that?"

"Transportation."

Chapter 7

It took Abby less than a quarter of an hour to slip on the clothes that Dante had brought for her and tie back her hair in a simple braid. Not surprising, really. There was nothing like a twice-dead body lying on the floor to kick a woman into turbo speed.

Not only was it disgusting, but the smell was certain to become ripe before long. Something she wasn't particularly anxious to experience.

Careful to avoid glancing in the mirror at the reflection that was no longer her own, she swiftly brushed her teeth and returned to the outer room where Dante awaited her.

A rueful flare of amusement rushed through her at the sight of him beside the door. While she looked as if she had spent the past two days rolling in alleys, being hunted by demons, and attacked by zombies, he was Versace perfect.

The raven hair was brushed from his lean, alabaster face to flow down his back. The black silk shirt was without a wrinkle as it shimmered over his chiseled torso, and a pair of black leather pants hugged his legs with oh-my-God results.

Even the wicked features were without fault. There were no shadows, no hint of weariness. Not even a five o'clock shadow.

It was damn well unfair, she decided as she continued forward. He could at least have bed head or a bit of sleep crusted in those magnificent eyes.

Oblivious to her ridiculous thoughts, Dante offered her an encouraging smile. "Are you ready?"

"Only in the proverbial 'as ready as I'll ever be' sense," she admitted wryly.

His pirate smile widened. "Good enough for now, I suppose. Let's go."

Together they left the apartment, moving down the hall to the elaborate lobby. Instead of heading toward the door, however, Dante led her toward the curved marble staircase. In silence they climbed to the top floor and toward the back of the building. Only when they stood before a pair of carved mahogany doors did Dante come to a halt.

She was trailing so closely behind him that she nearly ran into him when he abruptly turned to regard her with a frown.

"Look, Abby, I can't leave you on your own, not when we can't be certain it's safe."

Abby gave a lift of her brows. "Do you think I'm going to argue? After the past few hours, I plan to stick to you like glue."

"A very nice visualization. One I intend to ponder at length later, lover. Still . . ."

"What?"

His lips thinned. "This isn't the place for innocents."

Abby rolled her eyes heavenward. Were all vampires

demented? She hadn't been innocent since the day she left the cradle.

"I'm not a child, Dante," she retorted darkly. "I don't think I was ever a child. I've seen more evil in my life than most people can even dream of."

His expression softened as he reached out to brush his fingers over her cheek.

"I know that, lover. It doesn't mean that in your heart you're not still pure. Unfortunately at this point, we don't have much choice. Just . . . stay close."

Wondering what new horrors could possibly be beyond the door, Abby gave a slow nod as she stepped next to him and wrapped her arms tightly about his waist.

"You'll have to use a cattle prod to get me off."

Dante gave a low moan as he briefly closed his eyes. "Bloody hell."

Abby frowned at his odd behavior. "Is something the matter?"

"If I weren't already dead, you'd have me in the grave, lover," he muttered; then, reaching out, he wrenched open the door. "Let's do this."

She might have puzzled on his odd words if he hadn't swept her over the threshold and into a shadowed room that pulsed with the sound of Eastern music.

A sheik's harem, she realized as she glanced about the circular chamber that was draped in flimsy gauze and spangled silk. About the floor were tossed dozens of large pillows, several of them occupied by a variety of men and women who breathed deeply of the opium smoke coming from the brass braziers.

It was the corners, however, that drew her attention.

Although it was dark, there was no mistaking the writhing forms and loud groans that echoed through the shadows. She may have never attended an orgy, but she certainly recognized one when she stumbled across it.

Feeling her stomach twist with disgust, she clung even tighter to Dante. She had thought that nothing could bother her—well, at least nothing of the human variety—but there was a dark, hungry decadence in the room that made her skin crawl.

It was the hopeless desperation, she decided. That familiar sickness of the spirit that she had battled for longer than she wanted to consider.

Putting an arm about her shoulder, Dante did his best to block her view as he firmly led her toward an alcove at the side of the room.

"Viper will be in the back," he muttered. "That's where the—"

Whatever *the* might entail was sharply choked off by a sudden shriek that split the air, and Dante was pried away from Abby by a clearly furious woman.

Stunned by the unexpected attack, Abby stumbled backward, watching in amazement as the assailant gripped Dante by the neck and lifted him off his feet to pin him to the wall with astonishing ease.

A vampire, she swiftly recognized. Not only would a mortal woman be incapable of tossing a grown man about with such ease, but she possessed that alien beauty that marked her as something more than human.

Far more than human, Abby acknowledged as Dante held out a hand to keep her from approaching.

As tall as Dante, the female vampire possessed a willowy body barely covered by a token sheath of gauze and hair past her waist that contained the rare shade of a golden sunrise. Her face was thin, almost feline with smoldering green eyes and lush lips that could fulfill any man's fantasy.

And she was clearly in a PMS mood.

Not struggling, Dante nevertheless regarded his captor with a wary gaze.

"Sasha."

"Dante. Now this is a delicious surprise," the woman purred. "You can't imagine how many days I have dreamed of just this moment."

Abby stiffened at the unmistakable tone. Hell, she wasn't attacking Dante because he was protecting the Phoenix.

She was his ex.

A startling flare of something that might have been jealousy raced through Abby as she folded her arms over her chest. This was the sort of woman he desired? Gorgeous, powerful, and immortal?

The . . . toad.

"An old friend of yours?" Abby demanded.

"Something like that," Dante conceded, his lips twisting in wry humor. "Now, Sasha, this isn't the time for one of our petty spats."

"Petty?" The woman narrowed her gaze to dangerous slits. "You locked me in a cellar."

"Obviously you managed to escape. No harm done."

Sasha gave a low growl. "I was there for three weeks. I had to eat rats."

"I hear they're very nutritious." Dante grunted as the fingers tightened on his throat. "Dammit, Sasha, I wouldn't have locked you in that bloody cellar if you hadn't tried to stake me."

"You know I would never have done it. I was only playing."

"Playing?"

"You used to like our little games. Remember how you enjoyed being chained to the—"

"Chains are one thing, Sasha, but a stake is quite another," Dante hastily interrupted. "I didn't particularly care to stick around and discover where you intended to put it. Call me crazy."

Sasha gave a loud sniff. "It was still rude."

"You have my deepest apologies," Dante muttered. "As well as my solemn promise never to lock you in a cellar again."

There was a long pause before Sasha's features softened to a seductive pout, and she lowered Dante to the floor.

"I suppose I could be convinced to forgive you."

"You are nothing less than a saint."

Allowing the hand that had been choking Dante to smooth its way down his chest, the vampire leaned forward until she was pressed intimately against him.

"Now, do we kiss and make up?"

Abby discovered her fists clenching as the woman rubbed against Dante like a cat in heat. She wasn't sure if she wanted to smack Dante or Sasha the Slut. But she most certainly wanted to smack someone.

"Actually, I'm in rather a hurry. I need to speak with Viper."

The pout became more pronounced. "Always running off. And always with some worthless human," she accused, her cat eyes shifting toward the silent Abby. "Or is this dinner?"

With a smooth motion, Dante was moving to Abby's side, his expression stark with warning.

"She's not on the menu."

"Predictable." Sasha's voice was pure venom. "You really should spend more time with your own kind, Dante. These creatures make you weak."

"I'll keep that in mind."

With an angry sniff, Sasha turned to stalk away, her ivory curves perfectly visible beneath the thin gauze.

Alone with Dante, Abby shot him a disgruntled frown. "Charming."

"Sasha's a bit . . . emotional," he ruefully conceded.

"More than a bit if she tried to kill you."

He shrugged. "Every relationship has its share of danger. You admitted that yourself."

"Not death by wooden stake," she muttered, still battling the lingering sense of resentment at the thought of Dante being intimate with the beautiful vampire. "The woman was clearly demented."

A raven brow arched as Dante allowed his gaze to sweep over her stiff features.

"As I recall, you've threatened to stake me more than once."

"Yes, but that was different."

"How?"

"Because it was."

"Ah." Dante's lips twitched with a flare of wicked amusement. "I think I know what has you in such a twit. You're jealous."

She slapped her hands on her hips. Well, duh. Of course she was jealous. Sasha might be dead, but she was still disgustingly beautiful and drenched with the smoldering passion that made men drool.

More importantly, she had managed to ensnare Dante with her seductive skills. Or perhaps it was the chains, a nasty voice whispered in the back of her mind.

In any event, she had possessed what Abby had lusted after for months.

Of course she was damn well jealous.

Not that she was about to admit as much. She did have her pride. For whatever that was worth.

"Get over yourself, Dante. My only concern is knowing how many other ex-girlfriends might leap out of the woodwork. Things are bad enough without vindictive women stalking you."

He reached up to trace her lips with the tip of his finger. "You're a terrible liar, lover."

She instinctively stepped from the distracting touch. "Didn't we come here to find Viper?"

"Someday soon, Abby, we're going to have a long conversation. It should be quite interesting," he said softly. "Until then, you're right, we should be finding Viper and getting the hell out of here."

Despite a rather childish desire to linger and enjoy the sight of Abby's unmistakable fit of jealousy, Dante firmly took her arm to lead her toward the back of the room. Not only was this no place for an innocent, but he also possessed more than one disgruntled former lover, not to mention the numerous demons who harbored the annoying opinion that he owed them money.

The sooner he could get the keys to Viper's car, the better.

Stepping into a shadowed alcove, Dante paused to glance into the long hallway beyond. He was thankful that most of the doors were closed and that none of the perverse pleasures that Viper offered his customers could be readily detected. He was even more thankful to discover Viper leaning casually against the wall.

At least he wouldn't have to drag Abby through the lowest dregs of debauchery.

"There he is," he murmured, turning to place his hands on Abby's shoulders. "Wait right here. I'll only be a minute."

Her eyes widened as she glanced uneasily over her shoulder. "What if one of your friends gets hungry?"

"I will kill them," he promised with stark sincerity. "I'm not going to let anything happen to you."

Her gaze returned to meet his determined expression before she gave a slow nod. "Okay, but hurry."

"I will." Brushing his lips over her forehead, Dante turned and made his way toward his friend. Stopping at Viper's side, he waited until the vampire turned to regard him with a lift of his brow. "Viper, a moment please."

Flicking a glance toward the waiting Abby, Viper pushed away from the wall and folded his arms over his chest.

"I wish you would make up your mind, Dante. First you insist that your beauty be protected from my wicked clientele, and now you parade her about like a tempting fruit. Unless you desire a riot, I would suggest you take her out of here."

"Things have changed," Dante retorted, swiftly revealing the latest attack upon Abby in clipped tones.

A growing frown marred Viper's brow as he listened in silence. When Dante at last finished, he breathed out a furious curse. "Who would dare loosen such a creature?"

"A reckless fool."

"A human, no doubt," Viper gritted, never one to hide his disdain for mortals.

Dante shrugged. For the moment he didn't have the luxury of time to ponder who might be behind the attack.

"Perhaps. At the moment my only concern is keeping Abby safe."

Viper narrowed his gaze. "A worthy task; however, I hope that you have a miracle or two tucked up your sleeve, Dante. At the moment your companion is the Holy Grail for every creature in the underworld."

A miracle? Dante smiled wryly. The closest to a miracle he had was the fact that Abby was still alive and he hadn't yet ended up on the wrong end of a stake.

"No miracles, but I do have a plan," he reluctantly confessed.

"One that includes disappearing for the next few centuries, I hope."

"I'm taking her to the witches."

A sharp, disbelieving silence descended before Viper was abruptly grasping Dante's arm and pulling him into the darkest shadows of the hallway.

"Have you completely lost your mind?" his friend growled with a smoldering fury. "The last time you encountered those bitches they leashed you like a dog. This time they might very well kill you."

Dante shoved his hands into his pockets. Hellfire, he wasn't an idiot. Or at least not a complete idiot. He was fully aware that if it suited the witches, he could be back in shackles, if not worse.

"I have no choice," he said stiffly.

"Why?"

"They are the only ones who can remove the Phoenix from Abby."

Viper appeared far from impressed by his perfectly reasonable explanation. Instead he stared at Dante as if he were considering a straitjacket.

"Now I know you're mad," he seethed. "Why would you allow yourself to be bound to another? This woman at least cares for you."

Dante grimly closed his mind to temptation. He wasn't by nature noble. Or self-sacrificing. He took what he desired and to hell with morals.

But somehow the rules had changed. Abby had seen to that.

"It isn't her burden."

"It's not yours either," Viper countered with lethal softness. "Not by choice."

Slowly Dante turned his head to the slender form hovering anxiously by the door. His lips twisted in a wry smile.

"It is now."

"You will risk everything for this woman?"

"Everything," Dante admitted in low tones.

There was a short silence before Viper heaved a resigned sigh. "Madness. What can I do to help?"

Dante turned back with a determined expression. "For now all I need are your keys."

Chapter 8

Hours later, Dante continued his hunt through the silent fringes of the city. At his side, Abby sat in rare silence as she reluctantly swallowed the herbs he had insisted she drink.

Too silent, he realized as he glanced toward the delicate profile that was tinted silver by the moonlight.

Although Abby was always careful to keep others at a distance, it was unlike her to withdraw so completely. If nothing else, she should be complaining of their futile search for some hint of the witches. Or chastising him for possessing lethal ex-lovers. Or at least telling him how he should be driving.

Instead she slouched in her seat, drinking her herbs and . . .

Dante's frown abruptly deepened. Was she humming?

Devil's blood. There was something definitely wrong with the woman.

Slowing the car, Dante carefully cleared his throat. "Abby?"

"Mmmm?"

"Are you okay?"

"I was just thinking."

Well, that didn't seem so awfully bad. At least she hadn't tumbled into some catatonic state.

"What were you thinking?"

"Do all vampires have Porsches?"

He shot her a swift glance of puzzlement. That was what she had been brooding on? The preferred form of transport for vampires?

"Of course not," he said slowly. "I know several vampires who prefer Jags and even one who wouldn't be caught dead in anything but a Lamborghini. Pun intended."

"Ah." She wagged her finger in his general direction. "I knew there was something suspicious going on. I just supposed that the very rich had sold their souls to the devil. Instead they are all demons."

"Yes, it's all a vast conspiracy."

She actually giggled. Giggled. Then, taking another deep drink, she turned her head on the soft leather seat and regarded him with half-closed eyes.

"Whatever happened to the days when a vampire would skulk through the sewers and live in a damp crypt?"

He arched a brow. "I think they ended about the same time mortals decided to crawl out of their caves."

"Still, you should at least turn into a bat or have a bumpy forehead. Something vampirish."

Okay. It was official. Mortal women were without exception the most unpredictable, erratic, insane creatures ever to roam the earth.

And this woman was the champion of champions at driving a vampire insane. One minute she was terrified, the next she was angry, and then, bam, she was all soft and vulnerable.

Still, this giggling, almost giddy mood was a distinct change. He might have thought she was drunk as a skunk if it weren't . . .

Oh bloody hell. Dante's eyes narrowed as he watched her down another large gulp of her drink.

That was it.

It had been so long since Selena had become the Phoenix that he had forgotten the effects of the potent herbs. Over the years, she had become accustomed to the concoction, but for a time she had reacted with precisely the same woozy silliness.

"Abby," he murmured.

"Mmmm?"

"Are you drinking Selena's herbs?"

"Yes." She smiled blithely. "And you know, once you get past the vile taste and occasional lumps, it isn't entirely repulsive. It makes me feel . . . tingly."

"Tingly?"

She abruptly grimaced. "Except for my nose. I can't feel my nose at all. It's still there, isn't it?"

Dante swallowed a laugh as he reached out to lightly tap her nose. She was unexpectedly endearing when she was tanked.

"Safe and sound in the center of your face," he assured her.

"Good. I don't like it very much, but I wouldn't want to lose it."

"No, a nose is a good thing to have." He regarded the pale features a moment before returning his gaze to the darkened streets. "And it's a perfectly fine nose."

"It's too short, and it has freckles."

He tightened his fingers on the steering wheel as he turned onto a tree-lined boulevard.

"Mortals," he breathed in annoyance. "Why are

you so consumed with physical appearance? Not only does it swiftly fade, but it is also meaningless."

His words of wisdom were greeted with a disdainful raspberry. "Spoken like one of the truly beautiful people," she groused. "It's easy to condemn shallow vanity when you look like a Greek god."

"I merely . . ." He shot her a swift glance. "You think I look like a Greek god?"

"Actually, you look more like a pirate. A very, very wicked pirate."

A pirate? That didn't seem nearly as good as a Greek god. Of course, she had said that he was a wicked one.

"Okay, I'm going to take that as a compliment."

"You must know you are gorgeous."

"Well, there is that whole reflection thing, lover," he said in dry tones. "I don't spend a great deal of time preening before mirrors."

"Oh . . . I forgot." She hiccupped. "Sorry."

"Not as exciting as having a bumpy forehead or turning into a bat, but it's at least vampirish."

She gave a slow nod. "That's true, I suppose. And you do have the fangs."

"Yes, I do have the fangs."

She heaved a faint sigh. "Still, turning into a bat would be cool."

Dante's smile faded. She still had no clue of the monster he was capable of becoming. In her mind it was all myths and fairy tales.

"Abby."

"What?"

"I think perhaps you've had enough of those herbs for now."

There was a short pause before she struggled to

straighten in her seat. "You may be right. My head is starting to spin."

Dante flicked a switch to roll down her window, allowing a gust of fresh air to enter the car.

"Better?"

"Yes." She stuck her head out the window, breathing deeply. "Do you know, I think that muck might have been spiked."

Dante chuckled as he slowed and pulled the car to a halt. "Don't worry, lover, soon enough you'll be enjoying your hot fudge sundaes instead of spiked muck."

Pulling in her head, Abby regarded him with a lift of her brows. "Why are we stopping? Are we near the coven?"

"That's what I intend to find out."

She blinked in surprise. "You can sense it?"

"Actually, I hope to smell it."

"Ugh. Do witches stink?"

"Not the witches, but something near the coven," he explained with a smile. "When Selena would return from her visits, there was always a peculiar scent that would cling to her."

Abby tilted her head to one side. "What sort of scent?"

Dante gave a shrug. "I'm not sure. I only know that when she would return, I would avoid the house for days. It was very . . . distinctive."

Abby pondered for a long moment. "A butcher shop? Or tannery?"

He lifted his brows at her naïve words. "I would recognize the scent of blood, my sweet."

"Oh . . . right. What about an oil refinery or stockyard?"

"No, it was more like a rotting field of wheat."

She frowned. Dante didn't blame her. Even for a powerful vampire, a vague smell that he couldn't even identify was hardly much to go on. MacGyver he was not.

Then, without warning, she reached out to grasp his arm in a tight grip.

"Oh my God."

Instantly on alert, Dante glanced about to ensure they were not under attack. "What is it?"

"I know where it is," she breathed.

"The coven?"

"Yes."

"How?"

"Years ago, my oldest brother worked at the cereal factory," she explained. "When he would return, the entire house would reek of rotted wheat for hours."

There was rotted wheat in cereal? Hellfire. How dare humans shudder at vampires' preference for blood? At least he demanded it distinctly unrotted.

"It's worth a try," he concluded. "Which direction?"

"South."

Gunning the engine, Dante turned the car southward. There was no guarantee that the coven would be near the factory, but it was at least a place to start.

As silence once again descended, Dante shot a covert glance toward the woman at his side. On this occasion, Abby wasn't guzzling the potent herbs or humming in a pleasant cloud of fog. Instead her brow was furrowed, and she chewed upon her lower lip as if she were in deep thought.

With an effort, he resisted the urge to demand what was on her mind. If he had learned nothing else about this woman over the past few months, it was that she could write a thesis on stubbornness. She would reveal what she wanted to reveal, when she wanted to reveal it.

It was twenty minutes later before she at last turned her head to study him with a troubled expression.

"Dante?"

"Yes?"

"Viper seemed angry when you spoke with him earlier."

Dante abruptly clenched his fingers on the steering wheel. He had presumed that Abby had been far too occupied with ensuring none of the guests were creeping toward her neck to notice his confrontation with his fellow vampire. It seemed that not even a hotel filled with vampires and demons indulging in orgies could keep her properly distracted.

"He wasn't overly eager to hand over the keys to his favorite Porsche," he retorted in light tones. "He can be annoyingly possessive of his toys."

"No." She gave a decisive shake of her head. "I don't believe you."

"Rather harsh, lover," he protested.

"He didn't want you to take me to the coven. Why?"

Dante muttered a low curse. Damn Viper and his poor imitation of a mother hen.

"You could not possibly have heard what was said between us," he futilely attempted to bluster.

"I know you were arguing and that he was trying to convince you of something," she charged. "He's worried about what the coven will do to you, isn't he?"

"Viper has always distrusted magic."

"Dante, I want the truth." She folded her arms

over her chest, clearly taking on a don't-screw-with-me attitude. "Will they harm you?"

He shrugged. "They need me."

"They did need you, but now everything has changed," she muttered, striking far too close to the truth. "In fact, I think that we should reconsider seeking out the witches."

"What?"

"I won't have you hurt."

Dante grimly kept his gaze on the empty road. Despite his undeniable flare of pleasure at her concern, he wasn't about to make this woman into a martyr.

"Abby, we have no choice."

"There are always choices."

His expression hardened at her soft words. "Not if you are to be rid of the Phoenix. They're the only ones capable of transferring the power to another."

There was a long pause, and Dante had almost convinced himself that he had forced Abby to see reason when she cleared her throat.

"Then maybe I should just keep it."

The car dangerously swerved before Dante could regain command of himself. Bloody hell, the woman never failed to catch him off guard. Slowing to a mere crawl, he shot her a disgruntled frown.

"You don't know what you're saying," he growled. "You haven't been prepared to become the Chalice."

She gave a lift of her brows. "Was Selena?"

He grimaced as he recalled his former mistress. Although Selena had been human, she had always possessed the arrogant belief that she was above others. Not surprising for the daughter of a duke who considered himself on equal footing with his own god. Selena had viewed the power and immortality of the Phoenix as her right rather than her duty.

"She knew what she was getting into," he muttered.

Abby reached out to lightly touch his arm. "Then tell me."

Dante carefully chose his words. He didn't want to add to her terror, but then again, he had to make sure that she understood precisely why it was impossible for her to carry such a burden.

"Can you imagine what it is like to be immortal?" he at last demanded.

"Well, I can imagine it makes life insurance a rather moot point."

"Abby," he rasped.

She gave a lift of her shoulder. "I'll admit I've never had reason to give it much thought."

"It means watching your family and friends wither and die while you remain precisely the same," he informed her sharply. "It means watching life pass by without ever touching you. It means being utterly alone."

She offered a humorless laugh. "My so-called relatives could have posed for the poster of dysfunctional families. My father terrorized and then abandoned us, my mother drank herself into an early grave, and my brothers fled Chicago the moment they could escape." There was a brief silence. "I have always been alone," she whispered in the dark.

Dante flinched. "Abby."

She sucked in a sharp breath, clearly regretting her brief moment of vulnerability.

"What else?"

"You will always be hunted," he retorted starkly, thrusting aside the urge to offer her comfort. He had to make her see sense. "Every moment, some evil will be plotting your death."

She turned in her seat to regard him squarely. "But you said that the Phoenix is beginning to disguise itself."

"It is, but there are always those with enough power or desperation to track you down. That was why I was chained to the spirit as protection."

He could feel her gaze sweeping over his rigid profile.

"Then you can protect me."

Dante stiffened, his skin prickling with a sudden wave of self-disgust.

"Like I protected Selena?" he growled.

"Dante, you can't blame yourself—"

"It is not a matter of blame; it is a matter of knowledge," he retorted in black tones. "Bloody hell, I don't even know what killed her. Which means the sooner I get you to the witches, the better."

"Dante—"

"No." He turned his head to stab her with a fierce glare. "We must do this for the Phoenix, Abby. It must be protected by those who are best suited to keep it from harm."

Neatly outmaneuvered, Abby offered a frustrated scowl before throwing herself back into the soft leather of her seat.

"You don't fight entirely fair, you know."

His lips twisted with wry humor. "A vampire, sweetness, never fights fair. We only fight to win."

Nearly an hour later, Abby gamely battled her way through the weeds that had taken command of the fields about the industrial park.

Weeds and obnoxious, nuclear-mutant thorn bushes, she discovered as she halted for the hundredth time to salvage her jeans from destruction. Hell, she had never liked nature. It was dirty and filled with crawly creatures and things that made her sneeze. And this little jaunt wasn't making her any fonder. Why the witches couldn't have set up shop in the local mall defied her imagination.

Of course, the weeds and thorns were only a small part of her current discomfort, she ruefully conceded. The knots twisting her stomach and the dryness of her mouth was entirely due to the witches that they currently sought.

Dante was adamant that it was their only option, but she was not nearly so convinced. Whatever their noble motives, she had witnessed Selena's screams of mercy as they had forced the powerful spirit into her body, and worse, their contempt of Dante as they had bound him with their magic.

Could women capable of such acts truly be trusted?

Feeling a nervous sickness clenching her stomach, Abby turned to regard the man walking at her side. She was in dire need of a distraction if she didn't want to embarrass herself by running away in screeching terror.

"If you intended to sweep me off my feet with a moonlight stroll, Dante, I have to tell you that I'm not impressed," she teased in strained tones.

Turning his head, Dante flashed his familiar wicked grin. "For shame, lover. What could be more romantic than a gentle night breeze—"

"Perfumed with the rank stench of factories."

"Or being surrounded by the beauty of nature."

"Itchy, scratchy weeds that are going to leave a very unpleasant rash."

He chuckled at her tart words. "At least you must admit that you've never had a more handsome, charming, sexy companion."

Well, he had her there, she acknowledged wryly. Not in her wildest fantasies could she have ever imagined such a devilishly handsome man even existed.

"Perhaps," she grudgingly conceded. "But most of my dates don't come complete with packs of demons, monsters, and zombies."

A raven brow arched. "Dull bastards. They obviously don't understand the potent allure of a true adventure."

"Adventure?" Abby swatted at a biting mosquito with a grimace. "An adventure is walking through St. Mark's Square in Venice, or sipping coffee in a charming bistro in Paris. Not wading through a briar patch in search of witches."

"Actually, the last time I attempted to enjoy coffee in Paris, I nearly had my head lopped off by the guillotine," he murmured. "So you see, lover, it's all a matter of perspective."

Abby stumbled at the off-hand confession. "Good Lord, would you stop that?" she complained.

"What?"

"Mentioning the past so casually. I thought I was ancient because I can remember *Melrose Place*."

He merely laughed. Damn his vampire soul. "You were the one who brought up the subject of Paris. I was merely offering my own experiences there."

Her gaze swept over the beautiful features bathed in moonlight. "So you were really in Paris during the Reign of Terror?"

"For a few unforgettable months." He smiled

ruefully. "I would suggest that you visit when there isn't a revolution in progress."

Abby rolled her eyes. Her in glamorous, sophisticated Paris? Yeah, the same day that she sprouted wings and tattooed her butt.

"I'll keep that in mind when the destined-never-to-be opportunity rolls around," she said dryly.

His eyes smoldered like liquid silver in the shadows. "Who knows what the future might hold, lover? A few days ago you didn't expect to be on the run with a vampire or battling to save the world from evil."

"Actually, it would have seemed a lot more likely than a luxurious vacation in France."

Reaching out, he gave a tug on a curl that had strayed from her braid. "You're too young to be so cynical."

"I'm realistic, not cynical," she corrected firmly. "Vacations in Paris are not for women who make minimum wage and—" She came to an abrupt halt, her eyes widening in horror. "Holy hell."

A subtle tension prickled around Dante as he swept a searching gaze about them. "What is it?"

"I'm out of a job, and my rent is due."

There was a moment of sharp silence before Dante tilted back his head to offer a very unsympathetic laugh. With a frown, Abby slapped her hands on her hips.

"What's so funny?"

He reached up to grasp her chin with his slender fingers. "You've become a Chalice for a powerful spirit, confronted demons, and are about to place yourself in the hands of witches. Now you're worried about whether or not you can pay the rent?"

Her eyes narrowed at his amusement. "I'm

worried about spending my days pushing a shop-
ping cart down the streets and sleeping under a
park bench—very real possibilities that are as bad
as any demon or witch."

His brows drew together as his fingers strayed to
brush over her cheek. "You think I would allow you
to be tossed into the street?"

Something painful clenched in her heart. Soon
enough, the witches would remove the spell from
her and Dante would be bound to another. Why
would he ever give her another thought?

They were the proverbial ships, or in this case
vampire and mortal, who passed in the night.

Troubled more than she cared to admit at the
thought of being completely alone once again,
Abby forced a stiff smile to her lips.

"Well, you did lock you former lover in a cellar."

"Only in self-defense." His fingers tightened on
her face, his expression oddly somber. "I have
promised that nothing will harm you, Abby. Nothing. It's a promise I intend to keep no matter what
the future might hold."

She was forced to swallow the lump lodged in her
throat as her hand lifted to cover the fingers upon
her cheek. By God, but he knew how to steal a
woman's heart.

"Dante," she breathed softly.

A low groan was wrenched from his throat as
Dante pressed his forehead to her own.

"Oh, lover, if you have any pity in your heart, you
won't look at me like that. At least not now."

A dark sinful heat raced through Abby as she
pressed herself next to Dante's hard body. If they
weren't standing in a thorn briar, or if demons
weren't chasing them, or if there weren't witches

lurking nearby, she would have thrown him to the ground and have had her way with him.

Damn but he made her hot and bothered.

Unfortunately, no amount of wishing could change their situation, and with a shuddering sigh, she forced herself to step back.

"We should find the coven," she said with a resigned grimace.

Dante briefly closed his eyes, as if battling for control, before lifting his head and sweeping his gaze over the star-studded sky.

"Yes, dawn will come too soon. Let's get this done."

Chapter 9

The past centuries had taught Dante more than a few lessons.

Never dine upon drunkards. Never turn your back on an angry woman. Never bet on a horse named Lucky. Never wrestle a Chactol demon after a bottle of gin.

And never, never ignore pure instinct.

That last lesson had been the hardest and best learned, which was why he had not directly headed for the coven, although he had managed to catch its scent only a mile from the abandoned factories.

There was something not at all right, he decided as they drew closer. An icy chill prickled over his skin, and the smell of fresh blood filled the air.

A battle had been fought nearby. A battle that had involved powerful magic and undeniable slaughter.

Skirting the trees that hid the coven from view, Dante attempted to determine the danger ahead. He could sense no demons, but he was no longer certain that it was the creatures of the night who posed the greatest threat.

And that, of course, was what troubled him the most.
Devil spit.

He didn't like the feeling that he was being led by the nose by this unseen enemy. And yet, what choice did he have but to go forward?

He had to find the witches.

Even if it killed him.

A thought that pissed him off royally.

Glancing over his shoulder, he watched as Abby struggled to free her shirt from a clinging thorn bush. A faint smile twitched at his lips. She truly was the most unusual of creatures. As rare and precious as the finest jewel.

As if sensing his gaze, she abruptly jerked her head up to glare at him with that glorious annoyance that she seemed to reserve solely for him.

"Dammit, if we're going to walk in circles, can we at least do it somewhere that sells mocha ice cream and has air-conditioning?"

"We aren't walking in circles," he instinctively denied, only to give a faint grimace. "At least not precisely."

"I suppose you possess some sort of bat vision?"

He flicked his brow upward. "You do know that bats are blind?"

She gritted her teeth. "Vampire vision, then."

He gave a shrug. "I can see well enough, not that it truly matters. I'm not looking for the coven."

"What?" Her eyes glittered with danger in the fading moonlight. "I swear to God, Dante, if you've led me through this mutant briar patch for some sort of joke, I'll st—"

"Stake me, yes, I know," he drawled. "You might try to be a bit less predictable, lover."

"You didn't give me the chance to say *where* I'd stake you," she snapped.

A flare of humor raced through him. "True."

"For God's sake, if we're not looking for the coven, then what the hell are we doing out here?"

"I said I'm not *looking* for the coven and I'm not," he corrected smoothly. "I'm trying to smell it."

The prickly anger slowly faded as she realized her hasty mistake.

"Oh. Are you having any luck?"

That icy shiver once again crawled over his skin as Dante turned toward the hidden coven.

"It's just beyond that line of trees."

She followed his gaze, her eyes narrowing. "I'll have to take your word for it since I can't see jack crap."

"It's there."

"Then why are we waiting?" She sent him a puzzled frown. "I thought you wanted to get this over with?"

"Something is not right."

He felt her tension at his blunt admission. Obviously whatever her feelings for him, she at least had learned to trust his instincts.

A dark satisfaction lodged itself in his heart but was swallowed swiftly by an inner shudder.

Bloody hell, he was acting as sappy as any mortal. To imagine an immortal vampire scrounging about for pathetic scraps tossed at him by this woman.

Perhaps he should be staked.

"How do you know something's wrong?" she demanded in a soft whisper.

With an effort, Dante wrenched his thoughts back to the troubles at hand. They were surely enough to deal with.

"I smell blood."

"Blood?"

"Lots of blood."

"Oh God."

"I must find out what happened."

Without warning, she reached out to grasp his fingers with her own. The warmth of her swiftly traveled through his skin to heat his entire body.

"You think the witches have been attacked?"

There was no point in lying. Not when they would have to approach the coven.

"Yes."

"I . . ." She paused, tilting up her head to stab him with a narrowed gaze. "You're going to try and make me stay here, aren't you?"

"No." He made the decision swiftly. "Until I know what's happening, I can't be certain that there isn't something still creeping about."

Her grip abruptly tightened upon his fingers. "You had to say that, didn't you?"

"I want you to be on your guard."

She made a sound of disgust at his warning. "I'm wandering through the dark with a vampire, searching for a gaggle of witches who may or may not flay us alive. You think I'm not on my guard?"

He gave a small tug to pull her close, his hand gently cupping her face.

"What I think is that the worst is yet to come," he murmured.

"Perfect." Allowing her gaze to meet his own, she momentarily stilled. The stark awareness flared in her eyes then; with a faint shake of her head, she took an awkward step backward. "I suppose we might as well get this over with."

Swooping down, he pressed a swift kiss to her not-quite-steady lips.

"Stay behind me, and if you sense anything, let me know," he whispered against her mouth.

She swallowed heavily as he pulled back. "I promise you'll be the first to hear my scream."

"Right."

Keeping her fingers laced tightly in his, Dante moved directly toward the thicket of trees. Behind him Abby stumbled and occasionally cursed at the underbrush, but she managed to keep up with his smooth stride. Within a quarter of an hour, they at last stepped into a clearing.

Directly in the center was a plain three-story brick structure with several wooden outbuildings. There was nothing about it to suggest that it was anything other than a farmhouse. In fact, it was rather depressingly normal.

Precisely what the witches would desire.

Unlike vampires, they had no ability to disguise themselves from curious eyes. They were forced to hide in plain sight.

Abby hesitantly stepped to his side, her brow furrowed in puzzlement.

"You're certain this is the coven?"

"Yes," he murmured, keeping to the shadows as he cautiously led her closer to the structure.

"It seems—"

"Dead?" he finished, halting as they came to a large side window.

"Yeah, that about sums it up," she agreed in shaky tones.

A swift glance through the tinted panes also summed it up. The carnage was impressive, worthy of the darkest soul, but Dante did not allow his gaze to linger. No one within had been left to tell the tale.

Pulling back, he allowed his gaze to slide over the remaining buildings.

"Are you going inside?" Abby demanded from behind.

"No. I cannot enter."

"Damn."

He turned to offer her a wry smile. "Actually, it's a good thing."

"Why?"

"It means that at least some of the witches survived the attack," he explained. "Otherwise the barrier would be broken."

"What?"

His undead heart twitched at the sight of her features that were unbearably fragile.

"It doesn't matter. They must have fled. I'll see if I can pick up their trail."

Her mouth dropped open in dismay. "More walking?"

Dante considered the clearing. For the moment they were alone.

"You can wait here for me. I won't go far."

She bit her lip, the terror she was struggling to keep at bay almost visible as she considered the darkness shrouded about her.

"Your definition of *far* is considerably different than mine," she muttered.

He placed his fingers beneath her chin to tilt her head upward. He waited until she met his searching gaze and then offered her a comforting smile.

"You have only to call and I will come running."

"You promise?"

"Upon my quiche-hating heart," he said softly.

Her lips twitched, although her eyes remained dark with unease. "That'll do."

Framing her face in his hands, Dante crushed his lips to her forehead before pulling back to regard her with a somber expression.

"Abby."

"What?"

"I would suggest you stay away from the windows. It's bad in there. Really bad."

His warning delivered, Dante turned to make his way toward the outbuildings. If some of the witches had fled, he should be able to follow their scent. He supposed it was too much to hope that they might be hidden in the nearby trees.

In over three centuries, they had never made anything easy.

Don't look. Don't look. Don't look.

Dante's words echoed through Abby's mind.

She knew he was right. She didn't want to see whatever was inside. God knew she had seen enough in the past hours to last her a couple of lifetimes. Not the least of which was a walking corpse who refused to stay in his grave.

But the very fact that she shouldn't look naturally ensured that her feet were moving forward and she was pressing her face to the glass.

For a moment her eyes could make out nothing in the gloom, and a deep sense of relief shuddered through her. Then, even as she prepared to pull away, her gaze shifted toward a nearby wall and she was reeling backward in horror.

So much blood . . .

It had been splattered everywhere.

And . . . stuff she didn't even want to consider.

Bending over, she gagged at the rising nausea.

"You had to look, didn't you?" a dark voice drawled even as a strong arm encircled her shoulders and pulled her close.

"You shouldn't have told me not to."

He pressed her head into his shoulder. "Somehow I knew it would end up being my fault."

Comforted more than a rational woman should be by a vampire's touch, Abby slowly forced herself to pull away.

"Did you find the trail?"

Even in the darkness, she could see his grimace.

"It led as far as the nearest outbuilding, which happened to be a garage."

Her eyes lifted to the heavens. "Don't tell me. They took off in the witchmobile?"

"Something like that."

Abby sucked in a deep breath. She knew she should be disappointed.

Without the witches, her life remained in danger. All sorts of creepy, icky, semi-dead things would continue to hunt her. And the Phoenix that had taken up residence within her body would continue to refurbish her like she was a cheap dorm room.

But the disappointment that was lodged in her heart felt remarkably like relief.

"So, what now?" she demanded in an effort to sound resigned rather than certifiable.

Lifting his head, Dante sniffed the air. "Dawn will be approaching soon. I must find some place to wait out the day."

"Oh. We could return to the factories."

"I think there might be something closer. Can you walk?"

Her feet had gone beyond pain to a petulant numbness. "I'll make it."

A slow, enigmatic smile curved his lips. "You never fail to amaze me, lover."

Startled by the low words, Abby had no time to demand what he meant before he had a hold of her hand and was tugging her across the clearing to the woods on the other side.

In silence—well, Dante in silence and her with snapping twigs, squishing mud, muttered oaths, and a whimper of pain when she stubbed her toe on a fallen log—they made their way through the darkness. Abby swiftly lost track of time as she concentrated simply on keeping her feet moving forward, but eventually Dante slowed his swift pace.

"Here we are," he murmured, his hand reaching out to brush aside a heavy curtain of ivy that was growing upon the side of a low hill. "Not quite five-star material, but it's dark."

"And damp," Abby muttered as she bent low to follow Dante into the narrow tunnel that led to a small circular opening.

Seating himself on the sandy ground, he gave a tug on her hand, pulling her next to his hard length.

"Look at it this way, at least it's not a crypt," he pointed out in dry tones.

Although not overly impressed with the low ceiling and moss-covered walls, she did have to concede that it was a relief not to have a corpse lying about.

"Meaning I should be grateful for small favors?"

"Well, you also have the pleasure of my company. That should make even a damp cave seem like paradise."

"God, you really need to get over yourself, Dante," she muttered, pulling her knees close to her chest and wrapping her arms about them.

Clearly feeling the faint shiver that raced through Abby, Dante shifted to study her pale face.

"Are you cold?"

"A little."

"Here." Wrapping his arm about her shoulder, he tugged her close to his side, his cheek resting on top of her head. "It should warm up as the sun rises."

There was no warmth in his body, but that didn't stop a sudden heat from flaring through her blood. Damn, it had been so long since she had been held in a man's arms, alive or dead. So long since she had felt that heady sense of sated passion.

And she couldn't deny that she had lusted after Dante for months. The dull hunger that plagued her seemed to have no sense of timing, damn it all.

"You should try to sleep," Dante broke the silence, his fingers aimlessly toying with a strand of her hair. "I'll keep watch."

She sternly turned her thoughts to more pressing troubles. Having the hots for this vampire surely came second place to imminent peril.

"I'm too on edge to sleep."

"I can't imagine why," he said dryly.

"Shall I make you a list?"

"No need."

She heaved a faint sigh. "We are truly screwed, aren't we?"

There was a momentary pause, as if he were carefully considering his words.

"I'm not sure I would put it quite in those words,

but the attack on the witches has made our task more difficult."

"Who would do such a thing?"

"That is the question." His tone held a lethal edge, revealing he was not nearly so composed as he would have her believe. "A demon could not have passed through the barrier, and yet a human could never have caused such destruction."

She shuddered in horror. "God no, it was gruesome."

"Unless . . ."

"Unless what?"

"A human who worshipped the Prince might have been capable of summoning a great deal of power."

Abby didn't bother to hide her shock. She had never even considered the idea that it could be anything but a monster that could attack with such savagery.

"A human?"

He stiffened at her obvious surprise. "You believe only demons capable of evil?"

The rasp in his voice brought her gaze to his tight expression.

"No," she said softly. "I am well acquainted with the evil people are capable of."

He grimaced ruefully. "I'm sorry. I don't like mysteries."

"I've discovered I don't much care for them myself," she muttered, reluctantly forcing herself to consider the horrors that had been dogging them for the past days. "Do you think the same person who attacked the witches killed Selena?"

"I just don't know."

Abby gave a humorless chuckle. "Well, we've

nicely determined that we're not Nancy Drew and Hercule Poirot."

"No." She felt him stroke his cheek over her hair, his lips briefly pressing against her temple. "I'm not much of a champion, am I, my sweet?"

She tilted back her head to glare at his ridiculous words. "Don't say that. If it wasn't for you, I would be dead by now."

His lips twisted at her fierce defense. "Instead you're hiding in a cave, no closer to being rid of the Phoenix than when you started."

He shifted, his movement tugging her even more firmly against his hard body. Her heart skipped, kicked, and lodged somewhere near her throat.

Don't think about it, Abby, she sternly told herself. Don't think about those slender, skillful fingers skimming over your bare skin. Or those lips nuzzling at sensitive places. Or your legs wrapped about his waist as he . . .

Oh hell.

She melted against his hardness, her eyes darkening with the awareness that she was tired of battling.

"I thought you promised that being with you would make this cave a paradise?"

Quite intelligent, despite being male, Dante instantly sensed the change in the atmosphere. The silver eyes darkened to smoke as he allowed his gaze to slowly wander over her face.

"Abby?" he whispered.

Not giving herself time to consider her rash behavior, Abby reached up to thrust her hands into his glorious hair. Her heart was already racing and her breath impossible to capture.

"I don't want to think about demons or witches

or all the other horrid creatures that are trying to kill me."

His arms wrapped about her, tugging her easily to straddle his legs so they were face-to-face.

"What do you want?" he rasped, his fingers trailing up the length of her spine.

"You." She kissed him with all the yearning that was burning within her. "I want you."

Chapter 10

She heard his soft groan as his hands shifted to cup her hips, compulsively pressing her to his thickening cock.

"Abby?"

She arched forward, her body already on fire. Hell, at the moment she felt fully at home in this cave. Certainly her urges were as primitive as any Neanderthal.

She want. She take.

"What?" she muttered, tilting back her head as his lips nibbled their way down her throat.

"You know you are not thinking clearly?"

"I don't care."

His tongue ran a searing path along the line of her collarbone.

"I just don't want you to come to your senses and discover some creative spot for that stake that you keep threatening me with," he husked.

In response, she leaned back so that she could pull her shirt over her head. She tossed it aside and quickly followed it with her plain cotton bra.

"I've already accepted that I've gone completely insane. What is a little more madness?"

His agonized groan echoed through the shadowed cave, his eyes flashing silver fire as his hands moved to tenderly cup her breasts.

"Good madness, I hope," he muttered, clearly distracted as his thumbs brushed over her nipples.

She shivered with excitement. "Yes."

His head lowered, his lips closing over the tip of her breast.

"And better madness?"

Her eyes squeezed shut as a sharp, gnawing pleasure raced through her.

"Oh . . . God, yes."

"Bloody hell." Still tormenting her nipple with his tongue, Dante expertly attacked the fastening to her jeans and, with Abby's full cooperation, swiftly had her naked and back in his lap. Pulling her close, he kissed her with a desperate hunger. "I've dreamed of this so long, lover. I need to know this isn't just another fantasy."

"I'm no fantasy," she assured him.

He gave a soft chuckle, his hands trailing down her back and over her hips. "That's a matter of opinion."

"Dante," she whispered.

"You are so warm. I could drown in your heat."

"I think you would be warmer if you got rid of some of those clothes," she daringly offered.

"Much warmer." His movements were jerky as he helped her to remove the final barriers between them.

Her breath caught as she glimpsed his full arousal, a sudden ache clawing deep within her. She wanted to make this a slow, delicious seduction, but the thought of having him buried deep within her made her long to abandon her plan and simply join herself to him in a flurry of pagan heat.

Obviously misunderstanding her hesitation, Dante reached up to gently stroke her cheek. "Are you sure about this, Abby?"

"Yes," she managed to croak, wrestling control over her hot surge of desire. "At the moment it's the only thing I am sure of."

Giving her a long searching glance, Dante slowly framed her face in his hands, pulling her forward to kiss her with an aching sweetness. Abby melted toward him. She had not exaggerated. In this moment there seemed nothing more right than being in this vampire's arms.

Feeling a strange confidence that was usually lacking within her, Abby ran her hands lightly over his muscled chest. His skin was as smooth as silk, inviting a more intimate touch.

Without thought, she lowered her head to trail her lips over his shoulders, delighting in the erotic power that flowed through her blood.

"My champion," she whispered as she continued her persuasive caresses. "Do you like this?"

"Yes," he growled, his hands clutching her hips as he sought to remain in control of his building need.

"And this?" she whispered, moving steadily lower.

"God, yes."

"And this?"

"Abby," he choked as she reached the clenched muscles of his lower stomach.

"Yes, Dante?"

"Keep this up and it will be a fantasy for one," he ground out.

She gave a throaty chuckle as she deliberately rubbed her body back up the length of his chest.

Her every nerve felt alive, sensitized to the point of near pain.

"I'm only trying to convince you that I am no dream."

Without warning, he shifted her farther up his thighs. The air was wrenched from her body as the fierce jut of his erection settled in the damp heat between her legs.

She shifted experimentally, the dull throb in her lower body rejoicing as the tip of him slipped just inside her body. She was prevented from a complete entry, however, as he grasped her hips and regarded her with smoldering eyes.

"All you've done is made more certain this is a fantasy," he murmured.

"You need more proof?" she teased.

"Ah, no, my turn for kisses," he informed her, drawing her toward his waiting lips. "And I want to kiss you everywhere."

With a slow, deliberate motion, Dante branded her lips with a searing kiss. Then moving his mouth over her face, he stroked down the length of her arched neck. Abby's fingers dug into his shoulders as he pulled her relentlessly upward, catching the hardened nipple between his teeth. She gave a soft cry as he tugged and suckled her, her head thrown backward at the insistent pleasure crashing through her. He turned his attention to the other breast, relentlessly driving her need to a fever pitch.

She wanted him within her.

She wanted the powerful thrust of his erection driving her to that wondrous edge and tossing her over.

But even as she sought to bring them together, he was determinedly lifting her ever upward. She found herself on her unsteady feet as his mouth teased the contracted muscles of her stomach, occasionally nipping at the shivering flesh. She moaned in protest, and then her eyes flew open as he lowered even farther, and his seeking mouth found her moist parting.

She momentarily struggled to stay upright as his tongue reached out to stroke the highly sensitive flesh.

There was something utterly decadent about being poised above him as he expertly urged her to the point of no return.

But then sensation took over, and, closing her eyes, she simply allowed him to pleasure her.

With tantalizing care he searched to find her center of pleasure, holding her hips in firm hands. Abby gritted her teeth as he gently stroked the building pressure, so enthralled by the searing delight he was creating that she was nearly too late when she abruptly pulled away from his magical touch.

"No, Dante," she gasped.

As if sensing she wished to have him inside her when she came, Dante guided her back to her knees and positioned her so that he could slowly penetrate her softness.

Abby sighed in relief as she pressed herself ever deeper, knowing that nothing had ever felt so right as having him within her.

For a moment she merely savored the full sense of completion. But as he remained unnaturally still, she reluctantly lifted her heavy lids to send him a puzzled gaze.

"Dante?"

"You started this seduction, Abby," he rasped. "You can finish it."

With a slow smile, she placed her hands upon his chest and slightly lifted her hips before sliding back down.

Dante moaned, his fingers convulsively clutching her hips. "My God, you are going to kill me. Again."

Abby moved, pulling herself higher before plunging downward. His hips arched off the sand-covered ground, a pained frown forming on his forehead.

Abby smiled with heady satisfaction, thoroughly enjoying the knowledge that Dante was completely at her mercy.

For this moment he was hers. As intimately tied to her as if they were one.

One soul, regardless if he possessed one or not.

One heart, beating or not.

One body.

With slow, deliberate motions, she tormented them both to the edge of frenzy, refusing to increase the pace even as he gasped out a plea for mercy.

Only when she realized that her muscles were inevitably tightening to an explosive release did she give in to his broken commands and allow him to grasp her hips so he could pump himself forcefully within her.

He gave a shout of joy at the same moment she violently convulsed about him.

For a moment out of time, she floated in pure bliss, pressed against the impaling flesh until with a low moan she collapsed against him in utter exhaustion.

She was shaken by the force of her pleasure. But

oddly comforted by the arms that encircled her to press her close against the hardness of his body.

It was as if she had been thrown from the top of a skyscraper, only to discover she was being caught in the safety of Dante's embrace.

Perhaps sensing her tumultuous emotions, Dante softly stroked her tousled curls and placed a comforting kiss on her brow.

"Are you all right, Abby?"

She snuggled against his strength. "More than all right."

"And you aren't considering any wanton staking?"

"Not at the moment."

"Good." He gave a soft chuckle as his lips absently smoothed over her temple. "Unlike most vampires, I enjoy my passion without pain, bloodshed, or the threat of imminent staking."

Lazily tilting back her head, she met his glittering gaze. "What about Sasha?"

A decidedly smug smile curved his lips. "I've told you there's no need to be jealous, my sweet. I put Sasha in my past the moment you arrived on Selena's doorstep."

Her heart gave a jump even as she regarded him with a frown. "I don't believe you."

He arched a brow, his unworldly beauty starkly pronounced as the rosy dawn outside the cave began to dispel the gloom.

"That Sasha is in my past?"

"That you even noticed me when I arrived on Selena's doorstep," she clarified in dry tones.

His fingers traced aimless patterns over the bare skin of her back, his expression softened with amusement.

"Oh, I noticed. How could I not?" His lips twisted

with a hint of self-derision. "From the moment you arrived, I was plagued by that damnable purity. It taunted me until I couldn't get you out of my thoughts. I knew I was going to seduce you even before I knew your name."

She gave a choked laugh at his outrageous arrogance. "Could you possibly be a little more full of yourself?"

He shrugged. "There are some things that are inevitable."

Abby paused. She wasn't much of a philosopher. Hell, she didn't even know what a philosopher actually did. But she did know that *inevitable* or *fate* or *providence* were not words in her vocabulary.

"No, there is no such thing as inevitable," she said firmly.

"Why do you say that?" he demanded, more curious than offended.

"Because if fate was set in stone, then I would be a drunken whore working the streets for a cheap bottle of whiskey."

Her tone was light, but she felt him stiffen beneath her, his fingers pressing into her skin.

"Don't say that," he rasped.

She pulled back to regard him with a somber expression. "Why not? It's true enough. My parents were both alcoholics who shouldn't have been allowed to have a dog, let alone six children. My father spoke with his fists and did us all a favor when he forgot to return home after a drunken spree. And my mother left her bed only long enough to get a fresh bottle of whiskey. My brothers took off as quickly as they could, and I was left alone to watch my mother die. What sort of destiny do you think was waiting for me?"

With a firm tug of his hands, he pressed her back against his chest, his chin resting on the top of her head.

"Destiny has nothing to do with where you came from or who your parents might be," he said fiercely. "Destiny comes from the heart, and the soul. You could never be anything less than extraordinary, Abby Barlow."

Wrapped tightly in his arms, she did feel extraordinary. She wasn't the grubby little girl who roamed the streets because she was terrified to go home. Or the teenager who kept people at a distance because she didn't want them to know the truth of her family. Or even the tedious, rapidly aging woman who struggled just to keep a roof over her head.

She was bold and daring. A vampire's lover. The woman who held the fate of the world within her.

A weary smile tugged at her lips.

God save the world if she was its best hope.

"I don't know about extraordinary," she murmured, "but I'm definitely exhausted."

"Then sleep." His lips pressed gently to her hair. "I promise to keep you safe."

Abby allowed her heavy lids to fall shut.

No doubt she should be making plans and considering her options. Or even returning to the coven to discover if she could find any clue of where the witches might have fled.

Who knew what might be stalking and closing in on her even now?

At the moment, however, she preferred to play the role of Scarlett O'Hara to that of Lara Croft.

She would consider it all . . . tomorrow.

* * *

Dante was a card-carrying cynic.

How could he not be?

He was an immortal. He had done everything, seen everything, been with everything.

Most of them more than once.

There was nothing left to surprise him.

Nothing but the woman currently curled in his arms.

Bloody hell. He had already been amazed by her rare courage. And, of course, dazzled by her beauty. But to have her give herself to him with such raw, delicious abandon.

Well, that was enough to make even a jaded creature of the night feel a bit stunned.

A wry smile twisted his lips, and his hand ran softly over her curls. He was unaccustomed to holding a woman for hours as she slept. It was not the way of vampires. They were by nature solitary creatures. And even when together, they didn't seek such tender intimacy. Passion was all well and good, but once it was done, there was no reason to linger.

Only humans felt the need to hide animal instincts behind pretty emotional wrappings.

Perhaps vampires were not nearly as wise as they had always believed, he ruefully conceded.

Sensitive to Abby's slightest movement, Dante was aware the moment she began to stir. Tangled black lashes fluttered and then at last lifted to reveal sleepy blue eyes.

"Dante?" she murmured.

His arms instinctively tightened. "I'm here, lover."

"Did you sleep at all?"

Dante shrugged. "I have little need for sleep."

"Speaking of need, I have to step outside."

With a rueful grimace, Abby pulled out of his grasp and pulled on her scattered clothes. Dante rose as well, his gaze never straying from her awkward motions.

"You won't wander far?" he warned as she moved toward the entrance of the cave.

She tossed him a wry glance. "Don't worry."

She might as well have saved her breath, he acknowledged as she slipped out of the cave. He would of course worry. And fret. And damn the all-too-slow setting sun that prevented him from following after her.

If something happened, he would be utterly helpless to save Abby.

He paced the cave. That took all of five seconds. He rammed his fingers through his tangled hair and impatiently pulled it back to tie it at his nape. That took nearly three minutes. He paced again. And again. And again.

Ten minutes later, he was seriously considering the notion of marching from the cave to assure himself that Abby was still alive. Thankfully the sound of her pounding footsteps prevented any hasty death-by-setting-sun; moving as close to the entrance as he dared, he stood directly in her path as she barreled right into his waiting arms.

His brows swiftly pulled together as he felt her trembling against him.

"Abby? Is something wrong?"

She tilted back her head, her eyes wide. "I don't know. There were . . . shadows out there."

Dante tensed in reaction, already considering how he could protect this woman while they were virtually trapped in the cave. Damn, he had not counted on anyone finding them so swiftly.

"Shadows?"

"No, that's not exactly right." She gave a frustrated shake of her head. "They were more silvery thingamabobs."

He gave a lift of his brow. "Maybe it would be better if you tried to speak in English, my love. I don't know the translation for *thingamabobs.*"

Turning about, she pointed imperiously toward the mouth of the cave.

"There."

Edging dangerously close to the fading shaft of sunlight, Dante surveyed the nearby trees. His tension fled as he caught sight of the slender silver forms that darted through the shadows.

"Ah."

"What are they?"

Dante shrugged. "I suppose you would call them fey creatures."

She shifted to stand close at his side, seemingly unaware that her sweet heat was cloaking about him and causing all sorts of delicious reactions.

"Fairies?"

"Technically they're demons," he murmured in distracted tones.

"Just great."

He glanced down at her tight expression. "You don't have to worry; they're very gentle and very shy. Which is why they prefer such isolated places."

His words were meant to be comforting, but Abby lifted her hands to press them to her temples.

"This is insanity."

"What?"

She heaved a deep sigh. "Until two days ago, demons were nothing more than something from a B-rated horror show. Now I'm tripping over them every time I turn around. They can't just have suddenly appeared."

"No." With a rueful smile, Dante pulled her into his arms, his hands running a soothing path down her back. "They have always been here. Far longer than humans."

"Then why haven't I seen them before?"

"Because you weren't looking with those eyes."

"What?" She blinked before she was suddenly hit with comprehension. "Oh. You mean the Phoenix?"

"Yes." His hands continued to smooth over her slender back, although he couldn't fool even himself that it was any longer to offer reassurance. "Most mortals prefer to see only what they desire to see, and of course, most demons possess the ability to keep themselves hidden."

"Even vampires?" she demanded.

"When we choose." Hearing a faint hum in the air, Dante turned Abby back toward the narrow opening, locking his arms about her waist. "Watch."

"Watch what?"

He leaned down to whisper in her ear. "The dance."

For a moment nothing could be seen, and then, just as Abby was shifting impatiently, the sun slipped past the line of trees and in the growing darkness the silvery shapes began to glow with luminescent color.

Shimmering in shades of crimson and emerald and gold, they darted among one another, their playful antics creating a dazzling display of color.

"Oh my God," Abby breathed. "It's so beautiful."

"You sound surprised."

"It's just that I never expected . . ."

Her words trailed away as if she realized she was

about to reveal her instinctive prejudice. His lips twisted in a humorless smile. He couldn't blame her. She was still in shock from all that had happened. And the demons she had encountered so far had hardly been the sort to inspire warm, fuzzy feelings.

"Beauty among demons?" he finished in dry tones.

Slowly turning, she caught him off guard by pressing herself intimately against him as she smiled deep into his eyes.

"Actually, I've already discovered some demons can be incredibly beautiful." Her eyes darkened, and her hand moved to stroke him in a manner that Dante fully approved of. "And incredibly sexy."

He growled in fierce pleasure. "You're playing with fire, lover."

"Is that what I'm playing with?" she teased.

"Christ, I knew you would be a danger when you finally let loose," he rasped, catching her tightly in his arms and carrying her deeper into the cave.

Chapter 11

Abby felt . . . what?

Sated, certainly. Gloriously sated.

But it was more than that, she decided as she lay in Dante's arms and waited for the darkness to become complete.

She felt cherished. Yes, that was the word. As if what had just happened between the two of them had been more than just a means of passing the time or forgetting the horrors of the past hours or scratching the proverbial itch.

Maybe it was because he was a hell of a cuddler, or because he had centuries of practice, or just because he was Dante.

Whatever the case, she knew with absolute certainty she could spend an eternity with her head upon his shoulder and his hands softly stroking down her back.

Her dreamy thoughts were interrupted by a sharp jab to her neck. Lifting her hand, she slapped at the aggravating mosquito. Damn.

Well that was a pissy way to be jerked out of a rosy fantasy.

Probably not such a bad thing, she wryly acknowledged.

How delusional did she have to be to start dreaming of small bungalows, Sunday brunch, and nurseries with a vampire?

Obviously she had endured one zombie too many.

There was another fierce bite on her leg.

"Ow." She slapped at her calf.

"I hope you're not into some kinky self-flagellation," Dante murmured. "I suppose it's sexy enough, but it never turns out good."

She sat up and scratched at one of her endless bites. "I'm being eaten alive."

Although fully dressed, Dante still managed to look sinfully tempting as a lazy smile curved his lips.

"Not guilty . . . for a change." The silver eyes flashed in the shadows. "Not that I mind a nibble or two."

Abby might have shivered with pleasure if she hadn't been busy saving what was left of her blood.

"Mosquitoes," she retorted, her gaze skimming over his perfect features. Then it skimmed over the perfect hair that looked as if it had just been styled by Sassoon and the clothes that didn't have a damn wrinkle in sight. It was enough to make the most sated and cherished woman a bit grumpy. "I suppose you don't have to worry about the nasty bloodsuckers?"

His lips twitched at the edge in her voice. "Mosquitoes have never been a bother, but I can't say the same for all bloodsuckers."

She tilted her head to one side, her brief grumpiness forgotten.

"What's it like?"

"What's what like?"

"Being a vampire."

A raven brow lifted at her blunt question. "I think you're going to have to be more specific, lover. That's a rather big question."

Abby shrugged. "Is it a lot different from when you were human?"

There was a brief silence, as if he was considering precisely how much truth she could bear before folding his arms across his chest and meeting her curious gaze.

"I have no idea," he at last admitted.

Abby blinked, not expecting that. "You were born a vampire?"

"No, but it isn't like in the movies. I didn't crawl out of a grave and continue on as if I never died."

"Then what happened?"

His expression hardened as he dredged up his ancient memories. "I woke up one evening on the docks of London and couldn't remember my name or anything about my past. It was as if I had just been born without the slightest clue of who or what I was."

Abby frowned at the clipped words. Holy crap. He must have been terrified. It had been bad enough for her to accept she had a . . . thing rummaging around inside her. At least she hadn't woken up allergic to the sun, addicted to blood, and with her few brain cells wiped clean.

More importantly, she had Dante at her side to ease her fear.

That, of course, was the only reason she wasn't sitting in a padded room.

"Good God," she breathed.

"At first I thought I must have been on a bender and that my memories would eventually return," he said with a grimace. "I probably would have still been sitting on the docks when the dawn came if Viper hadn't stumbled across me and taken me into his clan."

Abby had an odd image of kilts and bagpipes. Not at all fitting with beautiful, deadly vampires.

"Clan?"

"A sort of family without all the guilt and drunken holiday brawls," he retorted.

Abby chuckled softly. "That sounds like my kind of family."

"Yeah, not bad if you can get it."

His tone was flippant, but Abby was not foolish enough to believe that it had been easy.

Unconsciously, she reached out to grasp his hand. "Still, you must have been curious about your past."

His gaze dropped as he interlocked her fingers with his own. "Not really. From my pungent scent and ragged clothes, I could guess I had been one of the endless hordes of undesirables that plagued the city."

"But what if you had a family?"

For the barest fraction of a second, his fingers squeezed her own almost painfully; then he was once again leaning against the cave wall with that coiled ease.

"What if I did?" he demanded. "I wouldn't have remembered them. They would have been strangers to me. Or worse."

"Worse?"

He deliberately held her gaze. "Dinner."

Her stomach clenched in horror. Damn. He warned her not to forget who, or what, he truly was. Unfortunately, he made it so damn easy.

"Oh."

"It was better for everyone to allow the man I had been to simply die."

She couldn't argue. She never had believed in all that Leave-it-to-Beaver crap anyway. There were definitely times when it was better for all when Daddy walked away and never looked back.

She tugged her legs up to her chest and rested her chin on her knee.

"It must have been so strange. To just wake up and be someone you didn't even know."

Almost absently he raised her fingers to his lips. "In the beginning, but Viper taught me to appreciate my new life. He was the one to give me the name Dante."

It was difficult to imagine Viper acting as a father figure. He seemed so remote and cold. Still, it was obvious that the older vampire had a great influence on Dante. And for that she had to be grateful.

"Why Dante?"

Dante smiled wryly. "He said that I needed to learn to be more a poet than a warrior."

"Ah, Dante, of course."

"He warned me that a predator was more than muscle and teeth. A predator must use his intelligence to observe his prey and learn their weaknesses. A kill is far easier when you can predict how your quarry is going to react."

Abby grimaced. "God, I thought my outlook was bleak."

He shrugged. "He wasn't all wrong."

"What do you mean?"

"If I had been quicker to sense a trap, then those witches would never have gotten their hands on me."

In a heartbeat, Abby was on her knees and had her hands framing his face. The thought that it might have been some other vampire besides Dante here with her was enough to make her stomach clench with horror.

"And you wouldn't be Dante," she said in stern tones.

An odd smile touched his lips. "And that would be a bad thing?"

"A very bad thing," she whispered.

Without warning, he leaned forward to plant a fierce, possessive kiss upon her lips before reluctantly pulling back to regard her with a searching gaze.

"As much as I would love to stay and play, I think we had better move along."

Abby stiffened. Move along? Go out into the dark and face whatever creepy crawlies were out there waiting?

It didn't sound at all appealing. Not when she could think of several other things she would rather be doing in the dark.

Things that involved one sexy vampire and maybe some scented oil . . .

"Do we have to leave?" she demanded. "We're at least safe here."

He gave a shake of his head. "No, we're very nicely trapped here. Especially once the sun rises."

Abby wrinkled her nose, accepting that he might have a point. "Where will we go?"

Rising to his feet, he reached out his hand to help her up. "First we find the car and then head back to Chicago."

Once on her feet, Abby made a hopeless stab at dusting off her pants. Stupid, of course. The dust helped to cover the wrinkles.

"Why Chicago?"

He tucked a stray curl behind her ear. "Because Viper can keep you protected while I try and find some means to trace the witches."

She jerked her head upward, her lips thinning into a line that should warn the most obtuse vampire she was not pleased.

"You're not thinking about going after them alone?"

Wise enough to sense trouble before it slapped him upside the head, Dante regarded her with a wary eye.

"I am the only one who knows their scent."

"Not the only one," she gritted. "There's something out there that is hunting them. Something that already found them once and gutted them like sushi. A trick I'm sure they would love to show you up close and personal."

"Graphic, but true," he conceded. "Which is why I need to get you to Viper."

She planted her hands on her hips. "And why you won't go after the witches alone."

"We can argue as we walk," he murmured, taking her hand and pulling her out of the cave. "It will make a nice change from your shrill complaints that I'm leading you in circles."

Abby took a moment to appreciate the faint breeze that stirred the air. It carried with it a scent she could only presume had something to do with nature. She had always made a point of never going anywhere that didn't have pavement and a Starbucks. It was rather strange to be surrounded by trees and stars.

Not strange enough, however, to make her forget that she was in the middle of correcting Dante's mistaken assumption that he could go about playing the Lone Ranger while she was around.

"There's not going to be an argument," she said in her best third-grade-teacher voice. "You're not going alone, and that's final."

He flashed a superior smile. "I'll admit you have stubbornness down to an art form, but I've had four centuries to perfect my own. You don't stand a chance."

Her smile was even more superior. "Four centuries is nothing. I'm a woman."

"So you are." His gaze made a lazy journey over her rumpled form. "A beautiful, glorious woman who purrs like a kitten when I stroke your—"

"Dante."

His lips twitched at her blush. "What? I like kittens."

She struggled to frown. "You're just trying to distract me."

"Is it working?"

"I—" Abby came to an abrupt halt as a cold chill feathered over her skin.

In less than a heartbeat, Dante was at her side, his body coiled and prepared to strike. All he needed was a victim.

"What is it?"

"There's something out there," she muttered.

His head tilted up, his eyes closing. For a long moment he remained silent, then he gave a slow shake of his head.

"I sense nothing."

Any other night, Abby would have shrugged and admitted she must have been imagining things. A brief cold chill was hardly something to get twisted over.

This was not any other night, however, and while

she might not be Mensa material, she wasn't entirely stupid. She wasn't about to ignore her instincts, which were making the hairs on the back of her neck stand on end.

"I think it's the same thing that attacked us at Viper's."

He gave a low growl deep in his throat. A sound that did nothing to help with the prickles.

"Abominations," he hissed. "Where?"

"In front of us," she promptly retorted, and then less certainly she swiveled about. "And I think behind us."

Dante took a quick glance around before grasping her hand and tugging her deeper into the trees.

"This way."

Abby had no intention of arguing. Her stomach was already clenched with an icy dread, and her heart lodged somewhere in her throat. At the moment she was quite willing to run all the way back to Chicago if necessary.

Keeping low to avoid the branches that blocked their paths, they scurried through the dark. Dante with his usual elegant silence and Abby crashing behind him like a bull elephant with a tranquilizer stuck in its butt.

Her prickles continued despite their swift flight, at times becoming more pronounced and then oddly fading. She didn't need her instincts, however, to tell her they were being chased. The living dead were no longer making a secret of their presence, and they stumbled after them making even more racket than she did.

Panting and grimly ignoring the stitch that was ripping through her side, Abby briefly wondered how the corpses could move with such speed. For God's sake, they were dead, weren't they? Most of them no doubt killed from an overdose of meat, cigarettes, and beer.

They should be shuffling along like proper zombies, not blazing through the woods as if they were the freaking Kenyan track team.

Struggling to keep up with Dante's numbing pace, Abby was unprepared for him to come to a sudden halt. Slamming into his back, she was only kept upright by the arm he was quick enough to wrap about her waist.

"Damn," she grunted, sucking in deep gasps of air. "Why did you stop?"

The silver eyes glittered in the darkness, his features set in hard lines.

"I don't like this."

Abby shivered, glancing over her shoulder at the unmistakable sound of an advancing horde.

"I don't particularly care for it either, but it's a hell of a lot better than those things catching us."

"That's the point," he rasped.

"What?"

"They could have surrounded us, cut off any escape. Why haven't they?"

Abby frowned, barely able to keep herself still when every instinct screamed at her to continue her willy-nilly bolt for safety.

"Because they're freaking brain dead."

Dante appeared stunningly unimpressed with her logic. "They may be dead, but they're being controlled by someone."

"And your point?"

There was a pause as his eyes narrowed to dangerous slits. "We're being herded."

"Herded?" It took a moment for Abby to collect a mental image. "You mean like sheep?"

"Exactly like sheep."

"But . . . why?"

Astonishingly the beautiful features managed to harden even further. "I don't think we want to find out."

Abby's heart sank from her throat to her lower stomach. If Dante was worried, then it had to be bad. Really, really bad.

"Oh God, what do we do?" she muttered.

"I suppose we either stand and fight or try to make a run for it."

Abby didn't even have to think about it.

"I'm voting on the run-for-it option."

"Let's do it, then." Tightening his arm about her waist, Dante pulled her upward, planting a too-brief kiss on her lips before tossing her over his shoulder like a sack of potatoes. "Hold on tight, lover."

Abby gave a startled squeak as he took off with a fluid speed that made the trees a mere blur in passing. It was certainly faster than having her blundering behind, slowing both of them to her human pace, but she discovered that the swaying was making her distinctly queasy.

Closing her eyes, she battled back the nausea and concentrated on anything but the rolling ground beneath her.

The rent was due on Friday. She didn't have a job. At least not one that paid. Unless of course there was something offered for saving the world from some creepy Prince. Her current lover was a vampire who was also unemployed. And her birthday was coming up in less than a month.

Those sorts of thoughts should easily have

distracted her. Unfortunately, her stomach continued to heave and rebel.

She wrenched open her eyes, hoping that would help.

Big mistake.

A scream was wrenched from her throat as she saw the rotting corpses beginning to close in.

With a large bound, Dante leaped over a fallen tree and with a motion that had her teeth crashing together, he had her back on her feet and shoved behind him.

"Dead end," he announced, his voice bleak, his hands clenched to strike.

Abby struggled to swallow. Slinking through the trees were a dozen, perhaps more, of the zombies. She could only thank God that it was too dark to see more than vague outlines. It was horrible enough to be attacked by the living dead without knowing first-hand how they met their end.

"Looks like we'll have to go the stand-and-fight route," she croaked.

"Abby." Dante turned to regard her with an anguished regret.

She could actually feel his fury and the biting guilt that raged through him. He held himself responsible, she knew. In his mind, he had failed her.

Lifting her hand, she gently laid it against his cheek.

"Dante," she whispered.

There was the sound of a cracking branch behind her. Instinctively she whirled about. And just as instinctively she screamed as a large stick came whizzing through the dark directly at her head.

Chapter 12

Dante knew he was going to die in the woods.

Vampire or not, he was no superhero. Hell, not even a superhero could battle off a dozen zombies and the dark wizard he could feel hiding among the trees.

But while he might not be capable of taking them all out, he could hope that he would destroy enough that Abby could use her powers to battle her way to safety.

It was a risky gamble.

It was also the only one they possessed.

He had managed to tear his way through the first wave of attackers and was desperately plowing a path toward the edge of the woods when the wizard had abruptly appeared before him. His hand lifted, and before Dante could dodge, he had struck him with a spell that sent him reeling into blackness.

He awoke to discover himself chained to a cold, barren stone floor.

He was alive, and he was not alone. He held himself utterly still, his mind already racing.

He hadn't died, but what of Abby?

Concentrating, he searched for her presence. Nothing. Not even the familiar chaffing of the Phoenix could be detected. If he had possessed a heart, it would have stopped beating.

Bloody hell.

Bloody, bloody hell.

With an effort, he collected his rising panic.

He couldn't allow himself to lose control. Not when he was not yet certain Abby was dead. If there was even the most remote chance she was still alive, he had to do whatever was necessary to rescue her.

Only when he knew there was no hope left would he allow himself the pleasure of ravaging everything and everyone in his path.

He hung grimly on to that thought as a soft, female hand ran an intimate path over his chest.

Dante clenched his teeth.

Once he might have found the lingering touch an invitation to full-blown debauchery.

Hell, at one time a mere glance was enough to stir his passions. A vampire was rarely particular when it came to sex.

Now, however, he barely hid his shudder of distaste.

There was something clammy and possessive about the stroking fingers. And, more importantly, they didn't belong to Abby.

"He's so beautiful," a voice crooned next to his ear. Dante did not stir so much as a muscle.

There was a rasping sound from farther away, but still too close for comfort.

"Stop jerking around, Kayla."

So, at least two, he acknowledged.

Two he could kill. Always presuming he could somehow free himself from the chains.

"You're the one who enjoys jerking around, Amil, or should I say jerking off?" the female drawled in mocking tones, obviously referring to the man's sexual preferences. "Some of us would rather have pretty toys when we play."

"In case you haven't noticed, this toy likes to bite."

"Not if I keep him in chains." The fingers toyed with the buttons on Dante's pants. "Besides, the danger is half the fun."

"You're sick; you know that, don't you?"

"We're all sick, you moron, or we wouldn't worship the Prince." The woman gave a soft chuckle, seemingly proud of her evil connections. "I'm just honest about my perversions. And this one could make the most perverse woman scream in pleasure."

Dante had every intention of making the woman scream, he thought. Only, pleasure would have nothing to do with it.

"The master said we are to leave him alone."

"What the master doesn't know—"

"Don't be an idiot. The master knows everything."

Ah. Dante silently tucked away the tidbit of information. This master was clearly the power he could sense in the distance. And as unloved as he was feared. Information he could use to his advantage.

"A pity. I suppose that bitch we captured has had her fill of vampire goodness."

"That bitch is about to be burned on the altar. I'm sure she'd change places with you if you want."

A tingle raced through Dante. They had to be speaking of Abby. She was alive. Freaking hell. He choked back a groan of painful relief.

He was not too late. Nothing else mattered.

This time he would not fail her.

He barely noted the hand that grabbed his crotch. "Having this between my legs might almost make it worthwhile."

"Shit, Kayla, do you ever think about anything else?" the man demanded in disgust.

"It's been a while."

"An hour?"

The woman gave a snort of ugly amusement. "Well, not long enough to consider your tiny cock as enticement."

"Like I'd risk my health with a whore who's been with every beast and demon this side of the Mississippi. Why don't you go do something useful and make sure the master has everything he needs for the ceremony?"

The fingers clutched his thigh, her nails sinking into his skin. "You're not going to do anything to him, are you? I don't want to come back and find him a pile of ashes."

"The master wants him alive and intact." There was no mistaking the edge in the man's voice or the fact that he held his master in little regard. A man who considered himself better suited to be tyrant than servant, Dante told himself. "No doubt the Prince will have something to say about that once he's returned."

"Maybe I can convince him to allow me some playtime before he has him toasted."

"And maybe he'll do us all a favor and have you turned into a goat."

"Eunuch."

"Slut."

The childish exchange completed, Dante felt the woman's fingers give a last longing sweep before she was lifting herself upright and walking away.

He longed to scrub away the feel of her touch, but he was sensible enough to resist the urge. Instead he slowly counted to one hundred. He wanted to ensure that he was truly alone with the man before revealing he was awake and aware of his surroundings.

At last, satisfied that the woman wasn't going to pop back in for a quickie with the unconscious vampire, Dante slit his eyes just enough to take a swift glance about.

There was not much to see.

As he had suspected, he was in a barren room that appeared to have been chiseled deep beneath the ground. His chains were attached to the stony floor, and a lone torch was stuck near the opening that led to a dark corridor beyond.

There were no chairs, no stray rocks, not even a stick that could be used to pry open the chains. Rather a pain in the ass since he would have to convince his guard to unlock him before he could break his neck.

His gaze shifted to the thin, startling young mortal attired in dark robes. He couldn't determine his magical abilities, but there was no missing the dark thread of power he received from the dark lord. Wild and untutored, but nothing that Dante intended to underestimate. Neither did he intend to underestimate the very large stake he had clutched in his hand.

He was desperate to get to Abby. But not so desperate as to get himself killed before he could save her.

Faking a low groan, Dante allowed his eyes to fully open. Across the chamber, the man clutched the stake even tighter while attempting to appear smug.

Dante resisted the urge to smile. There was a brittle arrogance about the man that would make his task all the easier.

Nothing like overweening pride to make a man act a fool.

"Ah, so the dead awakens." The man held up his stake, as if Dante might somehow have overlooked the lethal weapon. "I suggest you don't move. Not unless you have developed a liking for wood through the heart."

Dante curled his lips as he lifted himself enough to settle against the wall. His fangs he kept well hidden. No point in allowing the idiot to realize he was already dead.

"I get a lot of that."

His captor narrowed his gaze, no doubt surprised by Dante's casual indifference.

"Just don't make any hasty movements."

Dante flicked a brow upward. "Why would I make any hasty movements? I have nowhere to go." He took a moment to glance about, his nose wrinkling at the barren surroundings. "At least not at the moment."

Confusion flashed through the pale eyes before the man was pulling his lips into a tight smile.

"Nice try, but I was there when you tore apart six of my servants in an effort to save that woman."

Dante shrugged. Inwardly he was cursing himself. Six? Shit, he thought he had destroyed at least nine.

"I didn't have much of a choice. Those witches made sure of that."

"Just as they'll make sure you try to save her from the master."

Dante pretended to consider the accusation for a moment.

"Actually, I don't think so."

The man took an unconscious step closer. Unfortunately not close enough for Dante to get his teeth upon him.

"What do you mean?"

The chains rattled as Dante waved his hand toward the thick walls. "I don't know what it is about these caves, but the first time in three centuries that damn Phoenix doesn't have its claws stuck in me. I obviously owe you one. And a vampire always pays his debts." His smile widened. "Always."

A beat passed. Obviously his guardian was attempting to use what he loosely claimed as a brain.

"You're saying that you're free of the curse?"

"Who knows?" Dante leaned his head against the wall. "I'm just saying that I don't feel the least urge to lift a finger for that bitch who trapped me."

Another beat passed. "I don't believe you."

"Whatever." Dante shrugged. "At least tell me, is she dead?"

The man shot a revealing glance toward the darkened entrance.

"Not yet."

So, she must be near. A flare of anticipation raced through him before a warning voice reminded him that she might as well be a world away unless he could get the chains removed.

With an effort, he maintained his air of aloof curiosity. "Not yet? Why would you hesitate . . . ah. Of course. You're going to offer her up to the Prince, aren't you?"

The human stiffened at the hint of mockery in his voice. "When the time is right."

Dante casually studied his host, allowing his amusement to show.

"Let me give you a bit of advice, boy," he drawled softly. "Don't wait too long. There are all sorts of beasties out there who will kill you for the opportunity to be the one to give the Prince such a prize. The sooner you offer the sacrifice, the sooner you'll have glory beyond belief."

The stiffness increased as a hint of color touched the cheeks still rounded with youth.

"The glory belongs to my master."

"Master?" Dante gave a small snort of disbelief. "Are you telling me that you captured the Phoenix and handed her over for someone else to reap the rewards? Hell, don't you have a brain? Oh, maybe it's the balls you lack."

The color turned to purple as the man lifted the stake in a threatening motion.

"Watch your mouth, vampire. I would love nothing more than to stick this through your heart."

Dante merely laughed. He had hit a direct nerve. The man's frustrated ambition was nearly tangible in the air.

"God, I thought I had been pussy-whipped by those witches." He rubbed the salt a bit deeper into the open wound. "At least I never willingly allowed myself to be turned into a schmuck."

The pale eyes flashed with fury, but behind the anger was a cold hunger that he could not entirely conceal.

"I will have my rewards."

"A few crumbs dropped by the great master? Pathetic."

"Shut up."

Dante folded his arms over his chest, inwardly cursing the rattling chains. He hated chains. They made him want to bite something. Hard. Instead he smiled with mocking humor.

"You could have had it all. Power, glory, a place at the side of the Prince." His smile widened. "But then, maybe you like being a flunky. I've noticed most humans prefer being sheep to wolves."

A loud breath hissed through clenched teeth. "I know what you're trying to do, and it won't work."

Oh, it was working. The man was nearly drooling with the desire to snatch the power he felt being denied him.

"Look, I couldn't care less who manages to kill that bloody Phoenix, just as long as it's good and dead." Dante glanced down to inspect his fingernail. "I intend to walk out of this cave a free vampire."

The man gave a humorless laugh. "You think the Prince won't want a taste of you?"

"Why should he?"

Another step closer, but still out of reach.

"You protected the Chalice."

Dante didn't even bother to glance up. That didn't mean, however, he wasn't fiercely aware of the exact distance that separated them.

"I was compelled by the witches. It wasn't as if I wanted to be chained like a dog."

"I doubt he's that understanding."

"I'd say my chances of living through the night are considerably better than your own."

A shocked silence filled the chamber. It was obvious the fool had not even considered the cost of returning the dark power to the world. Typical. Most wizards were concerned only with the rewards, never the sacrifice that would be demanded.

And there was always a sacrifice.

"Now what are you babbling about?" he rasped.

Dante lazily lifted his head to regard him with a steady gaze.

"You do know that the Prince can't survive in this world without feeding?" he demanded. "He requires blood. A lot of blood. Thankfully, I'm fresh out."

A frown touched the young man's brow. "The woman holding the Phoenix will be the sacrifice."

"Abby? She's barely a snack, even for me."

"I . . ." His lips tightened. "There are servants."

Dante chuckled. "I hope for your sake there is a whole flock of servants. Otherwise you're about to find yourself laid over the altar with a knife carving out your heart."

Gripping the stake so tightly it threatened to snap in half, the mortal paced toward the narrow opening. Farther away from Dante but clearly unnerved by the thought of altars and knives and the ripping out of hearts.

"I suppose you think I should let you go so that you can help me overthrow the master?"

"Me?" Dante gave a sound of disgust. "Why the hell would I want to help you? It doesn't matter to me who kills the bitch. I'm free either way."

The decidedly nervous disciple whirled back. A tick in his left eye revealed his barely controlled emotions.

"I don't think you're nearly as unconcerned as you want me to believe. I think you have feelings for the woman."

Dante widened his eyes in mock disbelief even as

he inwardly conceded that the man was not quite the idiot he had supposed. Something to remember when it came time to kill him.

"I'm a vampire, you twit. I don't have feelings for anyone or anything. Although . . . ." He deliberately allowed his words to trail away.

"What?"

"She was a helluva lay," he drawled, hopefully cementing his seeming disregard for a mere mortal. The moment this fool was certain Dante would travel to the pits of hell to save Abby was the moment he lost all advantage. "The things she could do with her tongue could make a man explode like a volcano. I'll have to admit I wouldn't mind another couple of rounds before she's tossed to the Prince. You should try her."

A disdain marred the youthful features. "Not all of us are animals."

"Ah . . . a woman hater. You prefer men? Or is it something a little more exotic?" Dante gave a taunting smile. "I have a friend who could fix you right up."

His captor spit on floor. "Filth."

"I may be filth, but I'm not the one who's about to be fed to the Prince." Dante settled himself more comfortably. "Give him my regards, won't you?"

Pressed near to the breaking point, the man strode forward, his robes fluttering about his slender form.

"Shut up or I'll shut you up."

"Whatever you say."

When Abby had first awoken, she had been relieved to discover she was simply alive. There seemed to be few things worse than being eaten by ravaging zombies. None that came directly to mind anyway.

Then she opened her eyes.

It took only a moment to realize she had been moved from the woods to a dark cavern of some sort. And that she was tied to a post stuck near a brazier that was belching out a foul smoke.

And that she was not alone.

She might have screamed if a rough cloth had not been tied over her mouth.

A man was standing directly before her. Or at least he appeared to be a man. She was not about to be overly hasty in handing out species assignments after the past few days. And there was something very nonhumanlike about his pasty white skin and hairless head.

And of course there was his outfit.

What sort of man wore heavy robes and a medallion that looked as if it had been ripped off some sports car?

Even as the aimless thoughts floated through her mind the thing reached up to stroke a finger down her cheek. Abby gagged at the clammy feel of his touch, desperately wondering where Dante was.

He had to be near, she told herself. Perhaps even now plotting her rescue.

She didn't for a moment consider the fact he might be injured. Or, God forbid, dead.

That path only led to stark, raving madness.

Instead she glared at the man who was regarding her as though she were a bug pinned beneath a microscope. An apt description considering she was tied so tightly to the pole she could barely even blink.

"Such power," he purred in an oddly mesmerizing tone. "She hums with it. It seems almost a pity to have her slain."

Slain? Abby groaned through the rag stuffed in her mouth. She didn't think she was tied up for a surprise birthday party, but slain?

Damn Selena and those witches. She was obviously here to be served up like a Thanksgiving turkey for the Prince.

Hurry, Dante, she silently willed. Please, God, hurry.

Another face suddenly popped into view. This one belonged to a woman not much older than Abby with a pale, pointed face and a dark cloud of hair. She might have been attractive if it hadn't been for the unnatural glitter in her brown eyes.

"She doesn't look all that dangerous," the woman scoffed.

The man shot her a condemning glance. "Because, like most, you see only with your eyes, Kayla. A weakness that I have warned you of more than once."

"It hardly matters. She'll soon enough be dead."

Abby didn't like the woman's flippant tone. She made it sound as if they were taking out the trash rather than committing cold-blooded murder. With a flare of anger, she wondered if she could fry the bitch like she had those zombies.

"Yes, soon." The hairless stranger glanced toward the burning fire. "The summoning of the dark lord has begun."

"Shall I call for Amil and the vampire?"

Dante. Abby briefly closed her eyes as relief surged through her. He was near. And any moment he was going to charge through the door to kick some serious ass.

Unaware of his danger, the man allowed a peculiar smile to tug at his lips.

"Not just yet. I am waiting for the appropriate moment to . . . reward my loyal acolyte."

Something in the oily tone caught Abby's attention, stirring the hairs on the nape of her neck. The young woman, however, merely smiled.

"You have honored me by requesting my presence."

"I assure you that your presence is essential."

The dark eyes smoldered with a hectic fire. "We shall be blessed above all others."

"Yes, indeed."

There was a sound across the chamber, and Abby shifted her gaze to discover two shadowed forms standing near the corner. They were shrouded from head to foot in heavy robes. No doubt a good thing. Abby didn't hope for a moment they were actually human.

The woman seemed no more impressed than Abby, and her lips curled as she waved a hand toward the silent witnesses.

"Shouldn't you be sending away those . . . pests? You surely don't want them around when his lordship returns?"

"They are essential as well."

"Why?"

"You will discover soon enough."

The woman gave a harsh sound of annoyance. "I hate this waiting."

"Patience possesses its own rewards." Still studying Abby, the man seemed to stiffen, his head swiveling toward an opening near the servants.

The woman frowned. "What is it, master?"

"I sense a . . . disturbance. Return to Amil."

"Now? What if the Pr—"

A cold chill abruptly filled the air. "I said return to Amil."

Both Abby and the strange female blanched at the frozen edge in his voice. It was the voice of a man who would kill without thought or hesitation.

"Of course," she babbled as she gave a deep bow and hurried from the room.

Seemingly having forgotten Abby for the moment, the man studied the flickering flames.

"Nothing can stop me. Not now."

Chapter 13

Dante was waiting for the woman. She passed his shadowed form without noticing, and then it was far too late as he swiftly moved to sink his teeth deep into her throat. He was incapable of drinking human blood, thanks to the witches, but it didn't halt him from ripping out her throat.

Without even glancing down, he dropped her lifeless form to the ground and returned to the shadows to watch his arrogant partner in crime stride into the large chamber before them.

It had been child's play to convince Amil to release him from his chains. Evil always turned on itself, and the ambitious pup wasn't entirely stupid. He knew quite well his master wouldn't hesitate to feed him to the coming Prince. It was precisely what he would do given the chance.

And thankfully his puffed-up pride made him believe he could control a mere vampire.

A mistake Dante was quite willing to encourage. At least as long as he dutifully distracted the mysterious master and allowed Dante to slip away with Abby undeterred.

Should he stand in the way, Dante would ensure he made an early trip to hell.

Moving with a silence no human could match, Dante slipped behind Amil as he crossed to stand before a thin, older man draped in heavy robes. The master. Dante narrowed his gaze as he sensed the power that shimmered about the wizard.

Dangerous.

Very dangerous.

Dante slipped deep into the shadows that surrounded the cavern. He had no desire to confront the magician directly. Not when there was a danger he might be killed before freeing Abby.

The thought of Abby made his gaze instinctively move to where she was tied to the post. He had deliberately avoided regarding her too closely. It was enough to know she was alive and seemingly unharmed. To dwell upon her obvious distress would only distract him at a time when he desperately needed to keep his mind focused.

Clenching his teeth with a cold fury, he continued through the shadows, moving toward the two robed servants who stood only a few feet away.

Across the chamber, Amil at last confronted the dark wizard. "Master."

An icy tingle of power scoured the air, making even Dante shiver.

"Why are you here?" he charged. "Where is Kayla?"

Too stupid or too arrogant to realize just how overmatched he was, the younger wizard gave a low chuckle.

"The last I saw, she was being ripped into shreds by a very angry vampire."

There was a furious pause. "You allowed the beast to escape?"

"In a manner of speaking," Amil drawled.

Stepping directly behind the servants, who had not yet noticed his presence, Dante reached out to wrap his arms about their throats. With one smooth motion, he twisted both their necks until they cracked, and he lowered them to the floor.

They had never seen death coming, and he was one step closer to freedom.

There was a sharp hiss from the master. "You fool. You stupid, greedy fool."

"No, not a fool," Amil denied. "At least not fool enough to allow myself to become mere fodder so you can wallow in your own glory."

There was a startled beat, as if the master hadn't expected his student to realize his ultimate fate.

"Ah, perhaps not such a fool after all," he whispered in cold tones. "Tell me, Amil, what do you intend to do?"

"What I should have done to begin with. Kill you and offer the Phoenix to the dark lord myself."

Not surprisingly, the proud boast brought only a laugh from the older man. "Kill me? You?"

"You are weak from your battle with the witches," Amil boasted, causing Dante to pause in the shadows.

So, the wizard was responsible for the carnage at the coven. Bloody hell. The sooner he could get Abby out of this cavern the better.

Sinking back into the shadows, Dante began to inch his way behind the wizard.

"You can barely conjure enough power for a summoning spell," Amil continued his taunting.

What might have been a smile curved the thin

lips as the wizard grasped the medallion about his neck.

"Not so weak as you believe." Pointing toward the younger man, the wizard struck.

Abby was well aware there was some mystical battle brewing between the two robed men. It would be hard to miss when the younger of the two abruptly slammed against the far wall only to scramble to his feet and lunge toward the older man.

Her attention, however, was not on the dueling wizards.

She had sensed Dante the moment he had entered the room. Fierce, near-heart-stopping joy had rushed through her as she had at last spotted him creeping through the shadows.

He was alive and free and on his way to sweep her away from this horrible place.

Then her joy had faltered when the light had flickered and she had seen the wet crimson that stained his shirt. Vaguely she recalled the young man in robes claiming a vampire was ripping the woman Kayla to shreds, but somehow she had not connected it to Dante. Not until she watched as he slipped from the shadows to dispatch the servants with swift and lethal ease.

He was silent, gliding death. A ruthless killer who stalked his prey without mercy.

A chill shot down her spine as she studied the alabaster features set in a pitiless mask and the eyes that glittered with a frozen silver fire.

This was the vampire he had warned her of.

The demon who lurked beneath the image of a man.

Another chill shot through her.

But not out of physical fear. Perhaps it was ridiculously naïve, but she didn't believe he would harm her. Or at least not intentionally.

It was more the knowledge that she had come to think of Dante as . . . what?

Her boyfriend?

Her lover?

God, she didn't know.

And now was not the time to consider such idiotic thoughts, she told herself with a mental slap.

For God's sake, if Dante didn't get her untied and out of the cavern, she was about to become a midnight munchie for some evil spirit. Surely that was more important than her love life?

There was a furious screech and sounds of scuffling from the two men battling in the middle of the chamber and a prickling feel of electricity in the air, but Abby refused to take her gaze from the ever-approaching vampire.

As long as she kept Dante within sight, she knew she was safe.

A ridiculous certainty perhaps, but what was a terrified, soon-to-be-sacrificed woman to do?

Unable to even whimper with the gag stuck in her mouth, Abby watched Dante move closer. His silver gaze held her own, as if compelling her not to panic.

Yeah, right.

Only the ropes binding her to the post kept her from crumpling onto the ground so she could babble in terror.

Abby Barlow, savior of the world.

Careful to avoid the raging battle in the center of the chamber, Dante flowed through the shadows.

Her heart nearly halted when he disappeared behind her. Oh God. She couldn't see him. What if he disappeared? What if there were more evil baddies hiding . . .

The feel of cool, slender fingers on her wrist put a swift end to her crazed thoughts. Abby would have wept in relief if she hadn't realized they were still far from safe.

The ropes slithered to the floor, sending painful prickles through her arms as her blood was allowed to rush through her veins. She felt Dante's lips at her ear as he struggled to remove the gag from her mouth.

"Say nothing," he breathed, waiting for her nod before allowing the disgusting rag to fall away.

Abby sucked in several deep breaths as she stepped from the post and directly into Dante's welcoming arms. He gathered her close, as if sensing she would collapse without his support. Her weakened state, however, didn't keep him from forcing her wobbly legs to carry her toward the narrow opening across the chamber.

She bit her lip to halt her instinctive protest. She had been tied to the post for hours, and her entire body felt as if it had been ridden hard and put up wet. Still, she had no more desire than Dante to linger in this damp cell.

Not when that pasty-faced moron considered her a yummy treat for Prince Badass.

They had reached the narrow opening when a hair-raising scream rose behind them.

"No!" the younger man screeched. "I surrender! I—"

There was a horrid gurgling noise and then a whiff of what might have been scorched flesh.

Abby gagged even as Dante roughly tossed her over his shoulder and bolted down the dark corridor.

On this occasion she didn't even notice the nausea at the swaying motion. That was one good thing about absolute, mind-numbing fear. It tended to put everything else into perspective.

Moving through the darkness with a speed that defied the law of physics, Abby silently prayed to every god and deity she could think of. It seemed an appropriate moment to cover all the bases.

Really, when it came down to it, who knew?

Time had no meaning, but slowly she began to sense they were moving steadily upward. Then, without warning, she felt the unmistakable brush of fresh air upon her cheeks.

Oh, thank you, thank you, thank you, she breathed heavenward.

They were out of the dismal cavern.

And best of all, there seemed to be no sign of any sort of pursuit.

Still, Dante's pace never slowed. Seemingly unaffected by her weight (a sop to her vanity at any other time), he charged through an overgrown cemetery and past an abandoned church. She thought she caught sight of a handful of shabby houses, but they passed in such a blur it was impossible to be certain.

It was not until they were well away from the cavern that Dante at last slowed and gently lowered her to her feet. Abby instantly swayed, and his arm lashed about her waist to keep her upright.

"Are you harmed?" he growled, his hand grasping her chin to tip her face upward for his inspection.

She shivered beneath the compelling glitter of the silver gaze and then forced herself to relax.

This was Dante.

The beautiful, incredible vampire who had just saved her life.

"Nothing that twenty years of therapy won't cure," she retorted in a voice that was not quite steady. "Who were those freaks? Demons?"

His nose flared with smoldering fury. "They were human enough. Mortal disciples."

Well, that wouldn't have been her first guess.

"Disciples?"

"Worshippers of the Prince," he clarified. "You would call them wizards."

Her lips twisted. So much for kindly old men with long white beards and a twinkle in their eye.

"Which would explain the magic, I suppose."

"Magic more powerful than a mere human should be capable of possessing." His brows drew together as if the thought troubled him. Which in turn troubled her. A lot. "It was the elder wizard who attacked the coven."

"Dear God." She shuddered in horror at the memory of what he had done to the witches. How could any human commit such atrocities? "He was going to feed me to that . . . shadow."

"Yes. With the Phoenix destroyed, the Prince would walk the world freely once again."

"A wizard. Just perfect." She gave a shake of her head. "I suppose he'll be in line with the demons and zombies chasing us?"

"Hopefully not immediately. The battle with the witches and young Amil will have left him weak. I don't think he will be eager to face me just yet."

Her gaze unconsciously darkened. "No, I wouldn't think he would be in any hurry."

It took a beat before he abruptly grasped her

shoulders in a firm grip. His beautiful face was somber in the muted moonlight.

"I did warn you, Abby," he rasped. "I'm a vampire. A predator. Nothing can change that."

Instinctively she lifted her hand to place it against his cheek. His skin was chilled and smooth beneath her palm, sending a familiar excitement through her body.

"I know."

With a gentleness that made her heart leap, he smoothed her hair behind her ears.

"Did I frighten you?"

"Maybe a little," she admitted in low tones.

Something that might have been pain flared through his silver eyes.

"I would never harm you. No matter what happens."

Held close to his hard body, she didn't have a moment of doubt. "That is not what I feared."

"What is it?"

"I just realized you were right. We're very different. God, I'm not sure we're even the same species."

His arms shifted to tighten about her waist. "Different, but bound together, lover. At least until the Phoenix can be handed to another." He held her gaze with ease. "Will you trust me, Abby?"

There was no hesitation. "With my very life."

Oddly her swift assurance made him stiffen. As if he had been caught off guard by her ready trust.

"I . . . oh God, Abby, if only you knew," he muttered, lowering his head to press his lips tenderly against her mouth.

Abby readily arched against him, her arms encircling his neck. Dear God, she needed him. His touch. His strength. His comfort.

Softly he soothed the horror of the past few hours, his lips stroking over her mouth, his hands gripping her hips.

Tilting back her head, she moaned as he turned his attention to the sensitive curve of her neck, nibbling at the pulse that raced with soaring excitement.

"If only I knew what?" she questioned breathlessly.

His hands tightened upon her hips before he pulled back far enough to regard her with a smoky gaze.

"How long it's been since I've been treated as something other than a rabid animal."

Her heart wrenched as she brushed her fingers across his sensuous lips. She knew all too well the feeling of being despised and unwanted in her own home. Of being brutally kicked back into place when she dared to defy her father.

How Dante had managed to endure his captivity for centuries was beyond comprehension.

"I'm sorry," she husked. "No one deserves to be chained and held against their will." She framed his beautiful face in her hands. "I swear I will do whatever I can to release you."

His eyes flared as he claimed her lips in a kiss she felt to her very soul. Abby groaned, curling her toes in pleasure. Oh yeah, this vampire knew a thing or two about kissing. A woman could spend an eternity just being held in his arms.

Smoothing her hands through his satin hair, Abby sank into the sizzling heat. She was alive against all odds. She intended to appreciate every moment of what she had been given.

His hands slid slowly up the curve of her spine as

his kiss deepened. His erection pressed into her stomach.

Abby forgot about dark wizards, hideous zombies, and missing witches. She forgot about everything but the searing pleasure of Dante's touch.

For months she had fantasized about this man. Now that she knew up close and personal just what sort of lover he was, her hunger for him was near unbearable.

She heard his rasping groan as his hands shifted to cup the softness of her breasts. But even as she arched against his touch, he was reluctantly pulling away.

"Christ, what am I doing?" he muttered, shoving his hands roughly through his hair. "Let's go before I manage to get us captured again."

Taking her hand, Dante led her through the thickening trees, muttering beneath his breath at his brief distraction.

Abby did her own share of muttering. Certainly she was all for getting far away from the crazed wizard and his zombie posse. Putting several oceans between them didn't seem an overreaction.

But she couldn't deny a small measure of frustration.

Just once she wanted to be alone with Dante without the threat of horrible death hanging over their heads.

A few measly hours when they could enjoy each other in absolute peace.

It was enough to make any woman a bit grouchy.

They moved in silence for what seemed to be an eternity. Off and on, Dante would insist on carrying her so they could move quicker, but disliking the feel of being helpless, she preferred to trail behind him. Even if it meant tripping over every stray branch and bush that littered the woods. Damn nature.

At last she began to wonder if Dante intended for them to walk in circles for the rest of the night.

"Do you know where we're going?" she demanded in suspicion.

"For help," he retorted without missing a step. "The next time I face those zombies, I intend to have something that will frighten those sons of bitches back to the grave."

She couldn't argue with that.

"Good plan. Where is this something?"

"In Chicago."

"Let me guess . . . Viper," she said dryly.

That earned her a swift glance over his shoulder. "How did you know?"

"He seems the type to have a fascination with things that would frighten zombies."

"You have no idea." Without warning, he came to an abrupt halt. They had thankfully left behind the trees and now stood in what seemed to be an abandoned field. "Wait."

Brushing things from her hair that she hoped to God were bits of leaves and branches, Abby regarded Dante with a faint frown.

"Don't tell me you're lost."

Turning, he gave a lift of his perfect brows. "I'm never lost."

Abby rolled her eyes. "Spoken like a true male."

With a smug smile he once again took off. "This way."

"You're sure?" she demanded. "You aren't just leading me around until we stumble over the car?"

"Were you born this aggravating or is it a skill you've developed just to annoy me?"

Her lips twitched. She couldn't deny she enjoyed razzing Dante.

His own fault, of course.

He shouldn't be so arrogant.

"Don't flatter yourself. I've always been this aggravating."

"Now, that I believe," he muttered before tossing her a patronizing smile over his shoulder as he pointed to the outline of the abandoned factory buildings just off to the left. "There."

She gave a sniff although she inwardly sighed in relief as she realized they were only a short distance from Viper's car. She would give her soul to rest her aching legs.

"You don't have to smirk. It's unbecoming."

Dante chuckled as he reached the car and leaned his large form against the hood. Bathed in moonlight with his shirt half open and his hair flowing about his perfect face, he appeared tall, dark, and edible.

A tasty hood ornament, indeed.

Folding his arms over his chest, he allowed one of those slow, wickedly naughty smiles to curve his lips.

"I think you owe me an apology for doubting my extraordinary powers for even a moment."

Abby struggled not to melt at his feet.

She did have *some* pride.

"What sort of apology?"

The smile widened. "I have a few ideas. Unfortunately they include a soft bed, scented candles, and plenty of whipped cream. None of which I happen to have on hand."

Abby's mouth went dry. "Vampires eat whipped cream?"

"I don't plan on being the one eating it."

Oh. The air suddenly seemed too thick to breathe. No doubt it had something to do with the image of having Dante spread upon a bed as she licked a layer of whipped cream from his hard body.

"Shameless," she rasped.

He cast a glance toward the shadowed heavens. "Shameless and dead if we don't hurry. Chicago isn't getting any closer. It's going to be a near thing as it is."

Gathering her scattered thoughts, Abby attempted to determine how much of the night had passed. A stupid attempt. To her the morning arrived when her alarm went off, usually five or six times.

"If you're worried, why don't I drive and you hide in the trunk?"

"I don't think so."

"Why not?"

It was a perfectly reasonable solution.

Of course, he was a male despite the benefit of being a vampire. And in typical male fashion, he regarded her as if she had suggested he neuter himself.

"I prefer to risk the sun."

Her lips thinned. "Are you implying that a woman can't drive as well as a man?"

"I'm implying that the only way I'm getting into that trunk is if you join me," he said dryly. "Besides, if Viper finds so much as a scratch on his car, being a pile of dust will be the least of my concerns."

"And why would you think that I would scratch—"

Her words were brought to a rude halt by the simple means of Dante reaching out and hauling her against his chest. Once there, he sealed her lips with his own with a brief, scorching kiss.

"Please, lover, can we continue this argument in the car?" he murmured against her mouth.

"Oh, we'll continue it," she warned, not about to be so easily manipulated. At least not until they had that warm bed and whipped cream. "You can count on that."

Chapter 14

In the end, Abby's promise of a continuing argument proved to be an empty threat.

Her love for a rousing squabble was no match for her weariness. Dante had barely reached the interstate when her head had tilted to the side and her eyes slid closed.

Resisting the urge to halt the car and simply appreciate her peaceful beauty, Dante sped through the empty streets and reached Viper's lair well ahead of the sun. Parking in the private lot beneath the street, he carefully carried Abby to the room they had shared before.

He was beyond weary as he lowered Abby onto the wide bed. Not only from the exertions of the night, but also from the approaching dawn. Still, he forced himself to leave the room and search out Viper in his private chambers.

He found the vampire sprawled upon an antique chaise lounge attired in a brocade robe that was heavily embroidered with gold thread. The room itself would have made most collectors drool in envy.

Scattered over the priceless hand-woven carpets were carved and gilded furnishings that had once belonged to a Russian czar. The walls were decorated with hand-painted silk upholstery, the doors made of ebony inlaid with gold leaf, and the chandeliers studded with sapphires and pearls.

More stunning were the rare works of art that were carefully displayed behind temperature-controlled glass frames. Most were thought by the world to be lost, some even having been completely forgotten. Together they created a stunning beauty that was unsurpassed anywhere in the world.

Surrounded by furnishings fit for the finest palace and sipping a brandy that cost more than some small countries, Viper appeared every inch a pampered aristocrat.

It was only when one noted the cold, calculating glitter in his midnight eyes that the image of indolent hedonism was shattered.

A glitter that became even more pronounced as Dante briefly relayed what had occurred since he had left Chicago.

Rising to his feet, Viper regarded him with a sardonic expression. "Abominations, dark wizards, dead witches—I'll give you this, Dante, you really know how to pick your women."

"I didn't exactly pick Abby, the Phoenix did."

Perfect brows several shades darker than the silver hair slowly arched.

"You do realize you lost a perfect opportunity to be rid of your chains?"

Dante smiled wryly. The chains that held him to Abby would never be broken. No matter what happened to the bloody Phoenix.

"By allowing Abby to be sacrificed? Not a chance in hell."

"You have it bad, my friend." Viper stared at him for a long beat. "I know this voodoo priestess who has an incantation that could—"

"Thanks, but not necessary," Dante firmly interrupted. "What I need are those damn witches."

Viper's lips thinned, but for a pleasant change he didn't pursue his argument.

A relief, considering the elder vampire possessed the ability to bend others to his will whenever he desired to make the effort.

"You're sure some survived?" he instead demanded.

"At least a few of them. I followed their tracks to the garage."

"They could be anywhere."

"They won't go far from the Phoenix," Dante pointed out. "Even if they don't know the precise location or even who holds the Chalice, they sense its presence. Unfortunately I don't have any means of contacting them."

"I would hardly call that unfortunate." The thin nose flared with distaste. "A pity the wizard didn't wipe them out completely."

A sentiment Dante would have agreed with thoroughly until Abby was thrust into carrying the Phoenix. Now his only concern was finding the means to release her from her burden.

"We have already been through this, Viper."

"And you know my feelings."

"In gruesome detail." Dante raised a hand to rub the knotted muscles of his neck. "Will you help me?"

"You know you don't have to ask. I may

consider you all kinds of a fool, but I will always have your back."

"Thank you," Dante murmured with genuine sincerity.

"What do you need?"

"Protection." Dante promptly answered. "Something small enough to carry but able to deal with the zombies."

A smile twitched at the corners of Viper's lips.

"No doubt I have something suitable in my vault," he retorted. Dante knew Viper's vault could arm entire countries. His arsenal ranged from prototype weapons stolen from top scientists to ancient armaments blessed with powerful magic. "What else?"

"I think someone should keep an eye on the wizard. He was calling upon powers that have been forgotten for centuries. He could be a problem."

"Ah." The dark eyes abruptly glittered with anticipation. "Perhaps I will toddle over for a visit. I haven't gone against a decent wizard since the Middle Ages."

Dante frowned. As a rule, Viper managed to avoid petty confrontations. Unlike most vampires, he didn't feel the need to prove his balls by challenging every demon that crossed his path. Which was one of the reasons Dante preferred his company to others.

But there was a part of Viper that couldn't resist a challenge. If he thought there might be something out there to give him a worthy battle, he wouldn't hesitate to leap in with gun blazing.

Or fangs flashing.

"Be careful," Dante warned sternly. "I don't doubt he'll have a few nasty tricks up his sleeve."

Viper chuckled with cold amusement. "Trust me, Dante, no one can match me for nasty tricks."

"That I well believe," Dante muttered, reaching out to grasp his friend's shoulder as his knees threatened to buckle.

"God, you can barely stand," Viper growled, a hint of concern touching his lean features. "Go to bed. I will set a watch outside your rooms. You and your Abby are safe here."

Dante nodded in relief. "You're a good man, Viper."

"Spread that around and I'll chop you into bacon bits and leave you to the sun," the older vampire warned.

"It goes with me to the grave."

Feeling every one of his four hundred plus years, Dante made his way back through the darkened hallways. At least he would have a few hours of rest.

No wizards, witches, zombies, or demons.

Just Abby.

Heaven.

Entering the private apartment, he headed directly to the bedroom only to be halted by the unmistakable sound of splashing water.

The weariness slid away as a faint smile curved his lips. Altering his course, he moved toward the bathroom and stepped through the door to study the slender woman soaking in the vast tub.

Speaking of heaven . . .

If his heart still beat, it would have halted at the sight of the white skin glowing in the candlelight like the rarest pearl and her honey curls fanned about her gamine face. Thankfully the rest of his body functioned just fine. Dante allowed his gaze to trail over the soft thrust of her breasts to the tempting triangle of hair between her thighs, and he felt himself grow hard.

Painfully hard, he acknowledged as his erection bit into the buttons of his pants.

With perfect clarity, he recalled the feel of her warmth as she had held him in her arms and the aching pleasure as she had rode him to completion.

Ah, sweet heavens he wanted her.

No, he needed her.

With a desperation that made a mockery of mere lust.

Silently kicking off his boots and shrugging out of his shirt, Dante paced forward and settled on the edge of the tub.

"Is this a private party or can anyone join in?" he murmured softly.

With an obvious effort, Abby lifted her lids to regard him with a slumberous gaze.

"Dante," she husked, making no attempt to cover her delectable curves. "I didn't hear you return."

He choked back a curse as his erection swelled in response to the beautiful vision below him.

He wanted to kiss every inch of her wet, slick skin. To sink between her thighs and taste her heat. To watch her eyes widen with pleasure as he entered her and to thrust both of them into mindless bliss.

His hand trembled with the force of his desire as he reached out to stroke his fingers down the curve of her neck. He could feel the softness of her skin, the heat of her rushing blood.

"I thought you would be asleep by now," he murmured.

She heaved a soft sigh. "This feels so good, I can't make myself leave."

Dante slowly smiled. "I have something that would feel even better."

Her eyes darkened as a smile of pure temptation curved her lips.

"I don't know." Her gaze lingered on his bare chest. "This is pretty much at the top of the feel-good list."

Rising to his feet, Dante quickly rid himself of his pants before he joined her in the heated water. The steam clouded about him, filled with the scent of vanilla and woman, rousing the predator that always lurked just beneath the surface.

With a growl of satisfaction, Dante pulled her into his arms as he performed a smooth roll, anchoring her atop his aching body with her legs straddling his hips.

He smiled into her startled eyes as he carefully smoothed her damp curls behind her ears.

"Lover, you're just about to learn a whole new list."

Her breath caught as his hands skimmed down the curve of her back to cup her backside, pressing her firmly against his throbbing shaft.

"You think you're that good?" she breathed.

Dante chuckled as he lifted his head to nibble at the base of her throat.

"Oh, better. Much better."

"I . . ." Her head tilted back as he gave her a small nip, her hips moving in silent encouragement. "Oh."

Dante groaned. Her skin fascinated him. So soft. So warm.

He licked a hungry path to her breast.

The animal in him longed to simply thrust into

her and find his release. There was something to be said for a swift, sweaty orgasm.

But not with Abby, he conceded.

This was not sex.

Not mindless coupling.

It was a joining that he could feel right to his dead heart.

Savoring the sweet taste of her, Dante circled her tightening nipple with the tip of his tongue. With light strokes he teased her until he heard her hiss of breath, and she grasped his head in her hands.

"Please," she whispered.

"Is this what you want, lover?" he demanded, closing his lips about the peak to suckle her with gentle urgency.

"Yes."

Her fingers tangled in his hair, her legs parting until she could rub herself against the length of his erection.

Dante closed his eyes at the intense shock of pleasure that flared through him. Bloody hell. Nothing had ever felt so good. And he wasn't even inside her.

The warm water surged about them, and the candles flickered, adding to the erotic sensations. He arched his hips upward, his hands shifting to stroke over her inner thighs. Slowly he traced patterns on her wet skin, simply enjoying the feel of her. He could stay here an eternity, he realized with a tiny jolt of surprise.

Just the two of them, alone and at peace.

Still teasing the hard tip of her breast with his tongue, he slid his hands higher, tugging her legs farther apart until he discovered her center.

Her lashes lowered as he trailed a finger between her soft folds.

"Dante," she breathed.

Nibbling his way to her neglected breast, he lightly scoured his fangs over the sensitive swell even as his finger stroked into her sleek heat.

Abby moaned, tangling her hands in his hair. He leaned back to watch the flush darken across her cheekbones. God, but she was beautiful. An exotic angel that had tumbled into his grasp.

With a slow expertise, he stroked his finger deep within her. At the same time he used his thumb to caress her tiny nub of pleasure.

"You feel so good," he muttered, his tongue flicking over the tip of her nipple. "So ready for me."

"Don't stop," she gasped.

Dante gave a choked laugh. "There isn't a force on earth that could halt me now, lover."

Sighing softly, Abby allowed her hands to smooth down the length of his neck and over the muscles of his shoulders. Her touch was light, but a trail of fire followed in the wake of her fingers.

A shudder of pleasure arced through his body. For centuries he had sought out vampires and demons to ease his needs. The fierce, mindless sex suited his frustrated mood. Besides, human women were a complication he didn't need.

Now he realized just how much he had been missing.

The soft, lingering touch.

The scent of female desire.

The delicious foreplay that made him quiver with longing.

As if reading his mind, Abby lowered her head to press her lips to his chest. With open-mouthed kisses she moved to suckle his sensitive nipple, her hands stroking down the hard muscles of his stomach.

"Bloody hell," he groaned as she briefly hesitated and then grasped his straining erection in a tender grip.

"Maybe you're not the only one with skills, lover," she teased as she stroked him from top to bottom and back again.

Dante hissed at the exquisite sensations that jolted through him. Skills? No. Her touch was not mere skill. It was magic.

His hips instinctively rocked to thrust his cock in her grip. God, it felt so good.

Too good.

Astonishingly he could sense the delicious pressure building deep within him. His climax was already beaconing, and he was far from finished with this woman.

Gritting his teeth, Dante concentrated on the feel of her beneath his fingers. He conjured all the expertise he had gained over the centuries to heighten her stimulation. Her moan of pleasure was all he needed to assure him that he hadn't lost his touch.

"Come for me, Abby," he whispered softly.

Her breath quickened as her fingers tightened upon him.

"Dante . . ."

"That's it, lover," he encouraged, using his thumb to bring her to the edge.

Lost in the delight of watching her face as she neared her climax, Dante was unprepared when she suddenly stilled above him, a small smile touching her lips.

"Abby?" he questioned softly.

Her smile widened, and the water churned as she abruptly shifted her weight. With a speed that caught Dante off guard, she rolled to one side, easily pulling him atop her. He floundered for a moment and might have protested at the sudden interruption if her legs hadn't parted and wrapped about his waist.

Reaching up, she cupped his face in her hands. "You started this, Dante; you finish it," she murmured with a gleam in her eyes.

Dante chuckled as she tossed his words back into his face.

Oh yes.

He intended to finish this.

To both their satisfaction.

His chuckle became a groan as he pressed himself into her ready heat. She lifted her hips to meet his thrust, and he knew if he wasn't already dead, she would surely kill him.

What man could endure such bliss?

Thank God he was a vampire.

He intended to endure the bliss several more times before the day was through.

Some time later, Abby lay wrapped in Dante's arm in the middle of the vast bed.

She felt pleasantly weary and sated. Just as a woman should feel after a great bout of sex.

Unfortunately she also felt more than a little creeped out.

She cringed as she lightly stroked her fingers over Dante's shoulder, which was still reddened from the steam.

Who knew?

She had reached climax before. Well, at least what passed for a climax, considering the jerks she had dated. She had even reached climax with Dante. Glorious, wonderful, mind-numbing climax.

More than once.

And while she might have felt as if she were on fire whenever he touched her, she had never actually put out enough heat to boil water.

It was . . . unnatural. And embarrassing.

And, most of all, frightening.

Sensing Dante's curious gaze, Abby reluctantly lifted her head.

"I'm sorry," she said softly.

His brows drew together in puzzlement. "For what?"

She grimaced. "Nearly boiling you like a lobster."

A slow smile curved his lips as he pulled her even closer.

An instant jolt of excitement raced down her spine at the feel of his stirring body.

Jeez. Vampires seemed to be insatiable when it came to sex. Not that she was complaining. In fact, her first thought was, Yippee.

"A very, very happy lobster," he murmured. "I assure you that it was worth every singe."

She bit her bottom lip, her self-disgust returning with a vengeance.

"Dante."

He stroked a finger down her flushed cheek. "It wasn't your fault, Abby. You have powers now you don't even understand, let alone control. It's bound to cause a few side effects. Some of which are more pleasant than others."

Her flush deepened as he deliberately reminded

her of her brand-spanking-new strength and seemingly endless endurance.

All gifts of the Phoenix, it seemed.

And incredible bonuses when it came to making love.

"I'm glad you can find some humor in the situation."

The silver eyes glinted with amusement. "Trust me, lover, you can laugh or you can cry. It changes nothing."

"Easy for you to say," she grouched. "You don't know what it's like to have your body taken over and . . ." Her words abruptly trailed away as he arched a raven brow. "Oh."

"You were saying?"

"Something incredibly stupid," she muttered wryly. "I guess you do know."

He gave a slow nod. "Too well."

She blew out an exasperated breath. "You'd think if some being was going to take over your body, they'd at least have the decency to leave you a handbook. I could kill myself or, worse, someone else with my blundering about."

He absently toyed with a curl that lay against her cheek. "I suppose a higher being assumes that you should simply know the rules and regulations."

"A higher being?"

"The Phoenix is worshipped as a goddess by those who battle the dark lord."

Worshipped. Well. A girl could get used to something like that.

"A goddess, huh?" She attempted what she assumed to be a regal look. It had a lot of thin lips and flared nostrils. "Does that mean you have to bow down and pray to me?"

He chuckled softly, that wicked glint returning to his silver eyes.

"I don't battle the dark lord, lover," he murmured, his lips brushing her temple, her cheek, and down the curve of her neck, "but I don't mind bowing down and tasting this glorious sweetness."

Abby didn't mind his bowing down either. In fact, if she wasn't so freaked out, she would have told him to get on with the bowing down right quick.

Instead, she lightly touched his face. "Dante . . ."

Nibbling at her collarbone, he was already distracted. "Hmmm?"

"I don't want to hurt you," she said softly.

Dante stilled before he pulled back to regard her with a puzzled expression. Her heart gave a faint flutter. God, he was so beautiful. So perfect. She could spend the rest of eternity simply staring at him.

"You won't hurt me, Abby," he assured her in low tones.

"How do you know? When I . . ." Abby awkwardly hesitated. "When we're together, the powers just burst out of me."

His lips twitched at her shyness. No surprise there. She was lying naked in his arms after a three-hour bout of sex.

Now she couldn't say the word *orgasm* out loud.

Go figure.

"I'm willing to take the risk."

Her lips thinned at his hint of amusement. "This isn't a joke, Dante."

His eyes slowly narrowed. "Abby, what is it?"

"It's dangerous—"

"No," he interrupted. "You know I'm immortal. There's something else. You're frightened."

She shifted. He was probing into memories and emotions she had kept locked away for years.

Memories she would have seared out of her brain if she could have.

"Of course I'm frightened," she muttered. "I have this thing inside that's changing everything, and I can't do a damn thing to stop it."

His hand stroked a soothing path through her hair. "Understandable, but I think there's more here. Tell me what you fear."

She swallowed heavily before forcing herself to meet his probing gaze.

"Losing control."

"Control of what?"

"Of myself." She sucked in a deep breath. "What if I hurt someone?"

There was a brief silence as he brooded upon her words. Then with care he shifted to touch the ugly scar that marred her shoulder.

"Like someone hurt you?"

Abby flinched. Not from his touch, but from the pain of dredging up her violent past.

"Compliments of my father in one of his drunken furies," she said in clipped tones.

Dante's expression remained stoic, but there was no mistaking the lethal fury that flashed through his eyes.

"What did he do to you?"

"He took exception to my attempts to keep him from beating my mother and stabbed me with a broken beer bottle."

His fangs abruptly shimmered in the faint candlelight. He moved his hand to touch the tiny round scar on her upper arm.

"And here?"

Abby shuddered, her blood running cold.

The monster that walked in the night.

A child's fear.

For her it had never been the bogeyman.

It had been her father.

"A cigarette burn when I tried to hide his whiskey."

His features tightened, forcibly reminding her of the predator who had stalked through the wizard's cavern to rescue her.

"Where is he?" he growled, making the hairs on the back of her neck prickle.

"Dead."

His eyes were flat. "There are means to reach him even dead. Viper—"

"God, no," she breathed in genuine horror. "I don't even want to think he might be anywhere but rotting in his grave."

Easily sensing her distress, he pressed his lips to the top of her head.

"Shh . . . It's okay, Abby. He can't hurt you anymore."

She pressed her eyes closed. He didn't understand. But then, no one did.

No one who hadn't lived through her childhood.

"It's not that." She lifted her gaze. "I don't want to be like him."

He gave a jolt of surprise. "Bloody hell, Abby, you could never be like him."

She barely noticed the manner in which his accent thickened when his emotions were roused.

"How do you know?" she demanded starkly. "We don't know what this Phoenix might do to me."

He cupped his fingers beneath her chin, forcing her to meet his fierce gaze.

"I know that it will only strike out to protect itself. Selena was incapable of hurting anyone. A fact that annoyed the hell out of her. She came from a time when no one would blink if she wanted to beat a servant. Even if she beat him to death." He grimaced in reluctant memory. "There wasn't a day that went by she didn't long to have me tied to a post and have me properly whipped."

She regarded him warily, desperately wanting to believe his soft words.

"What about the water . . ."

He took her hand and firmly placed it against the smooth silk of his chest.

"It was no warmer than most spas. I just happen to possess a sensitivity to heat." He gave a shake of his head. "You are not your father, Abby. You could never be cruel. It's simply not in your nature."

She smiled wryly at his arrogant assurance. "You sound very certain for a vampire who has only known me a few months."

He arched a raven brow. "It's because I'm a vampire that I know. I can read your soul, Abby, and it is as pure and beautiful as any I have ever seen."

She became lost in his gaze. She had never had anyone tell her such amazing things. Not her worthless parents. Not her brothers.

Not even those rare handful of men who wanted to lift her skirt.

It made her feel warm and gooey and remarkably cherished.

It also eased the last of her lingering self-disgust.

She was not her father. She was pure and beautiful.

Well, that's what Dante believed.

And that was all that truly mattered.

Reaching up, she cupped his breathtaking face in her hands and pulled him down to her waiting lips.

Soon enough they would be battling the forces of evil. Damn the luck.

She would be a fool not to enjoy this rare moment of peace.

Dante's lips landed upon her mouth with a searing kiss, and her body reacted with its usual zing of excitement.

His fingers found her already-hard nipple, and the zings became zooms.

Arching toward his ready erection, Abby gave herself to the dark desire.

Chapter 15

Abby awoke naked and disoriented.

Not always a bad thing. Especially when she was still warm and tingly from Dante's touch. But she discovered that she didn't care for being naked, disoriented, and alone.

Crawling from beneath the covers, she discovered that someone had kindly left a pair of jeans and a T-shirt on top of the dresser. There was also a new white lace thong and matching bra.

She grimaced. She had never been much of a thong woman.

Probably because she hadn't been a size two since grade school.

Beggars, however, could not be choosers. After slipping on the tiny underwear, she pulled the T-shirt over her head before padding into the outer room.

A wave of relief rushed through her as she discovered Dante standing beside the wall refrigerator, looking extraordinarily fine in a pair of leather pants and black silk shirt he had yet to button. His silken hair was still loose about his alabaster face, and the candlelight shimmered in his silver eyes.

Fine, indeed.

So fine that Abby barely noted the empty cup of blood he set aside at her approach.

A smile twitched at his lips as he allowed his gaze to take a slow, appreciative survey of her scarcely covered body.

"Nice, lover. Very nice."

Abby rolled her eyes, although inwardly she did a bit of preening. And why not? No one but Dante had ever made her feel as if she were thong-worthy.

"What time is it?"

"Almost nine."

Abby blinked in surprise. "Why didn't you wake me?"

"You needed your rest." Dante reached into the refrigerator to pull out a plastic cup. "Here."

Abby regarded the offering with a wrinkled nose.

"I don't suppose it's that hot fudge sundae you've been promising?"

His smile widened. "The next best thing."

She thought of the green guck with a shudder. "Liar."

He moved forward to press the cup into her reluctant fingers, his lips brushing the top of her curls.

"I'll make you a deal. You finish that and I'll buy you as many hot fudge sundaes as you can eat."

Abby briefly sucked in the male scent of his cologne before stepping back to regard him with a suspicious glare.

"Okay, what's going on? Zombies? Wizards? The end of the world?"

A raven brow arched. "What are you talking about?"

"You're never this easy to get along with."

He gave a startled chuckle. "Me? Lover, I'm not the difficult one." Dipping his finger into the neckline of the T-shirt, he gave it a tug to inspect the barely-there bra. "Of course, there are moments when you are less difficult than others. Like when you—"

She swatted his hand away. "Dante, I'm not going to be distracted."

He gave his fangs a meaningful lick. "Actually, I think I'm already distracted."

Damn. Her nipples hardened. Determinedly she kept herself from melting into a puddle.

"You're up to something. What is it?"

"Nothing."

"Try again."

He hesitated and Abby felt her stomach muscles tighten. She wasn't going to like this.

"I have an errand I must run," he at last confessed.

"What sort of errand?"

"I'm returning to Selena's house to see if there are any clues to where the witches might have gone."

She considered his words a moment before giving a nod of her head and setting aside the cup o' goo.

"Not a bad idea. Let me take a shower and—"

He reached out to grasp her arms in a firm grip. "I'm going alone, Abby."

"No."

"Yes."

Her temper soared as she poked him in the chest. Hard.

"Dammit, Dante, it's a little too late to try and keep me out of danger."

"I will not have you taking unnecessary risks."

"The only risk is leaving me alone. You're supposed to be my guardian."

His expression hardened at her stubborn determination.

"You will not be alone here. Viper will keep you safe."

Abby was not impressed. Viper might be all kinds of delicious goodness, but the last time they had stayed at this hotel, they had nearly died.

"From zombies?" she demanded with a poke. "Dark wizards?" Poke, poke. "Creepy crawlies we don't even know about yet?"

Grasping her fingers, Dante lifted them to his mouth to give them a lingering kiss.

"He'll be on his guard this time, I swear. Nothing will get past him."

"I don't care."

"Abby—"

She threw her arms about his narrow waist and pressed her face to his chest.

"Damn you, I can't do this alone," she muttered. "If something happens to you, I won't be able to go on."

He lightly stroked her hair. "You will have to."

"No, I can't." She pulled back to regard him with a resolute frown. "We're in this together, buster, and if you leave here, I'll follow you. I swear I will."

His jaw briefly tightened before he gave a rueful shake of his head. "You truly are a pain in the ass, lover."

"But a most beautiful pain in the ass," a hypnotic voice husked from directly behind her.

"Exquisite," another deeply accented voice concurred.

With a jerk of surprise, Abby turned about to discover two male vampires standing far too close for comfort.

"Holy . . . freaking . . . cow," she breathed, her jaw dropping.

Dante was a dark and beautiful pirate. Viper was an exotic aristocrat.

These two . . .

They were sex magnets.

Gods of lust.

There were simply no other words.

Identical twins, they were tall with the polished golden skin of ancient Egyptians. Their faces were chiseled perfection. High cheekbones with hawkish noses and a noble brow. Their almond-shaped black eyes were outlined in heavy kohl, and there was a hint of color on their full lips. Their long ebony hair was pulled into a braid that hung down their backs, brushing the tiny white loincloth that was all that covered the most bodacious bodies ever seen.

King Tut, take me now, a renegade voice whispered in the back of her mind.

Abby gave a shake of her head, attempting to rid herself of her breathless reaction. A task more difficult than it should have been. Then Dante's arm curled about her shoulder, and the mystical tug of fascination was broken.

She sucked in a deep breath as Dante bristled at her side.

"What are you doing here?" he demanded, his voice cold.

"Master Viper requests your presence," one of the twins murmured.

"Master Viper?" Abby grimaced. "I bet he gets off on that."

Two sets of luscious black gazes moved in her direction, both spending an inordinate amount of time inspecting her half-clad form. Something that Abby might have taken as a compliment if she hadn't suspected that they were speculating upon whether her blood was A positive or B negative rather than her dubious attractions.

"We will protect the human while you are gone," Tut One claimed.

"It will be our pleasure," Tut Two echoed.

Abby stepped closer to the vampire at her side. "Dante?"

He pressed a comforting kiss to the top of her head. "Why don't you get dressed, and I'll find out what Viper wants?"

She shot him a wary glance. "They won't—"

"We have been commanded not to taste of you," the first of the intruders interrupted, stepping close enough for her to be cloaked in his rich, spicy scent.

"Or bed you." The second added with a hint of regret as he moved to take a deep sniff of her skin. "Unless it is what you desire."

They both smiled to reveal snowy-white fangs. "We possess many skills."

"Most will not harm a human."

Dante pulled her abruptly backward, his face the stark mask of a predator.

"Touch her and you'll wish you never rose from the dead."

The nearest twin merely shrugged, still sniffing at her hair. "Surely it is for the human to decide?"

"She's decided," Abby retorted as she grasped Dante's hand and pulled him toward the bedroom. Glancing over her shoulder, she pointed a finger at the carpet at the twins' bare feet. "Just . . . stay there and don't move."

"A waste," one of them murmured softly.

"Indeed," the second agreed.

Closing the door behind them, Dante pulled Abby to face him. "I must speak with Viper. Will you be okay?"

She bit her lip, glancing toward the door. "Can I trust them?"

His smile was without humor. "No, but they fear Viper and are not foolish enough to risk his wrath. They won't trouble you without invitation."

"Invitation?" She blinked in disbelief. "You think I'll invite them to . . . to . . . ?"

He gave a lift of his shoulder. "Few women can resist them. They have lured some of the most powerful and beautiful women to their bed. Cleopatra. The Queen of Sheba. It's rumored they've even seduced more than a few presidents' wives."

"Oh my God." Abby widened her gaze. "Which ones?"

"Does it matter?"

The edge in his voice warned Abby that now was not the time to press for juicy gossip.

"Only in a historical context."

A reluctant smile curved Dante's lips as he pulled her close. "Abby."

Her hand lifted to trace a light pattern upon his chest. "I'd be lying if I said they weren't gorgeous, but I don't want any vampire but you."

"Good." His lips nuzzled her temple. "It's not really good etiquette to dust a fellow vampire before dinner. Besides, Viper tends to get a bit cranky when he loses his goons."

She heaved a rueful sigh. "Speaking of Viper, I suppose you should go see what he wants."

He ran his tongue along the line of her jaw. "I'll be back as soon as I can."

A delicious shiver raced down her spine, but Abby refused to be entirely distracted. Grasping the front of his shirt, she pulled back to regard him with a warning frown.

"You're not going to try and sneak out behind my back?"

He arched a raven brow. "Would it do any good?"

"Absolutely not."

He sighed. "Don't worry, lover, as much as I hate to admit it, I can only search for what Selena might have left lying for anyone to find. To discover her secrets, I will need you."

"What do you mean?"

"I will explain later." He placed a branding kiss on her lips before moving toward the door. "Oh, you might want to wait until I return before you have your dinner." He flashed a dry smile over his shoulder. "The last time you sampled the herbs, they had a rather . . . potent effect on you. I wouldn't want your watchdogs to get the wrong idea."

He was gone before Abby could find something suitably heavy to toss at his head.

Damn vampire speed.

As he drove through the dark streets of Chicago, Dante found himself as twitchy as if he were standing in the midst of a lightning storm. An unfamiliar sensation and one that he found impossible to dismiss.

Bloody hell, what was the matter with him?

As promised, Viper had gathered a large canvas bag filled with a variety of mystical weapons. He had even given Dante a cell phone that was programmed with the numbers of various vampires and demons he could contact in case of an emergency.

Along with his supernatural powers, there were few things mortal or immortal that could hope to best him.

He was near invincible.

But near invincible was not good enough, he conceded, glancing to where Abby sat in the seat beside him.

There were too damn many creatures who wanted this woman dead.

One mistake, one miscalculation and . . .

His jaw tightened in grim determination.

No.

There would be no mistakes. No miscalculations.

Unaware of his brooding thoughts or just how easily she had managed to rattle his nerves, Abby poked at the heavy bag that Dante had placed in her lap.

"You haven't told me what's in the bag," she broke the silence.

"Protection."

With a curious lift of her brows, she pulled open the heavy zipper and gave a choked cough.

"Good God, are you sure Viper didn't make a mistake?"

"It would be refreshing to think Viper could occasionally make a mistake, but unfortunately it never happens. Why?"

"There's nothing in here but junk."

Dante hid his amusement. "Rare and priceless junk, I assure you."

Shaking her head at the amulets, talismans, and charms, she plucked out a delicate dagger with a serpentine blade that glowed with mystic symbols etched on the layered metal.

"What's this?"

Dante instinctively shuddered. "A keris."

"A what?"

"It's a blessed dagger from Bali."

"What does it do?"

He flashed a wry smile. "You use the pointy end to stab people."

She rolled her eyes. "Ha-ha."

"It possesses protection spells. Viper believes it will be effective against whatever evil the dark wizard might conjure."

"Oh." She held the weapon toward him. "Shouldn't you be carrying it?"

Dante flinched from the power of the blade. "Careful, lover, it works against me as well as other nasties, so you might not want to wave it in my direction."

"Oh, sorry." With a hurried motion, she dropped it back into the bag. "Why would Viper have a weapon that kills vampires?"

Dante shrugged as he turned the car toward the exclusive neighborhood that had once been his home.

"Better in his hands than in the hands of his enemies."

"Surely it would be better to have it destroyed completely?" she pointed out with indisputable logic.

"Viper is too fanatic a collector to ever destroy

such a priceless artifact." He flashed her a swift glance. "Besides, you never know when you might need such a weapon."

Her eyes widened. "You mean . . ."

"Battles between vampires are rare but not unheard of."

"Yikes."

Dante returned his attention to the road. "Indeed."

She fell silent as he pushed the remote keypad he held in his fingers and turned through the familiar iron gates. Slowly he drove up the long, tree-lined drive that eventually wound its way to Selena's secluded mansion.

Dante didn't need to see Abby's suddenly clenched fists or the tightening of her expression to sense her swelling tension.

This was where her life had been forever altered.

She hadn't forgotten.

Pulling the car to a halt and switching off the engine, he turned to study her fragile profile with a frown of concern.

"Abby?"

"It's a lot worse than I realized," she muttered, her gaze absorbing the broken windows and roof that had been half blown away.

Dante knew he would eventually have to deal with the estate, but he was in no hurry. The wards that Selena had placed about the house would keep out anyone not invited. Including the most desperate thieves.

He lightly touched her shoulder. "Do you want to remain in the car?"

She sucked in a deep breath, turning to meet his searching gaze. "No."

Gathering an amulet that Viper promised would counter the magic used to animate a zombie, Dante pushed it into the waistband of his pants. His daggers were already safely tucked into his boots, and with a motion of his hand, he indicated that Abby should place the keris in its sheath and belt it about her waist.

The sheath would protect him from the powerful blessing but would allow Abby easy access to the dagger should she have need.

Demon, witch, zombie, or wizard would get more than they bargained for on this occasion.

Together they left the car and headed up the sweeping terrace to the double doors. Entering the vast foyer, Dante instinctively headed for the main staircase when Abby abruptly stumbled over the broken bits of a vase upon the marble floor.

He placed an arm about her shoulders as she regarded the shattered porcelain with an odd fascination.

"Steady," he murmured.

It took a moment before she gave a shake of her head and turned her attention to the nearby stairs that were now charred and covered in plaster and chunks of wood from the ceiling.

"It's even worse than I remember. My God, how could this have happened?"

His jaw tightened as the image of Selena's lifeless body flashed through his mind. Nothing should have been capable of destroying her. Certainly not something that he had been incapable of sensing.

"I don't know, lover."

"Do you think it was the work of the wizard?" she demanded.

Dante frowned. "It's possible, I suppose."

"You don't sound very convinced."

"If it was a servant of the Prince, then Selena should have sensed its presence, just as you did with the zombies," he pointed out. "Besides, she had been the Chalice for a very long time and grown incredibly powerful. I cannot imagine even the elder wizard would dare to challenge her."

She gave a slow nod. "I think you're right, which means we're still no closer to discovering what happened to Selena."

"Do you sense anything?"

Abby closed her eyes and sucked in a deep breath. Dante realized she was attempting to focus her newfound powers to search the empty house.

At last her eyes opened, and she gave a faint shiver.

"No, there is nothing."

Dante stepped directly before her. He hadn't missed her faint tremor.

"What is it?"

She shrugged as she forced a smile to her lips. "I just have the creepy crawlies."

"The creepy crawlies?"

"The heebie-jeebies."

Dante gave a shake of his head. "Are you speaking English?"

"You know, like someone just walked over my grave."

Dante didn't even think as he abruptly lashed his arms around her and yanked her against his chest.

"Don't," he hissed.

Her eyes widened in shock, and he belatedly realized his fangs were fully extended and his face no doubt stark with warning.

He didn't care.

For the moment he was all vampire.

"Dante?" she husked uncertainly.

"Never tempt fate," he growled.

"It's just a saying."

"It's dangerous," he warned, his predatory instincts on full alert at the mere mention of Abby in her grave. "We mustn't do anything to call attention upon us."

She blinked, startled by his words. "You're superstitious?"

"I've lived for centuries. There are very few things I don't believe in."

"Oh." She mulled over his words before giving a nod. "I suppose you have a point."

His arms tightened as he pressed his forehead to her own. "I won't let anything harm you."

"I know," she said softly, her hands cupping his face.

"But if something should happen to me—"

His fierce command was brought to a halt. A highly unusual event, considering he rarely let anything or anyone interrupt a direct decree.

But then it was even more rare when Abby pressed her lips to his mouth. He found the entire world was brought to a halt.

Unfortunately her kiss was all too brief, and just as he was getting into the swing of things, she pulled back to regard him with a stern frown.

"No, Dante," she retorted, as always ignoring the fact that no one told him no. "You said yourself, we shouldn't tempt fate."

He didn't bother to argue. Why should he? It would be simpler to bash his head into the wall and be done with it.

Besides, Viper would know to come for her if something happened to him.

He would leave it at that.

"Enough." With a smooth motion, he hoisted her into his arms. Once assured she was secure, he easily moved toward the stairs. "I don't think it's wise to linger here any longer than we need."

Her arms instinctively looped around his neck. "What are we looking for?"

"Selena had a safe that she kept warded by powerful spells. I hope now that you carry the Phoenix, we can find a means to open it."

"If it survived the blast."

He smiled. Not even the end of the world would have affected the spell.

"It survived. Hold on."

She gave a small shriek as he crouched and then in one fluid bound had them at the top of the steps.

"Holy crap, I didn't know you could do that," she breathed. "What other surprises do you have?"

He slowly smiled. "Lover, I possess enough surprises to keep you guessing an eternity."

"And enough ego to last way beyond that."

"Would you have it any other way?"

She rolled her eyes. "I thought we were in a hurry?"

With reluctance he bent to set her upon her feet. He didn't sense any danger nearby, but he wasn't going to be caught off guard again. He wanted to be ready to strike if necessary.

"Be careful where you step. The floorboards are not entirely stable."

"Yeah, magical blasts tend to be hell on floorboards."

Despite her flippant tone, she was wise enough to be cautious as she made her way down the darkened hall. Dante was close behind her. So close that he easily sensed when the sudden chill shuddered through her body.

"What is it?" he demanded.

"Nothing."

"You felt something." He reached out to grasp her arm, pulling her to a halt. "Is there anything here?"

A frown marred her forehead. Not the pissy frown she reserved solely for him. But the one that warned she was sensing something she could not explain.

The one she had had too many occasions to use over the past few days.

"It's not that. It's . . . I don't know, like an echo."

"From the spell Selena cast?"

"Maybe." She abruptly rubbed her hands over her arms. "It feels wrong, somehow. Not evil, but . . ."

He tilted her chin, forcing her to meet his gaze. "Abby?"

"It's difficult to explain."

"Try."

Her eyes narrowed. A silent warning he would eventually pay for his arrogant tone.

Not at the moment, however.

"I once walked past a chemical plant that was pumping toxic waste into the river. It was nothing I could actually see, but there was a certain smell and foulness to the air that made my skin crawl. That's what I feel now."

"Foulness."

"Yes."

Dante growled low in his throat. He was a predator. A lethal killer. The fact that he could not sense the danger lurking in the air made him long to destroy something.

Something witchy.

"There is something I'm missing." He gave a sharp shake of his head. "Damn. This way."

Taking Abby's hand, he led her farther down the hall. He considered it a minor miracle they managed to make it over a dozen steps before Abby dug in her heels.

"Wait. Where are we going? Selena's rooms are down that wing."

He glanced over his shoulder. "Trust me."

Damn. Wrong words.

Her heels nearly made holes in the floor as she refused to budge.

"Trust you? Again?"

"Have I led you astray yet?" Her mouth flew open far too readily. A diversion was clearly in order. Never one to miss an opportunity, Dante glided forward to cover her mouth in a swift, hungry kiss. "Don't answer that," he murmured against her lips. Her hands clutched his arms as she instinctively arched against him. Devil spit. Dante felt her fiery heat sear through him. It licked over his skin and smoldered in his blood. His teeth clenched. The ache to gather her in his arms and take her against the wall was firmly thrust aside. He would never have enough of this woman. But now was not the time or place, he sternly chastised. Pulling back, he grasped her hand and pulled her firmly down the hall before she could come to her senses. Shoving aside a broken statue, he pointed at the wall. "This is it."

"This is what?"

"The safe."

"Where?"

He touched his finger to the center of the satin wallpaper. "There."

She shot him a narrowed glare. "Is this some sort of Abbott and Costello routine?"

His lips twitched despite the urgency of their situation. "The safe is set in the wall and has been warded. It's up to you to break the spell."

"Me? I'm no witch."

"Selena was not a witch, lover." He reached out to touch her cheek. "Her power came from the Phoenix."

"A power she had three hundred years to learn to control, not three days."

"You can do this."

Her frown threatened to become permanently engraved. "Easy for you to say. Hell, I don't even know how to start."

"Just concentrate," he urged softly.

"On the wall?"

"On the safe behind the wall." Dante stepped back to watch her closely. He hated putting such pressure on Abby. She had barely accepted that she carried the Phoenix. Now to be expected to wield its magic was rather like expecting a bird to fly only moments after it hatched. Unfortunately, there was no choice. They had to find the witches. A long silence filled the hall, and then her hand lifted, and she twitched her fingers. Dante frowned in confusion. "What are you doing?"

"Trying to cast a damn spell."

"By wiggling your fingers?"

"It's a . . . thing. A stupid thing, but a thing." She

angrily blew a stray curl from her forehead. "Now, do you mind? I'm trying to concentrate."

He held up his hands. "Please, concentrate all you need."

There was another silence. A long silence. And then a heavy sigh.

"Damn." She turned to regard him in defeat. "I can't do this."

He grasped her shoulders in his hands. This woman possessed enough power to rip apart the entire city. More power than he could ever dream of. He would not allow doubt to stand in her path.

"Abby, you have killed a hellhound, battled zombies, and escaped from a dark wizard. You can do this."

She grimaced. "What I've done is bumbled from one disaster to another, and the only miracle is that I haven't managed to kill both of us in the process."

"I believe in you, even if you don't believe in yourself."

"Which doesn't say much for your intelligence."

He gave her a slight shake. Why had Viper not warned him that mortal women were as stubborn as Stlantd demons?

"Abby."

She met him glare for glare before heaving a frustrated sigh. "Okay, okay. I'll try again."

Chapter 16

Abby squeezed her eyes shut. Even then she could feel Dante hovering beside her like a vulture. She could sense his tension. His fierce determination.

He was expecting her to perform some sort of hocus-pocus. A joke, of course. She was as likely to sprout daisies out of her ears as she was to magically open some mystical door.

Still, she had to try something. As long as she carried the Phoenix, she would be hunted. And worse, Dante would be forced to protect her, even if it meant the end of his own existence.

So far, stupid luck had kept them alive. But sooner or later, they would come up against something he could not defeat. Then they both would be dead.

She wouldn't let that happen.

Ignoring the feeling she was doing nothing but making an ass of herself, Abby sternly focused her thoughts. She had taken out a hellhound and had burned the zombie to a crisp. Granted, she hadn't known what the hell she was doing, but there had to be something inside her that she could use.

Imagine the wall, she told herself. And in the middle of the wall a safe. A safe like the ones in the old movies she loved. A big, silver safe with a black combination lock and slender handle . . .

Thoroughly concentrating upon the image, she didn't notice the faint buzzing in her ear. Not until the buzzing became a ringing. And then became a loud clap that sent her tumbling backward in shock.

Opening her eyes, she stared in wonder at the large safe now clearly visible in the wall and clearly open.

"Holy crap," she breathed.

The words had barely tumbled from her lips when Dante was at her side to gently lift her to her feet.

"Are you hurt?"

She pressed a hand to her heart, which she realized was nearly pounding out of her chest.

"I'll live. Is that the safe you wanted?"

"Yes."

"What's inside?"

"Books."

She turned to regard him in disbelief. "Are you kidding me? The woman leaves priceless Ming vases and Picassos lying about like they came off a sale rack at some discount store and she fills a hidden safe with musty old books?"

"They are spell books."

"Are you sure?"

A raven brow arched. "I'm a vampire; I can sense power, but not actual magic. You tell me."

She bit her lip before forcing herself to reach into the murky shadows and pluck out the handful of books.

She wasn't sure what she expected. Ancient manuscripts wrapped in leather and gold. Rolled parchments with heavy seals. Bed knobs and broomsticks.

Anything but the library rejects she held in her hands.

"They look like regular old books to me." She flipped open the top book only to sneeze as a cloud of dust filled the air. "Dirty old books."

"Don't tell me you're a philistine?"

"A what?"

He chuckled softly. "Never mind, lover."

Abby rubbed her nose as she shot Dante a puzzled glance. Once again she was rumpled and covered in dust while he stood there without a hair out of place.

Damn him.

"Will these help lead us to the witches?" she demanded.

"Is there anything hidden in the pages?"

"You mean like some sort of code?"

"Like telephone numbers or names or a map to a hidden coven?"

Well, duh. She busied herself with flipping through the pages to hide her blush. No one had ever accused her of being a budding genius, but she was not usually a total moron.

"No, no names or maps," she muttered. "Just a bunch of really bad poetry. Good God, listen to this stuff—"

"Abby," Dante abruptly interrupted. "I don't think—"

"'Circle of the sacred Chalice,
Turn your power to dark and malice.
Elements of earth and air,
Water and fire combine to share.

Hear our plea and know our cause . . .'"

Abby was uncertain when the words began to burn like fire upon the page. Or to echo eerily through the air as she mouthed the strange spell. She only knew that a powerful compulsion had suddenly taken her in its clutches, and the world about her disappeared.

She couldn't halt the words from flowing. Not even when a sharp, fierce pain began to pulse deep within her. It was like falling from a cliff. There was no halting until she hit the bottom.

Even if that bottom meant a jolting, bloody end.

She might have continued chanting for eternity if she had not suddenly been attacked from behind.

Given no warning, Abby found a pair of strong arms wrapped about her. She had time to grunt in confusion before she was being driven to the polished floor. Her head hit the boards with a sharp bang.

"Dammit." She blinked away the stars shooting in front of her eyes before struggling to her knees. "Dante, you could have just tapped me on the shoulder . . ."

Her words trailed away as she realized that Dante wasn't responsible for her near whiplash. Instead her gaze fell upon a strange woman crouched directly before her.

Oh yeah, definitely strange, she conceded.

Struggling through the fog that still clung to her brain, Abby studied the dark, slender woman.

She appeared human enough. Despite the exotic beauty of her long raven hair and perfectly crafted features, there was a smoldering vitality that seemed more mortal than immortal. And her hard muscles were the sort that belonged to a well-honed athlete rather than the fluid strength of a vampire.

Still, there was a barely tamed danger glowing in the slanted golden eyes and a tension in the coiled body that made her seem . . .

Deadly.

Covertly Abby cast a glance to the side, her heart faltering as she caught sight of Dante lying on the floor, his eyes closed.

Shit.

She didn't know what the creature had done to Dante, but if she was strong enough to knock out a vampire, what chance did a puny mortal stand in overcoming the intruder?

Not a chance in hell.

Her only hope of saving Dante seemed to be in talking her way out of danger. A frightening prospect.

Ignoring the instinct to rush to Dante's side, Abby sternly concentrated upon the woman before her. It had to be a good thing she hadn't already finished what she started.

Didn't it?

Careful to make no sudden movements, she sucked in a deep breath.

"Who are you?"

The golden eyes narrowed. "You must stop."

"Stop? Stop what?"

"The spell. It is dangerous."

Abby licked her dry lips, relieved to note that the wrenching pain that had been destroying her was starting to ease.

"Dangerous to whom?"

"Your mate, for one."

Mate? It took a moment for Abby to figure out she

was referring to Dante. Her eyes widened in horror as her gaze flew to the still-unconscious vampire.

"I did that?"

"The spell . . ." Without warning, the woman threw back her head and growled low in her throat. Abby stiffened as she watched the creature lift a hand to claw at her neck. Almost as if she was battling some unseen enemy.

Abby scooted forward with a frown, her hand reaching out. "Are you hurt?"

The woman hissed at her. She actually hissed. Just like a cat.

"Do not touch me."

Abby's hand wisely dropped, but her gaze remained upon the claw marks the woman had made on her neck.

"You're bleeding."

"They demand my return. I can't . . ."

There was another growl, and then with a blur of motion, the creature was on her feet and bounding down the hall. She disappeared into the darkness before Abby could open her lips to call out.

Well, that was creepy.

For a moment Abby remained frozen in place. She had seen enough horror shows to know that just because a beastie had left the room didn't mean it wasn't still lurking in the shadows.

When nothing lunged out with a butcher knife or breathed fire from the doorway, she awkwardly crawled to lean over Dante's horribly still body.

"Dante?" With great care she gently cradled his head in her lap, her hands frantically stroking his beautiful face. "Dante . . . Oh God, please wake up."

He didn't move. Didn't so much as twitch for what seemed an eternity. She called, she pleaded, and she even prayed. Panic was rearing its ugly head when his lashes at last lifted to reveal dazed silver eyes.

"Abby?" His silken voice was oddly husky. "What happened?"

Ridiculously she felt tears trickle down her cheeks even as she laughed in relief.

She hadn't killed him.

Thank the gods above.

"You're asking me?" she rasped. "I haven't had a clue what's going on since this madness started. One minute you were at my side and the next you were on the floor."

His brows drew together as he silently attempted to piece together his fractured thoughts.

"The spell," he at last breathed. "It was ripping me apart."

Abby grimaced. "I'm sorry. I didn't know what I was doing."

A faint smile touched his lips. "It doesn't matter. We need to get somewhere safe until I can recover my strength."

Abby was all for that. Especially when that strange woman might pop out of the woodwork at any moment. A story for Dante when he wasn't lying near death from her stupid attempt at abracadabra.

"Can you move?"

He closed his eyes to assess his injuries. "If you can help me to my feet."

Abby bit her lip as she slipped a hand beneath his shoulder and helped him struggle upright. If Dante actually lowered his testosterone enough to ask for help, it had to be bad.

He swayed heavily against her, and Abby battled to keep him upright.

"We'll never make it to the car," she said. "We should call Viper."

"No. If you can help me down to the basement, I can recover in my lair."

Abby gave a blink of surprise as she automatically led him toward the nearby servant's staircase.

"You have a lair?"

"Of course. A vampire needs more than tinted windows and a soft bed to feel comfortable."

"Oh." Abby felt incredibly stupid. Until this moment, she had never considered the fact that Dante had walked freely about the house during the day.

Reaching the stairs, she helped him grasp the railing and together they began the downward trek.

"Oh, what?" he demanded, his jaw locked to combat his obvious pain.

"I just realized that when I worked here, you were always awake during the day. The tinted windows protected you?"

He managed a strained smile. "As long as I didn't stand directly in front of the window."

Breathing hard, she pressed her hand to his chest to make sure he didn't tumble forward.

"Aren't vampires creatures of the night?"

"As a rule."

"But you prefer the day?"

"Let us that I possessed an irresistible desire to alter my habits."

Abby recalled their employer's demanding nature. The woman had been a despot when it came to her own comfort.

"I suppose Selena demanded you be available for her?"

"Whatever her demands, Selena was never

capable of forcing me to pander to her preference for day." His tone was arrogant as he shot her a glance from the corner of his eye. "Only one woman has ever managed that, lover."

Her eyes widened as a blush touched her cheeks. "Oh."

Despite the odd weakness that still clutched at his body, Dante found a smile curving his lips as Abby helped him to the deep basement. He reached out to press the hidden lever to his lair.

He had always delighted in bringing a hint of color to Abby's cheeks. For all she had endured in her life, and she had endured more than any woman should have to, she still managed to be enchantingly innocent.

The paneling swung inward to reveal the room he had called home since coming to Chicago. Switching on the light, he waited for Abby to step within before shutting the door and setting the invisible traps that should keep them safe for the moment.

"Don't touch the door," he warned Abby as he moved to the refrigerator and collected a bottle of blood. "I added a few surprises for anyone foolish enough to disturb me while I slept."

Wisely Abby backed away from the heavy steel door. "What sort of surprises?"

"Enough electricity to halt your heart, a poisoned dart that will turn your insides to mush, a curse that will shrivel a man's private jewels to—"

"Okay, that falls under the category of way too much information," she interrupted before her eyes abruptly widened. "Good God. What if I had accidentally stumbled across this door? I would have been fried or mushed or shriveled."

Taking a deep drink of the blood, Dante was relieved to find his strength swiftly returning. Whatever had happened to him at least was not permanent.

"Maybe mushed or fried." He cast a pointed glance below her waist. "You don't have the proper equipment to be shriveled."

"I'm serious." She planted her hands on her hips. "I could have been killed."

His lips twitched. He wasn't about to confess that he had been vividly aware of her presence in the house even during his deepest sleep. That there was not a step that she had taken that he hadn't followed. She could not possibly have come near his lair without his awareness.

It smacked too closely of obsession.

"You were living with a powerful Chalice and a vampire, lover. My private door was the least of your concerns."

Her lips twitched with grudging humor. "Are you feeling better?"

"Yes. Whatever happened seems to be fading."

"Thank God."

"Yes."

There was a moment of silence before curiosity at last overcame good manners, and Abby was covertly casting glances about his secret lair.

Dante drained the last of the blood as he watched her expressive features.

The room had little in common with the pretentious mansion. Unlike Selena, he preferred the elegant to the gaudy. The bed was wide but built of plain mahogany with a gold and black comforter to match the carpeting. The furnishings were sturdy and the walls nearly hidden by the heavy shelves that were filled from floor to ceiling with his collection of rare books.

Giving a faint shake of her head, Abby moved to his desk to touch his state-of-the-art laptop and printer.

Dante polished off another bottle of blood, his lips twitching. "Is something the matter?"

"It's not quite what I was expecting."

"You were hoping for dusty skeletons and bats?"

She turned to face him with a faint smile. "It seems more fitting for a college professor than a dangerous vampire."

Setting aside the bottle, Dante prowled toward the slender woman. "Are you implying that I'm dull?"

Sensing the sudden heat in the air, she eyed him warily. "Dante, we should be deciding what we are to do next."

She was right, of course.

Once again his brilliant notion had led to nothing more than nearly getting them killed. And the witches remained as elusive as ever.

Even worse, he was now completely out of ideas as to how to trace the coven.

But his thoughts refused to remain focused on the problems at hand.

How many nights had he lain sleepless in that bed tormented with fantasies of Abby? How often had he battled against the ache to lure her to his side?

She may never have stepped foot in this lair, but her presence haunted every inch of it.

He continued forward, not halting until he had her firmly wrapped in his arms.

"You didn't answer my question, lover. Do you find me dull?"

He felt her breath catch as the mystical blue eyes darkened with awareness.

"We shouldn't become distracted," she protested, although her hands were already smoothing up his chest to wrap about his neck.

"Too late."

With one smooth motion, he scooped her off her feet and laid her in the center of the bed. The breath rushed from her lungs as he busily set about ridding her of the annoying clothes.

"Dante."

Tossing aside her shoes and socks, his hands reached to remove the sheathed dagger and then returned to tug at the zipper of her pants.

"You don't know how many nights you tormented me, lover." The pants were swiftly jerked off her legs, and his attention turned to her shirt. "Watching you, smelling your scent, feeling your heat. It was truly enough to drive a vampire mad."

A flush touched her cheeks as he removed her shirt and regarded her with a slumberous gaze. Bloody hell but she was a delectable morsel.

Spread upon the gold and black cover wearing nothing more than her lacy bra and thong, she would have made the most discerning vampire pant with need.

His lingering weakness was washed aside by a tidal wave of sheer blinding need.

Holding his gaze, Abby slowly smiled. "Good."

Dante lifted his brows as he planted his hands on each side of her head and pressed his lower body against her.

"Good?"

Her hands skimmed up his arms and over his chest where she began tugging at the buttons of his shirt.

"You tormented me enough," she explained.

His head lowered to nuzzle at the sensitive spot just below her ear. "Why didn't you come to my bed?"

His shirt was roughly tugged off his body. "Do you think that I jump into bed with every vampire I meet?" she demanded.

The demon flared within him. "I think that any jumping of vampires you do from now on had better be with me."

He leaned down to nip at her ear and was rewarded by a sharp shudder of longing that raced through Abby's body.

His own body was already hard and aching as he kissed a path down her neck and struggled to rid himself of his remaining clothes. Then, using his fully extended fangs, he tugged aside the bra.

Abby caught her breath as his teeth grazed her delicate skin, and Dante choked back a groan.

"Bloody hell but I wish I could taste you," he muttered as he sought her hardened nipple with his tongue.

Her fingers tunneled into his hair as she arched upward. "Taste? You mean suck my blood?"

"There is nothing more intimate than the mingling of blood," he whispered. "And nothing more erotic."

"This seems plenty erotic," she moaned. "I'm not sure I could bear any more."

Dante licked the underside of her breast as his hands slid over her smooth skin. Her heat seeped into his body, into his dead heart.

"You'd be surprised, lover," he assured her as he settled more firmly between her legs. "We haven't even begun to explore the possibilities."

Her legs encircled his hips with blatant invitation. "You mean like whipping cream?"

"Whipping cream, strawberries . . . chains."

"Chains? In your dreams, bud. I—" With a soft laugh, Dante surged into her damp heat. Pure sensation rippled through him as her fingernails sank into his shoulders and she gasped with pleasure. "Oh yes."

"Oh yes," he breathed as he lowered his head to kiss her with tender need.

Buried deep inside her, Dante paused to savor the feel of being so intimately bound together. It wouldn't matter if they had an eternity to explore each other, he would never tire of this woman. Never have enough of her sweet heat.

He would never be close enough.

Opening her eyes at his hesitation, Abby regarded him with a searching gaze.

"Dante? Is something wrong?"

His lips touched her forehead. "Everything is perfect, my love," he whispered, his hips thrusting deeper before slowly pulling out to thrust again. "You are perfect."

Her legs tightened about his waist, her beautiful face flushed. "Hardly perfect."

"Never argue with a vampire. We are always right." A growl was wrenched from his throat as she lifted her hips and his cock sank to the heart of her. Bloody hell. He needed more. He needed to have her connected to him in a manner that would bind her forever. "Abby."

She was panting as he steadily pumped himself

into her. "Dante . . . can't this conversation wait? It's a little difficult to think right now."

He traced her lips with his tongue. "I want to give you something."

Her fingernails bit deeper, sending a thrill of pleasure through him. "What?"

"A gift."

She moaned. "Now?"

"Now."

"But—"

It was obvious she was swiftly climbing to a climax, and Dante slowed his pace.

"I want to give you my blood."

Her eyes widened, the hint of distaste revealing that she had no idea just what an honor he had just offered her.

"I . . . um . . . That's very nice, but I have to be honest and tell you that drinking blood rates pretty high on my ick meter."

He smiled gently. "Abby, a vampire does not easily offer his blood to another. It is a rare symbol of trust since it gives power to the one who ingests it."

"Power? Do you really think I need any more? I don't seem to be able to control what I have."

"Power over me."

She stilled beneath him. "How?"

He brushed his lips over her cheeks and gently nipped at her swollen lips.

"You will be a part of me. You will feel my emotions, know my heart, and sense me wherever I may be." He pulled back to peer deeply into her eyes. "Even if I am hidden deep within the ground to heal."

It took her a long moment to realize the extent of his faith in her.

To be able to sense his every emotion, to know if he was lying, to be able to discover him even when he was at his most vulnerable . . .

Few vampires would ever offer such trust.

Not to anyone.

Seeming to at last sense the depth of his offer, Abby gave a small frown.

"Why? Why would you do this?"

"Because it is how a vampire chooses his mate," he said without hesitation. "The woman he will love for all eternity."

Her blue eyes softened with a tenderness that shimmered through his entire body.

"Oh, Dante." Her hands moved to frame his face. "I would be honored to be your mate."

Holding her gaze, Dante lifted his hand to his neck. Before she could protest, he used his nail to make a small incision. Only after he felt the precious blood begin to trickle down his skin did he cup the back of Abby's head and press her mouth to the wound.

"Drink," he commanded softly.

There was a moment of hesitation before he felt her lips part and gently suck at his life force.

Dante nearly jolted off the bed as his body clenched in raw, primitive bliss. Holy hell.

He had known what Abby would experience. With his blood in her veins, her senses would be sharper, clearer, brighter. The world itself would seem to come into crisp focus. And, of course, she would become aware of him in a way that mortals could not imagine.

But he had not realized the sheer erotic nature of allowing her to feed from him.

Passion and hunger flooded through him. An overwhelming need to brand her as his own.

His fingers tangled in her hair as he pressed her even closer. He felt as if he was being consumed and nothing had ever been so glorious.

With every tug of her lips, his hips began to thrust forward, his need growing to an unbearable ache. She moaned. He growled. They clutched at each other. They surged together.

And then the powers of the Phoenix within Abby began to smolder and flare, engulfing them in a sizzling cloak of heat.

Dante choked out a groan of shocked pleasure as he thrust himself to the very heart of her. Mist-red desire clouded about them, driving them ever upward, until with an explosive climax they combusted in flames together.

Chapter 17

Still panting and drenched in sweat, Abby slowly floated back to earth.

"Yowza," she breathed.

Sex with Dante was like running a marathon. Only a lot more fun.

Rolling to his side, Dante gathered her in his arms. "Yowza, indeed."

She pressed her lips to his chest, absently noting his skin was cool and dry. She was afraid to glance higher. No doubt his hair was perfect as well.

Damn vampires.

A smile abruptly curved her lips.

Her vampire.

She briefly closed her eyes, absorbing the unfamiliar sensations that had settled deep within her. Like a whisper in the back of her mind, she could feel Dante. His small glow of sated pleasure. The fierce love that flowed through every part of him. And, overall, his gnawing concern that he wouldn't be capable of protecting her.

She wrenched open her eyes to discover Dante regarding her with a searching gaze.

"I had no idea." She gave a faint shake of her head. "It's so intense."

"How do you feel?"

"Amazing." She watched Dante smile his sexy pirate smile. Made even more sexy by the fangs that were still fully extended. How weird was that? Suddenly her eyes widened in horror. "Oh."

His arms tightened about her. "What is it?"

"I'm not going to turn into a vampire, am I?"

"No." He dropped a kiss on the top of her curls, thankfully not insulted. "Turning someone is a bit more complicated. And it would not even be possible as long as you are the Chalice. The Phoenix would do whatever necessary to protect itself."

Reassured that she wasn't about to morph into anything else inhuman for the moment, she snuggled closer to his hard body.

"I wish we could just stay here."

"Hide from the world?"

"At least an extended vacation." She pulled back her head to meet his silver gaze. "I think we deserve a few days off, don't you?"

He regarded her with a hint of regret. "I can't think of anything that would please me more."

"But?"

He blinked. "How did you know there was a but?"

Abby heaved a sigh. "In my world, there's always a but."

"You're a very odd woman at times, lover."

"I thought I was beautiful and courageous and sexy as hell?"

"All of the above," he swiftly agreed, a faint smile playing about his lips, "and occasionally odd."

"Rather ironic coming from a vampire."

He bent down to press a swift kiss to her lips. Too brief.

"As much as I hate to admit it, we must not linger any longer."

That wasn't what she wanted to hear. Not when she felt warm and fuzzy and, best of all, safe.

"We have to leave now?"

"It's too risky to stay here for long. If the house is being watched, then we could find ourselves surrounded by the sort of nasties that no one wants to meet on a dark night."

"They couldn't get in here, could they?"

He gave a lift of his shoulder. "Probably not, but we'll eventually have to leave."

Dante rolled off the bed, and before she could even appreciate the sight of his hard, alabaster body, he was impeccably attired and looking Gucci yummy.

Damn. That was starting to be a real sore spot with her.

"If we're safe, why do we have to leave?" she demanded.

He gave a lift of his raven brow. "You don't want to be locked in a room with a hungry vampire, lover. Even if I can't drink human blood, I don't doubt I might get a bit testy. Besides, I doubt that the witches will be considerate enough to make an appearance upon our doorstep."

Heaving a sigh, Abby sat up and pushed her tangled curls out of her face. "Fine, go ahead and make sense. At least you can hand me the clothes you ripped off me."

"Your wish is my command." With a flourishing bow, he bent to retrieve the clothing that had been scattered across the floor.

"Isn't that what a genie is supposed to—" Her teasing words trailed away as she watched Dante scoop the clothes in his hands and then slowly stiffen. With a strange expression, he pressed her shirt to his nose. "Dante? Are you sniffing my shirt?"

His silver eyes shimmered with a dangerous glow. "It smells of demon."

Abby stiffened. Did he just say she smelled like a demon?

She had probably suffered worse insults, but she couldn't think of one at the moment.

"Excuse me?"

He took another deep sniff. "I don't recognize the breed, but you have definitely been close to a demon."

Oh. Well, that was better.

Marginally.

"Yeah, I've been close to a demon." She gave him a pointed glance. "About as close as I could get. You don't remember? I know you're old, but holy crap."

His expression remained closed. Hard. "A demon, not a vampire."

His blood stirred within her. She could easily sense his lethal focus. A predator on the scent.

"That's impossible," she groused. She would have known if some demon had been rubbing on her shirt. That wasn't something a normal woman . . . "Oh."

"What?"

Abby slapped her forehead with her open hand. Christ. She must be losing her mind.

"There was this strange woman who interrupted my spell," she confessed.

"Upstairs?"

"Yes."

Abby shivered as Dante's blood heated with fury. "What did she look like?"

She struggled to recall. She had been just a little preoccupied at the time.

"Human, for the most part, although she was far more graceful than any mere mortal. And incredibly strong."

"She had the shape of a human?"

"Yes. A beautiful woman. She had dark hair and the most amazing gold eyes. Oh, and her skin had the strangest bronze glow to it."

His eyes widened as he lifted the shirt to his nose once again. "A Shalott demon? I thought they had all fled this world. She attacked you?"

"Yes . . . no."

He stabbed her with a piercing gaze. "Abby?"

She gave a helpless shrug. "I think she was just trying to stop the spell. She could have killed me while you were out, but she ran off. She said someone was calling her."

"Damn."

"What is it?" Abby scooted to the edge of the bed. "Is she dangerous?"

"I don't know, and that's what is driving me crazy." He gave a sharp shake of his head. "We must leave here now."

"Where are we going?"

"To see if I can pick up the trail of the Shalott. When they were in this world, they were assassins. If we can trace her back to her employer, we might discover what she was doing here."

There was an edge in his voice. A sharp thrill for the chase.

"Assassin?" she demanded.

"Very effective assassins. If either of us was her target, we wouldn't be here to tell the tale."

"Crap." Was there any end to the creepy crawlies that roamed the night? "Dante."

"Yes?"

She bit her bottom lip. If this assassin was so deadly, she had no desire to go chasing after it. "Does it matter why she was here? She can't have a connection to the witches."

"There is some connection."

"How do you know?"

"There is a spell upon her."

"You can smell that?"

"I can smell fear. And a Shalott demon fears nothing but magic."

Damn. He was good. "It could be that horrid wizard."

"We would be dead if it was."

There was a dark silence as Abby forced herself to swallow. Dante was right. The psychopathic wizard would have her roasting over a fire or in her grave.

"I suppose."

Dante moved forward to press her clothes into her reluctant hands. "It's the only lead we have at the moment, lover. I think we should follow it."

"Okay."

She knew she sounded petulant, but she couldn't help it as she pulled on her clothes and smoothed back her hair. Her idea of excitement was renting a movie and eating a bowl of popcorn. Not a gladiator session with a pack of demons.

Waiting in silence for her to recover from her bout of self-pity, Dante stepped forward to hand her the sheathed dagger.

"Don't forget this."

"Damn." She heaved a faint sigh. "I should have used it earlier. Some savior of the world I'm proving to be."

Suddenly she was in Dante's arms, and his cheek was rubbing against her own.

"Don't, Abby. There's not another mortal who would still be alive after what you've gone through."

It wasn't true, of course. But it made her feel better anyway.

She laid her head against his chest. "I don't understand how this happened to me. I'm not some chosen slayer or demon hunter. Hell, I didn't even know there were demons." Her lips twisted. "Unless you count my dad."

"Perhaps it was fate," he murmured.

"Then fate sucks."

A chuckle was wrenched from his throat as he pulled back to regard her with a searching gaze.

"Are you ready?"

"No."

He gave a tug on her hair. "Let's go."

Dante had even less desire than Abby to leave the peace of his lair.

What more could a vampire desire?

The woman he had chosen as his mate. A large comfortable bed. No phone, no neighbors, no relatives.

Satellite radio so he would never miss a Cubs game.

Paradise.

Unfortunately there were still hordes of demons,

wizards, and zombies just waiting for the opportunity to corner them.

Taking her hand, he led her to the door, pausing as he touched the lock and spoke a low word.

Silently the door slid open, and he took a step forward. At once he realized that something was wrong.

"Wait," he breathed softly.

Abby instinctively froze. "Is there something out there?"

He slowly tasted the air. There were humans near. At least four. And one of them was very familiar.

"The wizard is here. Upstairs."

"Crap." He heard her suck in a deep breath. "Do we wait here?"

He didn't hesitate. "No. The wizard has managed to tap into the power of the dark lord. Given time, he will be capable of discovering this lair."

Her face paled. If she didn't carry the Phoenix within her, he could remove her horrid memories of the wizard and his pack of zombies. For now it was just another burden she would have to shoulder.

"The door—"

"We can't allow ourselves to be trapped."

"Then we try to make a run for it?"

"I believe stealth will serve us better at this point."

Her eyes widened. She was thinking that he had lost his mind.

And she might be right.

"You intend to sneak past them?"

"Yes."

"Great."

"Trust me."

She gave a growl low in her throat. "One of these days."

"This way." He tightened his grip on her fingers

and led her from the room. In silence they moved toward the very back of the basement. Reaching the wall, Dante bent down to remove the grate that hid his secret passageway.

No vampire worth his salt was without a secret passageway.

Beside him Abby gave a faint gasp. "A tunnel?"

"It will lead you beyond the gates," he explained, holding her gaze. "Go two blocks north and wait on the corner behind the large oak. Can you remember that?"

It took a moment for his words to sink in. "No, Dante. I will not leave you."

"If I don't lay a false trail, then they will be upon us before we can reach safety. Besides, I must know which direction the Shalott took when she left the grounds."

She reached out to grip his arm. Dante flinched as he felt the heat from her fingers brand through his shirt.

The Phoenix would react to her emotions until she learned to control her powers.

"You can't—"

Gently he removed her hand, lifting the fingers to his lips. "Don't fear, lover. I'm far too swift for them to harm me."

He didn't feel the need to explain that he intended to confront the aggravating wizard and put an end to his interference. Full disclosure was for lawyers, not vampires.

Not that most people seemed to think there was much difference between the two.

One bloodsucker was much like the other.

"What if they have some magical trap?"

He cocked a brow. "I'm not completely helpless. This was once my home. I have a few traps of my own."

"Dante."

He pressed a kiss to her palm and stepped back. "There will be no argument."

She frowned at his stern tone. "You're far too fond of giving commands, vampire."

"And you're far too fond of ignoring them, Chalice." He held her gaze a long moment. "You must do this for me."

"I don't like it."

"Yeah, I got that." He bent beside the entrance to the tunnel and watched as she grudgingly crouched and stepped into the darkness. He pressed the cell phone he pulled from his pocket into her hand. "Don't leave the tunnel if you sense someone is near. Speed-dial Viper and he will come."

Her eyes glittered with frustration. "Don't you dare let anything happen to you or—"

"You'll stake me someplace unpleasant?" he finished for her.

"Yes."

He brushed her lips in a lingering kiss. "I will take the greatest care."

Chapter 18

Rafael chanted a simple spell as he moved through the shattered house. It was frustrating to depend upon magic that the rankest amateur could perform. Magic he hadn't used since he was a fledgling acolyte. But after the disaster of losing the Chalice when she was within his grasp, he was not foolish enough to dare calling upon the dark lord's powers.

He hadn't lived so many years by being stupid.

The Prince possessed a nasty habit of punishing those who disappointed him. There was no need to draw attention to himself.

Reaching the upstairs hallway, he paused and spread his hands. Giving a command, he studied the swirls of color that briefly appeared in the darkness.

"They have been here," he said in satisfaction to the three disciples who stood behind him in respectful silence. Or perhaps it was terrified silence. Since the death of Amil, a tense wariness had gripped the faithful. Which suited Rafael to perfection. He far preferred to be feared than respected. Fear only fed his power. He watched as the colors began to fade. "A vampire, a human and . . . ah, the witches' whelp."

"The witches have the Chalice?" a thin voice demanded from behind him.

A cold smile curved his lips as he turned toward his waiting servants. "No. She is still near. I can feel her power. Search the house. And remember, I wish the Chalice alive."

The oldest of the disciples stepped forward. "What of the vampire?"

"Kill him."

The three melted into the darkness even as a dark, terrifying laugh echoed through the hallway.

"Easy to say; much less easy to accomplish."

Rafael stiffened before he forced himself to pretend a nonchalance he was far from feeling. He could not afford to allow the vampire to realize he was without his powers. Not if he was to survive.

"Well, well," he drawled, placing his back against the wall. The animal wouldn't be allowed to sneak up from behind. "If it isn't the faithful hound. Have your mistresses grown so arrogant that they believe one pitiful vampire can defeat me? Or are they simply that desperate?"

"Neither," the disembodied voice floated through the air. "I merely have grown weary of your tedious pursuit."

"Then fortunately for you it's about to come to an end. It's time to be done with you once and for all, vampire."

Dante was prepared as the wizard thrust out his hand and sent a bolt of fire in his direction. With his inhuman speed, such parlor tricks were a wasted effort.

Something the wizard was bound to know.

Dante remained wary as he glided closer. He was not about to be lured into some unseen trap.

"Tell me, how is Amil?" he baited, reaching out with his senses to search for hidden dangers.

A smile touched the thin lips. "He found the duties of being a servant rather too much to handle. He decided becoming a sacrifice for the Prince was more to his taste."

"How very noble of him."

A sneer touched the pasty features. "He was a sniffling, spineless worm who should have been strangled at birth. Still, he served his purpose."

There was another bolt of energy that slammed into the wall and charred the wood. Annoyingly Dante could sense nothing more to warn him of the wizard's intention.

He would not commit himself until he was certain there were no nasty surprises.

"The Prince always did demand his share of bloody fodder to keep him satisfied. Still, it must be difficult to find willing victims in this day and age."

The wizard shrugged. "The Prince has never demanded a sacrifice be willing."

"A charming deity."

"A powerful deity."

Dante laughed with mocking amusement. He wanted the wizard distracted and off guard. Perfectly ripe to make a mistake.

His last mistake.

"So powerful he has been condemned to banishment by a handful of human witches."

The man growled deep in his throat. "He was

failed by his worshippers, who had been lured to complacency. I will ensure it doesn't happen again."

Dante was drifting ever closer. Once Dante had his fangs sunk deep in his throat, the wizard would be helpless. He would need his vocal cords to mumble his spells.

"And you believe he will reward you richly?"

A near-fanatical pride tightened the narrow face. "I shall rule at his side."

This time Dante's laughter was genuine. "You're even more a fool than Amil. The Prince rules alone, and those who worship him are no more than bugs beneath his notice."

"How would you know, vampire? You worship nothing. Believe in nothing."

"I'm at least wise enough not to barter my soul to a being who is certain to offer no more than betrayal."

The wizard reached into his pocket to pull out a small crystal. Dante hesitated. Why would he use a magical toy when he possessed the medallion of the dark lord?

A blue flame shot in his direction. It slammed into the floor, and the mansion groaned as if a breath from tumbling to the ground.

Dante easily shifted out of danger, his mind racing.

Although he couldn't detect magic, he could still feel the power that swirled about the wizard. There was a pulsing energy that could destroy the entire block, and yet he refused to reach for it.

Why?

It took a long moment before Dante at last realized the truth. Of course. With a low chuckle, he dismissed the shadows he had wrapped about himself.

The wizard didn't call upon the dark lord because he was terrified his god might be waiting to serve up a bit of revenge for having disappointed him.

It was perfect.

He stepped forward, his arms folded negligently over his chest. Watching his approach, the wizard licked his thin lips.

"I suppose you're attempting to keep me occupied so the woman can escape?" he blustered. "A worthless effort. My servants will soon have her in their grasp."

Dante merely smiled. "Having some acquaintance with your servants, I can't say that I'm overly concerned."

Without warning, he launched himself at the gaunt form. He wanted to be done with this. Abby was alone, and while he was fully confident in her ability to deal with her human enemies, there were still demons capable of detecting the presence of the Phoenix.

Sinking his nails deep into the arms of the man, he allowed his fangs to lengthen. Before he had been chained to the Chalice, he would have drained the man. Now he would have to settle for ripping out his throat.

A pity.

His head lowered. Unfortunately the wizard was not about to be sacrificed without a fight. With cold determination, the wizard battled back, his low chants filling the darkness even as he reached into his pocket to remove a smooth ebony stake.

A burst of light suddenly filled the hall, blinding Dante and forcing him to dodge backward. A stake was a stake, and he wasn't about to allow overconfidence to lead to his demise.

He carefully circled the man. Waiting for an opening.

The wizard glanced down at his bleeding arms. "You do know there is no need for us to be enemies? I could release you from your bondage. You give me the Chalice and I shall ensure you are set free."

Dante smoothly reached out to slash the man's face. "You think I would trust you?"

The wizard flinched but his composure never wavered. "Why not? There's no gain for me to kill you. For the moment, you stand in my way, but if you were to step aside, we could prove to be valuable allies."

"Tempting, but I don't think so."

"The witches have you that cowed?" he taunted, the stake held casually in his fingers as if he forgot he even held it. Dante was not stupid. The wizard hoped to rile his anger and give him the opportunity to strike. "Pathetic."

Dante shrugged. "It has nothing to do with the witches."

"Then . . ." The wizard gave a sudden laugh. "Ah, of course. You have come to care for the girl. You are worse than cowed; you're completely neutered."

"Actually, you have missed the most obvious reason I refuse to join forces with you."

The cold eyes narrowed. "And what would that be?"

"I don't like you."

At last realizing that Dante was not going to be bullied or coerced, the wizard grasped the medallion about his neck. He would have to risk the anger of his master if he were not to die in this hallway.

Dante crouched, preparing himself for the coming attack.

* * *

Despite the muggy night air, Abby was shivering.

It was more than the creepy trip through the spider-infested tunnel. Or the realization that by standing on the corner by herself she might as well be wearing a sign that said "Come Eat Me" to every demon in Chicago.

It was more the sense of Dante that coiled through the back of her mind.

She might not be able to read his thoughts, but his emotions were blatantly clear. He was not laying a false trail. Or even searching for the scent of the strange demon.

He was confronting the wizard.

She could feel his lethal intent as if it were her own.

Damn him to hell.

She was going to . . .

Her imagination failed her, but it was going to be really, really bad.

Stewing on potential repercussions, Abby froze as she heard the unmistakable sound of approaching footsteps.

"I'm tired of this shit. I'm not a freaking blood-hound," a male voice muttered. "We've lost her."

"Shut up and keep searching. Unless you want to return to the master and confess you have failed him?" an icy voice demanded.

Silently Abby pressed herself into the bush beside the tree. Her pursuers seemed to be human, but she wasn't overly relieved.

Not after she had seen what the wizard did to the coven.

Ick.

"She could be anywhere by now."

"Listen to me, you moron." Peering through the leaves, Abby watched a short, squat man grab a pimply faced boy by the throat. "When I found Amil, he was splattered over the altar like a slaughtered pig. I have no intention of joining him in hell. At least not yet."

Another man who was built like a linebacker and possessed the expression of savage stupidity curled his hands into fists.

"Perhaps the vampire will do us all a favor and kill the bastard," he growled.

The short man whirled to face him. "Are you willing to risk your life on an impotent vampire?" He waited for either man to speak. They were obviously not as stupid as they looked since both dropped their heads to study their toes. "Fine. Fan out and search the block."

There was a brief, tense moment as if the two goons were debating sticking a knife in the head goon. No honor among thieves and all that. Then, seemingly coming to their senses, they turned and grudgingly trudged down the street.

Abby forced herself to remain utterly still as she waited for the remaining merry man to be on his way. There were all sorts of hidey-holes to be searched.

Most of them far more intelligent spots for hide-and-seek than her own sad, scraggly bush.

He didn't scurry away. He didn't even meander away. He remained as rooted to the spot as the ancient oak. It seemed her streak of piss-poor luck was remaining firmly intact.

With a grand gesture that would have made Abby laugh under normal circumstances, the annoying twit reached into the pocket of his heavy robe and pulled out a strange rock that was hanging upon a chain. Holding it upward, he began to chant beneath his breath.

Abby didn't know what the rock did, but she was certain it couldn't be good.

Not good at all, she acknowledged as the rock glowed with a purple hue and a smirk touched the round face.

"You are near, Chalice. I can sense you." He moved to search the nearby parked cars. He peered into the branches of the tree. And inevitably he spread the leaves of the bush. "Hello. What do we have here?"

Abby should have been terrified. Or at the very least slightly fearful.

Instead she was really and truly pissed off.

Dammit. She wasn't out looking for trouble. All she wanted was to find the witches and be done with the whole ridiculous business.

Why the hell couldn't they just leave her alone?

As her temper mounted, so did the tingle of heat that was filling her blood. The Phoenix within her was preparing to take measures to protect itself.

And there wasn't a damn thing she could do to stop it.

Pressing herself into the prickly branches, she held out her hand. "Stay back."

"Or what? You'll scream?"

"I don't want to hurt you."

There was a beat before he gave an ugly laugh. "You hurt me?"

"Yes."

"You haven't got the skill or the nerve. That's the trouble with you Goody Two-shoes." He glanced deliberately downward. "No balls."

The fire burned even hotter. Freaking hell. Why wouldn't the idiot shut up and walk away? She had warned him, hadn't she?

Of course he possessed testosterone. A woman offering him a warning was as good as waving a red flag in front of his face.

"I'm telling you that you're the one who won't have any balls if you don't leave me alone."

"You think your vampire is going to come rushing to your rescue? I can promise you he's already back in his grave where he belongs."

Abby shook her head. She didn't know much, but she did know that Dante wasn't in any grave. Not until she got her hands upon him.

"No, he's very much alive."

The man shrugged. "It doesn't matter. He'll soon be dead or turned to our side. The master has a special talent for recruiting." The round face hardened. "Even those who never wanted to worship the dark lord."

"It's not too late," she urged. "You can walk away."

"Walk away? No one walks away. Not unless they have a death wish," he snarled. "You've wasted enough of my time. Let's go."

"No."

"Shit." He lifted a threatening fist. "Do you think I won't hurt you? The master said you were to be alive, but he didn't say anything about roughing you up."

Abby didn't doubt his willingness to hurt her for a moment. She sensed that he took a great deal of pleasure in slapping around those weaker than him.

Just like her father.

But he was no demon or zombie or even powerful wizard.

She knew deep in her heart she could kill him with horrible ease.

"Fine, I'll come, but you have to step back first," she retorted, hoping to gain some distance.

"Do you really think I'm that stupid?" The beady eyes narrowed as he reached out to grab a handful of her hair. "I've had enough, come on."

Abby's eyes watered as he gave a savage yank on her hair. She found herself tumbling forward, and out of sheer instinct, she reached up to grasp the man's arm. She had only intended to keep from planting her face in the ground, but the moment her hands touched his wrist, a burst of heat flared from her palms.

The man gave a keening cry as he snatched his hand free and cradled it to his chest.

"You . . . bitch. You stupid bitch," he gritted, a malevolent hatred glittering in his eyes. "You'll pay for that."

A sickness tightened Abby's stomach. She recognized that expression. She should. She had seen it often enough.

With a flashback of horror, she watched as the man curled his fist and raised it to strike.

No.

She rose to her feet.

Not again. Not ever again.

Preparing to launch a vicious right hook, the man was too blinded by fury to consider he might actually be outgunned by a woman four inches shorter and a hundred pounds lighter.

Not until she dived forward and planted her hands in the center of his chest.

Smoke began to rise as he howled in pain, but Abby didn't waver. The wizard wannabe would kill her given the chance. She didn't intend to give him the chance.

Somewhere in the back of her mind, Abby became aware of Dante swiftly approaching. Oddly he halted beside the tree rather than tossing himself into the fray.

Whether out of fear she might toast him in confusion or because he was alarmed he might distract her, she couldn't say. And at the moment she was a little too occupied to care.

Clutching at her arms, the man struggled to pull her closer.

"You'll pay for this," he panted.

Abby gritted her teeth as she pressed harder. A horrible stench began to fill the air. The smell of burning fabric. And what she suspected was searing flesh.

Then, just as she thought she could bear no more, her assailant gave a strangled cry and with a desperate wrench he was stumbling away from her.

Just for a moment she considered following after him. She didn't doubt he was an evil man who was capable of harming any number of innocent people. But, while she was prepared to protect herself, she knew she could not deliberately chase down a fleeing man and put an end to him.

That zoomed way beyond her comfort zone.

Instead she sank to her knees and sucked in a deep breath.

"You can come out now, Dante. I know you're here."

Chapter 19

Dante stepped from behind the tree with a faint smile. He recognized that peevish tone. It meant that Abby was well aware of his extracurricular activity with the dark wizard and was not a bit pleased with him.

"You did well, lover. That fool will think twice about coming after you again."

She stepped toward him, planting her hands on her hips. "Why didn't you help me?"

"Did you want my help?"

That made her briefly falter. Her independent nature made it nearly impossible for her to admit she might need assistance. From anyone.

At last she shrugged. "It's not like you to stand back and watch me duke it out."

Dante cocked a brow at the unfamiliar phrase. "Duke it out?"

"Fight off the bad guys."

He reached out to grasp her arms and tug her close. He breathed deeply of her warm scent. A scent that now held his own blood. That knowledge made a purely male pleasure race through him.

"You seemed to be holding your own."

She leaned back to stab him with a narrowed gaze. "Okay, what's going on?"

"Nothing."

"I could feel you behind the tree, and I know damn well you were itching to charge out and kill that man. What stopped you?"

He smoothed back a stray curl. "I needed to know that you wouldn't hesitate to fight."

She made a strangled sound. "God almighty, I've been in a full-scale war for days. Why would I hesitate now?"

"You've been fighting demons and zombies, not humans. In your mind there's a difference," he pointed out. "I needed to know you could overcome your fear of harming another."

A flush touched her cheeks. "Oh."

His finger brushed her lips. "Are you all right?"

Her lips twisted in a grim smile. "As all right as I can be right now."

"No regrets?" he pressed.

She took a moment as she glanced down the now-empty street. "Actually . . . no. This may be horrible of me, but it's nice to know that I didn't panic when the chips were down."

He tugged her closer. It was a lesson she needed to learn for herself. But it had been hell standing back and allowing her to discover her strength.

He would rather be staked than go through that again.

"A powerful woman. I like it." His lips skated over her temple. "Sexy."

"Is there anything you don't find sexy?"

"What can I say? Vampires are insatiable."

His hands were lowering to the flare of her hips when she was suddenly pushing against his chest.

"Wait."

"What?"

"You're not going to distract me."

His teeth nipped at the lobe of her ear. "It could be fun."

She gave a faint shiver before she was sternly stepping back and folding her arms over her chest.

"No. You lied to me."

Dante ruefully conceded that Abby wasn't going to be deflected. She was smoldering with the need to rake him over the coals. A pity. With the immediate threat gone, he could think of better means of passing the time.

"That's rather harsh," he mildly protested.

"You told me you were going to lay a false trail and pick up the scent of that demon." She poked her finger at his chest. "You didn't say anything about flexing your testosterone with that damn wizard."

"He's going to be a pain in the ass until we can get rid of him. I'm tired of looking over my shoulder."

"Did you . . . ?"

"No." Dante gave a disgusted shake of his head. He had been preparing for battle. He hadn't considered the notion the bastard would use his powers to elude him. "The coward scurried away rather than fight like a man."

More chest poking. "There was more than just him running away. I could feel you, and I know that there was some sort of fight."

"Hardly a fight. Or even a skirmish." He held out his arms. "Look at me, not a scratch."

Her eyes narrowed. "I've had your blood; I know there was some sort of fight."

His lips twitched. "More a minor disagreement."

"Dante . . ."

He cupped her chin in his hand. "Abby, I found the wizard, we exchanged a handful of threats, I had him in my grasp, and like a fool I allowed him to disappear. Nothing more."

"You're lucky he did disappear. I have warned you what will happen if you get yourself hurt."

Dante smiled as his gaze dropped to her mouth. Surely he had allowed her enough chiding? It was definitely time to move on to more interesting activities.

Debating whether he dared to pull her back in his arms and kiss away her temper, he was abruptly whirling, his fangs extended and his hands curled into claws. A vampire was near, and he wasn't about to take chances.

On cue, Viper stepped from the shadows and folded his arms over his chest. Even to Dante's eye he appeared a lethal threat with his large body attired in black and his pale hair pulled back with a heavy silver clasp. An ancient predator who wouldn't hesitate to kill.

The familiar mocking smile curved his lips.

"Really, Dante, I thought you would be knee-deep in witches by now, and here you are playing with your new toy."

Dante cocked a brow. "What are you doing here?"

"I was following the trail of your wizard."

"Too late." Dante glared toward Selena's dark estate. "He already made his grand appearance."

"And now?"

"His grand exit. He called upon the Prince."

Viper shrugged. "It's only a matter of time."

"He's proving to be a pain in the ass."

"Aren't all wizards?"

"I did manage to injure him. You should be able to follow the scent of his blood."

A beat passed as Viper slid his gaze to the silent Abby. "You aren't in a hurry to be rid of me, are you, Dante?"

He was, of course. He was possessive enough to resent the manner in which Viper watched Abby.

"I have my own trail to follow."

As if sensing Dante's prickling unease, Viper deliberately strolled toward Abby and lightly touched her hair.

"And games to play, eh?" He stilled, lowering his head to sniff at her neck before reaching to grasp her arm and turn it upward. "What is this?"

Never one to be manhandled by anyone, Abby was struggling against the vampire's hold.

"Hey. What are you doing?"

Viper's startled gaze cut toward Dante. "You mated her? Well, well. Congratulations."

Belatedly noticing what had captured Viper's attention, Abby regarded the intricate red scrolling that now tattooed the length of her inner forearm.

"Holy crap. What is that?"

Viper gave a short laugh. "She doesn't know?"

Abby stabbed him with a wide gaze. "Dante?"

Dante briefly considered the pleasure of tying Viper around the tree like a pretty bow.

"I did tell you that when you took my blood, we would be mated," he reminded Abby.

She appeared far from appeased. "You didn't tell

me that I was going to look like a biker babe from hell. Will it go away?"

"No."

"What does it mean?"

Dante opened his mouth, but Viper was quicker.

"That you have been branded. No other vampire may have you now."

Dante closed his eyes, perfectly prepared as he heard Abby suck in a deep breath.

He might not know a great deal about human women, but he did know they possessed a fierce dislike for being treated as property.

"Branded? You branded me?"

"For all eternity," Viper added in smooth tones.

Dante gave a low growl. "You are not helping, Viper."

Viper blinked with mock innocence. "Ah, you wanted me to lie to her? You should have given me some signal."

"Go." There was no mistaking the threat in his tone. "Go kill a wizard."

Viper's expression was suddenly somber as he moved to lay a hand on Dante's shoulder.

"Be careful. The Prince is calling on his minions. The town is crawling with demons. Most of them in a nasty temper."

Dante gave a small nod and watched Viper disappear into the shadows. Only when they were alone did he cautiously approach Abby and gently take her hand.

"Abby, it won't hurt you." His fingers ran over the scrolling mark. The demon inside him howled in triumph at the symbol of ownership, but he was wise enough to keep his expression sympathetic. "It's . . . like a wedding ring. A symbol of my love for you."

"A wedding ring can be removed. I'm marked forever."

Dante didn't need her blood to sense the tension that hummed about her stiff body. A frown tugged at his brows.

"Abby? This isn't about the brand, is it?"

She shivered as she forced herself to meet his searching gaze. "It didn't seem real until now. It's frightening."

"Me?"

"No, of course not. It's just that I never thought about spending my life with someone. After my parents' marriage . . ."

At last realizing the source of her sudden bout of nerves, Dante put an arm about her shoulder and pulled her close.

He hoped her father was burning in hell.

"We aren't your parents," he murmured softly. "I could never hurt you. Never."

She pressed her face into his chest. "I don't know how to be a mate. I've been alone all my life."

"Is that what you want? To be alone?"

He felt the shudder that raced through her. "No, but what if I disappoint you?"

Dante touched his lips to the top of her head. "Do you love me?"

"Yes, I love you."

"Then that's all that matters."

She pulled back, her face pale in the moonlight. "What if it's not enough?"

His hand cupped her neck. "The brand isn't a prison sentence, Abby. There is nothing to keep you from walking away whenever you want."

"And what about you?" she demanded. "What does the brand mean to you?"

He hesitated a moment before confessing the truth. "You are my mate. There will never be another."

His soft words seemed to catch her off guard. Then amazingly he felt the tension begin to ease from her body, and a rueful expression settled on her face.

"I'm sorry. I don't know what's wrong with me." Her arms encircled his waist. "I'm not usually the hysterical type."

Dante savored the feel of her heat pouring into his body. He wasn't sure how or why he had allowed her to become such a vital part of his life, but he knew he would never survive if anything happened to her.

"I can't imagine what's wrong," he teased, his fingers tangling in her hair as the familiar surge of desire began to harden his muscles. "It's not as if you have acquired an unwanted spirit or been hunted by demons or nearly sacrificed by a dark wizard."

She gave a reluctant chuckle as she snuggled close. "I think it was the tattoo that made me a little wacky."

"Not the thought of being my mate?"

A welcome amusement entered her eyes. "That depends."

"On what?"

"A mate isn't the same thing as a wife, is it?"

He gave a vague shrug. "Does it matter?"

"Of course it does. I have no intention of spending the rest of my life being some sort of unpaid servant to you."

Abby his servant?

He choked back a laugh of disbelief.

"Don't worry, lover, I'm fairly low maintenance," he assured her with a guileless expression. "Once you're done scrubbing the floors and washing my clothes and serving me blood while I sit in front of the television, you will have plenty of time to do your darning."

Her elbow dug into his side. "Darning? More likely I'll be sharpening my stakes."

With a chuckle Dante tapped the tip of her nose. "I've been taking care of myself for centuries, lover, and to be brutally honest, if I wanted a servant, I could enthrall any human to do my bidding."

"Enthrall?"

"A trick that all vampires possess."

Her brows lifted. "Did you ever try to enthrall me?"

His finger moved to outline her lips. "Never."

"Why not?"

"Because I liked you," he said simply.

She blinked. "You liked me?"

"I liked your innocence, your honesty, your refusal to feel sorry for yourself despite the rotten breaks you'd gotten, and of course"—he slowly smiled—"that delectable body didn't hurt anything. I didn't want you to become a mindless sycophant. I wanted you."

"Oh." She sucked in a deep breath. "You keep surprising me."

"And how is that?"

"When we first met, I expected you to be arrogant and dangerous and sexy."

"All true. Especially that sexy part."

"I never expected you to be kind."

Dante glanced down in astonishment. Kind? He had never been accused of that before. And with good reason.

Until the witches had captured him, he had been a hunter who preyed upon anyone foolish enough to cross his path. And even after being leashed, he had been a lethal warrior who could kill without mercy.

It was only with Abby that he discovered the softer emotions he didn't even realize he possessed.

"I wasn't until you."

They stood holding each other in the darkness, absorbing the pleasure of simply being together.

Abby at last pulled back with a grimace. "Do you want to go in search of the witches?"

"What I want is to have you naked and sweaty beneath me," he murmured.

She nudged him with her elbow. "Maybe I want to be naked and sweaty on top of you."

"God." Dante went hard at the visual. "Are you trying to kill me?"

"I thought you were immortal?"

"Not even immortals can take that sort of torture." He bent his head to snatch a brief searing kiss. "Let's go before I forget what the hell I'm supposed to be doing."

Abby absently allowed Dante to lead her back to the shattered mansion. A part of her knew that she should be on guard. She should be preparing for anything from zombies to hellhounds to wizards to leap from the bushes. Hell, at this point, she wouldn't be surprised if a leprechaun popped out to do a jig.

Her sense of self-preservation at the moment, however, couldn't compete with strange tattoos that shimmered with crimson fire beneath the moonlight.

Mate. Holy freaking cow.

Abruptly stopping in the shadows of the mansion, Dante turned to regard her with a smile that looked suspiciously smug.

"Stop scratching at it, lover. You'll make it sore."

"It looks strange." She held up her arm. "How am I supposed to go out in public like this?"

The smugness deepened. "No one will notice."

She shook her arm before his eyes. "Are you kidding me? I look like I got drunk on tequila and ended up in Shanghai."

"It's invisible to all but demons."

"Oh." Her arm dropped. "Really?"

"Really."

"Then why can I see it?"

He leaned forward to gaze directly into her eyes. "Because you're special."

Ridiculously it took a moment before realization hit.

"Great. First my eyes turn blue and now my arm is red. Are there any other bodily changes you should warn me about? A horn? Forked tongue? Cloven hooves?"

He shrugged, taking her arm and leading her into the house and toward the servant's staircase.

"Well, there is the tail, but once you get used to the wagging, you'll barely notice it's there."

She batted his arm. "You're lucky you're already dead."

He flashed a grin. "And you are already nagging like a wife."

Her own lips twitched. God, he was so beautiful. And intelligent and strong and tender and . . . and perfect.

A rush of heat raced through her before she was sternly turning her thoughts to the matter at hand.

"Why are we going upstairs?"

"We can't leave the spell books. They're too dangerous to have lying around."

"No kidding." She gave a shudder as she recalled the strange magic that had gripped her as she read the spell. That was an experience she'd just as soon not repeat. "What do you think Selena was doing with them?"

He paused on the landing and turned to face her. "That's the question, isn't it?"

"Maybe we should review what we know."

"Review what we know?" he repeated with a faint smile. "*Law & Order*? *CSI*? *Monk*?"

"Agatha Christie."

"Ah."

"It might help." She leaned against the wall, suddenly realizing how weary she was. The past few days had taken their toll on her body. "At the very least it couldn't hurt."

He gave a slow nod of his head. "True enough. Where do we start this review?"

Abby blinked. It always caught her off guard to discover Dante's willingness to listen to her opinion. No one, no one had ever done that before.

"I suppose with Selena," she said hesitantly. "You said you thought she was acting strangely before . . . the explosion? To be honest, I just thought she was crazy."

He narrowed his gaze as he remembered back. "She was more secretive than usual. She would come and go from the mansion without taking me and then disappear into her rooms for hours."

"You think she was visiting the witches?"

"Yes."

"Did she get the spell books from them?"

"That would be my guess."

Abby bit her lip as she attempted to make sense of the strange path of events.

"What sort of spell would she be working on? Was she afraid of something?"

His lips twisted as his gaze flashed over her. "At the time I didn't care. I had more . . . intriguing matters to consider."

The heat returned, with interest.

Damn but he shouldn't be so distracting.

"And now?" she grimly pressed.

"There's a possibility that the witches might have stumbled onto the wizard and his followers," he said. "If they sensed his power, they would have taken steps to protect themselves."

"That makes sense." She hesitated, sensing the frustration that simmered within him. "You don't think that's the answer."

He studied her a moment. "Giving you my blood was a dangerous thing."

"Tell me what's bothering you."

He shifted restlessly. "If they were worried about the wizard, they wouldn't have felt the need to hide it from me. More than likely I would have been sent in to deal with the threat."

"And?"

"And the spell you were chanting was obviously intended to harm demons, not humans."

She reached out to touch his arm. She had told him of the demon attacking her, but she had forgotten to confess the wrenching agony that had drilled through her just moments before the spell had been brought to an end.

"Maybe not."

"What do you mean?"

"When I was in the middle of that spell, I felt . . . pain."

His brows snapped together, his fingers reaching out to touch her face as if needing to reassure himself that she was unharmed.

"What sort of pain?"

She grimaced. "Like someone was shoving a hot poker through me."

"The Phoenix?"

She tried to remember back, only to give a shrug. "I don't know. There was just pain, and then the demon hit me from behind and it was gone."

His frustration deepened as he turned to pace across the landing. "This makes no sense."

"After the past few days, you're going to have to be a little more specific," she said wryly.

"We still don't know what the witches were up to, who killed Selena, or what the bloody hell the wizard has to do with all this."

"You're saying we don't know squat."

His low growl made the hair on the back of her neck prickle. "There's a connection. We just have to figure it out." Reaching out, he took her hand and pulled her down the hall. "We need to find those damn witches."

Chapter 20

They moved swiftly through the darkened house, only pausing when they reached the hall where Selena had hidden her safe.

Dante was intent on the scents that filled the air when he felt Abby dig in her heels. He turned to discover her peering uneasily through the shadows.

"You're sure the wizard is gone?" she demanded.

"One way to find out," he whispered directly in her ear. "You go first."

She rolled her eyes. "Very funny."

"If the wizard was near, we would hear him screaming for mercy," he assured her. "Viper doesn't screw around when he's on the hunt."

She sent him a knowing gaze. "Then what is bothering you?"

Dante gave rueful grimace. This mate thing was going to take a bit of getting used to.

"I smell something strange."

"It's not me is it?"

His lips quirked. "No."

"The demon?"

"No. The smell is human, although strangely masked."

Abby peered down the hall and oddly stiffened before stabbing him a glittering glare.

"What's with all the charred marks on the wall?"

He shrugged. "The house exploded, lover. There are a lot of charred marks."

"They weren't here earlier." Her hands landed on her hips. "The wizard did that when you were fighting, didn't he?"

"Abby, the wizard is no longer our concern. Viper will deal with him."

"The point is that you told me you had a minor disagreement."

"No one died," he pointed out in perfectly reasonable tones, flicking a glance over the unmistakable damage. His gaze lingered on the singed carpet before his teeth snapped together. "Damn."

"What is it?"

"The spell books are gone."

"The wizard?"

Dante gave a shake of his head. The wizard had shown no interest in the books.

"More likely the demon returned to retrieve them. Along with a witch."

"They were here and we missed them?"

Dante brooded for a long moment. Dammit, he hated this feeling he was stumbling about like an idiot. Especially when he feared he was putting Abby's life in danger.

"It was a foolish risk," he growled. "They must have known the dark wizard was near."

"They must really have wanted those books."

"Yes."

Abby abruptly grasped his arm. "Oh . . ."

"What?"

"Do you think they wanted the books enough to kill for them?"

Dante shrugged. "The witches would not hesitate to kill if they thought someone stood in their path. They are utterly ruthless."

"Even Selena?"

Dante frowned. "Selena?"

"Maybe they wanted the books and she wasn't in the mood to hand them over."

The memory of Selena's secretive manner flashed through his mind. The woman was certainly arrogant enough to be dabbling in magic the witches would have forbidden. Or even to seek powers that would have given her control of the coven.

But even as he considered the notion of a battle between the witches and Selena, he was giving a shake of his head.

"No. Selena was the Chalice. They would never put the Phoenix in danger. Protecting the spirit is their entire purpose in life."

Abby grimaced. "Oh. Just a thought."

"A very clever thought."

Her eyes narrowed. "Are you patronizing me?"

"Why would I wish to patronize you?" he demanded in startled curiosity.

"I know I'm not overly bright, but I'm not stupid."

Dante regarded her in astonishment. Devil spit, but she was the most baffling woman. "Of course you're not stupid. I always found it astonishing that such an intelligent woman would be content to work as a minion for someone like Selena when you could so obviously do better."

Her eyes darkened, almost as if she was relieved.

"It paid the bills. Trust me, it wasn't as bad as some places I've worked."

Taking her hand, he led her down the hall to the back staircase. The trail of the demon was growing ever fainter, and he had no intention of losing it.

At the moment it was their one and only lead to the coven.

"You could do anything with your life. Be anything," he told her softly.

Struggling to keep up with his long strides, she gave a short, humorless laugh.

"How? My father and brothers abandoned me when I was still a child, and my mother never left the couch until she drank herself into a grave when I was seventeen." He felt her shudder as she dredged up painful memories of her past. "I dropped out of school and got a job so I wouldn't be shuffled off to some foster home. I'm lucky I didn't end up walking the streets."

With one smooth motion, he reached down to scoop her in his arms and cradled her to his chest. Her fierce, relentless nature made him forget she possessed a human lack of endurance even with the additional power of the Phoenix. And God knew she was too stubborn to confess she might need to rest.

The fact that she didn't so much as mutter a protest at him taking matters into his own hands told him just how weary she must be.

Taking the stairs in a fluid bound, he studied her too-pale face.

"You would have never walked the streets. You have too much courage and power for such a fate."

Her features hardened. "It takes more than courage to survive."

In the blink of an eye, he was out of the house and swiftly moving down a back path.

"You need no longer fear. I will always be here."

"Not fear? A high school dropout who can't pay her rent is expected to save the world. How scary is that?"

"The world is in very good hands."

Her head rested against his chest as she gave a wry laugh. "You're demented."

He risked a glance downward as they left the estate, and he slowed to a more cautious pace. Even tired and rumpled as she was, he had never seen a more beautiful woman.

"What would you do if anything was possible?"

There was no hesitation. "Travel."

"Travel where?"

"Anywhere. Everywhere."

He paused at the road, sniffing the air until he caught the scent of the demon traveling away from the city.

"Very ambitious."

She snuggled closer, creating an aching heat that clenched the muscles of his thighs and an assortment of other pleasurable parts of his body.

"When I was little and my dad would come home in a drunken fury, I used to hide under my bed with an old globe that a teacher had given me," she murmured. "I would close my eyes and point at a spot, and then I'd imagine I was on a boat traveling there. In my mind I have been all over the world."

A sharp pain raced through him. This woman had been betrayed by those who should have protected and loved her. She had battled monsters in her own home and then been thrown into the world with no one to stand at her side.

But now that was all done.

She belonged to him.

He would devote his life, or even his death if necessary, to making sure she was never hurt or lonely or afraid again.

"Someday you will go," he swore softly. "I promise."

Her arms wrapped about his neck, almost as if she sensed his dark determination to do whatever necessary to keep her safe.

"*We* will go. After all, you owe me a honeymoon."

"Honeymoon. I like the sound of that." Without thinking, he reached out with his thoughts to gently stroke her face.

Her eyes widened in shock. "What did you just do?"

His lips twitched as he deliberately shifted his thoughts to cup her firm breast.

"You mean this?"

"I can feel you touch me. How can you do that?"

"You're my mate."

"But . . ." She gasped as he teased her nipple to a hard point. "Stop that."

"You don't like it?"

"Can I do that to you?"

"Not unless I take your blood."

Her gaze narrowed. "That's not fair."

He chuckled as he bent to press a kiss to her lips.

"Life is never fair, lover."

"Tell me about it," she groused, her gaze scanning the darkness about them. "Are we following the trail of the demon?"

"For now."

She turned her head to regard him with a frown. "You're worried."

He sniffed the air. The worrisome smell of blood

had been growing stronger. Now the ground seemed to reek of it.

"The Shalott has been injured."

"Viper?" she demanded.

"He is on the trail of the wizard."

Her breath caught. "The witches?"

"They may have punished her."

"Why?"

"You slipped through her clutches."

He slowly lowered her to her feet. A vague sense of menace was crawling over his skin. He couldn't yet pinpoint the source of unease, but he wanted to be able to strike swiftly.

Abby shifted close, no doubt feeling his own prickling alert. "You think she was sent to get me?"

"I think it's a possibility."

"Then why didn't she?"

Dante shrugged. At the moment all he could do was speculate.

"If she is in the power of the witches, it's not by choice. Shalott's are independent, fierce creatures, and she would struggle against her commands whenever she was able."

"Like you."

He smiled wryly. "Yes."

There was a moment of silence before Abby shifted to stand directly before him.

"We must rescue her."

"A demon?" he demanded in surprise.

"She could have killed both of us. Or at the very least taken me away while you were unconscious. I think we owe her."

He allowed his hand to drift over her tumbled curls. "If it is possible, we will release her. First we must find her."

* * *

Viper allowed the man to drop to the ground and licked his fangs clean. He had no real taste for wizard-wannabes, but the guard had to be eliminated, and he hated to waste perfectly good blood.

Not that the man had been much of a guard. A smile twisted Viper's lips. Despite the small medallion that had proclaimed the man a disciple of the Prince, he had been no match for Viper's strength. The battle had done nothing more than whet his appetite.

With a flick of his hand, he used his powers to sink the inert body into the ground. The fresh blood that coursed through his body elevated his strength and stirred the dark predator within. He was on the hunt, and he would kill anything in his path.

Sliding through the graveyard, he entered the large crypt and easily found the entrance to the tunnels beneath. He paused to sniff the air.

He could smell humans. And a handful of lesser demons who were willing to serve mortals in exchange for protection. Nothing that could prove a danger to him.

Nothing beyond the wizard.

Melting among the shadows, he slowly traveled down the steps. Although he was always confident, Viper wasn't stupid. A vampire did not live as many centuries as he had by blundering into danger.

If the wizard was tapping into the power of the dark lord, he would be a formidable enemy. It would take as much cunning as skill to best him.

A perfect means to spend the evening, he acknowledged with a cold smile.

He passed two more guards on his way to the inner sanctuary. On both occasions he killed with silent efficiency and moved forward without missing a step. The few demons he sensed were wise enough to scurry away before he could cross their paths.

With deadly speed he was at the entrance to the lowest chamber. He halted to carefully study the room before him.

It was a large room, but barren with a large brazier set in the center of the stone floor. Before the burning fire, a tall man knelt in obvious worship. The wizard. And in his hand he held a leather whip that he lashed against his own back in a steady rhythm.

Viper curled his lip in disdain.

He had encountered any number of humans who had willingly traded their souls to the dark lord. For power, for immortality, for their love of evil. They became willing servants who would sacrifice anything and anyone to please their vicious master.

Even themselves.

Pathetic creatures.

But dangerous, he reminded himself.

Very dangerous.

Despite the distance, he easily sensed the ancient force that radiated throughout the room. The sorcerer was obviously a favorite of the Prince and allowed to draw deeply upon his power.

It was little wonder he had proven to be such a nuisance to Dante.

Allowing his fangs to run out, Viper flexed his fingers and flowed into the shadows of the chamber.

"Fee Fie Foe Fum, I smell the blood of a . . . not

Englishman." He paused as he sniffed the air and gave a shudder. "Ah, a Saxon. A pity. The last Saxon I devoured made me ill for days. Filthy beast."

Scrambling to his feet, the wizard clutched the heavy medallion about his neck and scanned the room for the unexpected intruder.

A futile effort. Viper wouldn't be seen until he wanted to be seen.

"Cooper. Johnson." The man's voice held an unmistakable rasp as he called for his guards. Well, at least he was smart enough to be afraid. "Breckett."

"Dead, dead, and dead, I fear," Viper purred in cold tones.

The man gave a low growl as he backed close to the flames. "Show yourself, vampire."

"Later, perhaps. If you are very good."

"Coward."

Viper laughed as he drifted through the shadows. "I am intrigued. Why would an all-powerful wizard be hiding in these dark caves beating himself senseless? Are you the sort to delight in self-flagellation?" He paused as he easily read the dark, tangled thoughts that the wizard couldn't hide. "No, you prefer inflicting pain on others. It must be atonement for the dark lord."

"I have no business with you. Leave now and I will not try to halt you."

"But I have business with you."

"Do you think to challenge me?"

"No, I think to kill you."

"Fool." The wizard snarled. "You shall burn upon the Prince's altar."

"Actually, you shall be the one to burn. But not until we've had a little chat. Have a seat." Lifting his hand, Viper moved forward, forcing the wizard to his knees with the power of his glamour. He would not be capable of holding the man for any length of time. But he intended to have his questions answered before he took pleasure in the kill. "Now, tell me what you know of the witches."

Chapter 21

A shiver raced through Abby as she hovered close to Dante.

She seemed to be doing a lot of that lately.

Both the shivering and the hovering.

And standing in the dark wondering what the hell had happened to her life.

A week ago she would have already been in her cramped apartment tucked into her cramped bed.

She wouldn't have known about all the bad things that went bump in the night, or feared that she was about to become a roasted sacrifice for some nasty deity.

Her gaze slid upward to linger upon the tense, perfect profile of the vampire next to her.

Her heart gave a sudden jolt. She might have been safely tucked in her bed, but she would have been alone. And miserable.

Whatever happened, no matter how many beasts and demons and witches crossed her path, she would not regret the events that had led to this moment. Having Dante near her was worth any cost.

Even as the knowledge settled deep inside Abby, Dante stirred with a restless motion, and she sensed a surge of frustration ripple through him.

Her hand reached out to touch his arm.

"What do you sense?"

"The demon is near."

"How near?"

He flashed a wry smile. "Abby, I'm not a GPS. I can only say that she is close."

"Then the witches must be close."

"Yes."

Abby felt faintly nauseous. A sensation that was triggered each time she thought of the women who she had seen in her dream.

Women who would hold her life, as well as that of Dante, in their hands.

"Do we start searching houses?"

Dante angled his head and sniffed the air. She didn't know what he could smell, but he gave a sharp shake of his head.

"I don't want to blunder in blindly. I prefer to have some idea of what we're going to be facing."

"I could—"

"No."

Abby stiffened at his sharp tone. It wasn't that she particularly wanted to creep through the dark alone. Hell, she'd rather shove a fork in her eye. But she didn't take commands well. Never had, never would.

"Well, I'm not standing here in the dark all night," she informed him sharply. "I'm tired, I'm hungry, and my mood is taking a turn toward pissy."

He cocked a brow. "I'd say the turn has already been made."

"Dante."

His arm fell across her shoulders. "There is more than one means of discovering the witches."

"And they would be?"

He led her from the quiet back street toward the bustling thoroughfare just a block away.

"Trust me."

She rolled her eyes at the familiar words. "Can't you at least tell me where we're going?"

"You will see."

He turned the corner, and they walked past elegant restaurants with their discreet awnings and closed shops that didn't put price tags on their items.

The sort of neighborhood where women like her were followed by store security.

She wrinkled her nose as she found herself being relentlessly towed toward a sidewalk coffee shop that was still bustling with preps and corporate executives.

"I'm starting to rethink this whole mate thing."

"Really, lover, you should have more faith in me."

"I do, it's just . . ."

"Just what?"

Abby came to a sudden halt to meet his gaze squarely.

"I'm afraid," she abruptly admitted.

His arm pulled her close, his lips feathering over the top of her head.

"I won't let anything happen to you, Abby. You have my promise."

"But what of you?"

"I'm fairly fond of me as well. I intend to take great care."

She pulled back with a frown. "We don't know what the witches will do."

"They will discover a new Chalice, and you will be free of the Phoenix."

"And you will be the guardian for a new woman."

His expression eased. "Ah . . . you're jealous."

"Maybe a little."

His fingers cupped her chin. "You are my mate. Even if I wanted to be with another woman, I couldn't."

"But I will be mortal again."

"Those are worries for later. For now we must concentrate upon ridding you of the Phoenix. Until we do, you will be in danger." His lips lingered a moment on her forehead before he was once again pulling her down the street, pausing before the large window of the bustling shop. "This should do."

She glanced over the customers, who were all thinner, richer, and prettier than her.

"What is this place?"

"A coffee shop."

"I can see that. Why are we here?"

"Because of that."

He pointed to a spot directly over the window. For a moment Abby could see nothing but the red bricks that made up the building. Then as the clouds shifted, she could make out the strange hieroglyphics that glowed in the moonlight.

"Graffiti?"

"It's a symbol that the owner is . . . nonhuman."

His arm lowered to point toward the window where a tall man weaved between the tables. Abby's eyes widened. Yowza.

She had never seen anything like him. Large and muscular with the build a professional wrestler would have envied, he was attired in a loose, green, sequined shirt and leopard-print pants that appeared to have been spray painted on him. Even more eye-catching was the long, brilliant red hair that flowed down his back like a river of fire.

He was an exotic butterfly who oozed a sensuality that was nearly palpable in the air.

"Let me guess. E. T.?" she husked.

Dante grimaced. "Imp."

It wouldn't have been her first guess. Or hundredth.

"Isn't he kinda big for an imp?" she demanded, frowning as he passed out of sight and then without warning popped into the air directly before her.

"Not just an imp, I am a prince among imps," he corrected in rich tones, performing an elaborate bow. "Troy, at your service, and, sweet pea, big is most definitely better." He ran a hand down his stomach and then cupped himself with a seductive smile. "Of course, I don't expect you to take my word for it. I'm quite willing to display my goods if you want. I have the most darling room upstairs where you can taste my wares in private."

"That won't be necessary." Dante's voice sliced through the air with all the warmth of a snowball in Antarctica.

Turning about, the imp surveyed Dante with open appreciation. Obviously he was an imp with a varying range of taste.

"Well, hellooooooo. Preindustrial meat—just how I like it."

"Can we speak?"

The imp stepped closer with a lick of his lips. "I have better things we could be doing."

Dante didn't so much as blink. "This is important."

"Nummy." Running a hand down Dante's arm,

the imp leaned forward to give him a deep sniff. Suddenly the creature stiffened, and, pulling back, he offered them both an offended glare. "You've mated. Go away."

Abby was torn between disbelief and amusement. This was no mischievous sprite dancing about a garden or playing naughty tricks on the unwary. Still, there was something bizarrely fascinating about Troy, Prince of Imps.

There was no amusement in Dante. He was annoyed, pure and simple.

"This will only take a few moments." Dante pulled his watch off his wrist and held it out so the gold could glitter in the streetlight.

The imp's nose actually seemed to twitch as he leaned forward to study the expensive watch.

At last he straightened and waved a large hand toward the nearby alley.

"Go around back. There's a door that leads to the private rooms."

He disappeared as easily as he had appeared, but Abby had no opportunity to appreciate the startling trick as Dante gathered her hand and pulled her through the shadows to the back of the building.

"So what's with imps?" she demanded.

He gave a snort of distaste. "They're flighty, unreliable creatures who delight in pleasures of the flesh and, of course, creating chaos."

"And this one runs a coffeehouse?"

He shrugged. "Imps can pass as human when they want and are astonishingly very good at business."

"And we're here because . . . ?"

"Any demons in the neighborhood will gather here to share information."

Abby shuddered. Good Lord, the demons had

infiltrated the high-rent suburbs? What next? The White House?

Oh no. Don't even think about it, Abby, she sternly told herself.

"Dante, do you think it's entirely wise to spend any more time with demons while they consider me some sort of Holy Grail?"

"There are no other demons inside," he assured her. "I merely want to speak with the imp. He will have heard any rumors floating about."

"You're saying the demons come here to drink coffee and gossip?"

"That's one way to put it. If there are witches in the area, they will be keeping an eye on them." He halted to push open the door. He paused a moment to carefully scan the room before pulling her over the threshold and closing the door.

With a flick of his hand, the muted lights glowed to life and Abby gave a strangled gasp.

"Wow," she breathed, her gaze skimming over the vast room. She had never seen so much red velvet and lacquer gathered in one place.

Clearly demons had a taste for the lush and opulent.

Touching her arm, Dante flashed a warning frown. "Don't touch anything."

"Why?"

"Imps tend to have a few of their objects enchanted. One touch and you will find yourself compelled to return to this coffee shop over and over."

She wrinkled her nose. "No wonder they're such good businessmen."

"It doesn't hurt."

Less than a beat passed before Troy sashayed into the room, imperiously holding his hand out. Dante obligingly dropped his watch into the open palm, and the imp held it up to inspect it with an expert eye.

"Let me see. Gold . . . real. Diamonds . . . real. A small scratch on the crystal." He pursed his lips and dropped the watch into the pocket of his shirt. "I can give you half an hour. Will you have a seat? Some coffee?"

Dante gave Abby's arm a warning squeeze before he was offering a smooth shake of his head.

"Nothing, thank you. This won't take long."

Troy tossed back his fiery mane of hair. "What can I do for you?"

"We're looking for witches."

The emerald gaze shifted to Abby. "Ah. You desire a potion or perhaps a hex? I have a friend who I promise will not disappoint."

Dante answered, "These witches will be living in a coven, and they won't dabble in potions. They have power. A great deal of power."

The too-pretty features abruptly pinched into an expression of distaste. "Oh . . . those witches."

Dante took a step forward. "You know of them?"

"They arrived a few days ago. The worth of real estate has been plummeting ever since."

Abby blinked in confusion. "Real estate?"

"The demons are uneasy. These witches are not like others. They do not worship the beauty and glory of Mother Earth. They call their powers from the blood sacrifice. Already there have been several Sespi sprites who have simply disappeared."

Blood sacrifice? Abby bit her lower lip. That didn't sound good.

In fact, she was becoming more and more convinced that seeking out these witches was a very bad idea.

If Dante was shocked, he didn't show it. His alabaster face might have been carved from marble.

"What do you know of them?" he demanded.

"Their house is the large Victorian monstrosity at the end of Iris Avenue."

"How many?"

"Ten."

"Is the house guarded?"

The imp grimaced. "Well guarded. They have a tame Shalott that protects the grounds."

"Yeah, we've met," Abby muttered.

Dante took a moment to consider. "Any binding spells?"

"Not that anyone has detected."

"They must be conserving their strength," he murmured.

Troy moved forward, a smile on his lips and a wicked glint in his eyes as he lightly touched Dante's hair. "I do hope they are on your dinner plans, beautiful. They are beginning to affect business."

Dante smiled coldly. "For now I just want to speak with them."

"Pity." The imp heaved a dramatic sigh and moved toward Abby. He stroked her hair as he did Dante's. Then slowly he bent forward to sniff at her neck. Abby forced herself to remain still. The Prince of Imps seemed harmless, but he was large enough to crush her with one hand. "What is that smell? There is something within you . . ."

"That's all we needed." With a smooth motion, Dante was stepping between Abby and the imp, his entire body humming with danger. "Thank you for your time."

The emerald eyes narrowed, but with a sardonic smile the imp was performing a deep bow.

"The pleasure was all mine." He glanced over Dante's shoulder to stab Abby with a knowing smile. "Still, I think it best you not return. My establishment possesses a few minor spells to dampen the more feral tendencies of my customers, but I don't think anything could halt bloodshed if they caught scent of you, my precious."

"We won't be back," Dante promised, hustling Abby from the room and into the back alley. Once the door was shut, he peered into the shadows. "Well, we have the information we wanted. Now what the hell do we do with it?"

The cellar was straight off the set of a horror film.

The floor was packed dirt and littered with the droppings of mice and rats. The worn stone walls were damp with a slick layer of mold. Even the air was heavy and filled with a dark sense of menace.

It combined to create an atmosphere that would send most people fleeing in terror. But Edra was made of sterner stuff.

She had no love for the shadows, but she was willing to use them for her own purpose. And after centuries of battling the darkness, she had at last accepted that only by directly confronting evil could she put an end to it once and for all.

Setting her candle on the large altar she had commanded built after being forced to flee the secret coven outside the city, she reached into the pocket of her robe and pulled out a small amulet.

The darkness seemed to deepen, and the candle flickered. A bone-chilling cold crept through the air.

Edra smiled. So much power.

Enough power to alter the world.

The soft scrape of the door was the only warning that someone approached. With controlled haste, Edra slipped the amulet in her pocket and muttered a few words beneath her breath.

The few remaining witches could barely conjure a binding spell let alone be sensitive enough to the dark aura that clung to the amulet. Still, she wasn't about to take any risks. Not now.

Not when she was so close to success she could taste it.

With a groan, she forced her stiff joints to kneel before the altar and bent her head in prayer. It was not until she could sense the woman halt at her side that she at last lifted her head.

The intruder was thin with lank brown hair. She no doubt had a name, but Edra had never bothered to learn it. Most of those she had once loved were now dead and gone. The lesser witches in the coven were merely necessary inconveniences.

"The demon lives?"

"It lives, but her wounds are grievous," the woman reported with a frown. "Sally was forced to heal her."

"She shouldn't have bothered. Soon enough we will have no need of the creature." Edra didn't miss the annoyance that flashed through the dark eyes, and she rose to her feet. Deliberately she allowed her power to fill the room. There were times when her underlings needed to be reminded that beneath her aging frailty was a will that would destroy without mercy. "You have something to say?"

The witch momentarily faltered before she was squaring her shoulders.

"You have promised for the past year we would be rid of the demons, but we are no closer to achieving our goals, and now too many of us are dead."

"It was not my fault that Selena became greedy and used the spell books before I could assist her or that the wizard attacked without warning," she snapped in annoyance.

"We should have been better prepared."

Edra's hand dipped into her pocket to finger the amulet. "Are you suggesting that I failed?"

"I suggest that we became complacent."

"And you wish to challenge my authority?"

Perhaps sensing her imminent death, the witch took a hasty step back.

"No. I simply want to pull back and gather our strength. To continue with the plan while we are so weak is madness."

"Impossible. All the signs are in alignment. We must strike while we can."

"But we don't even know where the Phoenix is. The Shalott failed us."

A flare of anger raced through the ancient witch before she fiercely thrust it aside. She could not be distracted. Not now.

A cold smile touched her lips. "The Chalice is close. Even now she seeks us out."

The younger witch blinked in surprise. "You feel her?"

"Yes." A shiver of anticipation raced through her body. "Prepare the sacrifice. Our time is coming."

"But—"

"Do not make me repeat myself," Edra warned in a lethal voice. "Prepare the sacrifice."

Not entirely stupid, the younger woman was hastily backing toward the stairs. "Yes, mistress."

Dismissing her companion with a wave of her

hand, Edra concentrated upon the vague awareness that was becoming steadier with every passing
moment.

At last.

Despite all the grim setbacks. Despite the deaths.
Despite the failure of her underlings. Her dream
was about to become a reality.

"Come to me," she whispered softly.

Chapter 22

"This is it."

Squatting beside Dante in the overgrown hedges, Abby studied the house.

Set well away from the street and nearly hidden behind the hedges, it was an aging Victorian structure. Although *aging* seemed too kind a description. Crumbling to dust was more accurate.

Even in the shadows it was easy to spot the peeling paint and sagging porch. If Norman Bates needed a vacation home, she had just found if for him. Abby gave a shake of her head. Holy freaking cow. The only surprise would be if there wasn't a dead mother hidden in the bedroom and a homicidal maniac prowling the grounds.

"Yow," she breathed. "That's . . . spooky."

Dante was in full predator mode. With uncanny ease, he melted into the shadows and held himself motionless. There was none of her fidgeting, no muttered complaints of the hedge poking into his back. Hell, there wasn't even any tedious breathing to stir the air.

If she wasn't vibrantly aware of the tension coiled

within him, she might have thought he had been turned to stone.

Shifting slightly, she closely studied the alabaster features that were almost unrecognizable. This was not the tender lover or roguish pirate. This was the warrior vampire who still sent a tingle of unease down her spine.

Feeling her gaze, he turned to stab her with his silver gaze.

"Do you sense anything?"

"Yes." She absently rubbed her arms. The prickles racing over her skin had started the moment she had stepped onto the grounds of the house. "I just don't know what it is."

"Tell me." His voice was a whisper of velvet.

"It's like I can almost hear whispers in the back of my mind. I can't make out the words, but I know they're there."

"The witches?"

"That would be my guess." Her breath caught as the white fangs ran out and his hands curled to claws. The demon was in full force. "What was that?"

"What?"

"Did you just growl?"

"I don't like this." His gaze returned to the house, his tone flat. "It's too quiet."

"Hardly surprising they might want to keep a low profile after being attacked by the wizard. They're not likely to be having a party."

"And yet they have no spells to guard the house."

"What of the Shalott?"

He sniffed the air. "It must be within. Or dead."

Abby shivered. Or dead . . .

Those weren't exactly words to bolster a girl's confidence.

She licked her dry lips.

"Then I suppose there's nothing to stop us, right?"

He slowly turned back to her, his expression grim. "There is one thing."

Her head dropped into her hands as she heaved out a rasping sigh. "I knew it. I just knew it. What is this thing?"

"This is a private home."

"And?"

"And I can't enter without an invitation."

She jerked her head up. "You're kidding me?"

"No."

"You don't live in a crypt and you can't turn into a bat, but you have to have an invitation to enter a house?" Abby hissed.

A reluctant amusement softened the flat eyes. "You wanted me to be vampirish."

"Not when it's inconvenient."

"Sorry."

She wrinkled her nose, realizing just how ridiculous she was being. "No, this is for the best," she forced herself to say. "Until we know what's going to happen, I would rather you stay away from the witches."

He didn't so much as flick an eyelash, but Abby sensed his flare of anger. Great, just great. She had managed to rub against his vampire pride. A certain means to ensure he would bull his way headfirst into the nearest danger.

Sometimes her stupidity amazed even herself.

"You want me to hide in the bushes?"

"Dante, it only makes sense to split up," she

attempted to undue her unwitting damage. "I need you to be able to rescue me if I need help."

"I'm not letting you go in there alone."

She reached out to touch his arm. It was as cold and unyielding as granite.

"We don't have much choice."

His fangs flashed in the moonlight. Not the most reassuring of sights.

"The witches know you're here. They'll eventually come out to find you."

That wasn't reassuring either.

Especially if Dante was forced to retreat before the witches decided to make an appearance. She would rather go in now and know she had backup.

"We don't have that long. Dawn will be coming soon."

"Then we'll come back tomorrow night."

"Dante. I think—"

With a blurring speed, Dante had pinned her to his chest, the air shimmering and snapping about him.

"Dammit, Abby, I can't let you go in there," he rasped.

If she had a lick of sense, she would have been terrified. Mate or not, this man could crush her without effort. Or worse, rip out her throat.

But it was annoyance that stiffened her spine and brought a frown to her brow.

"I promise I won't take any risks. I will meet with the witches and—"

"No."

"Listen, Mr. Macho, I make my own decisions."

The arrogant nose flared. "Not on this."

Her teeth snapped together. "This argument is starting to get old, Dante. I'm not a child. To be honest, I don't think I was ever a child. I won't be dictated to, not by you or anyone else."

He studied her flushed features with a steady gaze. "If you die, I die," he said simply.

The wind was sucked efficiently from her sails.

She searched his hard features. "You will die because I'm your mate?"

"Because you're the reason I exist."

"Oh." Abby set back on her heels, stunned by the stark beauty of his words.

It was hard to remain all prickly and independent when he was making her heart melt.

Damn him.

"Dante—"

His finger touched her lips to halt her stumbling words, his head turning toward the unkempt yard that surrounded the house.

"Someone is approaching," he whispered directly in her ear.

Her fingers tightened on his arm as a sharp fear pierced her heart. This was why she was here, of course, but that didn't ease the chill that clutched at her stomach.

These women were not the local garden club. They weren't going to invite her in for crumpets and tea.

They were powerful witches who could chain a vampire with their spell and control an ancient spirit that kept the world safe from demons.

She would be a fool to underestimate them.

Ignoring the weakness in her knees, Abby forced herself upright. If nothing else, she would face whatever was coming on her feet. She didn't hear Dante move, but she knew he was standing directly behind her.

Within moments, a thin, narrow-faced woman appeared from the shadows. Halting before Abby, she astonishingly bent in a deep bow.

"My lady, you have arrived at last," she stated the obvious in somber tones.

Abby glanced at Dante over her shoulder. "My lady?"

"Selena never got over being a noblewoman. Obviously you inherited her title."

"I wish that was all I inherited," she muttered.

The witch cleared her throat, blatantly ignoring the vampire who stood only a handful of steps away.

"If you will you come with me, my lady? The mistress is waiting for you."

My lady? Mistress?

The woman must have spent her summers working at the local Renaissance Fair.

Abby squared her shoulders. "Only if Dante is invited as well."

The thin face briefly hardened with distaste. "Of course. The protector must accompany the Chalice. This way."

Turning, the woman headed back toward the dark house. So this was it. Abby pressed a hand to her quivering stomach.

Without a sound, Dante was standing directly before her. "You're ready?" he demanded.

For a moment she allowed her gaze to rest upon his impossibly beautiful features. Surely nothing horrible could happen as long as he was near?

"As ready as I can be," she retorted with a grimace.

"Don't let down your guard," he warned. "And stay close to me."

"I think I'm going to throw up."

He took a deliberate step backward. "Then that staying-close thing was more of a metaphor."

Grudgingly her lips twitched at his teasing. She knew he was attempting to ease the terrible tension that clutched at her.

"Love is supposed to be for better or worse."

He lifted his brows. "Love only goes so far."

"Thanks."

His hands framed her face with gentle care. "You can do this, lover."

Sucking in a deep breath, Abby gave a slow nod of her head. "Yes."

The silver eyes flared. "Then let's go make you human again."

Viper carefully adjusted his lace cuffs before returning his attention to the wizard huddled in the corner. The smell of blood was thick in the air. The wizard might be ancient, but he bled like any human when his head connected with the stone wall.

Unfortunately, despite the delicious scent, he felt no urge to drain the pathetic creature. The wizard's worship of the dark lord made his blood as tainted as his black soul.

Viper gave a flick of his hand as the wizard attempted a feeble ensnaring spell. The man had already been weak from his encounter with Dante. And oddly his few attempts to call upon his darker powers had been unsuccessful. Viper could only presume the Prince was not pleased with his disciple.

He had been no match for an ancient vampire.

"I think what we have here is a failure to communicate," Viper mocked as he regarded the pasty features.

"Go to hell," the wizard croaked.

"Eventually, no doubt." Viper heaved a sigh. "I did hope to do this without undue violence. This is, after all, my favorite jacket, and getting brain tissue out of velvet is a bitch. Still, the pleasure of killing will be worth the effort."

The once-proud man cringed in fear. "You're a vampire. Why do you care what happens to the witches?"

"Oh, I have no love for the hags. They can rot in hell for all I care. My only interest is for the welfare of my clansman. You seriously miscalculated when you attacked Dante."

"He is a pawn of the she-devils."

"Wrong answer." Faster than the mortal eye could follow, Viper slashed a deep cut in the man's cheek.

The wizard cried out, his eyes wide with terror. "If you kill me, then you will die."

"You believe your god will avenge the death of a pathetic sycophant like you?" Viper curled his lips into a sneer. "He's more likely to send me a fruit basket."

The man held up a hand of surrender. "You must listen. It's the witches."

"What about them?"

"They intend to murder you."

Viper narrowed his gaze. He had no trust for the human. Such a man would sell his soul if he still owned it to save his hide. But Viper could smell the sour desperation that oozed from his sweat. The wizard truly believed the witches were a danger.

"The witches intend to murder me? Why?"

"They want us dead. All of us."

Slowly crouching down, Viper reached out to

grasp the man by his throat. At the first hint of a lie, he would put an end to the miserable worm.

"Tell me."

Dante smoldered with violence as he grudgingly followed the witch leading them through the shadowed house. They had barely crossed the threshold when the familiar scent of brewing spells, drying herbs, and darker, less palatable odors clenched at his stomach.

It was a stench he knew all too well.

The witches were preparing a sacrifice.

He intended to ensure that the sacrifice didn't include Abby or himself.

No matter who or what he had to kill.

Staying close behind Abby, his senses swept the shadows. If you knew you were walking into a trap, was it still a trap?

Something to consider.

The rooms were large and empty with vaulted ceilings that gave the impression of space. The air, however, was close and thick with a cloaking heat that pressed uncomfortably on Dante. In his mind, it reeked of dusty cellars and prison walls.

Reaching what once must have been the formal drawing room, the witch paused at the doorway.

"Mistress, I have brought the Chalice," she said in reverent tones.

There was a rustle in the darkness and a low chant before the softness of candlelight chased away the gloom.

With stiff movements, a small, almost frail woman lifted herself from a chair. At a glance she might have been a sweet old grandmother with her fluff of gray hair and lined face. It was only when one noticed the hard brown eyes that the cold, relentless power became obvious.

Managing a tight-lipped smile, the old witch halted before Abby. "My lady. And the guardian." The hard gaze flicked over Dante before the woman waved a hand toward the cavernous room. "Come in and be welcome."

Dante felt Abby's hesitation before she was cautiously moving to take a seat on a leather chair beside the empty fireplace. Dante stood behind her, his body tense and ready to strike.

Just for a moment the unrelenting gaze of Edra weighed his protective stance, as if judging whether or not he would prove to be a hindrance to her plans.

Whatever she decided was not visible on the ancient face. But since he was still standing, he presumed she had concluded he was no threat.

For the moment.

In the blink of an eye, her attention returned to Abby's pale face.

"We have not yet been introduced, although I feel as if we are intimately acquainted. I am Edra." Her gaze narrowed. "And you are?"

"Abby Barlow."

"Ah, the servant," she murmured. "I should have realized you would be the only one near enough to have taken the Phoenix."

"I didn't mean to," Abby assured the woman dryly. "If I had realized what was going to happen, I would have run screaming in the opposite direction."

"Quite understandable." Something that was no doubt supposed to be sympathy touched the lined face. "You look exhausted, my dear. May I get you some wine?"

Abby nervously cleared her throat. "No, thank you."

"Very well." There was a short, thick silence. "You are well? You have had no difficulty in carrying the Phoenix?"

"Beyond being chased by every demon and dark wizard in Chicago?"

A gnarled hand waved in an imperious motion. "I mean physically. There is no pain? No sickness?"

"My eyes have turned blue, and I have a tendency to light people on fire, but besides that I feel all right."

"That is a relief. Still . . ." The woman moved close to bend over the chair, ignoring Dante's low growl as she reached out to touch Abby's cheek. "Perhaps you will not mind if I take a moment to ensure the Phoenix is unharmed by . . . recent events?"

Abby shuddered beneath the woman's touch but didn't pull away. "If you must."

Edra closed her eyes as she murmured beneath her breath. Dante couldn't feel the magic, but he knew it was being woven. His hands clenched at his side. Bloody hell, he hated this.

"It is well, thank the blessed Goddess," the woman breathed. Then, without warning, she gave a sharp gasp and stumbled backward, her hand pressed to her heart. "Oh . . ."

Abby clutched the arms of the chair. "What?"

With an effort, the witch wrestled control of her composure. Her hand, however, remained an angry red.

The Phoenix had struck out at her.

What the hell did that mean?

"You possess a great deal of power. More than Selena." She narrowed her gaze before she gave a faint nod. "You shall do well."

Never stupid, Abby regarded the witch with tense suspicion. "Do well?"

"As the Chalice, of course."

The words were smooth, but Dante didn't believe them for a moment. His hand dropped to Abby's shoulder as he regarded the witch with a cold threat.

"We are here for you to remove the spirit."

The candles abruptly flared. A not-so-subtle warning of her sheathed power.

"Impossible," Edra snapped. "The Phoenix has already taken possession of her body."

"Then bloody well find another body," he growled.

Her gnarled hand lifted. "Careful, beast."

Violence hung in the air, and with a nervous motion, Abby was out of the chair.

"Look, I understand your concern, but there's no way I can be your . . . Chalice," she muttered in an obvious attempt to halt bloodshed. "I didn't ask for this, I was never trained, and quite frankly I'm sick of scary things trying to kill me."

Edra sent her a fleeting gaze, her attention remaining on Dante. "You're with us now. We will see to your training as well as keep you safe."

"As you did Selena?" Dante mocked.

"Selena brought on her own demise."

"How?"

"It is not your place to question what occurs among the coven," Edra snapped.

"But it's mine," Abby intruded again. "And I want to know what happened to Selena."

"We shall discuss Selena later."

Dante hid a smile at the imperious command in the witch's voice. It was custom-designed to set Abby's teeth on edge.

He was not disappointed as his mate narrowed her gaze and mentally dug in her heels.

"No. I want to know how she died."

Edra stiffened. The old witch was accustomed to commanding her underlings with an iron fist. Even Selena had grudgingly conceded to her authority.

Surprisingly, however, something that might have been wariness flickered over the lined face as the witch studied the younger woman.

"She attempted a spell well beyond her capabilities," she abruptly confessed.

"What sort of spell?" Abby pressed. "What did it do?"

"It . . . protected her from demons."

She was lying.

The knowledge hung thick in the air.

"I thought the Phoenix could protect itself," Abby challenged.

"Against most enemies."

"Did she fear being attacked?"

"It is always a fear." The lined face hardened with hatred. "The darkness hovers and awaits the opportunity to regain what it has lost. There are evil forces in the world that will halt at nothing to destroy us."

"Yeah, I've been introduced to a few of them," Abby muttered. "Which is why I want this . . . this thing out of me and into someone who knows what they're doing."

There was a tense pause before the witch reached out to pat Abby's arm in an awkward motion.

"We will consider what is best to be done, but first you will desire a short rest. I can sense your weariness."

The woman turned and headed for the door before Abby could argue. Dante moved faster.

In the blink of an eye, he was standing in the doorway, his fangs exposed.

"Abby will need her herbs."

Edra gave a blink of shock at his sudden appearance before an expression of regal disdain settled on her thin face.

"Of course."

"And I will need blood."

The disdain deepened. "It will be attended to."

Dante waited a long beat before stepping aside and allowing the witch to leave the room.

He hoped that she sensed just how fiercely he desired to kill her on the spot.

Chapter 23

Abby felt like a bottle of champagne that had been shaken until it threatened to burst.

She didn't know her nerves could be wound so tightly. Or that she could feel so cold in a room that was smothering.

Worse, she didn't know if it was being in the lair of the witches that was making her so unnerved or the sight of her lover standing in the doorway.

In the shadows, he might have been carved from the purest marble. There was no expression on the alabaster features. No flicker of life in the flat silver eyes. Not a muscle twitched in the tall, elegant body.

He might have been a beautiful mannequin if not for the fangs that glittered in the candlelight.

She at last cleared her throat. "Dante?"

There was not a flicker of an eyelash. "Yes?"

"You're looking a bit fangy. Are you all right?"

There was a long moment before a ripple raced through him and he slowly turned to meet her gaze.

"I don't like being here."

"Neither do I," she muttered, wrapping her arms about her waist. "It's smothering in here but I'm freezing. It doesn't make any sense."

His brows lowered. "Magic?"

Abby considered. She was hardly an expert. Hell, she wasn't even an amateur. More like a bumbling buffoon.

Still, she could feel something in the air. A sense of foreboding that tingled over her skin and clutched at her stomach.

"More like magic waiting to happen," she attempted to explain the odd sensation. "It's like an approaching thunderstorm. You can feel the electricity in the air before it ever hits."

"So what are they brewing?"

She shivered as she moved to stand directly before Dante. She had hoped that meeting the witches would ease her vague fears. Instead the urge to flee was more overwhelming than ever.

There was something . . . foul in the air.

A hint of rotting disease just below the surface.

"I don't know." She laid her hand on his arm. "Maybe we should just go, Dante."

"No." He covered her hand with his own. His expression was grim. "Not until you're safe."

"She didn't sound like she's overly eager to rid me of the Phoenix."

"If you convince her that you won't be jerked around like a puppet on a string, she will be forced to find a new Chalice. The coven considers the Phoenix as their own, and they won't lose control. Even if it means endangering the spirit."

"You mean just be myself?"

The barest hint of a smile touched his lips. "Exactly."

"And what of you?"

His expression became shuttered. "I can take care of myself."

Abby swallowed a sigh. It was his me-Neanderthal-and-I'll-be-stupid-if-I-want expression.

Vampires.

"Not if they leash you to a new Chalice. You will be at their mercy."

His shoulder lifted. "I am already at their mercy. It won't change much."

Her brows snapped together. "I want you freed."

"One thing at a time, lover." His hand lifted to cup her cheek. "First we must make sure Edra understands you are serious about ridding yourself of the Phoenix. I had hoped she would have already chosen another Chalice and would be eager to assist us. As it is . . ."

"What?"

His fangs snapped together. "She may look old and fragile, but she wields magic like a gladiator wields a sword, and she doesn't care who gets hurt when she takes a swing. We must be careful to convince her to release you without making her fear you might be an enemy."

"So you want me to stand up to the witch but not stand up to the point that she wants my head in the stewpot."

"Something like that."

She wrinkled her nose. "You don't ask much."

His expression was somber. "This is important, lover."

"I know." With a sigh she leaned against his solid body and snuggled close as his arms wrapped about her.

In the distance she could feel the prickling

tension of a brewing spell and could smell the herbs and nastier ingredients that lay thick in the air. The thick mess crawled over her skin.

But being held tightly in Dante's arms kept the hovering darkness at bay.

How was that for an oxymoron?

Abby didn't know how much time had passed, but eventually Dante was gently tugging her to the center of the room and turning to regard the woman who entered the doorway carrying a silver tray.

Abby blinked in shock as the stranger settled the tray on a low table and straightened with a flip of her blond hair.

Good Lord, she looked like she should be flunking algebra class and flirting with the football quarterback, not playing servant to a pack of witches.

Of course, age was not necessarily an indication of maturity, she reminded herself wryly. By the time she was eighteen, Abby had seen more of life than most women twice her age.

Pressing her hands together, the girl kept her gaze glued to Abby's face. It took a moment for Abby to realize that Dante was probably the first vampire the girl had ever encountered.

Or at least the first vampire she knew was a vampire.

"The mistress requested that I bring you refreshments," she at last managed to stammer.

In spite of herself, Abby felt a pang of sympathy for the girl. Whatever her reason for joining with the witches, it was clear she was not happy. It was etched in the tension of her too-thin body.

"Thank you," Abby said softly. "It was very kind of you."

Something that might have been surprise flickered through the dark eyes before she was offering a tentative smile and turning toward the door.

Before Abby even realized what was happening, Dante was suddenly standing before the girl. Abby's lips parted to protest. The last thing they needed was a newbie witch having hysterics in the drawing room.

Astonishingly, however, the woman didn't scream in horror. She didn't even squeak.

Instead her features became slack and her eyes glazed as if she had taken a blow to the head.

"Do you not want to stay?" Dante breathed so softly that Abby barely heard his words.

"I . . . there is much to be done . . . I must . . ." the girl began to stutter.

Dante pointed a hand at a nearby chair. "Sit."

With jerky motions, she sat.

Abby caught her breath and stepped forward. "Dante? What did you do?"

He crouched before the chair, his gaze never leaving the witch. "She is young and not yet trained to avoid being enthralled."

"What does that mean?"

"For the moment she is in my power."

Abby studied the woman, who was pleasantly lost in her catatonic state, as a cold chill inched down her spine.

"Holy crap."

"I did tell you that I could do this."

She swallowed heavily. "Knowing you can do it and actually seeing it done are two entirely different things."

"And now you are afraid?"

She took a long moment before giving a shake of

her head. She could sense the truth written on his heart.

"No."

"Good." His lips curled into a wicked smile. "I would never enthrall you, lover. I don't want a mindless toy; I want you. No matter how stubborn or ill-tempered you can be at times."

She couldn't halt her own smile. "You always say the nicest things."

Slowly he turned his attention back to the silent girl in the chair.

"Tell me your name," he demanded. His tone was low and flowing. A golden voice that seemed to shimmer in the air.

The girl leaned forward with an eager need to please the man holding her so easily captive.

"Kristy."

"Kristy, how long have you been with the coven?"

"Not long." Her brow wrinkled as if she feared she might disappoint the vampire. "Just a few weeks."

Dante's gaze remained firmly locked with the witch. "You know of the Phoenix?"

"Of course. It is the reason the coven exists. It is the salvation of us all."

Dante arched a brow. "Salvation?"

A fervent glow touched the young face. "With the beloved Goddess, we will bring an end to the darkness. The light will shine for an eternity."

Abby crept closer. She didn't understand what the girl was babbling about. Eternal light, banish the darkness, yadda yadda.

But she did sense Dante's sudden tension. And that was enough to send up the proverbial red flag.

Ignoring Abby's approach, Dante leaned until he was nearly nose-to-nose with the witch.

"How will you bring an end to the darkness?"

"There is a spell. A spell to bring an end to the demon world forever."

"It must be very powerful."

"Yes." The girl gave a shudder. "Only the most talented witch can hope to perform the ritual. It killed . . . the last one to try."

"Who was the last one to try, Kristy?" Dante's hands tightened on the arms of the chair. "Was it Selena who attempted to cast the spell?"

"I . . ."

"And that's what killed her?" His voice held a lethal edge.

Abby's breath caught. Her thoughts flashed back to Selena's broken body and then leaped to the spell books that they had discovered in the mansion.

Damn. She had opened the safe and revealed them. God, she had even attempted to use them.

Now they were gone. If something bad was going to happen, it would be her fault.

A distressed expression rippled over the youthful face. "I . . . I am not to say her name. She betrayed the coven and was punished as she should have been. The mistress forbade us to speak of her."

"Sssh. All is well." Dante eased the girl's worry. "Is Edra planning to attempt the spell?"

The girl's expression cleared in relief. A question she could answer.

"Yes, she will use the Phoenix to battle the dark lord and bring an end to demons."

The tension in Dante became almost painful. "What demons?"

"All demons." The witch smiled with a near-sickening joy. "At last the world will be pure."

Abby frowned, rubbing her arms as Dante's flare of fury charged through her.

"Bloody hell," he breathed.

With a jerky motion the witch rose to her feet. Something that might have been pain twisted her lips.

"She calls me. I must go."

Smoothly Dante was on his feet, his hands framing her face. "Kristy, is there anything else you want to tell me?"

Even Abby shivered as his power pulsed through the air.

"The blood has been tainted with silver," the witch whispered.

Abby gasped but Dante merely nodded his head. It was precisely what he had suspected.

"You will go to Edra. You will not remember speaking with me. You brought the tray into the room and left. Do you understand?" he murmured.

"I brought the tray in and left," she parroted.

"Very good." Dante stepped back. "Now go."

The witch was walking woodenly from the room. With a shake of her head, Abby held out a hand.

Good God, there were so many questions that had to be answered. She had to know what was going on.

"Wait . . ."

Dante grasped her shoulder and kept her from running after the disappearing form.

"Let her go, lover. Edra will become suspicious if she does not answer her summons."

Abby whirled to meet his steady gaze. "What did she mean?"

"Wholesale slaughter," he rasped. "I didn't think even Edra could be quite so bloodthirsty."

"Could the witches really kill all the demons?"

"They seem to think so."

Abby struggled to breathe. She couldn't count how many times she had been terrified out of her mind over the past few days. How many times she thought some nasty creature might rip her limb from limb. But as horrible as it had been, she had discovered that not all demons were monsters.

My God, Dante was a demon. And Viper. And the beautiful fairies. And Troy, the ridiculous Prince of Imps. And the Shalott who was tortured rather than handing her over to the witches.

She would do whatever necessary to put a halt to the genocide.

"Shit. We have to stop her," she muttered without a clue as to how to accomplish such a lofty goal.

Half-expecting Dante to charge from the room like a raging madman, she was startled when he merely regarded her with a searching gaze.

"Is that what you want? To stop her?"

"What?"

His fingers touched her cheek. "Abby, if we battle Edra, you might never be able to rid yourself of the Phoenix."

Her eyes widened at the low words. "You think I would sacrifice you? For any reason?"

He gave an elegant lift of his shoulder. "To rid the world of evil? That seems a rather noble goal."

She stepped toward him and grasped the front of his silk shirt in an angry grasp.

If she could have, she would have given him a good shake. As it was, all she could do was wrinkle the beautiful material.

"Evil doesn't belong to demons, Dante. Humans are just as capable of sin as any creature."

The silver gaze never wavered. "Most would consider us monsters."

"No. Not all demons are monsters—no more than all humans are saints." She gave a faint shudder. "Besides, I would never agree to such a massacre. No matter how good the intention, it would be wrong. Evil."

There was a beat as if he was seeking to determine the depths of her determination. At last he gave a short nod.

"We need to get out of here."

Abby breathed a husky sigh. "Thank God."

Shifting to take her hand, Dante headed for the door only to come to an abrupt halt.

"Damn." He tugged her back toward the center of the room, not halting until they reached the low table that held the untouched tray.

"What is it?"

"Someone is approaching."

Her heart lodged in her throat as she watched him pick up the poisoned glass of blood.

"What are you doing?"

"Allowing Edra to believe she has been rid of one enemy." Moving so swiftly he was impossible to follow, he dumped the blood out the window and returned to her side. Then, startlingly, he stretched out on the bare floor. "If the witches believe me dead, then I will have a better way of seeking a means of escape."

Abby bit her lip. She didn't like this plan. Not when it might mean she would be separated from Dante.

"But won't Edra know?" she demanded.

He gave an arch of his brow. "That I'm not dead?"

"Yes."

"Abby, I am dead."

"Oh." She grimaced.

His beautiful features smoothed to somber lines. "Be careful, lover. I will get us out of here as swiftly as I can."

The footsteps were now close enough to be heard by her human ears.

"Make it very swiftly," she whispered.

Dante fell deep within himself. Unlike most humans, the ancient witch would need more than an unmoving corpse to convince her that he was dead.

Thankfully vampires could retreat far enough within themselves that only another vampire could sense the spark of life.

No spells or hocus-pocus would reveal the truth.

Reaching out with his senses, he monitored the steady approach of Edra and the feel of Abby as she bent beside him and touched his face. He could smell the sweet heat of her skin and beneath that the sharp scent of fear.

He battled every instinct not to reach out with his mind to comfort her. Even the smallest whiff of power would alert the witch.

The footsteps crossed the room, and Dante detected the scent of iron in the air. Odd. The woman must be carrying an amulet. And not the traditional wooden amulet.

This one was hard and dark and carried with it a feel of black shadows.

"My lady, is something wrong?" Edra cooed with false sympathy.

"Dear God, something has happened to Dante." There was no mistaking the fear in Abby's voice. Whether out of terror of being left to the clutches of the witch or because he did indeed appear remarkably dead was impossible to say. "You must help."

"Of course, I will call for a healer. Come with me."

Abby's hand tightened on his cheek. "I can't leave him here."

"You have a talent for treating the undead?"

"No, but—"

"Then we must seek out someone who does."

Her command was perfectly reasonable, and Dante felt Abby slowly rise to her feet.

"Very well."

It took every ounce of willpower he possessed to keep from leaping to his feet and halting Abby from her slow retreat.

He didn't want her to leave his side. To risk being alone with Edra.

But what choice did they have?

He couldn't directly attack the witch. Not as long as he remained bound to the Phoenix. And Abby was still fumbling to learn the powers she possessed.

All he could do was allow the coven to believe he was no longer a threat and wait for an opportunity to rescue Abby from their clutches.

After that . . . well.

He would deal with "after that" when it came along.

Forcing himself to wait and ensure that no one

else was about to enter the room, Dante was distracted by the faint tap on the window.

Warily he allowed his senses to reach out. His lips twitched as he flowed to his feet and crossed the room to regard the vampire standing just outside.

"Viper."

"Napping on the job?" the silver-haired vampire demanded as he slipped through the open window.

Dante raised his brows in surprise as Viper smoothed his velvet coat and adjusted the ruffles of his cuffs.

"How did you come in?"

A sly smile touched the too-beautiful features. Reaching beneath his shirt, he pulled out a small leather bag that was attached by a leather strap about his neck.

"A gift from a voodoo priestess."

Dante frowned. "What's in it?"

"A variety of nasty bits and pieces that are used to animate the dead," he drawled, a cynical smile tugging at his lips. "It allows me to pass as a living being."

A handy little object, Dante acknowledged. And precisely the sort of trinket that Viper would collect. He watched as Viper tucked the bag beneath his shirt. His brows abruptly snapped together.

"Bloody hell, what happened to you?" Dante demanded as he studied the charred burns on the smooth flesh.

With a flick of his hands, the older vampire closed his shirt to hide the marks.

"The dark wizard and I had a mild disagreement."

"What sort of disagreement?"

"I thought he should be dead and he disagreed."

Dante smiled wryly. There was little use in lecturing Viper in taking such risks. Once he was on the hunt, nothing could halt him.

"I presume you convinced him to your way of thinking?"

"Eventually." A flare of annoyance rippled over the pale features. "I was careless. His power was greater than I expected."

So the dark wizard was gone. One less problem to deal with.

"What are you doing here?"

Viper's presence suddenly seemed to fill the room. Even the candles dimmed.

"Before I ripped out his throat, the wizard swore that the witches intended to banish us all to the depths of hell. I decided that I wasn't ready to go yet."

Dante clapped a hand on Viper's shoulder. There was no need for words. They would hunt together as they had centuries before.

Few things could have given him more hope.

"The witches have Abby," he said.

"Where?"

Dante took a moment to reach out to his mate. "Below us. A cellar."

Viper gave a slow nod. "Can you fight?"

"I can't harm the witches who were part of the spell binding me to the Phoenix. The newer witches should prove no problem."

Viper smiled to reveal his fangs. "Leave them to me."

"There is also a demon," he warned. "We'll need to make sure it isn't planning a nasty surprise."

Viper tilted back his head to deeply sniff the air. The silver eyes widened in shock.

"A Shalott. So, they haven't all vanished. How very intriguing."

Dante grimaced at the fevered glitter in the midnight eyes. Shalott blood was rumored to be an aphrodisiac to vampires. Which no doubt explained why they had chosen to leave with the dark lord. Without his protection, they would be hunted to extinction by vampires.

"You take care of Edra; I will see to the demon," Dante said sternly.

"Why, Dante, don't tell me you've been seduced by the creature?" Viper mocked. "Whatever will Abby say?"

"She wants the demon spared."

Viper stilled. "Why?"

"Because she could have killed us and didn't."

"Humans." Viper gave a shake of his head even as an unreadable emotion darkened his eyes. "So weak."

Squaring his shoulders, Dante glanced toward the door.

"Are you up for this?"

Viper moved to stand at his side.

"What's the plan?"

Chapter 24

Abby bit her bottom lip as the hair on the nape of her neck stirred and her palms began to sweat.

It was the same sensation she had experienced when she had been five and had entered a carnival's haunted house and spent nearly two hours huddled in a dark corner, too afraid to move so she could bolt for the door.

She hadn't known why she was frightened. She had only known that she sensed something out in the darkness waiting to devour her.

Of course, with the wisdom of age, it was simple to look back and realize her fear had been caused by a combination of overstimulation, the smothering darkness, and being abandoned in the house by her mother.

Still, the sense of being devoured had been very real.

Just as it was at this moment.

Grimly squaring her shoulders, Abby allowed herself to be led through the dark, empty rooms until the elderly witch at last paused to open a door and began to climb down the narrow stairs.

She was no longer a child.

She didn't huddle in corners.

She fought back with a vengeance.

Well . . . maybe not a vengeance. More of a combination of bumbling, fumbling, and flaying.

But she would never again be a willing victim.

A musty smell of damp earth and mold rolled over Abby as they reached the bottom of the steps. She hesitated as the utter darkness momentarily blinded her.

"Don't be afraid," Edra whispered, her ancient face becoming suddenly visible as a fire bloomed to life in a large brazier. "There is nothing here that would ever harm you."

Nothing but you, Abby whispered silently.

"Why are we here?"

The witch moved across the floor. "I have something I wish to show you."

Edra was walking toward what appeared to be a large slab of marble set next to the brazier. It appeared all the world like something you would put on top of a grave.

Along the edge of the marble were precisely arranged black candles and dried herbs. And in the very center was a strange symbol drawn with a thick, clotted liquid that gleamed with a reddish-black hue.

Abby's stomach clenched as she reluctantly followed in the woman's wake.

"What is this?"

"My modest altar." The witch reached out to stroke the cold stone with a reverent hand. "Not what I desired to present to the beloved Goddess, but I was forced to leave much behind after the attack by the wizard."

"Why are we here?"

The tiny head turned to stab Abby with a glittering gaze. Abby grimaced. In the shifting candlelight, the woman looked like a shriveled lizard.

And just about as warm.

"To change the world, my lady."

Abby shifted uneasily. "That's a little vague."

"It's time that the full glory of the Phoenix be revealed. Her power will cleanse the world."

Cleanse the world.

It certainly sounded nicer than mass murder.

"Cleanse the world of what?" she demanded, needing to hear the woman admit her black-hearted intentions.

"Evil."

"Again, a little vague." She wrapped her arms about her waist. Any dark and dank cellar was creepy, but with the candles and mortician slab and some goo that might or might not be blood, this took creepy to a new level. "Precisely what evil are we cleansing?"

"The demons, of course. And those who worship the dark lord."

"The dark lord has been banished from this world."

Impatience as well as something that might have been anger tightened the older woman's lips. Obviously she was not a big fan of having her decisions put up for debate.

"His foulness still taints the very air we breathe. He calls to his disciples and they answer. They must all be brought to an end," she rasped.

Abby licked her lips. "And you expect the Phoenix to do this?"

"Of course. The beloved Goddess was meant to

rule." She held out her gnarled hands as if accepting worship from some unseen disciples. "Just as I was meant to rule. Our time has at last arrived."

Good God, the woman was certifiable.

Hurry, Dante, she silently breathed. *Please hurry.*

"I understand your desire. It is no doubt admirable, but there are surely other means of battling evil?" she attempted to soothe. Pacify the crazy person. That was always her motto.

Absurdly the witch appeared outraged rather than soothed.

"Understand?" She moved to stand directly before Abby. "What could you possibly understand, girl?"

"I understand right from wrong."

"Until a few days ago, you thought demons to be nothing more than fairy tales."

Abby found her terror being swallowed by a growing anger. Dammit. She hadn't wanted to be some stupid Chalice. Or to have monsters chasing her around. Or to be some sort of savior of the world.

But now that she had been forced into this position, she wasn't going to be bullied into becoming the evil they were supposed to be fighting.

"Perhaps I didn't know, but now I realize that there are many sorts of demons. Not all of them bad."

"The vampire," Edra hissed. "He has seduced you."

Abby clenched her hands. "This has nothing to do with Dante. I will not be a part of wholesale murder."

The witch stepped close enough to cloak Abby in the sour scent of sweat and cloves.

"Have you battled against darkness for the past three centuries?" she rasped. "Have you given your very soul to keep the horror at bay? Have you watched innocent women slaughtered like pigs beneath the magic of a foul wizard?"

In spite of herself, Abby stumbled backward. Her eyes might tell her that she could pick up the frail old woman and rattle her silly. Her heart warned her that the witch could wave a wand and squash her like a bug.

"I'm the Chalice," she bluffed. "You can't force me to perform a spell."

"I would prefer that you join with me." Edra raised a hand to point her finger directly between Abby's eyes. "But we can do this the hard way."

Oh God, here comes the bug-squashing part.

"No . . . wait . . ."

The words barely left her lips when a blinding pain exploded in her head.

Abby tumbled to her knees. She clutched her head as she realized she was going to die.

No one could survive such pain.

Dante, where the hell are you?

Viper and Dante slid into the shadows as the sound of noisy footsteps echoed through the hall.

Taking a deep sniff, Dante leaned close to his companion and whispered directly in his ear. "Two men, both human." His fangs lengthened. "I'll take care of them. You go to Abby."

Viper paused. "You're certain?"

"I can't harm Edra. You can."

A cold smile touched the elegant features. "It will be my pleasure."

Not even the air stirred as Viper disappeared from his side. Remaining in the shadows, Dante waited for the men to walk directly past him. Only then did he leap forward, taking the nearest guard to the floor with fluid strength.

He felt the second man reach to grasp his arm. Without even glancing in his direction, Dante threw him into the nearby wall. There was a thud and a groan as the attacker slid to the floor.

The man underneath him grimly struggled to reach beneath his bulky form. Dante smiled wryly, knowing the fool was no doubt reaching for a gun. He either didn't know a vampire held him or had no idea bullets couldn't harm the undead.

Grasping a handful of hair, he smacked the thick skull onto the floor, and then again. He felt the body beneath him go slack, and Dante was on his feet.

Both men were out cold, but he wasn't about to leave them behind. Opening a nearby door, he returned to the unconscious men and easily tossed them into the narrow room. With the same speed, he bound them with their belts and closed the door.

Silently he was once again moving forward. There was the sharp scent of blood ahead of him. Viper, no doubt. Unless the witches banded together, they would prove no match for the powerful vampire.

Ignoring the potent smell, Dante angled toward the back of the house. The fainter scent of the Shalott led him through the empty library to a small closet that had been locked with three iron bars.

Not a barrier to vampires, but Dante was willing to bet that iron was a threat to Shalotts.

With a grimace at the inevitable noise, Dante ripped the bars from the door, tossing them aside as he glanced over his shoulder to ensure that no one had come charging into the room to confront him.

The room was empty, but his momentary distraction didn't go unpunished as the door exploded outward and a slender form leapt forward to catch him on the chin with a sharp kick.

With a grunt that was as much annoyance as pain, Dante whirled to discover the demon bent in a menacing crouch.

There was a lethal, near-intoxicating beauty in her long, slender limbs and flowing black hair, but Dante had no interest in her physical attributes. Or even the cloud of pheromones that filled the room.

His bond with Abby made him impervious to her potent allure.

Instead he prepared himself for another attack. She wouldn't get another cheap shot.

Holding up a hand, he regarded her with a frown. "Let me speak."

Her hands flexed in warning. "Stay back, vampire."

"This may be difficult to believe, but I've come to help you."

Her lips curled. "And all I have to do is allow you to have a few sips, right? Thanks, but no thanks."

Dante gritted his teeth. Had there ever been a woman born—human, demon, or other—that didn't have to argue?

"I have no desire for your blood, Shalott," he rasped. "But I will need your skills."

"Forget it." She gently swayed, like a cobra preparing to strike. "I'll see you dead first."

Realizing she thought he meant her hereditary skills of seducing vampires, he gave an impatient wave of his hand.

"I need your fighting skills." He allowed his gaze to shift to the savage cuts that marred her arms and upper torso. He would bet she possessed a matching set on her back. She had been whipped as if she were an animal. "I intend to put an end to the witches."

She stilled, her brows snapping together. "It's impossible. They're too strong."

"Not after they were nearly wiped out by the wizard. They can't stand against two vampires and a Shalott."

She sniffed the air as if seeking to determine if he spoke the truth.

"Why should I trust you?"

"I'm chained just as you are."

Her breath caught. "The beast."

"Yes."

Without warning, she straightened and Dante bared his fangs. Promise or not, if the woman attacked him again, he would rip out her throat.

Instead she glared at him with a hint of fear.

"The Phoenix is here?" she demanded. "You must get her out."

"That's exactly what I intend to do. With your help."

"If they perform the ritual—"

"Can you fight?" he interrupted.

"Yes. The spell can only force me to come to them when they call."

He smiled wryly. "I meant are you well enough to fight? You've been injured."

She appeared momentarily startled by his concern.

As if it was the last thing she expected. Then, as if embarrassed by her display of vulnerability, her chin tilted to a proud angle.

"I can fight."

"Then let's go."

There was a tense beat before she gave a jerky nod of her head and they moved out of the room side by side. Neither was comfortable with having the other at their back.

"The cellar," he muttered, and with a nod she was headed down the hall toward what he hoped was the entrance to the stairs.

As they neared the kitchen, however, she slowed her pace as she shot him a warning frown.

"There is magic being used ahead."

Dante gave a grim nod as he bent down to pull the daggers from his boots. He could have taken a gun from the guards he had captured, but the last thing he wanted was some nosy neighbor calling the cops.

He doubted Chicago's finest could be convinced that two vampires and a demon were the good guys.

Slipping into the kitchen, Dante's gaze flashed over the circle of witches who currently held Viper in a binding spell. Snarling with fury, the elder vampire was battling with all he was worth, but it was obvious for the moment he was trapped.

Thankfully his struggles ensured that the witches were unaware of Dante's approach. It was taking everything they possessed to keep Viper caged.

Forced to halt as he determined which of the women had held his leash, Dante was briefly startled as a blur streaked past him and the Shalott was launching herself at the nearest witch. There was a loud shriek swiftly followed by another as Dante threw his dagger into the back of a chanting witch.

Belatedly realizing their danger, the witches turned to face their latest threat and the spell faltered. Dante flowed forward even as Viper smiled with vicious anticipation.

In the end, the battle was short and brutal. The older witches were dead at the hands of Viper and the Shalott while Dante had used his powers of enthrallment on the younger witches. They now sat huddled on the floor, nursing their injuries and obediently awaiting Dante's commands.

His hasty touch had been crushing as he had easily broken their spirit. They couldn't so much as stir from the floor without his permission.

Retrieving his dagger, he wiped the blood off before slipping it back into its sheath.

As he straightened, he watched Viper slowly stalk toward the female demon, the older vampire's eyes glittering with a dangerous fire.

"Ah, the Shalott," Viper murmured in silken tones. "Beautiful."

Moving until her back was to the wall, the demon held out a warning hand.

"Stay back."

Viper chuckled. "I won't harm you."

The Shalott tossed back her long mane of raven curls. Dante stifled a groan at the unconsciously provocative motion. With the bloodlust running hot in the air, the demon would be better served to play the role of a passive victim than to directly challenge Viper.

"Yeah, I've heard that a lot," she sneered. "Usually right before someone tries to harm me."

Not surprisingly, Viper slid forward and Dante hurriedly followed directly behind him.

Dammit, they didn't have time for this foolishness.

Debating how much force would be needed to halt the determined vampire, Dante found himself careening off Viper's wide back as he came to a sudden halt and sniffed the air.

"Human," he breathed.

The Shalott's eyes widened. "What?"

"You're a mongrel."

Without warning, the demon leaped on Viper and toppled him to the ground. She ended up seated on his chest.

"Don't push it, vamp," she growled.

Viper laughed as he twisted to send her to the floor with his larger body pinning her down.

"Don't take on more than you can chew, human."

Dante had endured enough. His entire body vibrated with the need to find Abby and carry her from this house.

"Are we going to fight the witches or each other?" he demanded sharply.

Viper gave a nod as he flowed to his feet and tugged the reluctant Shalott off the floor.

"We'll have to finish our game later, pet," he murmured as he moved directly to the door nearly hidden in the pantry. "Business first, I fear."

Chapter 25

It seemed a shame to leave the darkness.

The darkness was warm and soothing and didn't have one psychopathic witch or rampaging zombie.

And best of all, the darkness didn't have the throbbing pain that she could feel lurking in the back of her head.

Unfortunately, along with the throbbing in the back of her head was also the ever-present sense of Dante. Although they were separated, she could feel his cold fury as he battled to make his way to her side.

Until he could reach the basement, it would be up to her to keep Edra from using the Phoenix to perform her demented spell.

Damn.

Slowly absorbing the pounding pain that seized her head, Abby wrenched open her eyes to discover she was strapped onto the slab of marble.

Somehow she wasn't a bit surprised.

How sick was that?

She bit back a groan and then like any fool who ever found themselves tied up, she instinctively struggled against the leather straps that held her down.

It was a futile effort, of course. The straps were not overly tight, but they would hold her. Still, her movement had brushed her arm against her waist and reminded her of the dagger that was in its sheath. Her shirt had managed to hide the weapon, and thankfully the witch hadn't thought to check her.

Now if she could get her arms free to use it.

Covertly she scooted to one side. As she expected, the strap bit into her left arm, but it eased the pressure on the other. On the point of discovering if she could wiggle her arm free, she was halted as a shadow fell over the table.

"Ah, so you have awakened." Edra smiled with cold pleasure.

Forcing herself to hold perfectly still, Abby glared into the lizard eyes.

"You must stop this," she gritted.

"It is too late. The spell will soon be cast."

The witch stepped closer, holding what looked to be a silver goblet. Abby shrank against the cold marble. She didn't know what was in the strange goblet, but she was fairly certain she didn't want to find out.

At her movement, the candles flickered and her attention was captured by an unmoving lump in the middle of the floor.

Her heart halted as she blinked, and then blinked again.

It wasn't a lump. It was the body of a woman with short black hair and the sort of Goth make-up that made it impossible to determine anything more than that she was female and young.

And very, very dead.

Lying on the hard floor, her eyes were wide as if caught in eternal surprise and her mouth open. Most horrid of all was the ugly gash that marred her throat and allowed her thick blood to pool onto the dirt below her chin.

Abby gasped as she struggled against the rising nausea.

"Holy hell. Did you kill her?" she croaked.

"Such powerful magic demands blood."

Abby reluctantly turned back to the woman poised above her.

"You're crazy. You're stark raving mad."

A flare of color stained her pasty cheeks. "You will shut your mouth. You know nothing of the sacrifices I have endured," she hissed. "For three centuries I have devoted my life for this moment. While Selena pampered and preened and surrounded herself with luxury, I hid in the shadows and protected her. I faced the evil and kept it at bay. I looked into the heart of darkness to prepare myself to bring an end to those who would destroy the Phoenix. It is I who will save the world."

Abby shifted even farther to the side, further loosening her arm. She had to get free. There would be no reasoning with the lunatic. Whatever sanity she may once have possessed was long gone.

"And so you deserve to slice open the throat of some innocent young girl?" she demanded, determined to keep the woman too angry to notice her odd wiggles.

"Her death will serve a higher purpose." There was not a flicker of remorse. "It is a fate we should all aspire to."

"I noticed you didn't offer yourself up as the sacrifice."

The goblet trembled in Edra's hands. "Shut up, you filthy bitch. You have defiled yourself with a vampire. You are not worthy to be the Chalice."

"Tough luck. I'm all you got."

"I will soon enough teach you some respect, just as I taught Selena."

Wiggle, wiggle.

"Better bullies than you have tried."

Just for a moment, Abby thought she might have pushed the witch over the edge. The fevered glitter in her eyes was darkened to sheer fury, and her lips curled back into a snarl.

The temptation to say "the hell with saving the world and punish the bitch as she deserves" held Edra in its grip before she gave a shiver and pulled back from utter lunacy.

"No. You won't distract me. Not now."

She reached her hand into the pocket of her robe and pulled out a small metal object. Abby frowned. After all the horrid things she had endured over the past few days, she had half-expected the witch to pull out a knife or snake or at least a magic rabbit.

The small amulet seemed astonishingly harmless.

At least until it was laid on the middle of her chest.

At first there was nothing. Just a cold sensation that ran over her skin. Then, just when she began to hope that the piece of iron was a dud, the smell of smoke began to fill the air.

Abby screamed as the amulet easily burned through the light fabric of her shirt and hit her skin.

The metal was branding itself into her skin, and there was no guarantee it would halt before it managed to sear its way to her heart.

"What are you doing?" she panted, struggling to free the dagger from its sheath. She no longer cared if the witch realized what she was doing or not. If she didn't get free, the spell would be cast or she would be dead.

Neither of which were acceptable alternatives.

Thankfully Edra closed her eyes as she held the goblet directly over the amulet.

"The amulet will help me to draw upon the power of the Phoenix," she muttered.

"Stop, it's burning me."

The woman began to chant beneath her breath, and within the pain blazing through her body, Abby could sense the stirring of the spirit within her.

With a grim effort, she managed to slide the dagger free but her arm remained trapped by the straps.

Dear God, she wasn't going to be in time.

Sucking in a deep breath, she screamed for all she was worth.

"Dante!"

Already on the stairs, Dante moved with blurring speed to stand in the center of the cellar.

His hands clenched as he discovered Abby tied to the marble table with the witch hovering beside her. Even from a distance he could make out the stench of charred flesh.

"Abby . . ."

"Dante, she's doing the spell."

"The beast." Edra's eyes snapped open to pin Dante with a feverish glare. "I should have known you wouldn't die so easily. Well, never fear. I won't be so careless this time."

"Halt," Dante growled as he felt Viper and the Shalott at his back.

"We can't let her complete the ritual," Viper said in icy tones.

"There is a barrier."

Viper cursed in an ancient language. "I hate magic." He turned his head to the Shalott. "What of you? Can you breach the spell?"

The demon shook her head. "No."

Dante's teeth snapped together. He wanted to howl in frustration. Or kill someone.

To be so close and not able to reach Abby was unbearable.

Pacing the barrier, he growled low in his throat. The circle had been completed. It was closed until the witch had finished her spell.

He had never felt so helpless in his life.

And he bloody well didn't like it.

Continuing to follow the line of the circle, Dante searched for any means to distract the witch. If he could make her falter for even a moment, the barrier would be broken. She could never raise it before he and Viper were upon her.

Easier said than done, however. There was nothing in the cellar that offered any help.

Refusing to give up, he moved until he was standing directly behind the witch. There was a soft moan from Abby, and his gaze instinctively moved to where she was stretched on the slab.

For a moment he could see nothing through his red haze of fury. He had to get to her. Now.

Then his attention was captured by the glint of candlelight off the dagger in her hand. He stilled as he realized she was using the keris to cut through the leather strap.

His gaze locked with her own as he silently willed her to hurry. Already Edra was tilting the goblet to pour the blood on the amulet. She was completing the ritual that would allow her to bend the power of the Phoenix to her will.

If the spell was spoken, he wouldn't be able to rescue Abby.

Or himself.

He darted a sideways glance to make sure that Viper had noticed Abby's attempt to escape. The older vampire gave a slight nod of his head.

They moved together, ready to strike the moment the barrier was destroyed. The Shalott chose a spot directly in front of the witch. A demon with battle tactics.

Go figure.

Impervious to all but the spell she was casting, Edra held the goblet over her head and then slowly she lowered it to pour a measure of the thick blood directly onto the amulet.

Dante froze.

The spell was beginning.

He might very well be dead before Abby ever got herself loose.

The blood hit the amulet and sizzled against the searing heat. A strange humming filled Dante's ears, and he pounded his fists futilely against the barrier.

"Abby," he rasped.

As if sensing his rising panic, Abby gritted her teeth and sliced through the last bit of leather. The amulet on her chest seemed to flare as she knocked the smoldering iron off her skin and struggled to sit up.

From behind, Dante watched as Edra froze in shock.

In her arrogance, she thought that nothing could halt her glorious bid for power. Certainly not a mere slip of a woman with no ability to wield magic and no claim to the darker arts.

She hadn't counted on Abby's stubborn determination.

Something he had learned never to underestimate.

Ignoring the obvious pain wracking her body, Abby managed to lift herself upward, using her momentum to slash out with the keris. Belatedly sensing her danger, the witch leaped backward, avoiding a killing strike.

Thankfully the dagger managed to nick her upper arm, sending the goblet crashing to the floor.

More importantly, with her concentration destroyed, the barrier vanished into mist.

With a roar, Viper was across the floor and pinning the witch to the floor. Dante was at Abby's side, wrenching off the remaining straps and reaching to collect her in his arms.

"No." Holding out warning hands, Abby swung off the table and struggled to maintain her balance. "Don't touch me."

Dante slowly circled to face her, his brows pulled together. "Abby, what's wrong?"

She wrapped her hands about her waist. "I'm burning up."

Dante gave a slow nod. Even at a distance he could feel the heat rolling from her body.

"The Phoenix?"

"Yes." She turned toward the witch on the floor. "The spell has begun."

"Viper, kill her," Dante rasped.

"My pleasure."

Lowering his head to sink his fangs into the witch's neck, Viper gave a low grunt and then astonishingly was flying backward as Edra struggled to sit up. In her hand was the amulet.

"Shit." Dante was moving even as Edra lifted her hand to strike at Viper once again.

As fast as he moved, however, the blast of power was faster. He cursed as he realized that he would never arrive in time. Then, without warning, the Shalott was leaping onto Viper, taking the blow in her back and slumping over the startled vampire.

Dante whirled back to glare at the witch who was uneasily forcing herself to her feet.

"You can't harm me," she panted, perhaps more to reassure herself than to remind Dante of his impotency.

"Not yet, but soon I'll see you in hell."

She gave a wild laugh. "The spell has begun. No one can stop it now."

He rapidly turned his attention to Abby to discover her on her knees. She was moaning as she rocked back and forth.

"God . . . Abby."

"She can't hear you. The Phoenix has taken control, and soon the Goddess will release the power that I have called forth." The wild laugh came again. "She's about to kill you, vampire."

"No!" With a scream, Abby rose to her feet.

Dante stumbled back as the force of her presence abruptly flared through the room.

He could barely recognize his mate.

In the candlelight, her pale skin glowed with a strange luminescence, and the blue eyes had turned to a brilliant crimson, as if flames were lit behind them. Even her hair seemed to float on some unseen breeze as she lifted her arms wide and began to walk toward the witch.

"Beloved Goddess," the witch breathed as she sank slowly to her knees.

Dante tried to step forward only to cry out as a wave of heat slammed him to the ground. The very air was sizzling around Abby, making it impossible to reach her.

Bloody hell, she was going to burn the house down around them.

After she managed to kill every demon.

Starting with him.

Battling back the blackness that was threatening to overwhelm him, Dante forced himself to his knees.

"Abby, you must stop—" he rasped.

"No." Abby never took her attention off the kneeling witch. "This must end now."

Shit. He couldn't move. Couldn't do a damn thing.

"Abby."

Reaching the older woman, Abby held out her hand. "Rise."

"Yes." Awkwardly the witch managed to stand, an expression of adulation on her face. "I have waited so long to bathe in your glory. To see the full wonder of your powers."

"You shall know my powers to the fullest, Edra."

The words came out of Abby's mouth, but the voice didn't belong to her. She had been completely consumed by the spirit within her.

"Bless you, mistress. Bless you."

Caught and held by the smoldering fire in Abby's eyes, the witch stepped slowly forward. Dante frowned as Abby wrapped her arms about the woman. What the hell was the Phoenix up to?

He heard Viper and the Shalott groaning behind him, but his gaze never wavered from Abby as she closed her eyes and tilted back her head.

For a moment there was nothing.

Just the pulsing blackness that clutched at him with the promise of death. And then, from seemingly nowhere, there was a violent explosion.

Dante flew backward to land with a jarring impact against a mold-slick wall.

His ears were ringing, and he was fairly certain his brain had become dislodged. But amazingly he wasn't dead.

At least not yet.

Giving his head a shake to clear the fog, he frantically searched through the thick smoke that filled the air. A sharp fear flared through him as he realized the encroaching darkness had been seared away.

And even more frightening, the leash that had held him prisoner for the past three centuries had been sharply severed.

He was free. But at what cost?

No.

Hell no.

He wouldn't believe Abby was dead. He couldn't believe it.

Scrambling on his hands and knees, he crossed

the dirt floor to the last place he had seen Abby. It took less than a handful of seconds to move the short distance, but to Dante it seemed an eternity passed.

At last his searching hand encountered an outstretched arm. He gritted his teeth as he forced himself to touch the satin-soft skin.

A touch was enough.

He could feel her soul.

She was alive.

His head briefly touched the cool floor before he was moving to gather her still form in his arms. He ignored the mess that lay only a few feet away.

There was little left of Edra.

No doubt bits and pieces were scattered throughout the cellar. Certainly what was left of the charred lump couldn't possibly add up to a whole body.

A cold smile touched his lips.

It was a fitting end to the witch.

"Abby." He buried his face in her hair, holding her far too tight.

He felt her stir, and he pulled back to watch the brilliant blue eyes open.

"Dante?" Her face was covered in soot, her hair was singed, and there was blood on her chin.

And she had never looked so beautiful.

He pressed a careful kiss to her peeling lips.

"You did it, lover," he husked. "You put an end to the spell."

"Not me." Her voice was raw and raspy, as if her throat had been burnt. "The Phoenix. It wouldn't let itself be used to destroy without cause."

"Sssh. We'll discuss it later. For now all that matters is that you're alive."

The faintest smile touched her mouth. "And still a goddess."

He gave a soft chuckle. "So it would seem."

"Will you worship me?"

He brushed his lips on the dark bruises that marred her beautiful skin.

"Lover, I intend to worship you every night for the rest of eternity."

Epilogue

Two weeks later, Abby was lying on the bed in Dante's lair, watching as he carefully lit the candles he had placed about the room.

The witches had fled or been buried after Edra's death, bringing an end to the coven. Not a great loss to Abby, considering they intended to use her as some sort of catalyst for Armageddon.

Granted, she was now stuck carrying a mystical spirit, but she was becoming much better at disguising her powers from those who would like to see her dead, and there were a number of benefits to being a Chalice.

Not the least of which was the promise of an eternity with Dante.

Above them, Selena's mansion was slowly being reconstructed, complete with tinted windows and a new library for Dante's vast collection of books. And, of course, the newer travel catalogues that he had ordered for Abby.

For their honeymoon, Dante had promised to take her around the world.

But first they would share the ceremony that would make them truly mates.

Stirring on the pillows, Abby tugged at the black satin sheet that was all that covered her naked body.

"I get that Selena and Edra were in a power struggle to decide who would be allowed to rid the world of demons and become some sort of demigod," she murmured in lazy tones. "But I still don't understand why they waited so long to try and use the spell. You would think as soon as Selena became the Chalice they would have tried to flex their mojo."

Lighting the last of the candles, Dante turned to face her with a lift of his brow.

"Mojo?"

Her breath caught.

Wearing nothing more than a black silk robe and his hair framing his alabaster face, he looked every inch the wicked pirate.

Yum. Yum. Yum.

With an effort, she battled her attack of lust. "You know what I mean."

He shrugged. "From what I could discover among Edra's writings, it seems they were waiting for the stars to be in proper alignment."

"Oh."

"Clearly they didn't realize that the Phoenix possessed a mind of its own and that it would destroy anyone seeking to use it for such evil."

Abby shuddered. She still had nightmares of her time in the cellar with Edra.

"Not until too late."

"Enough, lover," he soothed. "We aren't going to ruin our night with thoughts of the witches."

No, they most certainly were not, Abby agreed, her gaze running over the perfect male body.

"You are looking way too sexy for anything to ruin the evening."

The silver eyes blazed as he moved to place himself on the bed beside her.

"How sexy?"

Abby smiled as she helpfully tugged the robe off. "Surely at your age you wouldn't be fishing for compliments?"

"I can't use a mirror to reassure myself, so I must depend upon you."

With the robe tossed onto the floor, Abby ran her hands over the smooth perfection of his back.

"Well, I suppose I won't be kicking you out of my bed any time soon."

His fangs flashed in the candlelight. Suddenly he looked incredibly exotic and every inch a vampire.

"Our bed," he softly corrected.

Her heart halted as she gazed into the silver eyes. "Our bed."

With a slow motion, Dante pulled the sheet aside to allow the cool air to rush over her bare skin.

"Are you prepared?"

Her hands tightened on his back.

With the death of Edra, the spell that prevented Dante from being able to drink human blood had been broken. He was now a fully functioning vampire.

And anxious to complete the ceremony that would bind them together.

She gave a firm nod. "I'm ready."

Easing himself on top of her, Dante settled between her legs. Then gently he brushed her hair from her neck.

Instinctively Abby stiffened.

"Don't be frightened," he husked. "I promise it won't hurt."

Breathing in deeply, Abby relaxed her tense muscles. "I'm not frightened."

"And you're certain that this is what you want? Once you have mated yourself to me, there is no going back."

It was a familiar warning. Had it been up to her, they would have been mated the moment they had pulled themselves out of the cellar. Dante, however, had proven to be remarkably stubborn, refusing her demands until she had ample time to consider the consequences.

"We've already been through all this."

"Yes, but—"

She reached up to frame his face in her hands. "Dante, shut up and make me yours."

The silver eyes flared as a wicked smile suddenly curved his lips.

"Yes, my goddess," he murmured, his head lowering to her exposed throat.

For all her words of bravery, Abby couldn't deny she expected at least some pain.

You didn't need to be a doctor to realize that shoving a pair of fangs through the skin was bound to cause a bit of discomfort.

Still, she didn't allow herself to flinch as she felt his tongue tenderly stroke over the pulse at the base of her neck. Dante would halt the moment he sensed her tension.

"My love," he whispered.

And then he bit.

Abby's eyes widened in amazement. It hadn't hurt. There was no more than a slide of cool pressure and then a jolt of pleasure so intense she jerked against Dante.

"Holy freaking cow," she breathed as the heat flared through her body to pool in a blaze of desire in the pit of her stomach.

Her fingers clutched at his back, drawing blood as she arched her hips upward in a silent plea for relief.

His hands tangled in her hair as he continued to drink of her blood, and with one smooth movement, he had plunged deep within her. Abby gasped, the sensations so intense she feared she might black out.

Nothing should surely feel so good?

And be legal.

Trembling, Abby opened herself to his masterful strokes. She groaned with each thrust, her hips lifting to meet him with wild abandon.

The building pressure was delicious. Astonishing. And if she didn't come soon, she feared she might actually explode.

"Dante . . . please."

His soft chuckle brushed her neck, but seeming to understand her desperation, his pace quickened until she was arching beneath him and with a faint scream found her release.

Panting in exhaustion, Abby slowly opened her eyes to discover Dante regarding his arm. Slowly she turned her head, watching as the familiar crimson tattooing began to wind its way along his forearm.

A smug smile touched his lips as he turned back to regard her with a glittering gaze.

"I knew I would make you mine," he murmured in arrogant tones.

Framing his face, she allowed her thumbs to run over the curve of his fangs.

"Dante, I've been yours from the moment I walked into this mansion and found a wicked pirate waiting for me."

"My lover . . . for all eternity."

"And goddess." She pulled his head down for a lingering kiss. "Don't forget goddess."

He laughed as his hands began to busily stir her body back to passionate life.

"How could I possibly forget?"

Please turn the page for an exciting sneak peek of

Alexandra Ivy's

EMBRACE THE DARKNESS,

now on sale!

Chapter 1

The auction house on the outskirts of Chicago didn't look like a cesspit.

Behind the iron fences, the elegant brick structure sprawled over the landscape with a visible arrogance. The rooms were large with vaulted ceilings that boasted beautiful murals and elegant chandeliers. And on the advice of a professional, they had been decorated with thick ivory carpets, glossy dark paneling, and hand-carved furniture.

The overall atmosphere was the sort of quiet hush that only money could buy. Lots and lots of money.

It was the sort of swanky place that should be peddling rare paintings, priceless jewels, and museum artifacts.

Instead, it was no more than a flesh market. A sewer where demons were sold like so much meat.

There was nothing pleasant about the slave trade. Not even when the trade involved demons rather than humans. It was a sordid business that attracted every decadent, demented slimeball in the country.

They came for all sorts of pathetic reasons.

Those who bought demons for mercenaries or bodyguards. Those who lusted after the more exotic sex slaves. Those who believed the blood of demons could bring them magic or eternal life.

And those who purchased demons to be released into their private lands and hunted like wild animals.

The bidders were men and women without conscience or morals. Only enough money to sate their twisted pleasures.

And at the top of the dung heap was the owner of the auction house, Evor. He was one of the lesser trolls who made his living upon the misery of others with a smile on his face.

Someday Shay intended to kill Evor.

Unfortunately, it would not be today.

Or rather tonight.

Attired in ridiculous harem pants and a tiny sequined top that revealed far more than it concealed, she paced the cramped cell behind the auction rooms. Her long raven hair had been pulled to a braid that hung nearly to her waist. Better to reveal her slanted golden eyes, the delicate cast to her features, and the bronzed skin that marked her as something other than human.

Less than two months before, she had been a slave to a coven of witches who intended to bring Armageddon to all demons. At the time she had thought anything was preferable to being their toady as she helplessly watched their evil plotting.

Hell, it's tough to top genocide.

It was only when she had been forced back to the power of Evor that she understood that death was not always the worst fate.

The grave was really nothing compared to what waited for her beyond the door.

Without thought, Shay struck out with her foot, sending the lone table sailing through the air to crash against the iron bars with astonishing force.

From behind her came a heavy sigh that had her spinning to regard the small gargoyle hiding behind a chair in the far corner.

Levet wasn't much of a gargoyle.

Oh, he possessed the traditional grotesque features. Thick gray skin, reptilian eyes, horns, and cloven hooves. He even possessed a long tail he polished and pampered with great pride. Unfortunately, despite his frightening appearance, he was barely three feet tall, and, worse, as far as he was concerned, he possessed a pair of delicate, gossamer wings that would have been more fitting on a sprite or fairy than a lethal creature of the dark.

As if to add to his humiliation, his powers were unpredictable under the best of circumstances, and his courage more often than not missing in action.

It was little wonder he had been voted out of the Gargoyle Guild and forced to fend for himself. They claimed he was an embarrassment to the entire community, and not one had stepped forward when he had been captured and made a slave by Evor.

Shay had taken the pathetic creature under her protection the moment she had been forced back to the auction house. Not only because she possessed a regrettable tendency to leap to the defense of anyone weaker than herself, but also because she knew that it aggravated Evor to have his favorite whipping boy taken away.

The troll might hold the curse that bound her, but if he pressed her far enough, she would be willing to kill him, even if it meant an end to her own life.

"*Cherie*, did the table do something I did not see or were you just attempting to teach it a lesson?" Levet demanded, his voice low and laced with a lilting French accent.

Not at all the sort of thing to improve his status among the gargoyles.

Shay smiled wryly. "I was imagining it was Evor."

"Strange, they do not greatly resemble each other."

"I have a good imagination."

"Ah." He gave a ridiculous wiggle of his thick brow. "In that case, I do not suppose you are imagining I'm Brad Pitt?"

Shay smiled. "I'm good, but not that good, gargoyle."

"A pity."

Her brief amusement faded. "No, the pity is that it was a table and not Evor smashed to pieces."

"A delightful notion, but a mere dream." The gray eyes slowly narrowed. "Unless you intend to be stupid?"

Shay deliberately widened her eyes. "Who, me?"

"*Mon dieu*," the demon growled. "You intend to fight him."

"I can't fight him. Not as long as I remain held by the curse."

"As if that has ever halted you." Levet tossed aside the pillow to reveal his tail furiously twitching about his hooves. A sure sign of distress. "You can't kill him, but that never keeps you from trying to kick his fat troll ass."

"It passes the time."

"And leaves you screaming in agony for hours."

He abruptly shuddered. "*Cherie*, I can't bear seeing you like that. Not again. It's insane to battle against fate."

Shay grimaced. As part of the curse, she was punished for any attempt to harm her master. The searing pain that gripped her body could leave her gasping on the ground or even passed out for hours. Lately, however, the punishment had become so brutal she feared that each time she pressed her luck might be the last.

She gave a tug on her braid. A gesture that revealed the frustration that smoldered just below the surface.

"You think I should just give in? Accept defeat?"

"What choice do you have? What choice do any of us have? Not all the fighting in the world can change the fact we belong . . ." Levet rubbed one of his stunted horns. "How do you say . . . lock, stock and jug—"

"Barrel."

"Ah, yes, barrel to Evor. And that he can do whatever he wants with us."

Shay gritted her teeth as she turned to glare at the iron bars that held her captive. "Shit. I hate this. I hate Evor. I hate this cell. I hate those pathetic demons up there waiting to bid on me. I almost wish I had let those witches bring an end to all of us."

"You will get no arguments from me, my sweet Shay," Levet agreed with a sigh.

Shay closed her eyes. Dammit. She hadn't meant the words. She was tired and frustrated, but she was no coward. Just the fact that she had survived the past century proved that.

"No," she muttered. "No."

Levet gave a flap of his wings. "And why not? We

are trapped here like rats in a maze until we can be sold to the highest bidder. What could be worse?"

Shay smiled without humor. "Allowing fate to win."

"What?"

"So far fate or destiny or fortune or whatever the hell you want to call it has done nothing but crap on us," Shay growled. "I'm not going to just give in and allow it to thumb its nose at me as I slink into my grave. One of these days I'm going to have an opportunity to spit fate in its face. That's what keeps me fighting."

There was a long silence before the gargoyle moved to stand near enough that he could rub his head on her leg. It was an unconscious gesture. A quest for reassurance that he would rather die than admit.

"I am uncertain I have ever heard such an inelegant speech, but I believe you. If anyone can get away from Evor, it's you."

Absently Shay shifted the horn poking into her thigh. "I'll come back for you, Levet, that much I promise."

"Well, well, isn't this touching?" Abruptly appearing before the iron bars of the cell, Evor smiled to reveal his pointed teeth. "Beauty and the Beast."

With a smooth motion, Shay pressed Levet behind her and turned to regard her captor.

A sneer touched her face as the troll stepped into the cell and locked the door behind him. Evor easily passed for human. An incredibly ugly human.

He was a short, pudgy man with a round, squishy face and heavy jowls. His hair was little more than tufts of stray strands that he carefully combed over his head. And his small black eyes had a tendency to flash red when he was annoyed.

The eyes he hid behind black-framed glasses.

The thickly fleshed body he hid behind an obscenely expensive tailored suit.

Only the teeth marked him for the troll he was.

That and his utter lack of morals.

"Screw you, Evor," Shay muttered.

The nasty smile widened. "You wish."

Shay narrowed her gaze. The troll had been trying to get into her bed since gaining control of her curse. The only thing that had halted him from forcing her was knowing she was quite willing to kill the both of them to prevent such a horror.

"I'll walk through the fires of hell before I let you touch me."

Fury rippled over the pudgy features before the oily smile returned. "Someday, my beauty, you'll be happy to be spread beneath me. We all have our breaking point. Eventually you'll reach yours."

"Not in this lifetime."

His tongue flicked out in an obscene motion. "So proud. So powerful. I shall enjoy pouring my seed into you. But not yet. There is still money to be made from you. And money always comes first." Lifting his hand, he revealed the heavy iron shackles that he had hidden behind his body. "Will you put these on or do I need to call for the boys?"

Shay crossed her arms over her chest. She might only be half Shalott, but she possessed all the strength and agility of her ancestors. They were not the favorite assassins of the demon world without cause.

"After all these years, you still think those goons can hurt me?"

"Oh, I have no intention of having them hurt you. I should hate to have you damaged before the bidding." Very deliberately his gaze shifted to where Levet was cowering behind her legs. "I merely wish them to encourage your good behavior."

The gargoyle gave a low moan. "Shay?"

Shit.

She battled back the instinctive urge to punch the pointed teeth down his throat. It would only put her on the ground in agony. Worse, it would leave Levet at the mercy of the hulking mountain trolls Evor used as protection.

They would take great delight in torturing the poor gargoyle.

As far as she knew, their only pleasure was giving pain to others.

Freaking trolls.

"Fine." She held out her arms with a furious scowl.

"A wise choice." Keeping a wary eye on her, Evor pressed the shackles over her wrists and locked them shut. "I knew you would understand the situation once it was properly explained."

Shay hissed as the iron bit into her skin. She could feel her power draining and her flesh chaffing beneath the metal. It was her one certain Achille's heel.

"All I understand is that someday I'm going to kill you."

He gave a jerk on the chain that draped between the shackles. "Behave yourself, bitch, or your little friend pays the consequences. Got it?"

Shay battled back the sickness that clutched at her stomach.

Once again she was going to be placed on the

stage and sold off to the highest bidder. She would be utterly at the mercy of some stranger who could do whatever he pleased with her.

And there wasn't a damn thing she could do to stop it.

"Yeah, I got it. Let's just get this over with."

Evor opened his mouth to make a smart-ass comment only to snap the fish lips shut when he caught sight of her expression. She was close enough to the edge that he was wary of pushing her over.

Which only proved that he wasn't quite as stupid as he looked.

In silence they left the cell and climbed the narrow stairs to the back of the stage. Evor paused only long enough to lock her shackles to a pole anchored in the floor before moving toward the closed curtains and slipping through them to face the crowd.

Alone in the darkness, Shay sucked in a deep breath and tried to ignore the rumblings of the crowd just beyond the curtain.

Even without being able to see the potential bidders, she could feel the presence of the gathering demons and humans. She could smell the stench of their sweat. Feel the smoldering impatience. Taste the depraved lust in the air.

She abruptly frowned. There was something else. Something that was subtly laced through it all.

A sense of decaying evil that sent a chill of horror over her skin.

It was vague. As if the being was not truly in the room in full form. More like a looming, intangible presence. An echo of foulness that made her stomach clench in fear.

Swallowing back her instinctive scream, she

closed her eyes and forced herself to take a deep, steadying breath. In the distance she heard Evor loudly clear his throat to command attention.

"And now, ladies and gentlemen, demons and fairies, dead and undead, it is time for our main attraction. Our pièce de résistance. An item so rare, so extraordinary that only those who possess a golden token may remain," he dramatically announced. "The rest may retire to our reception rooms where you will be offered your choice of refreshment."

Despite the lingering certainty that she had just been brushed by some malignant gaze, Shay managed a disgusted grimace. Evor was always a pompous blowhard. Tonight, however, he put even the cheesiest ringmaster to shame.

"Gather close, my friends," Evor commanded as the dregs of bidders were forced to leave the room. To be granted a golden ticket, a person or demon had to carry at least $50,000 in cash on them. The slave trade rarely accepted checks or credit cards. Go figure. "You will not wish to miss your first glimpse of my precious treasure. Do not fear, I have ensured that she is properly chained. She will offer no danger. No danger beyond her perilous charm. She will not rip your heart from your chest, but I do not promise she will not steal it with her beauty."

"Shut your mouth and open the curtain," a voice growled.

"You are impatient?" Evor demanded, his tone edged with anger. He didn't like his well-practiced act interrupted.

"I don't have all night. Get on with it."

"Ah, a premature . . . bidder. A pity. Let us hope for your sake that it is not an affliction that taints your performance in other areas," Evor sneered, pausing to allow the roar of coarse laughter to fade. "Now where was I? Oh yes. My prize. My most beloved slave. Demons and ghouls, allow me to introduce you to Lady Shay—the last Shalott to walk our world."

With a dramatic motion, the curtain disappeared in a puff of smoke, leaving Shay exposed to the nearly two dozen men and demons.

Deliberately she lowered her gaze as she heard the gasps echo through the room. It was humiliating enough to smell their rabid hunger. She didn't need to see it written on their faces.

"Is this a trick?" a dark voice demanded in disbelief. Hardly surprising. As far as Shay knew, she truly was the last Shalott remaining in the world.

"No trick, no illusion."

"As if I'd take your word for it, troll. I want proof."

"Proof? Very well." There was a momentary pause as Evor searched the crowd. "You there, come forward," he commanded.

Shay tensed as she felt the cold chill that warned her it was a vampire approaching. Her blood was more precious than gold to the undead. An aphrodisiac that they would kill to procure.

With her attention focused on the tall, gaunt vampire, Shay barely noticed when Evor grabbed her arm and used a knife to slice through the skin of her forearm. Hissing softly, the vamp leaned downward to lick the welling blood. His entire body shivered as he lifted his head to regard her with stark hunger.

"There is human blood, but she is genuine Shalott," he rasped.

With a smooth motion, Evor placed his pudgy form between the vamp and Shay, shooing the predator away with a wave of his hand. Reluctantly the undead creature left the stage, no doubt sensing the impending riot if he gave in to his impulse to sink his teeth into her and drain her dry.

Evor waited until the stage was cleared before moving to stand behind his podium. He grasped his gavel and lifted it over his head. Ridiculous twit.

"Satisfied? Good." Evor smacked the gavel onto the podium. "The bidding starts at fifty thousand dollars. Remember, gentlemen, cash only."

"Fifty-five thousand."

"Sixty thousand."

"Sixty-one thousand."

Shay's gaze once again dropped to her feet as the voices called out their bids. Soon enough she would be forced to confront her new master. She didn't want to watch as they wrangled over her like a pack of dogs slavering over a juicy bone.

"One hundred thousand dollars," a shrill voice shouted from the back of the room.

A sly smile touched Evor's thin lips. "A most generous bid, my good sir. Anyone else? No? Going once . . . Going twice . . ."

"Five hundred thousand."

A sharp silence filled the room. Without even realizing what she was doing, Shay lifted her head to stare into the crowd jamming the auction floor.

There was something about that silky dark voice. Something . . . familiar.

"Step forward," Evor demanded, his eyes shimmering red. "Step forward and offer your name."

There was a stir as the crowd parted. From the back shadows, a tall, elegant form glided forward.

A hushed whisper spread through the room as the muted light revealed the hauntingly beautiful face and satin curtain of silver hair that fell down his back.

It took only a glance to realize he was a vampire.

No human could so closely resemble an angel that had fallen from heaven. And fallen recently. Or move with such liquid grace. Or cause the demons to back away in wary fear.

Shay's breath caught in her throat. Not at his stunning beauty or powerful presence or even the flamboyant velvet cloak that shrouded his slender form.

It was the fact that she knew this vampire.

He had been at her side when they had battled the coven of witches weeks ago. And more importantly, he had been at her side when she had saved his life.

And now he was here bidding on her like she was no more than a piece of property.

Damn his rotten soul to hell.

Viper had been in the world for centuries. He had witnessed the rise and fall of empires. He had seduced the most beautiful women in the world. He had taken the blood of kings, czars, and pharaohs.

He had even changed the course of history at times.

Now he was sated, jaded, and magnificently bored.

He no longer struggled to broaden his power base. He didn't involve himself in battles with demons or humans. He didn't form alliances or interfere in politics.

His only concern was ensuring the safety of his

clan and keeping his business profitable enough to allow him the luxurious lifestyle he had grown accustomed to.

But somehow the Shalott demon had managed the impossible.

She had managed to linger in his thoughts long after she had disappeared.

For weeks she had haunted his memories and even invaded his dreams. She was like a thorn that had lodged beneath his skin and refused to be removed.

A realization that he wasn't sure pleased or annoyed him as he had scoured the streets of Chicago in search of the woman.

Glancing at his latest acquisition, he didn't have to wonder if Shay was pleased or annoyed. Even in the muted light, it was obvious her glorious golden eyes were flashing with fury.

Clearly she failed to fully appreciate the honor he was bestowing upon her.

His lips twitched with amusement before he was returning his attention to the troll standing behind the podium.

"You may call me Viper," he informed the lesser demon with cold dislike.

The red eyes briefly widened. It was a name that inspired fear throughout Chicago. "Of course. Forgive me for not recognizing you, sir. You . . . ah"—he swallowed heavily—"you have the cash upon you?"

With a motion too swift for most eyes, Viper reached beneath his cloak and tossed a large packet onto the stairs leading to the stage.

"I do."

With a flourish, Evor banged the gavel on the podium. "Sold."

There was a low hiss from the Shalott, but before

Viper could give her the proper attention, there was the sound of a low cursing and a small, wiry human was pushing his way through the crowd.

"Wait. The bidding is not yet closed," the stranger charged.

Viper narrowed his gaze. He might have laughed at the absurdity of the scrawny man attempting to bull his way through towering demons, but he didn't miss the scent of sour desperation that clouded about him, or the blackness that darkened his soul.

This was a man who had been touched by evil.

The troll, Evor, frowned as he regarded the man, clearly unimpressed by the cheap, baggy suit and secondhand shoes. "You wish to continue?"

"Yes."

"You have the cash upon you?"

The man swiped a hand over the sweat clinging to his bald head. "Not upon me but I can easily have it to you—"

"Cash and carry only," Evor growled, his gavel once again hitting the podium.

"No. I will get you the money."

"The bidding is over."

"Wait. You must wait. I—"

"Get out before I have you thrown out."

"No." Without warning, the man was racing up the stairs with a knife in his hand. "The demon is mine."

As quick as the man was, Viper had already moved to place himself between the stranger and his Shalott. The man gave a low growl before turning and stalking toward the troll. Easier prey than a determined vampire. But then again, most things were.

"Now, now. There is no need to become unreasonable." Evor hastily gestured toward the hulking bodyguards at the edge of the stage. "You knew the rules when you came."

With lumbering motions, the mountain trolls moved forward, their hulking size and skin as thick as tree bark making them near impossible to kill.

Viper folded his arms over his chest. His attention remained on the demented human, but he couldn't deny that he was disturbingly aware of the Shalott behind him.

It was in the sweet scent of her blood. The warmth of her skin. And the shimmering energy that swirled about her.

His entire body reacted to her proximity. It was as if he had stepped close to a smoldering fire that offered a promise of heat he had long forgotten.

Unfortunately his attention was forced to remain on the seeming madman waving the knife in a threatening motion. There was something decidedly strange in the human's determination. A stark panic that was out of place.

He would be an idiot to underestimate the danger of the sudden standoff.

"Stay back," the small man squeaked.

The trolls continued forward until Viper lifted a slender hand. "I would not come close to the knife. It is hexed."

"Hexed?" Evor's face hardened with fury. "Magical artifacts are forbidden. The punishment is death."

"You think a pathetic troll and his goons can frighten me?" The intruder lifted his knife to point it directly at Evor's face. "I came here for the Shalott, and I'm not leaving without it. I'll kill you all if I have to."

"You may try," Viper drawled.

The man spun about to confront him. "I have no fight with you, vampire."

"You are attempting to steal my demon."

"I'll pay you. Whatever you want."

"Whatever?" Viper flicked a brow upward. "A generous, if rather foolhardy, bargain."

"What is your price?"

Viper pretended to consider a moment. "Nothing you could offer."

That sour desperation thickened in the air. "How do you know? My employer is very rich . . . very powerful."

Ah. Now they were getting somewhere.

"Employer. So you are merely an envoy?"

The man nodded, his eyes burning like coals in their sunken sockets. "Yes."

"And your employer will no doubt be quite disappointed to learn you have failed in your task to gain the Shalott?"

The pale skin became a sickly gray. Viper suspected that the sense of darkness he could detect was directly related to the mysterious employer.

"He will kill me."

"Then you are in quite a quandary, my friend, because I have no intention of allowing you to leave the room with my prize."

"What do you care?"

Viper's smile was cold. "Surely you must know that Shalott blood is an aphrodisiac for vampires? It is a most rare treat that has been denied us for too long."

"You intend to drain her?"

"That is none of your concern. She is mine. Bought and paid for."

He heard a strangled curse from behind him,

along with the rattle of chains. His beauty was clearly unhappy with his response and anxious to prove her displeasure by ripping him limb from limb.

A tiny flicker of excitement raced through him.

Blood of the saints, but he liked his women dangerous.

About the Author

Alexandra Ivy lives with her family in Ewing, Missouri. She is currently working on the next installment of her Guardians of Eternity series, BOUND BY DARKNESS, which will be published in December 2011. Readers can visit her website at www.alexandraivy.com.

Romantic Suspense from
Lisa Jackson

Books by Bestselling Author
Fern Michaels

___The Jury	0-8217-7878-1	$6.99US/$9.99CAN
___Sweet Revenge	0-8217-7879-X	$6.99US/$9.99CAN
___Lethal Justice	0-8217-7880-3	$6.99US/$9.99CAN
___Free Fall	0-8217-7881-1	$6.99US/$9.99CAN
___Fool Me Once	0-8217-8071-9	$7.99US/$10.99CAN
___Vegas Rich	0-8217-8112-X	$7.99US/$10.99CAN
___Hide and Seek	1-4201-0184-6	$6.99US/$9.99CAN
___Hokus Pokus	1-4201-0185-4	$6.99US/$9.99CAN
___Fast Track	1-4201-0186-2	$6.99US/$9.99CAN
___Collateral Damage	1-4201-0187-0	$6.99US/$9.99CAN
___Final Justice	1-4201-0188-9	$6.99US/$9.99CAN
___Up Close and Personal	0-8217-7956-7	$7.99US/$9.99CAN
___Under the Radar	1-4201-0683-X	$6.99US/$9.99CAN
___Razor Sharp	1-4201-0684-8	$7.99US/$10.99CAN
___Yesterday	1-4201-1494-8	$5.99US/$6.99CAN
___Vanishing Act	1-4201-0685-6	$7.99US/$10.99CAN
___Sara's Song	1-4201-1493-X	$5.99US/$6.99CAN
___Deadly Deals	1-4201-0686-4	$7.99US/$10.99CAN
___Game Over	1-4201-0687-2	$7.99US/$10.99CAN
___Sins of Omission	1-4201-1153-1	$7.99US/$10.99CAN
___Sins of the Flesh	1-4201-1154-X	$7.99US/$10.99CAN
___Cross Roads	1-4201-1192-2	$7.99US/$10.99CAN

Available Wherever Books Are Sold!
Check out our website at www.kensingtonbooks.com